"Hurry, Julia. We don't have much time."

Abraham held out his hand to her. Fear flashed in Julia's eyes. Abraham's heart went out to her for the situation they were in. All she wanted to do was keep her son safe, yet they were walking into the middle of a clash between two street gangs. They were taking a big risk that could turn deadly.

"We have to keep going." Abraham put his hand on Julia's shoulder and guided her forward. She scooted William closer toward Abraham so the boy would be protected between them.

"We'll slip out along the side of the road," Abraham said. "Act nonchalant." They stayed on the sidewalk, keeping their eyes averted so they would not make eye contact.

"Hey, you!" someone shouted.

"They must have seen us!"

Debby Giusti is an award-winning Christian author who met and married her military husband at Fort Knox, Kentucky. Together they traveled the world, raised three wonderful children and have now settled in Atlanta, Georgia, where Debby spins tales of mystery and suspense that touch the heart and soul. Visit Debby online at debbygiusti.com, blog with her at seekerville.Blogspot.com and craftieladiesofromance.Blogspot.com, and email her at Debby@DebbyGiusti.com.

Carrie Lighte lives in Massachusetts next door to a Mennonite farming family, and she frequently spots deer, foxes, fisher cats, coyotes and turkeys in her backyard. Having enjoyed traveling to several Amish communities in the eastern United States, she looks forward to visiting settlements in the western states and in Canada. When she's not reading, writing or researching, Carrie likes to hike, kayak, bake and play word games.

DEBBY GIUSTI

Amish Safe House

&

CARRIE LIGHTE

Minding the Amish Baby

LOVE INSPIRED
INSPIRATIONAL ROMANCE

LOVE INSPIRED®
INSPIRATIONAL ROMANCE

Recycling programs
for this product may
not exist in your area.

ISBN-13: 978-1-335-22984-7

Amish Safe House and Minding the Amish Baby

Copyright © 2020 by Harlequin Books S.A.

Special thanks and acknowledgment are given to Debby Giusti
for her contribution to the Amish Witness Protection series.

Amish Safe House
First published in 2019. This edition published in 2020.
Copyright © 2019 by Harlequin Books S.A.

Minding the Amish Baby
First published in 2018. This edition published in 2020.
Copyright © 2018 by Carrie Lighte

This edition published by arrangement with Harlequin Books S.A.

For questions and comments about the quality of this book,
please contact us at CustomerService@Harlequin.com.

Harlequin Enterprises ULC
22 Adelaide St. West, 40th Floor
Toronto, Ontario M5H 4E3, Canada
www.Harlequin.com

Printed in U.S.A.

CONTENTS

AMISH SAFE HOUSE

Debby Giusti

To our law enforcement heroes.
May God bless them and keep them in His care.

Trust in the Lord with all thine heart; and lean not unto thine own understanding. In all thy ways acknowledge him, and he shall direct thy paths.
—*Proverbs* 3:5–6

Prologue

Gunfire!

Julia Bradford's pulse raced. "Kayla, where's your brother?"

"He took out the trash."

Julia rinsed the plate she was washing and glanced at the overflowing trash bag still on the floor by the kitchen counter, then peered through the window at the dumpster in the empty alleyway below.

Another round of gunshots. Her heart thumped a warning. She wiped her hand on a dish towel and hurried into the living area. "When did he leave?"

Her seven-year-old daughter clutched her doll and shrugged. Thankfully, Kayla seemed oblivious to the gang warfare that held this part of the inner city hostage.

"Come with me." Julia reached for her daughter's hand.

Kayla reluctantly rose from the floor, still holding her doll, and slipped her small hand into her mother's. "Where are we going?"

"To Mrs. Fielding's apartment."

Kayla's face broke into a wide smile. "Maybe she baked cookies today."

If only all of life's problems could be solved with a cookie.

"Hurry." Julia ushered her daughter into the stairwell and up one flight of steps.

She knocked on the apartment door. "Mrs. Fielding?"

Relieved when the sweet neighbor with the warm gaze and understanding smile opened the door, Julia gently guided Kayla through the doorway.

"William's outside," she explained. "I heard gunshots."

The older woman's brown eyes widened. "Lord, protect that boy."

"Can you watch Kayla?"

"Of course, dear."

"Lock the door, Mrs. Fielding. The gangs have started following their victims into stairwells."

"God help us." The woman moaned as she pointed Kayla toward the table. "Sit there, baby. I'll get you a cookie."

Once the door closed, Julia waited to hear the click of the dead bolt fall into place before she raced down the stairs, pushed on the outer door and stepped into the cool night air.

A *pop-pop-pop* sounded, followed by a rapid burst of semiautomatic gunfire. Heart in her throat, Julia ran toward the sound.

"William?" She glanced into the alley, the neighboring apartment, the small grocery on the corner with its windows barred to stop the rampant crime.

"Thank you, Charlie," Julia spat out, her hands fisted. Anger at her ex-husband bubbled up anew.

More gunfire, peppered with angry shouts.

Where's Will?

She turned left at the intersection, then right onto a side street. Her gut tightened. Halfway down the block two bodies lay sprawled on the roadway. Dark swaths of blood pooled on the pavement.

Fear tangled her spine.

William!

She wanted to scream his name, but her outcry would draw attention to a fourteen-year-old enamored of punk teens and twentysomethings who flaunted knives and guns and endless cash.

She blamed Charlie, her ex, who was serving time. So much for fatherly love. The only thing he had provided for his children was a heritage of crime.

Slipping into a nearby alleyway, she peered at the thugs marked with tattoos and piercings milling around their fallen comrades.

More shots. A man gasped, his face caught in the headlights of an oncoming car. He clutched his chest and collapsed to the pavement. Just that quickly, the rival gangs scattered.

Footsteps sounded. Julia held her breath and narrowed her gaze, trying to determine who was approaching.

Her eyes widened.

William!

She stepped from the darkness and grabbed her son's hand. "Where were you?"

"Mom, please." He jerked free.

"You snuck out."

"I told Kayla."

"You didn't tell me."

She glanced back. Three men stood staring at them.

Julia's heart lurched. She motioned William forward. "Go home. Now."

Footsteps slapped the pavement behind them. She turned again. Her heart stopped. The men were running toward them.

"Hurry, Will."

With his long legs and easy gait, her son moved ahead of her. They turned left at the corner and right at the next intersection. Her lungs burned. She gasped for air.

William climbed the stairs to their apartment building and plugged in the code. The door clicked open. He disappeared into the stairwell.

Julia followed him inside and up the stairs. He stood at the door of their apartment, fumbling with the key.

Shouts sounded below.

"Where is he?" Male voices. "Where's that punk kid? David's friend. He saw it all go down."

Another voice, coming from the same group. "I know his apartment number. Follow me."

Heavy footfalls pounded the stairs.

Julia's heart stopped. She reached around William and jiggled the key. The door to their apartment opened. She shoved him into the living room, slammed the door behind her and engaged the lock.

"Hide, Will. In the bathroom."

She grabbed her cell phone off a side table and followed her son through the bedroom to the bath beyond, locking both doors behind them just as the gang members crashed through the front door and entered the apartment.

"Lay down." She motioned William into the tub. "Cover your head with your hands."

Trembling, Julia punched 911 into her cell. "The

Philador gang," she said, breathless, once the operator answered. "Three of them...in my apartment."

She gave the address, the words spilling out one after another. "My son and I...locked in the bath. Hurry."

Angry shouts. Glass shattered. A heavy object clattered to the floor.

God, can You hear me? Protect my child.

Julia pushed her weight against the bathroom door, hoping it would hold. Her heart raced. A roar filled her ears.

If only the police...

Sirens sounded.

Would they get there in time?

Voices in the bedroom. Something or someone rammed the bathroom door.

"You're dead, punk."

William glanced up, his face twisted with fear.

Another crash to the door.

She thought of her daughter with Mrs. Fielding in the upstairs apartment.

Keep them safe.

"Police!" a voice shouted.

A shot, followed in a nanosecond by another. A scream. Then the scurry of feet.

Someone pounded on the door. "Ma'am, it's the police. Unlock the door."

Could she trust the voice? Could she trust anyone?

Will climbed from the tub, his cheeks wet with tears, his nose running. He touched her hand.

She saw his lips move, but she couldn't understand what he was saying.

He nudged her aside, undid the lock and slowly opened the door.

Hands grabbed both of them and pulled them through the bedroom, past two bleeding bodies on the floor, past the group of officers huddled around another gang member. His wrists were cuffed behind his back. Curly black hair, a mustache and goatee, deep-set eyes that stared at her as they passed.

Recognition flickered in the back of Julia's mind.

A female officer introduced herself and held up a badge. "We're taking you someplace safe."

Julia shook her head. She reached for William and pulled him close. "My son?"

"He's going with you."

"Kayla? My…my daughter—"

"Where is she, ma'am?"

"Upstairs."

Without letting go of William's hand, Julia climbed the stairs, pulling her son behind her. The officer followed.

"It's Julia." She tapped on Mrs. Fielding's door. "I need my daughter."

The door cracked open. Mrs. Fielding peered through the narrow crevice.

"Where's Kayla?"

"Mama!" The child yanked on the door. Her eyes widened as she glanced at the throng of police swarming the stairwell. "What's wrong, Mama?"

Julia pointed to the female officer. "We're going someplace with this lady."

"I don't wanna go."

"Shhh, Kayla. It'll be okay."

"My dolly."

"Kayla, please."

She ran back into the apartment and returned with the doll clutched in her arms.

Julia squeezed Mrs. Fielding's hand. "Thank you."

"God keep you safe," the older woman said. "I'm praying for you."

If only God would listen.

The officer touched Julia's arm. "We need to leave now."

"My purse?"

"I'll have someone retrieve your things."

"I homeschool my children. There are books and—"

"I'll tell them to bring the schoolbooks and supplies." The officer put her hand on Julia's shoulder and pointed her down the stairs.

Outside, the flashing lights of the ambulance and police squad cars captured them in their glare. Julia pulled her children close and ran toward the waiting car, her head lowered as the officer had instructed.

They slid into the back seat of the large sedan. Heat pumped from air vents. Julia buckled seat belts and wrapped her arms around the children, her heart nearly pounding out of her chest.

The officer glanced at William. "Did you see anyone shot this evening?"

He lowered his gaze and nodded. "Oscar… Oscar de la Rosa."

"Who shot him?"

William glanced at Julia before he answered, his voice little more than a whisper. "Frankie Fuentes."

Julia's heart broke. Her son was caught in the middle of a Philadelphia turf war between the Philadores and Delphis. Both gangs killed in cold blood and left no witnesses.

Kayla snuggled closer, her eyes heavy.

"Everything's all right, sweetie," Julia assured her.

But it wasn't. Nothing was right and everything was wrong.

Chapter One

❧

"I have your new identities." US Marshal Jonathan Mast sat across the table from Julia in the hotel, situated on the outskirts of Philadelphia, where she and her children had been holed up for the last five days. He was a pensive man with a dark beard and equally dark eyes.

"The night of the shooting I asked you to be patient, Mrs. Bradford, and you have been, which we all appreciate." He glanced at the two other marshals at the table. Both Stacy Porter, slender and focused on her job, and Karl Adams, more laid-back with an easy smile, nodded in agreement.

Julie didn't feel patient. She felt frustrated and stir-crazy. Keeping her children content in a two-room suite had been a challenge. Plus, she was scared to death about their safety.

The Philadores wanted to kill William so he wouldn't testify against their leader. As much as Julia didn't trust law enforcement, she had to rely on the US Marshals and their witness protection program to keep her family safe. No wonder her nerves were stretched thin. She had slept little over the last four nights, and the nagging headache and dark circles under her eyes were proof of her struggle to maintain some semblance of normalcy in her children's lives.

As efficient as Marshal Mast seemed, he failed to realize how antsy kids could be without sunshine and fresh air. Fortunately, Stacy and Karl had seemed more empathetic. Both in their early thirties, they had played games with William and Kayla and had provided pizza and colas and an abundance of snacks. But even a diet of junk food got old.

"We're ready to transport you and the children," Jonathan Mast continued. "We'll fly into Kansas City tonight, then drive to Topeka and north to Yoder."

"What's in Kansas?"

"What's *not* there is more important. Kansas is one of the few states where the Philadores don't have a strong presence. As I've mentioned previously, Frankie Fuentes is a killer. He runs drugs, has his hand in prostitution, trafficking and illegal gambling. Three weeks ago, he gunned down two cops in cold blood. No witnesses and no way to bring him to justice. Your son saw him kill Oscar de la Rosa. William's testimony will send Fuentes to jail for a long time."

Jonathan pulled out his phone and accessed a photograph. He handed the cell to Julia. "Abraham King will watch over you in Kansas."

Julia studied the picture. The man looked to be in his midthirties with a square face and deep-set eyes beneath dark brows. His nose appeared a bit off center, as if it had been broken. Lips pulled tight, and no hint of a smile on his angular face.

"Mr. King doesn't look happy."

Jonathan shrugged. "Law enforcement photos are never flattering."

Her stomach tightened. "He's a cop?"

"Past tense. He left the force three years ago."

Once a cop, always a cop. Her ex had been a police officer. He protected others but failed to show that same sense of concern when it came to his own family. After Charlie, she wanted nothing to do with men in uniform.

The marshal seemed oblivious to her unease.

"Abe is an old friend," Jonathan continued. "A widower from my police-force days who owns a farm and has a sparc house on his property. He lives in a rural Amish community."

"Amish?"

"That's right."

"Bonnets and buggies?" she asked.

He smiled weakly. "You'll be off the grid, Mrs. Bradford. No one will look for you there. If anyone asks, you'll be working as Abraham's housekeeper, at least until the trial."

"Has a date been set?"

"Not yet. Everything takes time."

Julia tried to get her mind around a new identity in a new state. She didn't understand the Amish connection, but she was okay with anything that meant William and Kayla would be safe.

"My ex-husband…"

She glanced into the adjoining bedroom where William was watching a sporting event on ESPN. Kayla stood nearby and pretended to feed her doll.

Julia lowered her voice. "My ex-husband won't know of our whereabouts?"

"That's correct."

"He won't be able to find us," she repeated, needing the reassurance she hoped the marshal would provide.

"No one will find you, ma'am."

"William will be safe in Kansas?"

"Yes, ma'am."

"As you probably know, my husband was a cop." She glanced again at the photo. "I'm… I'm hesitant to rely on someone with that background. Do you know why Mr. King was forced to resign?"

Jonathan stiffened. "Abraham had a stellar record with law enforcement, Mrs. Bradford."

"I didn't mean to imply…" She held up her hand. "I'm just worried about the safety of my children. They come first."

"Of course they do, but let me assure you, their safety, as well as yours, is our top priority."

He retrieved his phone from her outstretched hand and tucked it into his pocket. "Abraham put a criminal in jail who wanted payback after he was paroled. The guy planted an explosive device in Abe's car. The next morning, his wife tried to drive their daughter to daycare. The car exploded, and his wife and four-year-old child were killed."

The marshal's matter-of-fact disclosure of the tragedy hit Julia hard. She glanced down at the table, fighting back tears that welled up in her eyes at the senseless loss of life. "I'm sorry."

Jonathan nodded. "It was a tough time for him, as you can imagine."

"Did Mr. King agree to shelter us?"

"He did. Your identities and location will probably change again after William testifies, but for now, you'll be Julia Stolz."

"A German name."

"Yes, ma'am. The area has a large German as well as Amish population. Stolz will fit in."

"I don't speak German."

"That won't be a problem." He pulled a manila folder from his briefcase and placed it on the table in front of her.

"Here's the paperwork you need for your new identities. Social security cards with new names and numbers for you and the children. Birth certificates. A high school graduation diploma for Julia Stolz."

Jonathan glanced into the bedroom. "William and Kayla need to understand the importance of not revealing their old identities."

Kayla wouldn't be a problem, but William was going through a defiant stage where he rebelled against everything.

As if reading her mind, Mast added, "William needs to know that his safety as well as yours and your daughter's depends on him agreeing to this new life."

Julia nodded. "I'll talk to him."

But would he listen?

Pushing his chair back from the table, Jonathan glanced at his fellow marshals. "We'll leave at nine tonight."

"Why so late?" Julia asked.

"At the present time, the Philadores don't know your whereabouts. We don't want that to change." He stood. "Stacy and Karl will drive you to the airport. I'll meet you there."

True to his word, Marshal Mast was waiting on the tarmac when Karl pulled the sedan to a stop next to the small charter plane that night.

Julia and her children were ushered onboard. Kayla fell asleep not long after the plane was airborne. William nodded off soon thereafter. Julia stared out the window, peering into the dark sky. Her head throbbed, her eyes burned and she was cold, too cold.

Stacy handed her blankets. "You've been very brave."

Julia covered her children and herself with the blankets and almost laughed. Not brave, but maybe foolish to think she could outsmart the Philadores. Her eyes closed. The jerk of the plane when the wheels touched down forced them open again.

"We've landed." Stacy patted Julia's arm. "A van will take us to your final destination."

Julia ushered her children off the plane and into the vehicle parked on the tarmac.

Karl slipped behind the wheel. Jonathan sat in the passenger's seat, and Stacy climbed into the rear.

Kayla fell asleep again, her head on Julia's lap. William leaned against her shoulder. Soon, he too drifted off.

Julia watched the lights of the city fade from view as they headed into the country. She quickly lost track of the twists and turns in the road and slipped into a half sleep.

A hand tapped her shoulder. "We're almost to our destination."

The car turned off the paved road onto a dirt drive that led to a two-story house with a porch and overhanging tin roof. A small light glowed in a downstairs window.

A second house, similar in style but a bit larger, sat not more than twenty feet away.

Stacy slipped out from the rear. "I'll carry Kayla." She lifted the girl into her arms.

"William, wake up." Julia patted her son's arm. "We're going inside."

He rubbed his eyes and followed her out of the van. Julia took Kayla from the marshal and then grabbed William's hand, surprised that he didn't balk. Most days, he objected to any show of affection.

Julia's stomach churned. She hugged Kayla closer and gripped her son's hand more tightly as they followed Stacy up the steps to the porch.

The door opened. A man stood backlit on the threshold. "You made good time," he said in greeting.

"No traffic this late at night." Marshal Mast extended his hand. The two men shook, then embraced in a back-slapping half-hug of sorts that confirmed the friendship Jonathan had mentioned.

The homeowner shook hands with the two other marshals and invited them inside. "There's coffee. I placed ham and cheese and bread on the table, in case you're hungry."

He glanced at her and nodded. "Ma'am."

Stepping inside, she narrowed her gaze and studied the sparse accommodations. A table, sideboard, a wood-burning stove. Glancing into another room, she saw two rockers, a bench, a chest of drawers and another table.

She focused again on the man who had welcomed them to his house. He wore a white shirt and trousers held up with suspenders. No collar on the shirt. No buttons. No belt. Work boots scuffed with mud. Turning she saw the pegs on the wall by the door and the black, wide-brimmed felt hat and the short black waistcoat.

She glanced at the marshals who were pouring coffee and helping themselves to the bread and cold cuts on the table. The only person who noticed her discomfort was the man whose photo she had seen earlier today.

His deep-set eyes stared at her as if questioning why she was there.

Julia wanted to ask the same question. Jonathan had mentioned that Abraham was living Amish, but the stark reality of what that meant hit her like a sledgehammer. No phone, no electrical power, no technology. *Off the grid,* as Jonathan had mentioned, was an understatement. Plus, the Amish were pacifists. If they didn't believe in violence or raising a hand against another, then what if the Philadores discovered where she and her children were hiding?

Her heart sank as she looked at the tall man with the questioning gaze. A former cop who didn't fit the law enforcement model. No matter what Jonathan claimed, she didn't see how Abraham King could protect her and her children if he was Amish.

Abraham had made a mistake. As much as he owed Jonathan, he never should have agreed to bring a woman into his life.

Losing everyone he had ever loved had taken him to the brink of despair. Jonathan had saved him and brought him back to life, a life of hard work and isolation. A life without a woman to stir up memories of Marianne and their precious little girl, Becca. His breath caught as he thought of the pain that never seemed to end.

Surely Jonathan would understand if Abraham backed out of their agreement. Then he glanced at Julia. Too thin, too afraid, too lost. He knew the signs of a person holding on by a whisper. He had been that person three years ago.

The boy standing next to her was tall and gangly, as if a growth spurt had caught him unawares. His brown eyes, like his mother's, peered warily at the three marshals gathered around the table. The kid looked tired and confused and ready to bolt if given the chance.

"His dad's doing time," Jonathan had shared. "Wouldn't take much for the kid to follow in his father's footsteps from what we know. You're the family's last hope, Abraham."

Abraham sighed. How could he turn his back on a woman and two children in such need?

"The bedrooms are upstairs." Abraham stepped toward her. "I can show you the way. Perhaps the children would like to go to sleep."

"I'm sure they would." Clutching her daughter in her arms, she nodded to her son, and the weary threesome followed Abraham up the stairs.

Carrying an oil lamp to light the way, he chastised himself for not placing a lit lamp in each of the bedrooms. Darkness could be frightening, especially to children in new surroundings.

He opened the first door on the right. "I thought your daughter could sleep here."

The woman hesitated a moment and stared at the furnishings. A single bed, small dresser, and a side table with a water pitcher and basin.

She moved into the room, pulled back the covers and laid her little girl on the bed. Quickly, she removed Kayla's shoes and covered her with a quilt.

Abraham glanced down at the child's blond hair and chubby cheeks. A knife stabbed his heart as Becca's face filled his vision. He turned away and headed to the door.

"William, your mother will sleep across the hall. The room next door is for you." Thankfully, the boy followed.

"I will leave the lamp in the hallway."

"You…you don't have electricity?" the boy asked, his voice filled with wonder.

"We use oil lamps."

The boy frowned.

Abraham stepped back into the hallway to give the lad privacy as he untied his shoes and got ready for bed.

Julia stepped past him and entered the room. She pulled the covers around her son's shoulders and brushed the hair from his forehead. "Go to sleep, William. We'll talk tomorrow. I'll be across the hall."

"I don't wanna stay here."

She nodded. "I know."

The boy's eyes closed and he was soon asleep.

Abraham placed the lamp on a small table in the hallway. Julia joined him there.

"I appreciate you taking us in, Mr. King."

"Please, my name is Abraham. Some call me Abe."

"I hate to disturb your life, but Marshal Mast—"

"You have disturbed nothing, Ms. Stolz."

Her brow wrinkled.

"Perhaps Jonathan did not provide your new name?"

"He did. It's just that…" She raked her hand through her golden-brown hair. "So much has happened."

"We can review the information you will need tomorrow."

"Thank you, Abraham." She glanced into her room and then hurried downstairs.

The marshals were eating sandwiches and finishing their coffee. They stood when she entered the kitchen.

Stacy pointed to a plastic bag sitting next to the luggage by the door. "I brought a few games for the kids."

Julia offered a weak smile. "That was very thoughtful."

"William and Kayla will adjust." Stacy squeezed her arm. "You will, too."

"I hope so."

Jonathan shook hands with Abraham. "Thanks for the chow."

"You are traveling back to Philadelphia tonight?"

"We'll be at our desks before dawn." The marshal turned to Julia. "You can call us if you need anything. Abraham's neighbor has a phone. Do you have any questions?"

"None that I can think of at the moment."

The marshals shook her hand and then left the house. Stacy and Karl climbed into the van. Jonathan hung back.

"I'll leave the coded message on your neighbor's answering machine if anything new develops," he told Abraham, who had followed them outside. "Let me know if you notice anything suspicious. The Philadores don't have much of a foothold in Kansas, but that could change."

He slapped Abraham's shoulder. "Nice seeing you, Abe. Looks like you've settled into Amish life."

"Coming back was a good decision for me." Abraham hesitated. "I will always be grateful."

"You saved my hide a few times. The least I could do was reciprocate."

Jonathan glanced back at the house before adding, "I know this is hard, but the kid's in danger. I don't have to tell you the woman looks fragile and at the end of her rope. The boy could be the biggest problem. The cops in Philly found him on the street a couple times and took him home. The mom's trying hard, but we both know sometimes that's not good enough. Plus, her ex-husband came after her following their divorce. She got a restraining order and changed locations twice. Each time he found her. He eventually went to prison, but he talked about getting even. She's carrying a lot of worry, especially concerning her son. Maybe you can redirect the kid and focus him on something other than gangs and crime."

"The Amish way is not for everyone, Jonathan. You know that."

"*Yah.*" The marshal slipped into his own Amish roots. "But for a kid who doesn't know where to turn, the hard work and strong sense of community might give him a new outlook on life. As I mentioned when I first contacted you, my wife was in WitSec and was placed within the Amish community, which proved successful. I have confidence you'll make this work as well, Abraham."

"When I agreed to help, I thought there would be a husband." Abraham tugged on his jaw. "A husband who would follow his wife here at some later time, instead of an ex locked away in prison."

"I may have skipped over that detail."

Abraham chuckled. "You knew I would never agree to a woman without a husband."

"You'll be in the house next door."

"Of course I will, but she was hurt by her ex and probably struggles to trust men."

"Wouldn't you struggle, if you had been through what she has? Her husband had a passion for gambling. Too much debt and to the wrong people. Then he embezzled funds to cover his habit."

"Being placed with a female might have been a better fit."

"Encourage her to call Stacy if she needs to talk to

another woman. In the meantime, you're our man on this case, Abe. The family needs you."

Again the two men shook hands. As Jonathan turned toward the car, his cell rang. He pulled it out, pushed Talk and raised the phone to his ear. "Mast." He nodded. "You're sure? Thanks. I'll pass that on."

Pocketing his phone, Jonathan turned worried eyes to Abraham. "We picked up an informant who was eager to talk. Fuentes got wind of us moving William out of Philadelphia."

"How?"

Jonathan shrugged. "Beats me, but it compounds the situation. Not that they suspect Kansas. Still, stay alert. His people could be anywhere and anyone."

"Are you sure the informant is legit?"

"As sure as we can be. I'll call you if we get more information."

Jonathan hurried to the van and climbed into the front seat. The three marshals nodded their farewells before the vehicle drove away, leaving Abraham to think of the family he had not been able to protect.

His own family.

He turned and, with a heavy heart, entered the kitchen. The woman stood by the table.

"I live in the house next door," he said. "I will leave you to your rest now. Tomorrow we will talk about this new arrangement."

He touched the dead bolt on the kitchen door. "The front door is locked. Do the same with the dead bolt once I leave. Do not worry. The only person prowling the grounds tonight will be me. I will not let harm come to you or your children."

Without waiting for her to comment, Abraham

grabbed his hat and coat from the wall pegs and stepped outside.

He paused and listened for the door to lock.

Silence.

He knocked. "Lock the door, Mrs. Stolz, for your own peace of mind."

The lock clicked into place. With a heavy sigh, he headed home.

He was glad he had bought the main house and the *dawdy*, or grandparents' house, next door. Abraham had not needed two houses, but he had wanted the land. One hundred twenty acres to farm and to exhaust him so he would forget about Marianne and Becca. Except he could never forget his wife and child.

Now this woman had stepped into his quiet world with her two children and all he could think about was what he had lost.

He had made a mistake agreeing to help Jonathan. In a few days Abraham would tell him the setup was not working and insist he find somewhere else to place Julia and her children.

Abraham kicked a clod of dirt with his boot and sighed, knowing that if the Philador gang was after them, there would be no place safe for Julia and her children to hide.

Chapter Two

Julia awoke to someone pounding on the door.

She blinked her eyes open to see a blue curtain covering the bedroom window and tried to remember where she was.

Not the apartment in Philly.

Kansas.

Her heart sank. For a moment, she had hoped everything had been a dream.

Rising from the bed, she slipped into her jeans and pulled on the sweater she had worn last night. Hunger nagged at her stomach and made her hurry that much faster down the stairs. She wanted the children to sleep in, at least until she'd had a cup of coffee.

Another rap sounded at the kitchen door. She glanced out the window, relieved to see the tall Amish man standing on the porch. She raked her hair out of her face, twisted the lock and pulled open the door.

Her breath hitched. She hadn't realized how tall he was or how muscular. She pulled the sweater across her chest and took a step back, needing to distance herself from his bulk and his pensive eyes that stared down at her.

He held out a large ceramic mug. "Coffee?"

In his other hand, he held a jug of milk that he gave her. "There's sugar in the kitchen. Breakfast will be ready in fifteen minutes."

"The children are still asleep."

"Wake them so they can eat."

"I wanted to let them sleep."

"Chores need to be done."

"Chores?"

He nodded. "A farm does not run on its own. To eat, we must work."

She glanced around his broad chest and scanned the surrounding area. Horses grazed in a nearby pasture. Cattle waited at a feed trough in the distance.

"Okay," she said. "We'll see you in fifteen minutes."

"*Gut.*" He turned and headed back to his house.

Julia inhaled the rich aroma of the coffee, added a dollop of milk and sighed with the first sip. Strong and hot, just the way she liked it.

Turning back to the kitchen, she spied a wooden box and opened the lid, seeing the insulation and feeling the coolness. She bent to examine a trap door that she slid open to find a chunk of ice.

"Who needs electricity?" She placed the milk in the aluminum-lined icebox and then tugged their suitcases upstairs. She rummaged through the contents until she found her toiletries.

Using the water in the pitcher, she washed her face and hands and brushed her teeth, then pulled her hair into a knot at the base of her neck.

Taking another sip of coffee, she knocked on William's open door and stepped toward the bed. "Time to get up, sleepyhead."

She brushed her hand over his hair, wishing he could always be so calm and peaceful. "Abraham is fixing breakfast. I'm sure you're hungry."

William opened one eye. "That big dude cooks?"

Julia tried to squelch a smile. "That dude is named Abraham. I have a feeling he can do a lot of things, and it sounds as though if you miss breakfast, you won't eat until lunch."

Both eyes opened. "Okay. I'm outta here."

"I put a clean shirt on the chair. There's water in the pitcher. Pour it into the basin to wash your hands and face and brush your teeth."

"Rules, Mom. Too many."

No doubt their host would have more rules for them to follow.

Kayla woke with a smile and hopped out of bed without needing to be told twice. She slipped into a fresh blouse and jeans and reached for her doll, tucked under the quilt. "I hope Mr. Abraham makes something good for breakfast. My tummy is hungry."

"Whatever he prepares will be appreciated, Kayla. Be sure to say please and thank you."

"I always remember even if Will doesn't."

"You set a good example for your brother."

The child smiled as if they shared a secret. Julia brushed Kayla's hair and helped her wash her face. "You look lovely."

Hand in hand, they headed downstairs, where William waited in the kitchen. "It's weird, Mom."

"What is?"

"The fridge looks like a box cooled with a big chunk of ice."

"That's what it is, Will. An icebox. The Amish don't use electricity."

"That's crazy."

"Maybe to you, but many people enjoy the *plain* life as it's called."

"Plain and stupid," Will grumbled under his breath. Julia chose to ignore the remark as she pulled open the kitchen door and guided the children into the cool springtime morning.

The musky smell of the rich soil and fresh air greeted them. She peered at the sun, which was peeking through an overcast sky. A crow cawed from the branches of a gnarled oak in the front yard. The irony wasn't lost on her. For so long, she had yearned to live in the country where the air wasn't stagnant with car exhaust and a crowd of buildings didn't block the sun. Strange that her son being caught in the middle of a gang war would lead them to this remote Amish farm.

Then she thought of the Philadores, who wouldn't give up their search until they found William. Narrowing her gaze, she stared at the distant road where a pickup truck traveled well over the speed limit. Someone local, no doubt, yet instinctively, she put her arm around Will's shoulder and pulled him close.

God, if you're listening, protect my child.

He shrugged out of her hold just as the door to the nearby house opened and Abraham stepped onto the porch.

"I had planned to ring the dinner bell to summon you," he said, his voice warm with welcome. "Your timing is perfect. Breakfast is on the table."

Kayla ran ahead and climbed the stairs. "I'm hungry, Mr. Abraham."

"What about your dolly?" Abraham asked, eyeing the doll she clutched in her arm.

Kayla smiled. "She's hungry, too."

"Does she have a name?"

"Marianne. My daddy gave her to me."

Abraham's face clouded. He glanced at Julia, pain visible in his gaze.

"Mr. Abraham might not want a doll at the breakfast table," Julia said to ease his upset. Then, fearing they may have offended his faith, she added, "As I recall, Amish dolls don't have faces, although I'm not sure why."

"It has to do with graven images, but only in certain communities." Abraham held up his hand. "Having a doll with a face is not a problem here in Yoder."

He glanced down at Kayla and smiled. "If you do not mind, I will call your doll Annie."

The child shrugged. "That's a pretty name, too."

"What do you and Annie usually eat for breakfast?" he asked.

Kayla scrunched up her sweet face. "Mom makes us eat oatmeal."

"Does she?" He laughed, and the pain evaporated. "It appears from your expression that you do not like oatmeal."

"Oatmeal's okay and it's cheap. That's why we eat it."

"Kayla May, you don't need to bore Mr. King with our family's financial situation."

He held the door open and motioned them inside.

A man's house. Sparse but tidy. Two wooden rockers sat near the wood-burning stove in the middle of the room. A long table with chairs on one side and a bench by the wall divided the kitchen from the living area. A hutch and sideboard sat in the kitchen, a blanket chest and bookshelf in the larger living area.

Blue curtains, just as in the smaller house, were pulled back from the windows, a cloth covered the table, and oil lamps sat on a shelf in the kitchen.

"Sit on the bench, children," he directed. "Your mother can take the chair across from me."

"May I help serve the food?" she asked.

"Everyone likes pancakes?" He raised a brow.

Kayla's eyes widened. "I do."

"William, what about you?"

He shrugged. "They're okay."

"I also scrambled eggs and fried some slices of ham." Abraham handed Julia a plate. "Give the children as much as they can eat."

While she put pancakes and a slice of ham on each plate along with a spoonful of scrambled eggs, Abraham poured milk for the children and coffee for the adults.

He held her chair, which she hadn't expected. How long had it been since anyone had done that for her?

Shaking off the memory of Charlie on one of their first dates, she slid onto the chair and placed her napkin on her lap.

William reached for his fork. She held up her hand, waiting as Abraham sat and bowed his head. Eyeing her son, she nodded for him to follow Abraham's lead and hoped both children would remember how to give thanks.

Not that God would be listening to Julia's prayer. Still, she was grateful. *Keep us safe*, she thought before grabbing a fork and lifting a portion of the sweet and savory pancake into her mouth.

"Breakfast is delicious," she said between bites.

William, usually a picky eater, gobbled down everything on his plate and asked for more.

Abraham nodded his approval. "You have a good appetite, *yah*?"

Will wrinkled his brow and chuckled. "*Yah.*"

Julia frowned at her son. She was grateful Abraham either hadn't realized or chose to ignore William's disrespect.

Once they had eaten, she helped Abraham clear the table. "I can wash the dishes. You mentioned having chores to do."

"The soap is under the sink." He grabbed a hat hanging on a wall peg. "Come with me, William. We need to feed the neighbor's livestock."

The boy hesitated.

"William," he called again.

Slowly, the boy rose and shuffled to the door.

Abraham grabbed a basket from the sideboard. "Kayla, you can gather eggs."

"What about Annie?"

He smiled. "Annie should stay inside and help your mother with the dishes."

Satisfied with the response, Kayla sat the doll on a chair and hurried after Abraham.

"Is gathering eggs like an Easter egg hunt, Mr. Abraham?"

"Perhaps a bit. I will show you." He motioned the child toward the door and then glanced at Julia. "After Kayla collects the eggs, she will return to the house. Then William and I will go to the farm across the road. Harvey Raber and his sons are delivering the furniture they make to customers who placed orders. The neighbors lend a hand while they are gone."

Julia glanced quickly around the tidy kitchen and peered into the living area. "Shall I start cleaning?"

"You are a housekeeper in name only, Julia. You and Kayla can return to your house. I am sure you have things to do there."

She appreciated his thoughtfulness. "I'd like to unpack."

"Lock the door. If there is a problem, ring the dinner bell. I will hear you."

In spite of the peaceful setting and Abraham's attempt to welcome them to farm life, his mention of using a bell if she or Kayla had a problem, made the anxiety Julia had felt in Philadelphia return. She and the children had traveled over a thousand miles to elude the Philadores, yet the truth remained. Frankie Fuentes was a killer, and he was after her son.

Abraham hurried Kayla to the henhouse while William sat on the porch steps, looking totally uninterested in anything about the farm. From what he had seen so far, the two children seemed to be complete opposites. Kayla embraced life to the full, while William hung back and needed to be coaxed into new endeavors.

Kayla's eyes were wide with wonder as she stood on tiptoe and peered into one of the nests. She spied an egg and placed it in her basket.

"Don't the chickens get upset that their eggs are gone?" she asked.

"They will lay more tomorrow, Kayla." Abraham pointed to the corner of the henhouse. "Check there. I usually find an egg or two hidden under the hay."

The child's search proved fruitful and soon she was

headed back to the house with a smile of contentment on her pretty face and a basket full of eggs.

"I'll tell Mama to make something with the eggs like Mrs. Fielding did."

"Mrs. Fielding?" Abraham asked.

"She lived in an upstairs apartment and used to take care of William and me when Mama had to work."

"I am sure she was a good woman."

"Mrs. Fielding told me she was a God-fearing woman. I wasn't sure what that meant, but I told her I didn't fear God because I loved Him."

Abraham tried not to smile, but Kayla's sincerity touched his heart. "Hurry into the house and tell your mother that William and I are going to Mr. Raber's farm."

"Can I go with you?"

"Maybe next time."

She skipped toward the house and stopped on the porch step to wave goodbye.

"Go inside, Kayla," he called to her.

The child climbed the stairs, knocked and scooted into the house when Julia opened the door. She stood for a long moment in the doorway, staring at him. The breeze pulled at her golden hair. She caught the elusive strands and tugged them back into place before she closed the door again, leaving Abraham with a curious sensation in the pit of his stomach.

He glanced at William, who shuffled along the drive, his head down and shoulders slumped. "You act as if you would rather have stayed with your mother."

"I would rather have stayed in Philadelphia," the boy said with a huff. "Besides, I don't like to get up early."

"You are tired from your journey?"

The boy nodded. "Tired and bored."

Abraham chuckled under his breath. With all the chores that needed to be done on the farm, William would not be bored for long.

"Grab that bucket and fill it with feed for the horses in the paddock," Abraham said when they entered the neighbor's barn. The bucket was heavy when filled, but William carried it to the trough and then repeated the process.

"Now we will muck the stalls." Abraham handed the boy a pitchfork and pointed to an empty stall. "Start there."

From the look on William's face, Abraham knew he was not happy, but he worked hard, and if he complained, he did so under his breath.

"Next we will lay fresh straw."

William followed Abraham's lead and a bed of straw soon covered the floor of the stalls.

"You have done a good job." Abraham patted the boy's shoulder. "We will go home and do the same in my barn."

An almost imperceptible groan escaped Will's lips. Abraham pretended not to notice and led the way back to the country road that divided the two farms.

Raber's phone shack sat at the edge of the road. "Wait here, William."

Abraham opened the door and stepped into the booth. He checked the answering machine to ensure Jonathan had not called and left a message.

"Is that where the Amish keep their phones?" William asked when Abraham joined him again.

"*Yah*, Mr. Raber takes orders by phone for the furniture he makes. The *Ordnung,* the rules by which various Amish communities live, forbids phones within the home. Keeping the phone away from the house and near the property line allows Mr. Raber to stay in contact with his customers while also obeying the rule."

William pointed to the roof. "Are those solar panels?"

Abraham nodded. "They run the answering machine. You know about solar energy?"

William shrugged. "A little."

"Perhaps you will be an engineer when you get older."

The boy shook his head. "I don't think so."

"Why not?" Abraham asked.

"School's not cool."

Abraham would not ask what the boy thought was cool. From what Jonathan had said, William was drawn to the street gangs with their rap music and fast cars and even faster lifestyle. Was that what William thought was cool?

The sound of a car engine drew Abraham's attention to the road. A souped-up sedan raced over the crest of a distant rise, going much too fast along the narrow country lane.

William stared at the car, no doubt attracted to the gaudy chrome and the heavy bass destroying the peaceful quiet.

"Hide in the phone shack." Abraham opened the door and nudged William inside.

The car approached. Abraham walked to the curb. The driver stopped and rolled down the passenger window. "I'm looking for Yoder. Made a few wrong turns, it seems. Can you give me directions?"

"You are headed the right way. The town is about four miles ahead."

"I'll need a room. Can you recommend lodging?"

"There is a hotel south of town. At the intersection of

Main and High, turn left. The hotel sits about five blocks south on the left." Abraham stepped closer. "You are not from this area."

"I was in Kansas City on business and had a few days off so I decided to explore this part of the state. My hobby is writing articles for travel magazines. A story on Yoder and the Amish people might sell. If you have time, we could schedule an interview."

The last thing Abraham wanted was publicity about Yoder or his Amish neighbors. "Not much is going on around here. You might find more tourist attractions in Hutchison. They have an Amish community there."

"I'll check it out. Thanks for the information about the hotel." The man handed a business card to Abraham. "You know where to find me for the next few days in case you have time for a cup of coffee, or we could talk over lunch."

The driver waved and drove away.

Abraham made a mental note of the license plate before he opened the door to the phone booth. His heart stopped. William stood with the phone to his ear. His eyes widened and his face flushed. He dropped the receiver onto the cradle and lowered his gaze.

"Who did you call?"

The boy shook his head. "No one."

"I will ask you once more, William. Who did you call?"

"I… I thought about calling a friend of mine from Philly."

"What is his name?"

"David."

"His full name."

"David Davila."

"Did the call connect?"

Will shook his head. "No way. There wasn't time."

"Did you call your friend from the hotel in Philadelphia?"

The boy's face reddened.

"What did you tell David?"

"Only that we were moving, but I didn't tell him where."

"Did you mention Kansas?"

"I just said we were leaving the city."

Abraham pointed the boy toward the road. "The phone is off-limits. Is that understood?"

"Yeah, sure." William pushed past Abraham.

Abraham glanced back at the phone. William was his own worst enemy. The Philadores did not care if the boy was fourteen or forty-three. He was on their hit list. If Abraham could not protect William from himself, the boy and his sweet sister and pretty mother might die.

Chapter Three

Julia felt a swell of relief when she spied William and Abraham return to the farm and enter the barn.

A short time later, the clip-clop of horses' hooves pulled her attention back to the road. A buggy turned into the drive and stopped near the barn. A woman dressed in the typical Amish calf-length blue dress, black cape and matching black bonnet climbed to the ground.

Abraham stepped from the barn and greeted her with a welcoming smile. Julia wished she could hear their conversation and wondered what she should do if the woman came inside. Was she supposed to hide?

William stood at the barn entrance. From the way his arms moved, Abraham appeared to be introducing her son to the woman. Taking that as a sign she could go outside, Julia called for Kayla to join her and they both stepped onto the porch.

Abraham glanced up and nodded. "Sarah, this is Julia. She will be staying in the *dawdy* house for a bit of time and helping with the cleaning and cooking. Her daughter's name is Kayla."

Sarah looked perplexed, but she covered her confusion with a weak smile of welcome. "Abraham said you needed a place to stay."

How should she answer? "He has been most generous to us."

"I… I brought clothing."

The Amish woman glanced at Abraham, said something that sounded German and then reached into the buggy and pulled forth a basket. "Perhaps I should show you how to pin the dress?"

Julia didn't understand.

Abraham must have noticed her confusion. He stepped closer. "I saw Sarah yesterday before you arrived and asked her to bring Amish clothing, which will be good for you to wear."

"You want me to dress Amish?"

He nodded. "For now. So you can fit in."

"And the children?"

"They should, also."

Julia glanced at Kayla who clapped her hands and jumped up and down. William frowned and wrapped his arms across his chest.

Seemed there were complications to their new environment. Julia tried to recall if the marshals had said they would be living *with* the Amish or living Amish.

A huge difference, which she would need to explain to her children. Would William listen? From the scowl on his face, probably not.

Abraham poured another cup of coffee and waited in the kitchen as Sarah ushered Julia and Kayla into a spare bedroom and helped them dress. William headed for a small room off the main living area.

"You would like help?" Abraham asked.

The boy shook his head. "I've got it."

But evidently he did not *have it* because he remained in the room far longer than Abraham had expected. Before he could check on the boy, the bedroom door opened and Kayla skipped into the kitchen. Seeing Abraham, she stopped short.

Her cheeks were flushed, and her eyes twinkled as she smiled shyly. "Sarah said she has a daughter who used to wear this dress. Now she's grown taller. Sarah said I look like an Amish girl."

Abraham had to smile. "You look very pretty, Kayla, and very Amish." Her hair was braided and pulled into a bun. "We must get you a white *kapp* in town."

"Sarah said girls cover their heads when they pray and since they always pray, they always wear their hats."

"Called a *kapp*," he instructed.

"William wears baseball caps sometimes."

"That is not the same thing."

The girl nodded. "Sarah's fixing Mama's hair so she can look Amish, too."

Footsteps sounded. Abraham looked up to see Julia standing in the hallway, eyes downcast and a troubled frown on her oval face. She wore the typical Amish blue dress with white apron tied around her slender waist. Any self-sufficiency he had noticed earlier in her demeanor had been replaced with an alluring femininity that caused his gut to tighten. He also noted a hint of confusion that creased her brow, as if leaving her ordinary world and stepping into the Amish realm had thrown her off-kilter. Perhaps dressing Amish was too much too soon. The woman had been through so much.

Sarah encouraged her forward. "Trotter's Dry Goods

sells *kapps*. You must go to town and buy one for Kayla and Julia. Another dress, too, and a second apron."

He nodded. "We will go soon."

"I could meet you there and help with the selection."

"If we need help, I will let you know."

Sarah nodded and glanced at Kayla. "Tell me which you like best, apple pie or sweet potato?"

"Apple," Kayla said.

"I have an extra pie in the wagon."

Abraham smiled. "Thank you, Sarah."

"It is the least I can do." She turned and grabbed Julia's hand. "I do not know the reason you are here, but I know it must be important. Embracing the Amish life is not easy. Should you need another woman with whom to talk, tell Abraham you would like to visit. Perhaps one day this week. I will be finishing one of my quilts and could use help."

"I'm not sure you would approve of my stitches."

"We all must learn, *yah*?"

Julia smiled. "I hope someday to find a way to repay you."

"Payment is not necessary. We are neighbors and now friends. My help is freely given."

Sarah stepped toward Abraham and took his hand. "It is always good to see you, Abraham."

"Thank you, Sarah."

"You will come for dinner on Sunday?" she asked. "The bishop and his wife will be at my house."

"Not this week. Perhaps some other time."

She stepped closer and smiled knowingly. "Someday you will be ready, *yah*?"

Then she hurried around him and patted Kayla's

shoulder. "Come with me, child. You can bring the pie into the house."

Abraham watched her climb into the buggy and hand a pie to Kayla. The girl hurried back inside.

"Place the pie on the counter," Abraham instructed. "We will have a slice after we eat this evening."

Kayla returned to the porch and waved goodbye to Sarah. Julia stood near the sink as if glued in place.

"I am sure wearing an Amish dress is not what you expected." Abraham tried to explain. "Jonathan felt the disguise would add another layer of protection."

"He's right. It's just a change." She offered him a weak smile, and then, with a sigh, stepped closer to the sink and washed a glass left on the counter. "Sarah seems like a nice woman."

"She goes out of her way to be helpful." Abraham took another sip of coffee.

"You are courting, perhaps?"

He furrowed his brow. "Did she say this?"

"No, of course not. It's just she mentioned her husband had died." Julia reached for the towel and dried her hands. "I saw Sarah's expression when she looked at you. I thought—"

"You thought wrong." For whatever reason, Julia's comment irritated him. "William is still in the small room at the front of the house, probably refusing to change clothes. You best check on him."

Abraham grabbed his hat from the wall peg and stomped outside. His anger changed to concern when he spotted William heading into the barn from the driveway, still wearing his *Englisch* clothing. Abraham glanced back at his house and then at the phone shack in the distance. The door he had closed earlier now hung open.

His heart stopped. The boy had left Abraham's house through the front door and had returned to the phone booth, probably to call his friend. If William had shared his whereabouts with David, the information could easily spread throughout the Philadelphia neighborhood and eventually to the Philadores. Within a day or two at the most, the gang would descend on Yoder, Kansas, in search of a fourteen-year-old boy who, in their opinion, needed to be offed.

Abraham would talk to William, but first he had to alert Jonathan. He hurried to the phone shack, stepped inside and hit the button that would reveal the last number called. He jotted down the sequence of digits on a piece of scratch paper and tapped in Jonathan's number.

"We have a problem," Abraham said in greeting. He quickly relayed what had happened and provided the phone number William had contacted. "Have Karl pick up the family and find another safe place for them to hide out."

"No can do, Abe, at least not now. Fuentes is beating the bushes, trying to find Will. Moving the family would be too dangerous. They have to stay with you until things calm down."

"You are taking too big of a risk, Jonathan."

"I'm keying the phone number William called into my computer. Give me a minute or two and we'll see what I can find."

"Find a new hiding place for Julia and her children. If the gang learns their whereabouts, they will be sitting ducks, as the saying goes."

"Hopefully the kid in Philly will keep his mouth shut."

Abraham let out a frustrated breath. "The kid's name is David Davila. If you count on him keeping silent, you are toying with William's life."

"We'll work as fast as we can, Abe, but nothing is done in the blink of an eye. You know that."

"I know when someone is in danger and needs protection."

"That's why I placed them with you."

"While you are checking, run the name Nelson Turner. He asked for directions to Yoder. Said he was a writer." Abraham provided the license plate number for the sports car.

"Writer or journalist? I'll check the plates, but my advice is to stay clear of anyone involved with the media. The last thing we want is Julia or her children's photo in the paper or on some online news blog."

"That was my thought, as well."

Jonathan clucked his tongue. "I found the address associated with the phone number William called. Now I'll cross-check it with known gang members in the area."

A sigh filled the line.

Abraham pushed the receiver closer to his ear. "What?"

"William's friend, David, lives at the same address as a low-level punk who we think has ties to the Philadores. Pablo... Pablo Davila. They must be brothers."

"David is probably filling his brother in on William's whereabouts as we speak."

"Point taken. I'll pull some strings and see if we can speed up the process of creating new identities for the family. But remember, Abraham, Kansas is a big state. Fuentes is looking for a woman and kids wearing jeans and sweaters. Keep them dressed Amish for their own safety. As we both know, Fuentes is a killer. The last thing we want is for Julia and her son William to be injured or end up dead."

Dead, like Marianne and Becca. Abraham's stomach soured. "Move mountains, Jonathan, and get this family to a more secure location."

"We'll work this end, Abe, but I'm relying on you to keep them safe until then."

Safe and alive. Was Jonathan counting too heavily on Abraham? He had not been able to protect his own family. Would he be able to protect Julia and her children?

Chapter Four

Julia had watched her son scurry into the barn. Abraham had then raced across the country road to the neighbor's farm. When she stretched on tiptoe, she could see to the end of the neighbor's driveway where the small guardhouse-like building stood near the two-lane road.

At first glance, she'd thought it an outhouse, but realizing the location was much too public for the modest Amish, she ran off a checklist of what could be contained within the shelter and came up empty. What she did realize was that something was wrong when Abraham bounded back across the road and followed the path her son had taken into the barn. Her stomach tightened as concern swept over her.

She could tell Abraham was upset from the way he held himself, tense, unsettled and she feared angry, as well.

She glanced down at the Amish clothing she was wearing and wondered yet again at the circumstances that had led her to Kansas. At least she and her children had eluded the Philadores and had escaped from the inner city. Yet, at the present moment, she questioned their security here on this Amish farm. If their generous host was upset with William, he could easily call Jonathan and ask that they be moved to another location.

She let out a lungful of pent-up air, conjuring up memories of their five days in the hotel and the uncertainty of not knowing where they would be placed. As much as she appreciated the marshals' desire to keep them safe, she did not want to face that uncertainty again.

She glanced at the table where Kayla was pretending to feed her doll baby with wood chips she had collected from the box near the stove.

"Stay inside with Marianne while I see what William is doing in the barn."

"Her name is Annie."

"What?" Julia stepped closer. "Who's Annie?"

"My doll. Abraham said he would call her Annie so I'm calling her Annie, too. It's her Amish name. Plus, she's in witness protection so she needed a new name."

"You aren't to mention WitSec, Kayla."

"I won't say anything to anyone except you and William and Mr. Abraham. And Marshal Preston and Marshal Adams and Marshal Mast, too. Will we see them again, Mama?"

"I'm sure we will, but right now, I need to talk to William. You and Annie stay inside. I'll be in the barn."

"Did William do something wrong?"

"Why do you ask?"

"Because he's acting like he's not happy here. I told him living on a farm is better than in the city."

"What was William's reply?"

Kayla shook her head. "He didn't say anything. He's pretending he doesn't want to talk to me 'cause he had to leave his friends. Only they weren't really his friends."

"Why do you say that?"

"They weren't nice to me."

Concerned, Julia threaded her fingers through her daughter's blond hair. "Did something happen while I was at work? Something you didn't tell me?"

"No, Mama. It's just that David wanted Will to sneak out of Ms. Fielding's apartment. But I told him he had to stay inside so you didn't have to worry."

At least one of her children had a good head on her shoulders. Kayla was wise beyond her years.

"Your brother will get his life straightened out one of these days, Kayla."

"I hope so."

Julia hoped so, too.

She opened the kitchen door and hurried to the barn. Her stomach roiled as she thought of what might be transpiring between their Amish host and her son. Worried, she stepped into the darkened interior and narrowed her gaze, hoping to see William before he saw her.

He stood in one of the stalls, holding a pitchfork in his hands and staring up at Abraham.

"You were not thinking of your mother and sister and of their safety, were you?" Abraham asked.

Will shrugged.

"When I ask you a question I expect more than a shrug."

"I dunno."

"I think you do know, William. Did you tell David you were in Kansas?"

William shook his head.

"I did not hear you."

Her son blinked. His face was pale and his eyes wide,

as if he realized Abraham expected obedience even if William did not see the need to make a verbal reply.

"I am waiting for your response." Abraham's voice was firm, yet Julia heard no hint of anger, only a man who expected an honest answer.

"I...I might have mentioned Kansas," William said in a timid voice.

"Might you have mentioned the town of Yoder, and that you were staying on an Amish farm?"

"No, sir." Her son's response was immediate. If she could trust her mother's instincts, William was telling the truth.

"So your friend does not know where in Kansas, just that you and your mother and sister are living in Kansas."

"I didn't mention Kayla or my mom."

Abraham nodded. "I see. So does David think you are living alone in Kansas?"

"I don't think so."

Abraham leaned in closer. "Does David know anything about the witness protection program?"

"Maybe, but not from me. I didn't say we had a new name or that the marshals flew us here. I just said I was in Kansas."

"You called David's cell phone?"

William shook his head. "I called his house landline."

"That has Caller ID and would register the phone number you used."

"David's mom won't pay for anything extra," Will insisted. "They don't have Caller ID or Call Waiting or any other add-on."

"He could have punched in *69."

"Yes, sir, but I don't think knowing the phone number was important to Davey. I told him I'd call him back."

Abraham studied him for a long moment and then gave a quick nod of his head. "Is there anything else you think I should know?"

"Only that the Philadores are looking for me."

Julia's heart broke, seeing the downward cast of William's eyes and the pull at his mouth. When was the last time her son had been a happy, carefree boy? Would he ever be one again?

"That is why you are here, William. You understand that, do you not? You are here so the Philadores cannot find you. That is why we do not want them to have any phone numbers they could trace."

"Even if Davey knew the phone number, he wouldn't give it to his brother or to any of the gang members."

Abraham's shoulders sagged with frustration, as if, at that moment, he realized William truly did not comprehend the danger he was in.

No one should feel hunted or preyed upon. Especially not a fourteen-year-old boy who did not understand the full meaning of gang warfare and retaliation.

"No more phone calls, William. Is that understood?"

"Yes, sir. I understand."

"*Gut*." Abraham hesitated a moment before adding, "I expect you to wear Amish clothing. After you finish mucking the stall, go inside and change your clothes."

He turned and walked toward the open barn door with determined steps, nearly bumping into Julia who hovered in the shadows just inside the entrance.

She put her finger to his lips, motioned him outside and stopped when they were halfway to the house. "I overheard you talking to William. Did he call David?"

"He did." Abraham pointed to the shack at the edge of his neighbor's property. "On Harvey Raber's phone."

"You're pointing to the little house by the road?" she asked.

Abraham nodded. "The phone shack. Harvey uses the phone for business and emergency needs. He allows his neighbors to make calls, too."

"I apologize for William's actions. He has changed over the last year or so. Age has a lot to do with it, but so does where we lived. Now the people he wanted to associate with in the city are after him."

"Yet he does not understand the danger, Julia."

Which was exactly what she had been thinking.

"It is the problem with youth," Abraham continued. "Especially *Englisch* youth. They live in the moment and act irrationally. Someone hurts a kid on the street and they strike back, then they get their friends to strike back. That only escalates the unrest and violence."

"And mushrooms into gang warfare in the inner city." She knew it all too well.

"I saw it when I was a cop. Boys grow up without fathers and without good role models who provide sound advice and guidance. Children—most especially boys—need a strong male presence in their lives so they can understand what it means to be a man."

"I agree, but some fathers are not good role models. William's father is in jail. That's hard for a kid to overcome."

Abraham nodded. "Yet I can see that you have tried to be what he was not. William is at a difficult time of life and questioning everything. I did the same at his age."

"I'm sure you weren't attracted to gangs and violence."

"Only because I had a faith that served as a moral compass. Plus, the people I knew—my father and uncles and other leaders in my community—were strong men. I wanted to work for good and not evil and knew this, even though I longed to experience life outside the Amish community."

"What made you want to leave?"

He shrugged. "I was looking at the world through teenage eyes and did not see the big picture, as the saying goes. A young Amish boy had been kidnapped. The parents listened to the bishop who did not believe the *Englisch* authorities needed to be notified."

"And the child?"

"Was never found. Growing up, I always wondered what would have happened if law enforcement had been called in to investigate. I wanted to be the man who saved that little boy."

Julia touched his arm. "Jonathan told me about your wife and daughter. I'm sorry."

"Sometimes Jonathan talks too much."

He started to walk away, but she tugged on his arm. "Don't be upset. Jonathan knew I would understand a portion of your pain. He said a paroled criminal came after you and killed your family. That's my fear. I can never stop thinking about William, knowing he could end up dead. Kayla, too. I don't know how you survived."

"The truth is that I wanted to die, but God did not grant me that desire. Instead He sent Jonathan to help me heal."

"Perhaps God knew my children and I would need you."

Abraham tilted his head, as if pondering what she had said, and stared down at her for a long moment. The intensity of his gaze filled her with sorrow at the depth of pain he carried.

Then, with a jerk of his head, he glanced back at the barn. "William will finish cleaning one of the stalls soon. I noticed the schoolbooks you brought from Philadelphia. If you have work for him to do, it must wait until after we go to town. The sole on one of his shoes has ripped apart. He needs work boots to protect his feet."

"Town?"

"Yoder. It is not far. Kayla needs new shoes, and so do you."

Julia glanced down at her flats. "I have shoes."

"Those will not last long on a farm. As Sarah mentioned, you and Kayla also need *kapps*."

"Are you sure?"

"*Yah*, I am sure. When we come home, I will prepare the evening meal and will ring the dinner bell at six o'clock. This will give you enough time for the schoolwork."

"It will. Thank you. Tomorrow I will cook."

"We will wait until tomorrow to decide on the day's meals. A lot can happen in the next few hours."

He turned and walked to the paddock, leaving her to ponder his words, which hopefully were not prophetic. William and Kayla were safe on this Amish farm, at least for now.

She could breathe easy, although Julia was still concerned about her children's well-being. The Philadores were a vile gang that would stop at nothing to get her son.

Keep William safe, she prayed, knowing God wouldn't be listening. He had other people He loved more and who were more important to Him.

Julia was a woman who had made too many mistakes. Her own father had called her a mistake, and she'd never been able to shed the label.

She had a lot to learn about faith and putting her trust in God. She watched as Abraham harnessed one of the horses. She needed to trust God and Abraham. If only she could.

Kayla tugged at Abraham's heart. Her blue eyes and sweet smile brought back memories of Becca. His daughter had been only four years old, but she had wrapped Abraham around her little finger. Like his daughter, Kayla was bubbly and energetic, and the opposite of William, who slumped into periods of moodiness. The boy needed to learn the benefits of hard work. He would forget about what he had left behind when he started to feel proud of what he was able to accomplish on the farm.

"Sit next to your sister," Abraham instructed as the boy climbed into the buggy dressed in the Amish shirt and trousers Sarah had gotten from a neighbor. "You need a hat, William."

"A *kapp*?"

"*Kapps* are for the ladies. You need a felt hat. Once warm weather arrives, the men switch from felt to straw hats."

"I don't want a hat."

"*Yah*?"

The boy nodded. "*Yah*."

William's tone was emphatic and sarcastic. Abraham ignored the disrespect. A headstrong horse was hard to break. A boy could be the same. Abraham would be patient and consistent in both discipline and praise.

He glanced at the *dawdy* house. What was keeping Julia?

The door opened and she stepped onto the porch. As she neared, he noticed a hint of excitement in her eyes.

Unlike the boy, Julia and her daughter seemed more eager to embrace the Amish way.

He took her hand and helped her into the buggy.

"Sit in front next to me," he suggested.

"Thank you." She lowered her gaze and adjusted her skirt. "I've never ridden in a buggy before."

"You will find it enjoyable, I hope."

"What's the horse's name?" Kayla asked from the rear.

"Buttercup."

"Mama said my daddy called me Butterbean."

Julia sighed ever so slightly.

"Your father loved you, I am sure," Abraham said, hoping to assuage the child's need for acceptance and affirmation.

"Sometimes I have trouble remembering him." Her tone was grown-up and matter-of-fact, yet she was never without the doll her father had given her clasped tightly in her arms.

Abraham glanced at Julia. From the struggle he saw in her eyes, he wondered again about the husband. Both Jonathan and Julia had mentioned he was serving time. Hard for kids to know their father was in jail.

"What should we expect in town?" Julia asked as Abraham flicked the reins and turned the mare onto the main road. Buttercup's hooves pounded over the pavement.

"Remember your new last name in Stolz," he said. "I do not think people will ask, but you are my sister Susan's friend. She knew I needed help with my house."

"Why do we have to make up a story?" Kayla asked.

"Because the Philadores want to hurt me," William mumbled.

"You never should have gone outside the night of the street fight."

"Be quiet, Kayla."

"Children!" Julia turned, her finger raised. "We will not say anything unless it is something positive about the other. Is that understood?"

"Yes, Mama," Kayla replied.

"Whatever," William groaned.

Julia turned back to the road. "What if people ask me about being Amish?"

"You can say you are deciding whether to join the faith."

"I don't speak German, Abraham. You said a few things to Sarah I couldn't understand."

"The dialect is Pennsylvania Dutch. You will be fine speaking English. Just say you are studying to become Amish if anyone quizzes you."

"William doesn't like quizzes," Kayla tattled.

"I do, too."

"Not when you don't know the answers."

Julia raised her hand again. The children quieted.

"I'm sorry, Abraham, about their outbursts."

He smiled. "My sister and I were the same."

"I've heard the Amish practice shunning when they leave the faith. Is that what happened to you?"

"I was not baptized, so I was not actually shunned. Although my *datt*, my father, refused to speak to me after I left home."

"I'm sure he was overjoyed when you returned to your faith."

"He died the year before I returned to be baptized."

"I'm sorry."

So was Abraham. He glanced back to ensure the road

behind them was clear. "We'll stop at a store on the outskirts of town."

"The one Sarah mentioned?"

"*Yah*. It is just ahead."

He guided Buttercup around a bend in the road and into the store's parking area. After tethering the horse to the hitching rail, he lifted Kayla from the buggy. Julia climbed down after William. Her foot slipped. Abraham wrapped his arms around her waist and guided her to the ground.

"You must be careful," he cautioned.

"I tripped on my skirt. Jeans would be less of a problem."

"You are right." He motioned them toward the door.

The clerk, a young Amish woman, approached as they entered. "May I help you find something?"

"I need a *kapp*." Julia pointed to Kayla. "And so does my daughter."

"What size do you wear?"

Julia looked quizzically at Abraham who shrugged.

"I came from another area," Julia said, covering her confusion. "Our sizes were different. Not too small. Not too large."

"You can see them in the back. There is a mirror." The clerk pointed Julia to the small dressing room. Kayla skipped behind them.

"We must find a hat for you." Abraham put his hand on William's slender shoulder. The boy balked, but Abraham ushered him toward the far side of the store where the men's hats hung on the wall.

The scowl on William's face lifted after he checked the price tag on one of the hats. Money talked in the gang world, and whether the boy equated the expensive hat with status in the Amish world, Abraham would never know, but William's negative attitude softened somewhat.

After trying on a number of wide-brimmed, felt hats, they decided on one that fit. "It suits you well," Abraham said once they made the selection.

The door to the dressing room opened and Kayla came out smiling. The white starched *kapp* covered her bun. "*Mamm* says I look lovely."

"*Mamm*?" Kayla had used the Amish word for mom or mama.

"*Yah*." She dipped her head and smiled, as if proud of the newly acquired word she had evidently picked up from the clerk.

"There is a flea market in town next week," the woman said to Julia as they joined Abraham and William. "It is a nice day for families."

The clerk glanced at Abraham. "You are going, perhaps?"

"Perhaps. How much do I owe you?" He paid with cash and hurried Julia and the children outside.

A siren sounded and lights flashed. The sheriff had pulled a red sports car to the side of the road. A tall, slender teen with tattoos and piercings glanced at them. His gaze lingered on Julia. A second, equally tatted kid stared through the passenger window.

A buggy, driven by an older Amish man, turned into the lot and parked next to Abraham's rig. "Trouble has come to Yoder," the elderly man grumbled.

"What happened?" Abraham asked.

"The driver was speeding through town, but the sheriff will set him straight, *yah*? Samuel Hershberger's buggy was run off the road last week when a red sports car cut him off. My guess it is the same car. Why do the *Englisch* not let us live in peace?"

Abraham had often wondered the same thing.

He helped Julia into the buggy.

"We should go home," she said, her face tight with worry.

"After we buy shoes."

As the buggy passed the stopped car, Abraham made a mental note of the license plate.

"Did you see an *P* monogramed on the baseball hat the guy in the car was wearing?" Julia bit her lip and glanced back, her eyes wide. "He could have been a Philador. They sometimes tattoo an *P* on their hands."

"The car has a Kansas plate, Julia. They are local punks. Do not worry."

Philadelphia was over a thousand miles away, and the Philadores had yet to set up a presence in this part of the country. Still, Fuentes could have expanded his reach. While Abraham wanted to soothe Julia's concerns, he would keep watch for the sports car and the two teens. Better safe than sorry, especially when a woman and her two children were in danger.

Chapter Five

Julia wanted to go back to the farm. The men who'd been stopped by the sheriff had unsettled her. Plus, she didn't want to pretend to be Amish and have to fend off questions like the ones the clerk at the store had asked about where she was from and how she knew Abraham. She hoped her responses had been general enough to not raise the clerk's suspicions.

But she worried about the next person who questioned her. Surely she would say something wrong that would give away their identities. If she didn't, her children would.

How could the marshals think this was a good way to keep them safe? Instead of feeling protected, Julia felt exposed and vulnerable.

"The shoes can wait until another day," she said to Abraham.

"We are already in town. There is no reason to turn back now."

Once again, she glanced around the side of the buggy and stared at the flashing lights on the sheriff's sedan. "Does the sheriff know you work for the marshals?"

"I do not work for them, Julia. Jonathan is a friend who asked if I could help. No one here knows about either of us being involved with witness protection, so it is not something we should discuss."

"I wasn't discussing it, I was merely asking a question." Frustration bubbled up. Did Abraham not realize how dangerous it was to be riding through town in a buggy? Surely everyone would stare at them.

But when Julia looked at the people milling around on the street, they seemed oblivious to her and her children. Perhaps because many of the other people were dressed in Amish clothing, and everywhere she looked, she saw buggies. Some driven by women, most driven by men. Children sat perched in the rear and stared at the passing cars.

The scene was as foreign to her as living in the inner city had been when she and the children had first moved there. Maybe more so.

She wrung her hands and tried to calm her unease by reading the signs that hung above the shops—The Tack Shop, Eicher's Feed, *Yoder Gazette*.

Abraham seemed oblivious to her concerns.

"Where's the shoe store?" she finally asked.

"On the next block."

She stretched to see into the distance. "I only see a hardware store and restaurant."

"The hardware store sells shoes, Julia."

"Only in Yoder, right?"

He looked at her and smiled. "You will get used to the local ways."

Abraham parked the buggy in the rear of the store and pointed them through a side door. The expansive interior was paneled in knotty pine and lit with bright fluorescent lighting.

The clerk nodded a greeting. "Morning, Abraham."

"Silas." Abraham motioned the children and Julia forward. "We are in need of shoes for these children and their mother."

"I will measure their feet."

Once the measurements were taken, Silas brought out boxes of shoes. William's eyes brightened when he spied a pair of work books. "They look like Doc Martens."

"Only they will hold up better," the clerk assured him.

Kayla tried on a pair of leather shoes with laces. "They fit, *Mamm.*"

Julia leaned closer. "Did your last shoes not fit?"

"They pinched my toes, but I didn't want to tell you."

Seven years old, yet sensitive beyond her age.

"My feet are happy in these shoes," Kayla said with a wide smile. "I'll be able to run and skip and jump again."

Julia's heart hurt. Tears burned her eyes. What kind of mother was she not to have realized her daughter needed new shoes? Money had been tight, but she would have cut back on something else. If there had been anything else to cut back on.

Abraham was staring at her.

She averted her gaze, feeling foolish and emotional. Plus, she was still so tired.

He stepped closer. "You need shoes. Something sturdy."

She looked down at her flats. The aches in her legs were, no doubt, from wearing shoes without support and too many hours on her feet working in the diner while Mrs. Fielding watched the children.

"What do Amish women usually wear?" Julia asked.

He held up a pair of black leather lace-up shoes.

"They're not very fashionable."

He laughed. "The farm is not a place for fashion."

"You're probably right."

She tried on the shoes and was surprised at how the soft leather cushioned her feet. Now she understood what Kayla was saying about her feet feeling happy.

"May I wear them home?" she asked.

"*Yah.*" Abraham paid for the shoes. "Now we will get ice cream for an afternoon treat."

Kayla's eyes widened. "Mr. Abraham, that sounds *gut.*"

He chuckled. "You are quite the linguist, Kayla."

"*Mamm* says I'm smart."

"Your mother is right."

He smiled at Julia, and for a moment she felt the weight lift from her shoulders. Then she thought again of the gang that was after her son.

Her pulse raced as she glanced around the store. "Where's William?"

Abraham's face drained of color. He turned to look. "Stay here."

But she couldn't. Not when her son was missing.

She grabbed Kayla's hand and followed Abraham out of the store. Her heart pounded a warning when she thought of the men in the sports car.

"Where's William?" Kayla asked.

"I don't know, honey."

Why had she let him out of her sight?

Abraham hurried around the corner and headed to the rear of the building.

"*Please!*" Julia lifted up a partial prayer to a God who never listened.

She turned the corner with Kayla in tow and stopped short, seeing Abraham a few feet ahead. He was staring at the buggy where William stood, raking his fingers through Buttercup's mane.

Stepping closer to Abraham, she sighed. "My heart stopped beating about two minutes ago."

"I should have looked here first. He loves the animals."

"I…I thought something had happened to him."

"We could not find you, William," Abraham said when the boy looked up and noticed them. "Next time, you must tell your mother where you are going."

"I don't have to ask her permission."

"A child does not disrespect a parent." Abraham's voice was firm. He pointed to the buggy. "Get in."

The boy huffed and climbed all the way into the rear.

Abraham hefted Kayla onto the second seat.

"What about getting ice cream, Mr. Abraham?"

"Not today, Kayla."

William slumped in the back of the buggy, his eyes downcast, looking sullen and unresponsive. A look Julia knew too well.

Julia climbed in beside her daughter. She didn't want to sit next to Abraham. Not when her son had caused them such a scare and had been so disrespectful.

She wrapped her arm around Kayla and pulled her close.

Abraham flipped the reins and turned the buggy onto the main road. Buttercup began to trot as they left town.

Clouds covered the once-bright sun and warned of an encroaching storm. Everything had gone from bad to worse in the blink of an eye.

After what William had done today, Julia was sure Abraham would insist they leave, but if he forced them away, where would they go?

Chapter Six

Julia had trouble falling asleep that night. She kept hearing footsteps and imagining her son had left the house and was now in the middle of a street fight just as had happened in Philadelphia.

She got up twice and each time stared out the window, seeing the main house and the still countryside. Surely she and her family were safe here in Kansas, yet the Philadores were looking for her son. A heaviness settled on her shoulders as she thought of William's phone call to David and how easily one slip of the tongue could have revealed their whereabouts. How had life gotten so complicated?

Returning to bed, she pounded her fist into her pillow and flipped onto her side, facing away from the window and the first light of dawn that peeked around the edge of the curtain.

She dozed for all too short a time and then jerked awake, still fearful for William's well-being. After pulling herself from bed, she slipped on her robe and stepped into the hallway where she glanced at Kayla, sleeping peacefully in the room across the hallway. The doll Charlie had given her was still clutched in her arms.

Julia shook her head at the sad irony of a child who clung to a doll as a substitute for the love she longed to receive from her father.

She continued along the hall and stopped on the threshold of William's room, noting how high his bedding was piled. She moved quietly into the room and lifted the edge of the quilt, expecting to see William. Instead of her son, she found two pillows waded into a ball.

Her heart stopped.

She threw the quilt off the bed, then turned and ran down the steps. Fighting back tears, she checked the remaining rooms before she returned to the kitchen. She pulled open the door and raced across the yard to the main house.

"Abraham, wake up." She pounded on his door. "Abraham."

The door flew open. His hair was tousled, his face puffy with sleep. "What is wrong?"

"William." Tears filled her eyes. "He's gone."

Adrenaline had kicked in as soon as Abraham heard the insistent knocking on the door. Seeing Julia, her eyes wide with fear, her mouth drawn and her face pale, sent a jolt of panic to wrap around his heart.

"Did you search the house?" he asked.

"I did."

She glanced back at the *dawdy* house. "I heard something a few hours ago that sounded like footsteps, only I talked myself into believing it was just the house creaking." She put her hand to her mouth. "Oh, Abraham, how could I have been so foolish?"

"I will search the grounds. Change into street clothes, then wake Kayla and get her dressed. She can wear her Amish dress, if she wants. We will ask Sarah to watch her while we look for William."

Grabbing a flashlight, Abraham raced to the barn and outbuildings, calling William's name. From there, he crossed the road and entered his neighbor's barn. He checked the stalls to make certain the boy was not hiding in one of the dark corners and then ran to the phone shack.

The answering machine blinked.

He entered the code and listened as a male voice left a message. "William, this is David. Look, I can't get to Kansas City in time, but my brother Pablo will be there. He'll meet your bus. You can fly with him back to Philly. Pablo said he'll keep you safe."

Either William had lied or somehow David had gotten Harvey Raber's phone number. Abraham made a fist and wanted to smash his hand through the wall. Instead, he reached for the phone and tapped in the number for the Amish taxi, grateful that the taxi driver prided himself on being available around the clock.

"Randy, this is Abraham King. I need your services. Come as quickly as possible."

The taxi pulled into the driveway not more than twenty minutes later. Abraham forsook his waistcoat and grabbed a black hooded sweatshirt from his room and slipped it on as he hurried to the *dawdy* house.

Julia opened the door before he knocked. She was dressed in jeans and a sweater with a lightweight jacket. "Did you find him?"

He shook his head and explained about David's message on the answering machine.

A faint gasp escaped Julia's lips, then she turned to where Kayla sat at the table, rubbing her eyes, and motioned the child forward. Her hair was pulled into a makeshift bun. She wore her Amish dress and carried her *kapp* in one hand and her doll in the other.

"You called a cab?" Julia asked, seeing the car in the drive.

"An Amish cab. Randy is a good driver. We will go first to Sarah's house. Kayla can stay there while we look for William."

Julia nodded and ushered Kayla into the car. Randy seemed to understand that speed was of the essence. He turned the car radio to an easy listening channel, which would ensure Abraham and Julia could talk without being overheard. Instead of conversing, both of them seemed lost in their own thoughts and were silent as Randy pulled the taxi onto the main road and drove quickly to Sarah's farm.

Abraham was the first to alight from the car once it stopped in front of the farmhouse. Julia and Kayla followed close behind him. He knocked on the door, hoping Sarah was in the kitchen preparing breakfast.

She peered through the window before opening the door. "What's wrong?"

"William left the house sometime in the night. We need to find him. He may have taken a bus to another city. Can you watch Kayla while we are gone?"

"*Yah*, of course." Sarah reached out to Julia and squeezed her hand. "Do not worry. Kayla will be fine with us."

"Thank you, Sarah."

Julia hugged her daughter. "We'll be back as soon as possible. Mind Miss Sarah."

"I will, Mama."

As soon as the door closed, Julia hurried back to the car. Abraham climbed in next to her. "The bus station in town, Randy. As fast as you can."

Julia dropped her head into her hands. "I'm so worried."

"We will find him." Abraham wanted to reassure her, but he was worried, as well.

"Why would David leave a message on your neighbor's phone?" she asked.

"He probably thought William had access to the voice mail. The boys cooked up this rendezvous in Kansas City, never realizing the implications." Or the danger to William, he failed to add. Thankfully, the outgoing message on Harvey's answering machine was generic and did not mention his business or its location.

"David's brother is working with the Philadores," Julia said, her voice low. "I saw him a few times and knew his mother. She's a nice woman, struggling to keep her kids safe. William didn't have much to do with Pablo, which doesn't bode well for the two of them meeting up in Kansas City." She shook her head. "How does William plan to get there?"

"I keep the motor coach schedule on the bookshelf in the main room. William must have seen it yesterday before he called David. A bus left the Yoder station at six this morning, heading first to Topeka and then on to Kansas City."

"He doesn't have money to buy a ticket."

"Check your wallet."

She opened her purse and pulled out her wallet. Her face dropped. "He took money from my purse."

Julia shook her head. "I never thought my son would steal from me."

"He probably plans to pay you back, although I am not sure how he will earn the money. But then, kids do not think things through."

"Oh, Abraham. What am I to do?"

"We'll check at the bus station. Surely the clerk will remember if a young boy bought a ticket. If he did not, then we will search through Yoder and the surrounding area."

"And if he bought a ticket?" she asked, her eyes filled with worry.

"Then we will go to Kansas City."

"What if Pablo is waiting there for him?"

"We will face that when it happens. Right now, wc need to determine if William was on that bus." Abraham reached for her hand. "We will find him, Julia."

"I was too hard on him."

He shook his head. "The boy needs to understand what is expected. This is not your fault."

"He's a child."

"At fourteen, he is almost a man. An Amish youth would be plowing fields, driving wagons and taking care of livestock. You underestimate your son."

"He didn't grow up on a farm. He grew up in a middle class neighborhood outside of Philadelphia, until his father gambled away everything we had."

She raked her hand through her hair. "Charlie didn't want children. He said I never gave him any time after William was born. He didn't realize what parenting involved and thought only of what he wanted."

"What happened after you had Kayla?"

"That's the irony," she said with a sigh. "He adored

his daughter while ignoring William. He knew his father didn't love him. He didn't hold that against Kayla, but he held it against Charlie."

"Your husband left you soon after Kayla was born?"

"Not until she was in preschool. I kicked him out. He was taking all the money he earned along with whatever he could find from my paycheck. He gave me no choice."

She turned to look out the window and lowered her voice. "Plus he became abusive."

"What?"

She held up her hand. "Not physically, although he threatened me. That's when we moved. I didn't think he could find me, but he sent a package to the new house. It was a present for Kayla. She opened it before I realized what she was doing and found the doll she now calls Annie."

Julia tugged at a strand of hair and glanced at Randy, who was oblivious to their discussion.

"William looked into the box," she continued. "I knew he was searching for a gift for himself, but there was nothing. We moved again, this time into the city. I didn't want Charlie to know where we were. Not long after that, I saw in the paper that he had been arrested for embezzling money from a police department fund for officers who had been wounded or killed in the line of duty."

"He was found guilty?"

She nodded. "And sent to prison. Soon after that, William started talking about various gang members and what the Philadores were doing in the neighborhood. He only saw what he wanted to see. He didn't realize how they intimidated people and shoved their weight around. That's when I took both children out of school and taught them at home. A sweet neighbor watched them while I worked at night. I kept my thumb on William, only he still slipped away from me at times, which is what he's done again."

Abraham glanced out the window. "The bus station is on the corner of the next block. You stay with Randy while I check inside."

"I want to go with you."

As the taxi pulled to a stop, Julia stared through the car window. "How did William find his way here?"

"Probably from the bus brochure. A map on the back of the brochure shows where the station is located. The Amish rely on buses to visit relatives and friends in neighboring towns, and the buses run frequently."

"He can't be gone, Abraham. I can't lose him."

But when they entered the station and saw only a few Amish people waiting for the next bus, Abraham had a sick feeling in the pit of his stomach. He headed for the clerk.

"We are looking for a young boy, age fourteen, who may have bought a ticket to Kansas City in the last few hours."

The clerk nodded. "Brown hair, wearing a Philadelphia Eagles sweatshirt?"

"William loves that sweatshirt. You saw him?" Julia glanced around the small station. "Is he still here?"

"He took the earlier bus to Topeka and then on to Kansas City, which was his destination. Is there a problem?"

"What time will that bus arrive in Kansas City?"

"With all the stops along the way, it won't get there until eleven this morning. You're looking for him, I presume? Might be able to catch up to him in Topeka."

The clerk glanced at his watch. "On second thought, I doubt you'll get there in time. If you've got a car, my suggestion would be to take the back roads to Kansas City. You should arrive just before the bus. The next motor coach heading that way leaves here in an hour, but it won't arrive in Kansas City until later this afternoon."

"Thanks for your help." Abraham grabbed Julia's hand and they hurried outside and back to the cab.

"How do we get to the city?" she asked.

Abraham peered through the open passenger window at the driver and raised his voice to be heard. "Hopefully, Randy will drive us to Kansas City."

"I haven't been to the city in almost a year, but I know the back roads," the taxi driver acknowledged with a nod. "Climb in. I'll get you there."

Abraham glanced at the sky, where dark clouds hovered on the horizon. They would be driving into a storm. But that was the least of their problems. They had to find William, and find him before Pablo Davila did.

Chapter Seven

Julia wanted to get behind the wheel and drive, only she would probably exceed the speed limit and crash into another vehicle, as jumpy as she felt. Why were the miles passing so slowly and the minutes so quickly?

William was on a bus heading straight into the hands of the Philadores. Maybe they should have called law enforcement, but she didn't trust cops. She glanced at Abraham who stared out the front window, his jaw tight and neck tense. He looked as worried as she felt.

She rubbed her hand over her stomach and tried to calm the nervous jitters that wreaked havoc with her composure. She wanted to cry and scream at the same time, although she continued to sit still and stare at the road, knowing if they didn't get to Kansas City in time, they wouldn't find William and her life would be over. She would have to go on because of Kayla, but losing her son would break her heart in two.

She must have groaned. Abraham turned to look at her, his eyes filled with understanding that almost crashed through the dam she had placed on her tears. She couldn't cry now. It wouldn't help anything and would make her seem weak, which she never wanted to be. Plus, it wouldn't help William. The only thing that would help him was arriving at the station before the bus.

"How much longer?" she asked, her voice little more than a whisper.

"Randy, how far are we from the city?"

The driver turned down the radio and waited until Abraham repeated the question, then he shrugged. "We're not far in miles, but you never know about traffic. Especially around midday. What time was the bus supposed to arrive?"

"Eleven."

Randy glanced at the clock. "We might make it."

"Might?" Her voice was pinched tight.

She closed her eyes, bringing to mind thoughts of when William was a little boy, thoughts of the good times instead of the bad.

Fortunately, the storm they had expected blew past, traffic moved and Randy skillfully got them to the city. They crossed over the river and onto the Missouri side.

"Which bus station?" Randy asked.

Abraham provided the address.

"We're not far from there. I'll drop you off in front. Should I hang around for a while?"

"If you can. As soon as we spot William, I will find a pay phone and call you."

"You've got my number?"

"I do."

Julia glanced at the clock on the dashboard. Eleven-fifteen. If only the bus was running behind schedule.

"Ready?" Abraham asked when the taxi pulled to the curb.

She nodded. He opened the door and stepped to the

sidewalk. Julia followed, her eyes on the people exiting the bus station. She hurried through the doors with Abraham close behind her.

Both of them stopped short.

Julia's heart pounded as she searched the folks milling around the central waiting area. "I don't see him."

Abraham guided her to the information desk. "Has the bus from Yoder, Kansas, arrived yet?"

The guy checked his computer screen. "About twenty minutes ago."

Julia leaned into the counter. "Did you see a young boy, fourteen years old, brown hair, five-six and slender?"

The guy frowned. "Lady, do you know how many people come through this station each day?"

"He was wearing a gray Philadelphia Eagles sweatshirt."

"I didn't see him, ma'am, but that doesn't mean he wasn't here."

She turned away from the man who offered no help and pointed to a vending machine area. "Knowing William, he's probably hungry. I'll check the vending machines. You look in the restroom."

Julia was downcast when she met up with Abraham again. "You didn't find him either?"

"There is a fast-food restaurant at the end of the block."

Julia's spirits brightened. "He's probably eating a burger and fries. We need to hurry."

They walked rapidly along the street and soon arrived at the corner eatery. Julia peered through the tinted windows. The day was overcast, but the glare from the sun made it difficult to see inside.

"There." She spotted William. "He's at a table in the corner."

She hurried toward the door but stopped before she entered and grabbed Abraham's hand. "Pablo's inside. I don't think he's seen William yet. He's with another gang member from our neighborhood. His name's Mateo Gonzales."

Julia pointed out both guys to Abraham. Just as in Philadelphia, they wore their gang's so-called uniform— white T-shirts, sagging pants, baseball caps turned backward and silk team jackets with *Philador* embroidered on one of the sleeves.

"You grab William and leave by that side door," Abraham said. "We passed a small inside shopping mall on the way here. Right hand side of the street, two blocks down. I will meet you there."

Abraham needed to distract Pablo and his buddy to give Julia time to grab William and hustle him out of the restaurant. If only the kid would go with her willingly and not give his mother a hard time.

Pablo elbowed Mateo and nodded in Julia's direction. Before Abraham could get around an elderly woman who stepped in front of him, Pablo grabbed Julia's arm.

She turned on him, eyes wide, and tried to pull her arm free. "No!" she cried.

A beefy guy, twice Pablo's size, stepped in front of him. "Hey, buddy. The lady doesn't want you touching her."

Pablo laughed nervously and dropped his hold. Mateo edged around the big guy and moved toward Julia. Abraham barreled into him, throwing him off balance.

Mateo fell back against a teenage girl. Her tray flew

into the air, spilling French fries and a burger onto the floor. The plastic top sailed off her mega soft drink, spewing cola and ice.

A rush of customers came to the young woman's aid. In so doing, they surrounded Mateo and boxed him in.

Julia grabbed William. They left through a side door and hurried along the street, heading north to the rendezvous area Abraham had mentioned.

Disengaging himself from the gathering, he slipped out the front door and crossed the street, hoping to throw off the gang members if they connected him with Julia or the boy.

He glanced back just as the two men hurried outside. They looked both directions and then split up. Pablo headed north. Mateo turned south toward the bus station. Abraham pretended to examine merchandise in a store window until Pablo passed by on the opposite side of the street.

The punk was medium height but built like a tank. More than likely, he had flown into Kansas City. From the bulge at his waist, he must have picked up a weapon on the street. The east side was known for gang activity where money could buy anything.

Pablo gazed into the stores he passed and entered a number of them. Each time, he quickly returned to the street and continued walking. A game arcade appeared ahead. The perfect place for a young teen with money in his pocket to pass the time.

Pablo glanced over his shoulder. Abraham slipped into an alleyway, fearing he had been seen. He counted to ten under his breath and then peered from his hiding spot. Pablo was gone. Probably into the arcade, searching for William.

Abraham sauntered along the sidewalk toward the arcade, peered through the window and then stepped inside the darkened interior. A strobe light twirled overhead and mixed with the flashing lights from the machines. A number of adults and a few teens dropped coins into slots and pressed buttons or pulled on levers that activated the various games, filling the arcade with pings and dings and all types of other sounds.

Abraham kept his head down and his gaze focused on the various patrons as he slowly circled through the rows of machines. At the rear of the arcade, he spied Pablo. The punk opened a door and slipped into an adjoining area.

Abraham's heart stopped. Pablo had gone from the game arcade through a back door into the shopping area where Julia and William would be waiting. Abraham's plan had backfired. He should have hurried to meet Julia instead of tailing Pablo. By now, the three of them could have been far from either Pablo or his friend. Instead, Julia and her son were in the gang member's crosshairs.

Abraham's police skills were rusty at best, but Julia and William were in danger, imminent danger, and Abraham needed to save them.

Chapter Eight

Julia spotted Pablo. She and William had been in a sporting goods store, trying to act nonchalant like the other shoppers all the while they stared at the door, waiting for Abraham. Only their Amish friend hadn't entered the store. Pablo had.

William tensed. "I'll talk to him, Mom, and tell him I'm not going with him."

"You will do nothing to alert him to your whereabouts, William. What don't you understand about being in danger?"

"Pablo was always nice to me. He's Davey's brother."

"And a member of the Philadores."

"Davey said he's getting out."

"Getting out so he can join another gang?" she asked.

"Maybe, but the other gang isn't looking for me, Mom."

"The Delphis want to get back at the Philadores. What better way than to capture the witness who can testify against the rival gang's leader? You'd be a pawn, William, a bargaining chip to be used by one gang against the other."

They'd keep her son alive as long as they needed him and then dispose of him once he was no longer of use.

She grabbed a pair of sweatpants off a rack, handed them to William and pushed him toward the dressing area. "Stay in the men's dressing room until I tell you to come out."

"Mom, you're getting carried away."

She leaned into his face. "I love you, William. I gave you life, and I will do anything to ensure you remain alive. Is that understood?"

He blinked.

"Get into the dressing room. Now. No arguments and don't come out until I give you the all clear."

Once William was gone, Julia glanced back at Pablo. He was walking through the shoe section, staring at the customers. Her heart stopped when he turned and started walking toward where she stood.

Julia grabbed a tennis outfit off a rack, slipped past a sales clerk who was arranging clothing on a nearby mannequin and hurried into the women's dressing area.

Heavy footsteps sounded behind her.

"Is anyone in there?" Pablo called into the dressing room from the entrance.

"Sir." A woman's voice. "I'm the sales clerk in charge of this area. Are you looking for someone?"

"My kid." Pablo grunted. "She's ten. I'm worried about her safety."

"We've never had a problem in this store. Wait out here, sir. I'll check the dressing rooms as soon as I help a customer find her size."

The click of high heels signaled the clerk had left to help her customer. Almost immediately, Pablo entered the changing area. Julia could see his shoes under the swinging, saloon-style door of the small dressing room where she hid. If she could see his feet, he could see hers. She climbed onto the ledge that doubled as a seat and held her breath. Her heart pounded like a jack hammer.

"Did you find your daughter, sir?" The click of high heels signaled the clerk's return. "Sir?"

The door to Julia's dressing room started to swing open.

"Men are not allowed in the women's changing area, sir." The clerk sounded indignant. "Leave now or I'll call security."

Pablo backed away from where Julia hid. "I'll check the guy's dressing room."

"Your daughter wouldn't go in there, sir. If you think there's a problem, I'll call security."

"Maybe she's in another store." He stomped off with the clerk clicking her heels after him.

Julia peered from the dressing area and spied Pablo heading to the front of the store.

"Mom?"

William was staring at her.

"What are you doing out here?" she demanded. "I told you to stay in the dressing room."

"Pablo was in the women's dressing room. I thought he'd come into the men's area next." William reached for her hand. "Come on, Mom. There's an emergency side exit."

Julia glanced at the front of the store. Seeing Pablo, she turned and hurried after her son. Just as he had said, there was an emergency exit. William pushed it open and stepped into a narrow passageway that ran behind the shops.

"Pablo won't find us here." He squeezed her hand. "We're safe."

"You were ready to go with Pablo not long ago. What changed your mind?"

"You did, Mom. You said you would do anything to keep me alive. I don't think Pablo would hurt me, but I don't want to hurt you."

She put her hands on his shoulders and stared into his eyes. "Promise you'll never run away again and you'll never take money from my purse."

He hung his head and nodded. "I'll pay the money back."

The door they had just come through opened. Julia shoved William protectively behind herself.

A man stepped into the passageway.

She gasped, not from fear but with relief.

"Oh, Abraham, I didn't know if we'd ever see you again."

Abraham let out a deep sigh and pulled them both into his embrace. "I thought I had lost you."

"Did you see Pablo?"

"He left the mall and headed back toward the bus station. I just called Randy. We need to hurry to where he plans to meet us."

Abraham pointed to a side door that led to the street. "I will check outside and motion you both forward if the street is clear. Turn right, walk to the next intersection and make a left. The spot where Randy said he would be waiting will be at the end of the block."

He opened the door and stood for a long moment, eyeing the flow of traffic and the people on the street. Convinced that Pablo and Mateo were not in sight, Abraham motioned Julia and William forward. They turned right and then left at the intersection. Abraham looked repeatedly over his shoulder to ensure they were not being followed.

His heart pounded. They were too visible and so vulnerable. Any car driving by could see them, but Pablo and his buddy were on foot. At least, Abraham hoped they were.

The drive-through burger joint sat on the corner. Abraham's spirits took a nose dive as he studied the cars in the parking lot. The Amish taxi was nowhere to be seen.

"We could go inside, but I do not want a repeat of what happened at the restaurant earlier." He spotted a small, rundown hotel across the street that would provide a place to wait until the taxi appeared.

He hurried Julia and William to the corner and across the street once the light turned.

"Where are we going?" she asked.

"Into the hotel. We can wait inside and watch the flow of cars without being so conspicuous."

"What happened to Randy?"

"I am not sure. He might be held up in traffic."

"I'm worried, Abraham."

Abraham was worried too. Without transportation, they were trapped in the city with Pablo and his buddy, Mateo, searching for them.

Chapter Nine

Julia scooted closer to William. They both sat on a small settee in the hotel lobby while Abraham stood by the window, watching traffic. His last attempt to contact Randy had gone to voice mail.

The clerk at the desk had ignored them for almost an hour. Now he glanced repeatedly at them over his bifocals and finally asked, "You folks need a room?"

"We're waiting for someone," Julia said, offering a smile.

"Someone staying at the hotel?" the clerk asked.

"We're not sure."

Traffic on the street slowed to a standstill.

Abraham stepped toward Julia and lowered his voice. "Stay here while I phone Randy again. Maybe his cell phone is on by now."

He headed to the pay phone in the nearby alcove and returned some minutes later. "There is a problem with the taxi's engine," Abraham said under his breath. "Randy found a mechanic who called it a big job that will take hours. The guy said he would work late if Randy was willing to pay time and a half."

"Did Randy agree?"

"I told him I would cover the extra expense. I also talked to Jonathan and filled him in on what had happened. He was in his car, trying to get home. A spring snowstorm is blanketing Philadelphia, and his office is closed."

Julia's already faltering spirits plummeted even lower. "So, the US Marshals' office is brought to a halt by Mother Nature?" she whispered.

"Evidently."

The clerk cleared his throat. "I know you folks are watching for a friend of yours, but the lobby is reserved for hotel patrons only."

"I understand, sir." Abraham looked at Julia. "We will take two adjoining rooms."

She titled her head, confused.

"You and William can rest."

Which was a good plan. Her son's eyes were puffy and bloodshot. He probably hadn't slept last night nor on the bus ride to Kansas City.

Julia moved closer to the window as Abraham approached the registration desk to check them in.

An ambulance snaked through the traffic, its siren blaring.

Abraham turned to look at her.

She shrugged. "Maybe an accident."

"Any sign of Pablo or Mateo?"

Julia shook her head. "The only thing I see—"

Flicking her gaze to the far side of the street, she gasped and drew away from the window. She grabbed William's hand and motioned him to where Abraham stood by the registration desk. A phone rang in a back office. The clerk disappeared to answer the call.

"We've got a problem," Julia told Abraham, her voice low.

He glanced out the front window.

Pablo and Mateo were walking across the street toward the hotel.

"There's Davey's brother," William said, pointing to the picture window. "He's probably worried about me. Maybe I should tell him I'm with you, Mom, and not to worry."

She grabbed her son's arm. "You won't tell him anything, William. He and his friend came to Kansas City to find you and take you back to Philadelphia. They'll use you as a bargaining tool to improve their standing in one of the gangs."

Staring into William's troubled eyes, she added, "Don't you understand, son? Pablo doesn't care about you or your well-being. He's only thinking of himself."

"But I need to get a message to Davey."

"The only message you need to give anyone is that you're safely hidden, far from where any gang member can find you."

Abraham pointed to a side exit. "We need to leave the hotel."

Julia put her hand on William's shoulder. "Follow Abraham."

William glanced again through the large picture window. "They're coming inside, Mom."

"Go, William. Now."

Abraham grabbed William's arm and hurried him along a side hallway. Julia kept up with them, then looked back as the door into the hotel opened.

Just as the two men entered the lobby, Abraham and William turned into a side passageway. Julia ran after them. Abraham pushed on the door at the end of the corridor.

He looked back. His face tightened. "Hurry, Julia."

She glanced over her shoulder and saw Pablo. He called to his friend and pointed to Julia. She followed Abraham and William out the door that slammed closed behind them.

"Down this alley." Abraham grabbed her hand and William's and hurried them along.

"Now left at the corner."

The street loomed ahead. They slowed to a fast walk so as not to draw attention and hurried around the corner.

"Cross the street, then turn right and left at the next corner."

Abraham glanced back. "Keep moving. Pablo and his friend are still in the alley."

Julia saw the fatigue that pulled at William's shoulders. She could tell from his eyes that he was frightened and tired.

"We need someplace to hole up," she said.

"What about there?" William pointed to a brick church on the next block.

"You think we should hide in the church?" Julia asked.

"In the basement, Mom. Some lady gave me a card in the bus station." He pulled it from his pocket. "The church has a night shelter for people who don't have a place to stay."

Abraham read over William's shoulder. "Fellowship Church Shelter opens at two. We need to hurry."

A small sign pointed to the rear of the church but when they rounded to the back of the property, Julia almost cried. A throng of people waited in line for the doors to open.

"Is it closed today?" she asked a woman standing in line.

"Opens at two. We've got a few minutes to wait."

"How many people do they take?"

"Thirty-five most days."

Julia started to count the people in the long line that snaked along the back of the church.

Abraham peered around the building in the direction from which they had just come. He moved closer to Julia. "Pablo and his friend are at the corner, heading this way."

If only the doors to the shelter would open and they could get inside. But as she counted off the number of people already in line, Julia's heart sank, realizing thirty-five people were ahead of them. They would be turned away and back on the street where Pablo would find them. She wrapped her arm around William's shoulder and grabbed Abraham's hand. They had to get inside.

The door to the shelter opened.

The woman admitting those in line was middle aged with a kind smile and understanding eyes. She welcomed many of the homeless as old friends and invited them in, and at the same time she gave them a number. Abraham stepped away for a minute and checked the street. His face was pulled tight when he returned to her side.

"You saw Pablo?" Julia asked.

"He is standing on the sidewalk just before the church, staring at the traffic."

"If he sees the sign for the shelter, he'll come around to the rear of the property and find us."

"You and William run if that happens. I'll try to slow him down."

"What if we're separated? Where can we meet up again?"

"Back at the corner where Randy said he would pick us up. Can you find it?"

"We'll try to get there."

The line moved slowly toward the back door.

"Welcome." The woman warmly greeted each person.

Julia stared at the side of the church, afraid she would see Pablo coming toward them.

Her heart stopped.

She could see his baseball cap over the fencing.

The woman counted to thirty-two. Three men stood between Julia, Abraham and William. The men would take the last spaces.

Tears burned Julia's eyes. "Please," she murmured.

She grabbed Abraham's hand and nodded toward the sidewalk where Pablo stood, looking back at the street.

The woman at the door of the shelter held up her hand. "Sorry, Norman, you and your friends can't stay here after the fight you started last week. I told you what would happen."

The three guys groused, but the woman held her ground. "Check with me next week and I'll see what I can do."

The men turned away and headed out along the sidewalk. Pablo started walking toward the rear of the church.

"Welcome," the woman said to Julia and Abraham with a wide smile as she handed them the last three numbers. "My name is Muriel. Make yourselves at home. Dinner will be served at five."

Julia hurried William inside.

"Restrooms," Abraham suggested, following close behind them. "William, come with me. We'll wait in the stalls in case Pablo comes into the shelter."

Julia hated to leave her son, but he was with Abraham. She had to trust they would remain safe. She hurried toward the ladies' room and glanced back as Pablo approached the door to the shelter, demanding entry.

"Sir, you're not allowed to be here." Muriel barred his entrance. "This is an overnight shelter for people who don't have a place to stay. We don't accept anyone who cuts in line or tries to force themselves inside."

Pablo grumbled, but he walked away.

Julia let out a sigh of relief. They had found shelter in the church, at least for the moment.

Abraham and William stepped out from the restroom. Abraham stared at her, his gaze cutting into her heart. He had tried to live a peaceful life after his daughter and wife had been killed. He had offered Julia and her children shelter out of the goodness of his heart. He didn't deserve anything bad to befall him.

Keep him safe, Lord, Julia prayed. *Keep us all safe.*

Abraham motioned them to a sofa in the corner of the large central common area where Julia and William could relax. The boy's eyes drooped soon after they sat down. He placed his head on Julia's shoulder and within a few minutes he had drifted to sleep. Julia rested her head against the back of the seat and closed her eyes. Every so often, she blinked her eyes open and peered at the various people gathered in the basement area.

A number of the men were middle-aged with graying hair. They shuffled as they walked and chatted amicably with some of the others gathered. The homeless women stayed in a corner, talking softly among themselves. A number of volunteers worked in the kitchen, preparing the meal they would soon serve. Showers were available and the homeless signed up for a time slot.

The woman who had greeted them at the door came by and smiled at the sight of William sleeping on Julia's shoulder.

"We're glad you're here," Muriel said to Abraham.

"Thank you, ma'am."

"You and your family are most welcome."

Family?

He started to correct her but stopped himself. He wanted to tell her his family had been murdered by a man who sought revenge for being incarcerated.

For too long, Abraham had felt that same desire for revenge against the man who had planted the explosive in Abraham's car. He should have been the one to die and not his precious daughter and beautiful wife. The memory of all that had happened cut through him again and opened the wound he tried to keep bandaged. Today he felt raw. Maybe because he had not been able to help Julia and William.

What was wrong with him? He had wanted to find the boy and take him back to Yoder, but they were holed up in a homeless shelter with two punk gang members looking for them on the street. Abraham had lost his edge. He had gone soft and was an ineffective protector.

Turning to gaze at Julia and William, his heart warmed. The boy had been obstinate and had made a huge mistake in calling his friend and running away, but he was basically a good kid. The hurt and anger he carried seemed aimed at his father. If only Will could realize how much his mother loved him and how much she had sacrificed to keep him safe. Maybe then he would understand the danger he was in and see the Philadores for who they truly were.

As she slept, the worry lines on Julia's face softened and she appeared more peaceful than Abraham had seen her thus far. Her eyes fluttered open and his chest constricted. He did not expect to react to the emotion that soared through him for one brief moment.

She pulled herself upright, smoothed her sweater and then tugged her hand through her hair. She glanced at William, still asleep, his head still on her shoulder.

"I must have dozed off."

"Rest longer, Julia. We seemed to have found a good place to wait until the taxi is fixed."

"You'll call Randy?"

"If I can find a phone. Randy said the mechanic would work until eleven. We will know then if we have to spend the night here or whether we can meet up with Randy."

Julia glanced at the kitchen. "Something smells good."

"You must be hungry."

"A little." She brushed the hair out of William's eyes and smiled at her sleeping son. "I'm sure he'll enjoy dinner, too."

Abraham went to the far side of the basement and peered out the window. Traffic was still bad. Hopefully Pablo and his friend had moved on. They would not give up, of that he could be certain. He had to get Julia and William out of the city and back to Yoder and the safety of the Amish community.

The woman who had welcomed them was wiping down the tables for dinner. Abraham approached her. "Ma'am, is there a pay phone at the shelter?"

She stopped working and smiled. "You're new here."

"It is our first time."

"How long have you been on the street?"

"Just today. We are traveling and ran into some difficulty."

"I know a construction company that hires day laborers if you're willing to work."

"I appreciate the offer, ma'am, but we plan to leave as soon as our ride can get here, today or tonight."

"We have beds if you need a place to sleep." She pointed to doors that led out of the common area to the right and the left. "Women on one side, men on the other. Your son will need to stay with you. We provide bedding and showers as well as breakfast in the morning."

"You provide a much-needed ministry."

"Just doing the Lord's work." She tilted her head. "Are you a believer?"

"I am."

She nodded. "I could tell. Glad you're here. Stay as long as you like."

"Thank you, ma'am. What about the pay phone?"

"A door on each side of this common area leads to a hallway outside the men's and women's dorm rooms. You'll find the phones there."

"Thank you." Abraham pushed through the swinging door, relieved to see the phones.

Randy's voice was tense when he answered. "I'm with the mechanic. He's working as fast as he can, but I still don't know when he'll finish. Can I reach you on this phone?"

"You can try calling. I might hear it ring, but I cannot say for sure."

"Then you call me, Abraham."

"I appreciate all you have done, Randy."

"You've been a friend for a lot of years, right?"

"*Yah*, since we were boys."

"I liked your *datt*. He was a good man. A bit pig-headed at times, but still a good man. The least I can do is help his son."

Julia's eyes blinked open when Abraham settled into the chair next to her.

"You don't look happy," she said. "Evidently Randy didn't provide good news."

"The mechanic continues to work on the problem. I will call again later."

"I'm not sure staying here is a good idea."

"We could try the hotel," he suggested.

She held up her hand. "Just kidding. The shelter works for me. I wonder if the hotel clerk told Pablo that his friends had been waiting for him."

"Maybe. The clerk made it clear he did not like us hanging around. At least here we are welcome."

"And fed."

"I can see the street from the window at the front of the church. Traffic is still bad."

"Did you see Pablo?"

"I did not."

"Would I be too optimistic to think he might have left town?"

"Yes." Abraham smiled. "Much too optimistic. My guess is that he will remain in this area at least until to-morrow."

She nodded. "When the children and I were trying to get away from Charlie, I considered staying at a shelter for a night or two. Somehow I was always able to scrape up enough money for a hotel. Not necessarily the nicest of hotels, but we were together in a room, and I could watch over both children. Most of the shelters, like this one, divide the men and women into two areas so William would have been taken away from me. I couldn't bear for that to happen."

"He will have to sleep in the men's dorm tonight, Julia, but I will be there with him."

"I know and I appreciate all you've done for us, Abraham."

"I am not sure if I have helped or hurt your chances of getting free of the Philadores."

"Why do you say that?"

"Because you are being hunted still."

"But this time we're not alone. You are with us, Abraham, to guide us."

"You have needed no guidance except at which corner to turn."

She laughed. William stirred. He blinked his eyes open and glanced at both of them before he drifted back to sleep.

"When I checked my purse earlier, I found a note Mrs. Fielding had given me when we were in Philadelphia."

"The lady who lived in your apartment building?" he asked.

"That's right. She watched the children for me when I worked at a neighborhood diner."

Julia opened her purse and pulled out a piece of folded notepaper. "It's a short prayer Mrs. Fielding said whenever she was worried or in trouble. *Jesus, I trust in You*."

"Sounds like she was a woman of faith."

"Indeed. She'd been through hard times. Her husband died some years back. They'd lost a son to a drug overdose, but she kept her faith and her trust in the Lord. She taught me a lot about believing in God's abundant mercy."

"When Marianne and Becca died, I railed at God and blamed Him for their deaths. I did not want to live and could not understand why I had been the one to live."

"Jonathan said a paroled criminal was trying to get back at you for arresting him."

"He thought I would be driving the car instead of my wife. Her car needed an oil change. I took it to the mechanic that morning so she would not have to deal with the problem."

The memory of kissing Marianne goodbye before he had left the house flooded over him. Becca had run from her room and grabbed his legs. He had lifted her into his arms and kissed her cheek. She had wrapped her arms around his neck and giggled. The last words he had heard from her sweet mouth were "Daddy, I love you."

Julia reached out her hand and took his. "Losing those we love, especially an innocent child, is the hardest thing anyone has to do. God watched His son suffer and die on the cross, Abraham. He understands your pain."

"That is what Jonathan tried to make me realize. He was there when I needed him."

"Which is why you took us into your home. I'm very grateful, and I'm also sorry that you had to leave your peaceful farm to help me find my son."

Abraham offered a weak smile. "William is a good boy. He has been hurt and feels abandoned by his father. That is a hard place for a boy to be."

"I know you were a good father, Abraham. I can tell by the way you interact with Kayla and William."

"Kayla never met a stranger, as the saying goes."

Julia nodded. "Which is not always good. Plus, she's wise beyond her years. I'm glad we left Philadelphia. It wasn't a good environment. I tried to keep the children at home as much as possible, but that's not the best, either. I kept blaming Charlie for everything that had happened, yet I was the one who married him. That mistake was totally mine."

"You have two wonderful children, so good came from your marriage."

"That's true. I'm blessed beyond words, thanks to them."

William stirred again and blinked open his eyes. "Did you say something?" he asked.

"Only that I'm glad you're my son."

The boy smiled. "I…I'm sorry about running away."

"Right now we need to give thanks for finding you and for keeping you safe." She glanced at Abraham. "We have someone to thank for that."

William hung his head and then glanced up. His gaze was sincere when he spoke. "Thank you both for coming after me. I wasn't thinking about anyone but myself, like you said back in the barn, Abraham. I was wrong."

"*Yah*, we have all made mistakes. This one will end well. You have a lifetime ahead of you, William, and much for which to be thankful. You are a good young man. You will grow into a strong man who makes good decisions."

"Do you really think so?" The boy seemed hungry for affirmation.

"I know it is so."

A bell rang. The woman who had welcomed them stepped to the middle of the room. "The meal will be served soon. Let us give thanks, then if you want to wash up before eating, the restrooms are on either side of the living area."

She waited for everyone to settle and then bowed her

head. "Dear God, we thank You for all those who are here today. We ask Your blessing on each of them, on the volunteers and on the generous people who provided the food for this meal. Touch each person with Your love and with Your mercy. Allow us to place our trust in You, Lord. Amen."

Julia nodded. "Amen,"

"A good prayer," Abraham said.

"And another confirmation about the importance of trust."

William took her hand. "You can trust me, Mom." He looked at Abraham. "I learned an important lesson."

"*Yah*, to trust *Gott* and those who love you. You need to also trust yourself, William. This will come with time."

Abraham glanced at the people who were headed to the wash area. "Now, let us prepare to eat. I know you are hungry."

William nodded. "I am starving. I could eat a cow."

Abraham laughed. "You have ambition, William."

"That's good, isn't it?" the boy asked.

"Yes, William. It is very *gut*."

Chapter Ten

Julia hadn't realized how hungry she was until she went through the food line. When a server asked if anyone wanted seconds, both Abraham and William went back for another helping of meat loaf and green beans. William asked for more bread and received an extra dollop of whipped butter to put on the homemade rolls.

An assortment of desserts was on a side table, which interested Julia. The gut-wrenching fear that had hovered over her for so long had lifted, and she was relieved they were in what seemed like a secure environment, at least for the evening.

The older men—regulars, as Muriel called them—took a liking to William. A number of them reached out to her son and encouraged him to get his education and a good job so he could do something worthwhile with his life. The regulars weren't speaking poorly of those in the shelter but rather bolstering William's morale and letting him know that he could dream big dreams and follow his heart.

After everyone had eaten, Muriel asked William to help her clear the tables. Instead of rejecting the offer, he eagerly jumped up and started to work. Julia and Abraham both offered to help, but she insisted the kitchen was in good hands.

"You folks relax. We have a number of volunteers. We'll let them do the work, along with William. I thought he might enjoy being of service." She patted Julia's hand. "You have a good boy there. He'll make you proud someday."

The woman's words touched Julia's heart. For too long, she had worried about William's future. Having pride in her son was something she had not even dared imagine.

She watched him follow Muriel to the kitchen and felt a swell of optimism in her heart. Things were starting to change, which gave her hope.

"I never thought my son would flourish in a shelter," she told Abraham. "If I had realized how much he enjoyed working with folks who were down and out, we might have visited them earlier."

"It does seem that he has had a change of heart, Julia. Once we get back to Yoder, I will assign him jobs to do. He showed an interest in Buttercup and was eager to work in the barn—even mucking out the stalls did not seem to bother him. Being successful at small tasks in the beginning will build his self-confidence. Once he becomes proficient at the initial jobs, others will be added. You will see a change in him within the month."

If only what Abraham said would prove true. She thought back over the last few years when the future had seemed so hopeless. Mrs. Fielding had prayed for them, and in her own way, Julia had sought help from the Lord. Although she'd never thought He heard her prayers. Maybe she hadn't been patient enough. Plus she never would have imagined the Lord could provide what William needed in not only a distant state but also in a homeless shelter with an Amish man who had cut himself off from the world.

She glanced at Abraham as he walked to the far end of the common area and peered out the window. His height and build always surprised Julia, as if she could never remember how strong and big he really was until he stepped away from her and she saw him from a distance.

He was handsome in a clean, outdoorsy way, a wholesome look that made her heart flutter when he glanced over his shoulder and caught her staring at him. She should not be thinking of his looks or his strength at this particular time. She should be focused on protecting her son instead of thinking about the man who made her heart skip a beat.

Looking around, she studied the other men. No one came close to having Abraham's charisma. Her cheeks burned and she shook her head ever so slightly, needing to focus on something else instead of on Abraham.

Once the kitchen was tidy, the men gathered at various tables and played chess and checkers. William joined in the fun. The men enjoyed his enthusiasm and a number of them patted his back when he made good plays and captured his opponent's pieces.

Julia glanced at the window, seeing the night fall, and thought of Kayla. Although she knew her daughter was well cared for, she still hated to be away from her.

Keep her safe, Lord, she prayed. *Let no harm come to my sweet little one.*

By nine o'clock, Julia knew many of the people would head to the dorm rooms soon to claim their beds. She didn't want to leave Abraham and William.

"Perhaps we can stay in this common area tonight," she said.

"You need a bed, Julia. The couch worked for a short nap, but for a longer sleep you need to lie down."

Muriel approached them. "I placed a reserved sign on two of the cots near the entrance and close to the hallway and the phones, Abraham. I know you've been waiting for a call."

"From the man who will drive us home," Julia said.

"You're welcome to stay out here for a while. By ten-thirty, we ask that everyone retire to the dorm areas."

"Thank you for providing such a lovely shelter and the delicious dinner," Julia said. "Your hospitality and understanding have touched us deeply."

"The Lord calls all of us to welcome the stranger and to feed the hungry. You'll take what you received here and pass it on to others in your lives who will need help at another time. I see great love between you all." Muriel's smile was warm and sincere.

Julia looked down, unable to face Abraham. He was a good man, thrown into this situation due to his own desire to help another person in need. He had not realized what saying yes to Jonathan would entail.

"We will try to reach out as beautifully as you have done, ma'am." Abraham stood. "I need to make another phone call in case the car is ready."

He entered the dorm area. Muriel patted Julia's hand. "He is a good man. I do not see a ring on your finger so I presume you are not married. This is something you should consider."

Embarrassed by the woman's words, Julia shook her head. "It's not what you think. He is helping me escape a bad situation, and regrettably, we have pulled him into the danger that surrounds us."

"He cares for you. I can see it in his eyes."

"Maybe you see his inability to leave us. Two gang members are after my son."

"Which gang?"

"The Philadores."

The manager nodded. "I've heard of them, but they aren't prevalent in the local area."

Muriel glanced at a couple of men sitting in the far corner of the room. "Grant's the guy with the scar on his face. He was a gang member until he found Jesus. Now he tries to help the kids get off the street."

"Yet he's homeless himself?"

"He calls himself a vagabond for the Lord. He might know a way to get you safely out of town and away from the Philadores."

"I'm not sure you should mention our situation to him. I probably said more than I should have."

"Don't worry. Grant can be trusted. I would do nothing to place you or your son in danger."

Muriel did as she had mentioned and talked quietly with Grant. The man put down the newspaper he was reading and approached Julia. "Muriel told me about your problem with the Philador gang. That's a presence no one wants to have get a foothold in Kansas City. We have our own problems with gangs and do not need more bad actors stealing our youth and wreaking havoc in our city."

"I'm sorry that we might have brought them here."

"Do you have a picture of the gang members?"

"No, but their names are Pablo Davila and Mateo Gonzales." She described what they were wearing.

"The Philadores usually have a script *P* tattooed on their left hands."

"Yes." Julia nodded. "That's correct. Pablo has one. I'm not sure about Mateo."

"They wish to harm your son, Muriel told me, which means he's seen something or knows something that could cause them problems."

Julia refused to comment on Grant's last statement. She had already told him more than she should. Instead, she said, "The two men have been searching for us on the street. We need to meet a car as soon as it gets out of the mechanic's shop, but I fear we will be seen and followed."

"What time are you leaving here?"

She shrugged. "That depends on how fast the mechanic works."

"A few hours?" he asked.

She glanced at the clock on the wall. "The mechanic said he would keep working until eleven. If the work isn't completed by then, he'll have to finish the job tomorrow."

"Everyone has to leave the shelter in the morning by eight." Grant pursed his full lips. "Muriel needs time to have the place cleaned and the sheets washed before the doors open again at two tomorrow afternoon."

Julia signed. Eight o'clock seemed early. Where would they go? "I don't want to think about being on the street again tomorrow."

"Then let's hope your mechanic gets the job done."

Abraham hurried back into the room and looked concerned when he saw Grant talking to Julia.

She introduced her new acquaintance and tried to sooth Abraham's unease. "This gentleman knows some of the local gangs. He tries to get kids off the street. I told him two Philadores were searching for us."

Abraham's gaze narrowed. "I hope you are a trustworthy man, Grant. Julia seems to think you can help us, instead of doing us harm."

"I'll make a few phone calls. Let me know before you head onto the street. I'll see if the people I know can provide some cover for you."

Abraham stared at him for a long moment and then stretched out his hand. The two men shook. "Any help you can provide will be greatly appreciated."

Grant glanced first at where William sat playing chess, then back at Julia. His wide smile touched her heart.

"Your boy has made an impact on a number of people here this evening," Grant said. "We see some kids, but usually they stay to themselves and don't wish to interact. Your son has a big heart."

"You can thank his mother for that," Abraham added. "She has raised him well."

Grant nodded. "A mother's love makes all the difference." He turned to Abraham. "Young men also need strong fathers who can guide their sons and be a role model for them. You've done a good job yourself."

Abraham started to object, but Julia shook her head.

If Grant considered Abraham the father of her child, she didn't want anyone to set him straight. Abraham had all the qualities that would make a good father and William seemed drawn to him. If only they could stay with Abraham long enough for William to get on his feet and directed to the right path.

"I'll make those phone calls now." Grant stood. "Let me know before you leave."

Once he returned to his seat on the far side of the room, Abraham scooted closer to Julia. "I hope we can trust him."

"We need help, Abraham. Muriel mentioned that Grant could be of assistance. We have to trust him."

Trust. What Julia struggled to accept in her own life. Perhaps being with Abraham was also rubbing off on her.

Muriel blinked the lights. "It's time to put the games away so we can pray together before everyone gets a good night's sleep."

The men did as she asked. Working together, they returned the board games and magazines and books to the cupboards.

"We close each day with night prayer," Muriel said once the room was tidy. "I hope you'll all join us."

She looked around the room. "Who would like to read the scripture to us this evening?"

Most of the people glanced down as if unwilling to volunteer. She nodded to Julia and then Abraham.

He stood and walked to the Bible and read from Psalm 33. The verse, "Let thy mercy, O Lord, be upon us, according as we hope in thee," resonated with Julia.

Hope and trust were similar. Was the Lord telling her something and speaking to her heart? Could she trust the Lord? Was He telling her she could also trust Abraham?

Muriel prayed a blessing over all of them for the night ahead, for their safety, for peace and for an end to misery and heartache.

The prayer seemed aimed directly at Julia.

"Amen," they all said in unison.

She hugged William. "Stay with Abraham. I'll be in the other dorm room."

"Don't worry, Mom. I won't run away again."

She looked into his eyes and saw the truthfulness of his statement. "I trust you, William, and I love you."

Abraham waited nearby. "Do not worry," he told her when William stepped out of her embrace. "I will have Muriel contact you if Randy calls tonight."

"Thank you, Abraham. Keep William safe."

But when he and her son headed to the men's dorm, she started thinking of what could happen. What if someone broke in and found them? What if Grant warned the other gang members and they worked with the Philadores? What if the safety of this shelter wasn't real?

Muriel stepped toward her. "You're worried. I see it written on your face."

"Leaving my son is hard."

"I'll be up for a few more hours and promise to wake you if something changes."

"I hate to act like I'm not grateful, Muriel. It's just that so much has happened."

"Have you given it to God?"

Julia didn't understand.

"Give Him your worries and your fears. Give Him your son. After all we're all God's children. His love is unconditional so we know He loves William even more than you do, and He wants only good for all of us. Trust in the Lord, Julia. Let Him carry the burdens that weigh you down now. He can handle everything perfectly and in His perfect time."

"I have problems trusting Him, Muriel. He turned away from me when I was in need."

"Did the Lord turn away from you or did you turn away from Him, which is usually the case?"

"I'm not sure." Julia hesitated for a moment. "You've given me something to think about."

"Well, tonight try not to think about anything. Just get some rest. Things will seem better in the morning."

If only that would be true.

Chapter Eleven

Muriel woke Julia in the night. She hurried to join Abraham and William in the main room. Grant was there, cautioning Abraham to wait inside the shelter until the older man received a phone call.

Randy had called. He had paid the mechanic even more money to keep working past the eleven o'clock cutoff.

William looked tired and worried. He'd changed out of his sweatshirt into a dark jacket and baseball cap Muriel had provided so he wouldn't be recognized.

Shouts sounded from the street.

"What's going on?" Julia asked Abraham.

"The gangs are rallying. Seems someone warned them that the Philadores were infiltrating the city and ready to start up a group here."

"What about Pablo and Mateo?"

"They are outside somewhere. Grant's getting us an escort to the intersection where Randy will meet us."

Muriel gave Julia a small bag. "I made sandwiches for all of you and added some cookies and water. You'll need food once you get to your car."

"You've thought of everything."

Muriel turned to glance at Grant. "You've had help from some good people this evening. It's going to work out."

Grant's phone rang. He pulled it to his ear and nodded. "Thanks."

He pocketed his phone and approached Abraham. "It's time. My contacts spotted Pablo and Mateo. The description you gave was perfect. They'll keep them occupied while you slip outside and down the street. An escort will be waiting at the corner. They'll ensure you don't have trouble meeting your ride."

"Thanks, Grant."

"Just trying to help. Pass it on, like Muriel always tells us."

Julia squeezed his hand. "We will."

She hugged Muriel.

"Go with God," the woman said.

Julia grabbed William's hand. Abraham ushered them toward the door. She glanced back to see Muriel's encouraging smile. Grant gave them a thumbs-up as Abraham opened the door and slipped into the cool night. He motioned them forward.

The door shut behind them. Rounding the corner of the church, Julia gasped, seeing the swarms of teens and twentysomethings gathered. Their taunts made her heart race, fearing a fight was about to ensue.

She pulled William close to her side. What had she done to place her child in danger? Abraham had said they could get away without being stopped, but heading into the middle of a gang fight was asking for trouble that could end up badly for all of them. She should have stayed in the shelter with William.

"Hurry, Julia." Abraham motioned her forward. "We only have a short window of time to get to the intersection where we will meet Randy." He held out his hand to her. "Trust me."

If only she could.

Fear flashed in Julia's eyes. Abraham's heart went out to her for the situation there were in. All she wanted to do was keep her son safe, yet they were walking into the middle of what appeared to be a clash between two street gangs. They were taking a big risk that could turn deadly.

"We have to keep walking." Abraham put his hand on Julia's shoulder and guided her forward. She scooted William closer to Abraham so the boy would be protected between both of them.

"Keep your head down," Abraham said. "We will slip out along the side of the road. Act nonchalant."

William looked as frightened as his mother. If they got out of this alive, the boy might understand the reality of being in a gang and change his mind about having anything to do with the Philadores.

The shouts on the street escalated. Abraham walked on the outside to protect Julia and William. Once they rounded the church, they stayed on the sidewalk, keeping their eyes averted so they would not make eye contact with any of the punks who might want to have fun at their expense.

"What about Pablo and Mateo?" Julia whispered.

"Grant said the people he called had spotted them."

Julia glanced over her shoulder. "Pablo and his buddy are on the far side of the street." Her voice was shaky and laced with fear.

"Keep walking." Abraham wanted to look back as Julia had done, but he would not risk Pablo seeing him.

"Hey, you!" someone shouted.

"Stay calm," Abraham cautioned.

"Pablo must have seen us," Julia whispered.

"Just keep walking. If I say run, you and William head to the intersection where Randy will be waiting."

"We won't go without you," William said.

The boy's words touched Abraham's heart. "You have to get your mom out of danger, William. I will stay back and distract anyone who tries to follow you. Can you protect her?"

"I can try."

"Hey, you guys." The voice came again.

Abraham glanced back. Two men were heading straight for them.

"Grant sent us," the taller of the two men said as they approached. "The Philadores who followed you are being detained by some of our local guys. We'll stay with you until we get to a safer area."

A gunshot rang out. Abraham's heart stopped.

"Sounds like things have gone south," one of the guys said. "Let's pick up the pace."

Abraham, Julia and William started to run. Grant's friends followed close behind.

"Cross here," one of them said. "The street's clear."

Sirens sounded in the distance. More volleys of gunfire. "Did Grant order the violence?" Abraham asked.

"No way, man. Grant's cool. He works to keep peace in the hood. It's the local gangs. They're fighting for their own turf. That area around the shelter can get bad. We watch out for Muriel, and Grant calls us in if anything comes too close to the shelter. Tonight, we didn't expect gunfire."

The other man pointed to an alleyway. "Head between those buildings, it leads to the intersection. Grant said you need to meet your driver there."

Abraham glanced at Julia, worried that the pace was too much for her. She was keeping up but winded and, from the look on her face, scared to death.

William stayed close to his mom as if he was taking to heart Abraham's suggestion to protect her.

The alley was narrow and the main road appeared ahead. Traffic whizzed by. Abraham hoped they would be able to find Randy.

One of the guys held up his hand. "Wait here. I'll check the street."

Julia leaned into Abraham. He put his hand on her shoulder.

"Did we escape without Pablo seeing us?" she asked.

"I hope so."

"A car just pulled to the curb," the guy announced. "Looks like your ride has arrived."

Abraham squeezed Julia's shoulder. "Let me go first." But when he peered around the corner, his heart stopped. He did not recognize the car or the man sitting behind the wheel.

"Wrong car. We will wait in the alley."

"Is it the gang member who's after you?" Grant's friend asked.

Abraham shook his head. "Someone new."

"We'll check it out."

Grant's friends walked toward the street and stopped near the car. They started laughing and making a ruckus, which gave Abraham a chance to study the car and driver. Finally, the vehicle drove off.

Abraham let out a deep breath.

Grant's friends returned. "I don't know who the driver was, but he had a Glock sitting in the passenger seat."

Julia grabbed Abraham's hand. "It could have been someone from the Philadores."

Abraham spied Randy's car across the street. "There is our ride."

He turned to the two men and shook their hands. "Thanks, guys. You saved us."

"Hey, you're a friend of Grant's. That's all we need to know."

"We appreciate the escort and help. I doubt we would have made it here unharmed without you."

Their new friends looked up and down the street. "Get going now. The street's clear. Things could change in a heartbeat."

Abraham ushered Julia and William across the roadway. He opened the back door of the Amish taxi, and they all slipped into the rear.

"Do you know how glad we are to see you?" he asked Randy as he closed the door and buckled his seat belt.

Randy laughed. "The feeling's mutual. This city isn't for me, Abraham. Let's get outta here."

Gunshots echoed. "Sounds as if things haven't calmed down near the shelter," Julia said, glancing back.

"Stay down," Abraham warned. "Until we are out of this area."

Randy pulled onto the main road. Another car pulled in behind them. Abraham glanced over his shoulder. "That looks like the sedan that was parked on the road earlier. The driver has a Glock on the seat next to him,

Randy. Probably a nine millimeter strapped to his hip. He might have an ankle holster, as well. See if you can lose him."

Randy accelerated.

"Who is it?" Julia asked, her voice tight.

"No clue."

Randy increased his speed even more.

"Hang a left at the next intersection," Abraham suggested.

The light started to change. Randy accelerated through the yellow and turned left. The car behind them was forced to stop.

"Hit it, Randy."

Traffic was light, and Randy pushed down on the accelerator, but before long Abraham spotted the car again.

They needed to dump the tail. "Take a right and a left. See if you can lose him."

Randy nodded and followed Abraham's promptings. Eventually they ended up on a four-lane boulevard lined with homes.

Before they had gone more than half a mile, the car reappeared behind them.

"The guy's sticking like glue," Randy said.

Julia groaned. "I'm scared, Abraham."

"We are in good hands with Randy at the wheel, Julia. We will get through this."

"You're sure?" she asked.

"Absolutely."

But he was not sure of anything, especially since the tail kept coming after them.

More sirens. Two police cars flew past, heading in the opposite direction.

Randy turned on the car radio and found the news.

"Police are advising everyone to stay clear of the area near the Fellowship Church Shelter," the radio news commentator said. "Fighting has broken out between rival gangs. At this point, there are two confirmed dead with a number of life-threatening injuries."

"What about the men who helped us?" Julia said. "I pray they weren't hurt."

"They seemed to know their way around the city. My hunch is they stayed clear of the violence."

"What about Grant and Muriel?" William asked.

"From what Grant said, the church is a neutral zone. I doubt anyone holed up inside would be hurt. The fighting would have been on the street."

Randy turned off the radio and glanced over his shoulder. "I don't see the car."

"Which worries me," Abraham admitted.

"Do we cross the bridge and head west or chill around here and kill time?"

"Bad choice of words," Abraham said with a wry smile.

"Your call."

"Take the bridge."

Randy pulled into the turn lane and rounded the curve aimed toward the water. Abraham glanced over his shoulder and stared behind them.

"See anything?" Randy asked.

"Headlights, but I am not sure about the car."

"Traffic on the bridge is light, which is good."

The headlights were catching up to them. "Check the right-hand lane."

Randy nodded. "Our tail doesn't realize we're exiting. Hold on, everyone."

The car sped along the exit ramp.

Abraham grabbed the front seat to keep from slamming against the door.

William groaned.

"You doing okay over there?" Abraham asked.

"Even with my seatbelt buckled, I crashed into Mom."

"No harm done," she said. "Although I'd like to straighten up."

"Keep your head down a few minutes more, Julia."

Abraham patted Randy's back as they crossed the bridge to the Kansas side of the city without their tail.

"That is what I call too close for comfort." Randy let out a deep sigh and eased up on the gas.

Abraham looked back again to ensure they truly were free of the tail before he helped Julia straighten up.

"Are you okay?" he asked.

"A little shaken but no harm done."

She looked at William. "What about you, hon?"

"I'm okay, Mom."

"Sure?"

"Just worried about Grant."

"Grant knows how to take care of himself," Abraham said. "Plus he has friends who work with him seemingly for good. You need not worry, William, but instead offer a prayer of gratitude that God led us to the shelter."

Julia took her son's hands and both of them closed their eyes for a long moment. Abraham silently lifted up his own words of thanks to the Lord.

He smiled at Julia when she opened her eyes, but she was not smiling. She was tense and scared.

If they could get out of the city and onto the back roads, everyone could relax. It had been three years since he left law enforcement. Some days he had longed to put on his badge again, but being with Julia and fearing for her safety, as well as William's, made him realize he was well ensconced in the Amish life and farming. He no longer wanted to fight crime.

Abraham wanted peace and tranquility, but he did not want the loneliness that he often felt on the farm. Julia and William and Kayla had awakened a need within him for companionship. He glanced at Julia. She had closed her eyes, her arm around William who rested his head on her shoulder.

Abraham had feelings for Julia and her children, although he could not put a name to those feelings. But he cared about them and he was relieved that they were headed back to Yoder. He prayed trouble would not follow them.

Chapter Twelve

Randy turned the car radio back on to the easy listening station, but even with the restful music, Julia's pulse continued to race. Mentally she knew they were safe, at least for now, but knowing what had happened and the memory of how close they had come to being caught in the middle of two warring gangs circled through her mind.

William's breathing became shallow as he drifted to sleep. A swell of gratitude rose within her for all Abraham had done to keep them safe. A warmth filtered over her as he turned to her, his eyes filled with concern.

"I thought you were asleep," he said in a soft voice so as not to wake William or distract Randy.

"Just grateful we made it out of the city."

He nodded. "I will call Jonathan and let him know."

"Tell him you kept us safe."

"We worked together, Julia. I will tell Jonathan we make a good team."

"He asked you to take care of us because he knew you were a good man, Abraham." She smiled and then glanced at her son. "I hope William has learned his lesson. He was more frightened than I've ever seen him.

Plus, Grant made a good impression on him, along with Muriel."

"William made a good impression on them. He is a fine boy, Julia. Your hard work has paid off."

Abraham's words brought comfort. "For so long I didn't know if William believed what I was telling him," she said. "The street was a bigger draw than staying home with his mom and sister. I was afraid I would lose him."

"But you did not lose him. Even when he ran away, you were able to find him."

"Because of you, Abraham. If not for you, I would have lost my son."

He took her hand and held it as the car traveled along the back roads. Julia's pulse calmed and the tension that had gripped her eased. Abraham had come to her rescue. He had arranged for Randy to drive them, for Kayla to be cared for by Sarah and for ways to keep them away from the Philador gang in Kansas City. Julia would always be grateful.

Once they were out of the city, Abraham called Jonathan on Randy's phone. He kept his voice low to keep from being heard by the taxi driver. "We are heading back to Yoder," Abraham told Jonathan.

"That's good news. You have William?"

"We do. We holed up in a church shelter not far from the bus station. A woman named Muriel runs the shelter in the basement of the Fellowship Church. Turns out some former gang members, who found the Lord and work to get kids off the street, came to our aid and arranged an escort. They got us to where we had arranged to meet our taxi."

"You had the marshal's office in Kansas City worried."

Abraham pushed the phone close to his ear. "Did you contact them?"

"They sent a man to pick you up at the intersection where you planned to connect with Randy. The marshal followed you for a short time but eventually lost you." Abraham smiled to himself. "The guy was driving a black Buick."

"You saw him?"

Abraham glanced at Randy, grateful that he was focused on the road, and lowered his voice even more. "And the Glock he had on his passenger seat. We thought he was associated with the Philadores."

"Since when does a US Marshal look like a street thug?"

"After everything that happened, we did not hang around to ask questions."

"I'm sorry we couldn't be more help. We'll all breathe more easily once you're back at the farm."

Abraham would, too. He was ready for the danger to end, although Julia and her children would be looking over their shoulders for years to come. Would it ever end?

Abraham thought again of the people they had met at the shelter. Muriel was a good woman who helped so many. As Grant had mentioned, Abraham would endeavor to pay forward the outreach that had benefitted them. Many people were down and out. Instead of being reclusive and only interested in his own needs, Abraham vowed to get out more and help others.

Right now he was helping Julia, but she would not remain on his farm forever, much as he enjoyed having her and her family stay with him.

He turned to stare out the window and thought about what he had lost and what had returned to his life.

Could Julia ever fill the void left by his wife?

She could. In fact, she had already done so.

Chapter Thirteen

Julia blinked her eyes open when Randy turned the taxi onto the road leading to Sarah's house. She rubbed her eyes and sat up straighter.

"I hope we don't frighten Sarah, knocking at her door at this hour."

Abraham patted her hand. "She should be expecting us."

The house sat dark at the end of the drive.

"I'll wait here," Randy said when he pulled the taxi to a stop.

Abraham helped Julia from the car. Together they walked to the porch where Abraham rapped gently on the door.

When no one answered, he peered through a window.

"Do you see anyone?" Julia asked.

"Sarah is probably sleeping upstairs with her daughter and Kayla." He knocked harder, and when that failed to summon anyone, he rapped again.

Julia turned to glance over her shoulder, her heart pounding. "Why doesn't Sarah answer the door?"

He shook his head and tried knocking again.

"Tell me everything is okay, Abraham, and that Mateo and Pablo haven't been here."

"Just as you mentioned, Julia. Everything is fine. We have to be patient."

"Patient? I'm scared."

"I will check the barn and see whether the buggy is there."

"Would she have taken Kayla with her?"

"She would not have left the child here alone."

Tears burned Julia's eyes. She thought of everything that had happened. Now Sarah and Kayla were gone. How could anything worse happen?

After checking the barn, Abraham hurried back to the car where Julia stood waiting. "Something must have happened," he told her. "Sarah's buggy is gone. Perhaps she needed to visit an aging relative and took Kayla and her daughter with her. She would have left a note on the door of my house with information about their where-abouts."

"If only that could be, Abraham."

Julia climbed back into the rear seat. Her heart pounded. William was still asleep, oblivious to what was happening. She had worried about him so much while they were in the city, but she never thought any-thing untoward would happen to Kayla. Her mistake.

She had made so many.

Why had she left Kayla with a woman she didn't even know? In hindsight, she should have taken Kayla with them to look for William. Then she thought about grab-bing William in the fast food restaurant and running from Pablo and Mateo, and the unfriendly clerk at the hotel. Kayla would have gotten too tired and too frightened, plus she would have slowed them down.

No, Julia had been right to leave Kayla. But where was her daughter now?

Oh, Lord, please. I feel overwhelmed by what has happened and so very fearful. I am trying to trust, which is what I believe You want me to do, but I'm shaking inside.

If anything happened to Kayla…

She looked at Abraham. He had lost his four-year-old daughter and his wife. How had he survived all that pain?

She didn't want to be strong like he had been. She wanted to burst into tears and rail at God for putting her child in danger, although she only had herself to blame.

A hole formed in her heart and the pain of what might have happened was so powerful, she could hardly breathe.

Abraham wrapped his arm about her shoulders.

"Hurry, Randy. Take us to my farm. Sarah was not at her house. I am hopeful she left a message on my door."

Randy must have heard the fear in Abraham's voice. He turned sharply out of Sarah's property and accelerated. At this time of night, they were the only car on the country road. Darkness surrounded them, as dark as Julia's heart that was ready to break.

"Do not think of what might have happened until we have more information," Abraham said, his voice filled with compassion.

He must have known what she was thinking and that made Julia even more afraid. She could not answer him for fear her voice would turn into a scream from her heart.

The farm appeared. Randy turned the car into the drive and pulled to a stop in front of Abraham's house.

Abraham jumped out, ran up the stairs and unlocked the door. He lit an oil lamp and returned to look for a note left by the door.

Then he glanced at the taxi, his face fearful and illuminated by the flickering light. There was no note and no information about Kayla or where Sarah had taken her.

Julia climbed from the car, tears streaming from her eyes. Her life as she knew it was about to change forever and she couldn't go on.

"Oh, Abraham." She fell into his arms and sobbed.

"Kayla is all right," he assured her.

"I don't believe you." She gasped. "Where's my baby girl?"

Abraham rubbed her shoulders. "We will find her."

"First William and now Kayla. When will it end?"

"Julia."

Hearing her name, she turned to find Sarah running toward them from the *dawdy* house.

"Where's Kayla?"

"Asleep in her room," Sarah said as she neared. "She was upset you were not home. Some of my relatives stayed at Abraham's spare house when my husband died. I still have the key, so we came here to bring comfort to Kayla. My daughter, Ella, is asleep in the bed with her. I stayed downstairs, hoping to hear you return."

Julia ran past Sarah to the porch of the *dawdy* house. She pushed open the kitchen door and took the stairs two at a time. Opening the bedroom door, she gasped with relief when she saw Kayla sleeping peacefully in her own bed. Julia dropped to her knees, tears of relief falling from her eyes. She brushed the hair off her daughter's face and kissed her cheek. Sarah's daughter was sleeping next to her, both girls oblivious to the fear and terrible thoughts that had rumbled through Julia's mind.

She stumbled into the hallway so her sobs of relief wouldn't wake the girls. Suddenly Abraham was there again, pulling her into his arms, the smell of him so masculine and strong. She never wanted to leave him.

Kayla had not been hurt or captured or harmed in any way. William was asleep in the taxi downstairs. The two Philadores were still in Kansas City, or perhaps they were already on their way back to Philadelphia. Her ex-husband was behind bars where he couldn't hurt them and she wasn't alone. She had a wonderful man who was strong and honest and understanding, who didn't laugh at her for getting upset or for fearing the worst. A man who had lost everything he had ever loved, but who still was able to open his heart to her.

"I'm sorry I got so carried away. I…I thought…"

"I know, Julia. You have had so much happen recently and you have been so strong. But everything is going to be okay. I will not let anything happened to you or to the children."

She could hear his heart beat as he held her tight, her head on his chest. Her sobs subsided, and her thoughts turned from her children, who she knew were safe, to Abraham, the man who was very much present with her now.

He pulled back ever so slightly and stared down at her. Everything stopped for one long moment, even her heart that had pounded so hard just moments earlier. The whole world seemed to be on pause as she looked into his eyes. His lips twitched, as if he didn't know whether or not he should draw her closer. All she wanted was for him to lower his lips to hers. Although she didn't know if she could survive if he did.

"Julia." He whispered her name, yet so much more was contained in that one word than she had ever heard from anyone.

She stretched toward him, wanting nothing to keep them apart. All she wanted was for his mouth to touch hers.

Her heart pounded in anticipation. She reached her hands around his neck and buried her fingers in his hair as his lips slowly descended to—

"Abraham?"

Sarah was on the stairs, calling up to them.

He pulled back, startled.

Julia's heart stopped, this time with regret.

She backed away, unable to speak, feeling drained and tired. Her mind swirled with confusion wondering how she had gone from tears of fear to a yearning to remain in this man's arms forever.

"I need to bring William inside." She pushed past Abraham and hurried down the stairs, her hand gripping the railing lest she lose her balance. She felt weak and confused.

"Is everything all right?" Sarah asked as Julia hurried toward the kitchen door.

"Yes. Thank you for caring for Kayla. She's sound asleep. I need to bring William inside."

"I am sorry to have frightened you when you found no one home at my house," Sarah said, following her.

Julia turned and took the woman's hand. "You have been so gracious, and I am grateful. But today has been long and troubling. That everything turned out all right brings me comfort. Your friendship and help does, as well, Sarah. Please let me know how I can repay you for your kindness."

The Amish woman smiled. "No payment is needed. You would help me in the same way if I had a need."

Julia nodded. "That's true."

Abraham came down the stairs. "I must pay Randy." He looked at Sarah. "Would you like to stay the night here?"

She shook her head. "Ella and I should get home. Would you hitch my horse to the buggy?"

"Of course, it is not a problem. I will ask Randy to follow your buggy to ensure you and Ella arrive home safely."

Julia helped her sleepy son from the car and guided him upstairs to bed. By the time she left his room, Sarah's horse and buggy were waiting in the driveway. Her daughter slipped easily from bed and smiled sweetly as she and her mother left the *dawdy* house to return home.

Once they had driven off, followed by the Amish taxi, Abraham stepped back into the kitchen. He looked expectantly at Julia, as if he wanted to take her in his arms again, but the moment had passed and she had returned to her senses.

She was grateful to Abraham, and he was a man who made her think of being open to love again, although that still seemed almost impossible. She would never be able to trust anyone with her heart, even an Amish man who had saved her son.

The realization that she would go through life alone brought a sense of sorrow again.

But she had her children. What more could she want?

As Abraham left the house and she closed and locked

the door behind him, Julia realized that she did want something more. She wanted someone like Abraham to be a part of her life.

But that could never be, and that thought brought tears to her eyes as she climbed the stairs and slipped into her bedroom.

Tomorrow would be a new day. Everything would look brighter in the sunlight. She would be rid of foolish thoughts about love and happiness, things she wanted but would never have.

Chapter Fourteen

Abraham headed to the barn early the next morning to catch up on the chores that had not been done while he was gone. He had moved the horses to the pasture so they could graze and get water from the pond and they had fared well, but a farm took work, as he had told Julia the first morning she was here, and there was much to do.

He tried to focus on his labor, but he kept thinking of when she had been in his arms and the way she had felt so soft and warm and inviting. More than anything he had wanted to kiss her. Then Sarah had called out to them.

Too quickly, Julia had pulled free from his embrace, which left him feeling empty and flummoxed by all that had happened. Today he would behave more appropriately and stay more aloof. Clearly that was what Julia wanted, judging by the way she had rushed away from him.

He stopped for a minute and peered out the open door of the barn toward the house where she and her children slept. He would not wake them for breakfast this morning. They needed to sleep.

Just as long as Julia did not hole up inside the house and ignore him. He could not endure that, yet that might occur and if so, he would handle it as best he could.

The day was overcast and fit his mood. He should be giving thanks for their success in finding William and bringing him back home. Abraham was grateful, and he knew too well how things could have turned out, especially with two opposing gangs up in arms.

He had filled the troughs with water and mangers with feed, spread hay for the cattle and mended a broken patch of fencing before anyone stirred in the *dawdy* house.

A door slammed and he turned to see William dressed in Amish clothing heading toward him. The boy still looked tired, but he nodded a greeting and reached for a shovel that rested against the side of the barn.

"I'll muck out the stalls," the boy stated without preamble.

"How are you today, William?"

The boy shrugged. "I am glad to be here."

"Your clothes look good on you. Was it a problem to dress?"

"*Mamm* helped me hook the suspenders."

Mamm? He had used the Pennsylvania Dutch term for mother.

"Your mother is up?" Abraham asked, hoping the feelings he had for Julia were not evident in his tone.

"She is making breakfast. Kayla is helping her. She said she will ring the dinner bell when the food is ready."

"You are hungry, I am sure."

The boy smiled. "I am very hungry, but we will work first and then eat."

Abraham nodded, grateful to hear a new energy in William's voice. Much had happened to him on his trip to Kansas City, probably more than the boy realized. He had left Yoder in the middle of the night as a youth yearning to join a gang of street thugs, and in less than twenty-four hours he had turned into a level-headed young man. It was almost too much to believe could be true.

"*Danke, Gott*," Abraham said under his breath.

Within the hour, the door of the *dawdy* house opened and Kayla rang the dinner bell.

"Your mother has timed breakfast perfectly," he told William. "We have finished the morning chores. After we eat, we will check on Mr. Raber's animals."

"And the phone to see if any calls have come through?"

"We will certainly do that." Abraham pointed to the corner of the barn. "Leave the shovel. We must wash up at the pump and then enjoy the food your mother has prepared."

The water from the pump was cold. Abraham handed William the bar of soap and watched with approval as the boy rolled up his sleeves and scrubbed his arms up to his elbows in the chilly water to ensure the muck from the barn did not come with them to the dining table. Once they had washed, they dried their hands and arms on the towel that hung near the pump and headed to the house. Abraham wiped his boots on the rug by the door and smiled when William did the same.

Opening the door, Abraham was pleasantly accosted by the hearty smell of coffee, and bacon and eggs, and biscuits, hot from the oven. He stepped inside and searched for Julia, but the kitchen was empty.

"*Mamm*?" William called.

She came running down the stairs, looking bright-eyed and beautiful. Abraham's breath hitched, and he was taken aback by the flush in her cheeks and the twinkle in her eyes. She had pulled her hair into a bun at the base of her neck and had settled the *kapp* on her head, the strings hanging loose at her neck along with a long strand of hair that had either pulled free or had escaped capture when she first fixed her hair.

She straightened her apron and smiled in welcome. "You are hungry, I'm sure."

Abraham nodded. "The kitchen is filled with wonderful smells. You have been working hard to provide a hearty breakfast, for which I am grateful, Julia."

"It is the least I can do after what you have done for us, Abraham. Sit at the table and I will pour coffee and then fix the plates."

She brought a filled mug to the table. Her coffee tasted far better than the bitter brew he sometimes made. "Good coffee," he said with gratitude.

"I'm still not used to boiling water and pouring it over the grounds in the drip coffee pot. I tried to keep it hot on the back burner but fear the heat was too high. I am glad it meets your approval."

Kayla raced downstairs and ran to Abraham with her arms open wide. He had not expected her exuberant hello or the warm hugs she gave him. "You were gone so long," the child said. "I was worried."

"But you were okay staying with Sarah and her daughter."

"Yes, but I wanted to be here at your house so I could see you as soon as you returned. That's why Miss Sarah brought me here to sleep last night. When I woke this morning, I saw *Mamm* smiling down at me."

Kayla's statement that she had wanted to be at his

house touched Abraham, as well as her waking to find Julia.

Noting her empty arms, Abraham asked, "Where is your doll?"

"Ella said Amish girls don't play with dolls because they are busy helping their mothers with their own sisters and brothers."

"That does not mean you cannot play with your doll."

"Annie is resting. She didn't sleep well last night."

"You are still calling her Annie?" he asked.

"*Yah.*"

He smiled as she used the Amish word for *yes*.

"*Yah,*" Kayla repeated. "Annie is her name. We have all changed and you said you would call her Annie, so I will, too. It is a *gut* name, *yah?*"

"For sure, Kayla." He chuckled. "It is a *gut* name."

"Ella said that Amish girls my age cook and do housework."

He winked. "They also find time to play. You have years to work. Plus, now you must do your studies."

"Kayla, you are full of energy this morning," Julia called from the stove. "Come and take this plate to Abraham."

The plate was heaped high with food, and Kayla set it on the table in front of him.

William slipped onto the bench after he poured milk for Kayla and himself.

"*Danke,*" he said when Kayla brought his plate to the table.

She took her own plate from her mother and sat next to her brother.

Julia checked the stove and then stepped to the table. Abraham stood and helped her with her chair.

William stood, too.

Kayla smiled. "William, tomorrow you can help me with my chair."

The boy laughed and then returned to the bench.

"The food looks delicious. Let us give thanks." Abraham bowed his head, but before he could offer a silent prayer, Kayla nudged him. "Why don't you pray out loud and then we can all pray together."

He glanced at Julia, who looked expectantly back at him.

Kayla wrinkled her brow. "Miss Sarah said praying out loud is not the Amish way, but maybe just this once we could, please, Abraham?"

"That would be nice, Kayla." He held out his hand to the child. She took his and William's. The boy reached for one of Julia's hands, and Abraham held the other.

Warm contentment swept over him as he bowed his head. "Thank you, *Gott*, for bringing us together and for keeping us safe. We give You thanks for this food and for all who worked to provide this meal. May it nourish us so we can do the work You have called us to do. Amen."

The others intoned *amen* and without taking a breath, the children reached for their forks and started eating.

Abraham smiled at Julia. "Thank you for preparing such a delicious breakfast for us, Julia."

"You're most welcome, Abraham. Thank you for providing this nice house in which to stay."

"I hope we stay here forever," Kayla said as she swallowed a forkful of egg and then reached for her glass of milk.

"Abraham does not need us underfoot that long, Kayla," Julia said.

Her words brought Abraham back to the reality of

their situation. Just as Julia mentioned, she and the children would eventually move on to another location and another identity once the danger eased. He doubted Jonathan wanted them to stay here indefinitely. Still, it was something he might mention to his friend.

"I need to call Jonathan and check on a few things with him. William and I will tend to the farm across the way and then we can all go to town so I can make the phone call. We will also stop at the grocery for supplies."

"Ice cream, too?" Kayla asked.

"We will see about the ice cream, Kayla."

"Are you sure we should go into town?" Julia asked. "Can't you use your neighbor's phone?"

"I could, but it might be smarter to use a pay phone, in case anyone is tracking Mr. Raber's number. Using a pay phone in town will be an added precaution."

Julia's face clouded.

"Do not worry," he assured her. "Besides, a trip to town will be enjoyable."

"What if it rains?" Kayla asked.

Abraham glanced out the window. "It is cloudy, but I do not think we will have rain. Are you made of sugar?" he teased.

"Sugar?"

"I thought all little girls were sweet as sugar."

She giggled. "No, Mr. Abraham. I am not made of sugar. I am made of flesh and blood."

"And you are smart, too. You take after your mother."

Kayla grinned and looked at Julia. "Then William takes after our father."

"I do not," the boy insisted.

"Do too," Kayla replied. "You're a boy. That means you take after him."

"Enough, Kayla," Julia said. "You are each unique and special. Is that understood?"

"Still—"

Julia tilted her head. "It's time to eat instead of talk, young lady."

The child sighed with exasperation. Abraham squelched a smile. Kayla was precocious, which was cute at this age. Just as long as she learned how to temper her remarks as she aged.

He glanced at William with his downcast eyes and flushed face. Kayla's comment seemed to have cut William to the quick.

"The chores in the barn were done more quickly today because William helped me." The boy glanced up. Abraham nodded his appreciation. "You have a fine worker in your son, Julia. I know you are proud of him."

She smiled. "I'm glad you recognize his willingness to serve, Abraham. Both my children are eager to help whenever they can."

Kayla's eyes widened as she accepted her mother's praise and seemed less interested in her brother and more in her breakfast.

Children made life interesting and challenging, but also filled it with joy and love. Abraham thought of his Becca with her big blue eyes and curly blond hair. The pain was real as he thought of all he had lost.

"You look sad, Mr. Abraham."

Kayla was staring at him, her eyes wide. The concern he read in her sweet gaze was like salve to his wounded heart.

He forced a smile, not wanting to pull Julia or her children into his own sorrow. "I am fine, Kayla, but food remains on your plate. You need to eat now so you can go with us to town."

"Will we stop at the store where we bought our *kapps*?"

He glanced at Julia. "Is there something you need?"

"I need nothing." She turned to her daughter. "Is there some reason you wanted to return to the store?"

"I wanted to get another *kapp* in case I lose this one. Ella said they get dirty when we play outside and sometimes the wind pulls them off our heads and into the air." She touched her *kapp*. "I do not want to lose mine, but it might happen."

"If so, we will get another one then, Kayla. For now, just be careful when you go outside to play."

"Did you enjoy Sarah's daughter?" Abraham asked.

"Ella's nice. I helped her do her chores. After that, we played tag. Miss Sarah said I will need a larger dress soon, and if so, she has one that her daughter can no longer wear."

"Miss Sarah is very thoughtful," Julia said.

"She also will get some clothes for William."

"I don't need more clothing," he insisted.

Julia looked sharply at her son. "We will be grateful for anything Miss Sarah provides. Isn't that right, William?"

He shrugged. "I guess so. Maybe she will bake another pie." The boy glanced at his mother and widened his eyes. "Mom, you used to bake. A cherry pie would be good."

"With ice cream," Kayla added.

Julia laughed. "We can look for canned cherries at the grocery store."

"Yum." Kayla smiled as she scooped the last of her eggs into her mouth.

Once everyone had eaten, Julia stood and began to clear the table. "If you would like more coffee, Abraham…"

He held up his hand. "I have had enough. William and I will go to my neighbor's farm. When we return, we will prepare for our trip to town."

"Yay!"

"Finish your milk, Kayla, and help clear the table."

"Yes, *Mamm*."

Abraham smiled. Julia did, as well. If only children could remain innocent longer, he thought.

He glanced back and waited as William drank the last of his milk. The boy carried his plate and glass to the sink, rinsed the dishes and placed them on the counter.

"See you soon," Julia said as she carted another plate to the sink.

Abraham put his hand on the boy's shoulder as they walked outside. The pain he had felt earlier eased and was replaced with a sense of well-being.

Working together, they fed and watered the livestock at the neighbor's house. On the way back, they stopped at the phone shack. William stayed outside as Abraham checked the answering machine. The one voicemail was from a telemarketer.

After deleting the message, Abraham stepped from the shack. "Let us go home, William. You can help me harness Buttercup for our trip to town."

The boy nodded, then he glanced again at the phone shack. "Were there any messages?"

"Are you expecting a phone call?" Abraham asked.

William shook his head and hung his head. "No, but

I thought David might call since I never met up with his brother."

"Maybe David realizes being in the gang is not a good thing."

"Maybe. David's mother never wanted him to get involved with anything Pablo did. She said someday they would leave the city and go to live with her sister in the country."

"What did David think about that?"

William shrugged. "He said the country might be nice, especially if he could be outside more and if there were animals to play with. He always wanted a dog."

"What about you, William?"

"I wanted a dog, too, but now I would tell him about Buttercup and the other horses and cows, and what I've learned to do."

"You have learned much because you are a good listener."

"That's what Mrs. Fielding said. Kayla talks a lot, but I talk when I have something important to say."

Abraham put his hand on the boy's back as they walked back to the farm. "You are becoming very wise, William."

The boy smiled and nodded as if he thought the same thing.

William seemed to have learned the importance of having a home and a mother who loved him. If only he could have felt love from his father, too. Maybe the pain of that loss would ease with time. Until then, Abraham would try to offer good advice for as long as William and his mother stayed with him.

Right now, he wished they would stay for a very long time.

Chapter Fifteen

The wind had picked up, and Julia held on to her *kapp* as the buggy headed toward town.

"Perhaps Kayla was right," she said to Abraham. "I may need to get a second *kapp* in case this one blows away in the wind."

He looked at the sky. "The strong wind brings a chill to the air. You and the children might want to cover your legs with blankets. They are behind the last seat."

Without being told, William stretched back and retrieved two blankets. He handed one to his mother and the other to Kayla.

Julia helped her daughter arrange the covering over her legs. "William, do you want to cover your legs?"

"I'm not cold," he said.

Julia enjoyed the warmth of the blanket and draped part of it over Abraham's legs.

He smiled at her and nodded. "You are very thoughtful, but I am not cold. We will be in town soon."

"The wind is brisk, Abraham. You do not want to get sick."

"I am more concerned about you and Kayla." He

glanced over his shoulder at her son. "William and I will be fine."

"*Yah*," the boy answered with his new attempt at using Pennsylvania Dutch. "Abraham taught me a few phrases when we were working in the barn. *Es ist heute nicht so kalt.*"

Julia lifted her brow. "Would someone translate?"

Abraham laughed. "William said it is not so cold today in German. Meaning we do not need the blanket."

"What about Pennsylvania Dutch?"

Abraham nodded. "We will work on that soon."

"Someday I will need to learn the Amish language if I want to understand my own son."

William patted her shoulder. "Don't worry, *Mamm*. I will always tell you what I'm saying."

She grabbed his hand and felt a swell of gratitude.

"When will we be in town?" Kayla asked.

"Soon, Kayla."

"Do I need an Amish first name?" the child asked.

"Your name is Kayla," Julia said. "It's a lovely name and suits you well. We'll stick with that one."

"You and William will keep your names, too?" the child asked.

"Don't talk about new names," her brother warned. "You never know who will hear you."

"You called Davey Davila," she said with a huff.

"I made a mistake, okay? We move on when we make a mistake. That's what Abraham told me. We don't look to the past. We look to the future."

Julia reached for Abraham's hand and squeezed it. William had been listening. Whether their Amish protector realized it or not, her son was drawn to Abraham and wanted to do what was right in his eyes. His own father had never given him attention, and the boy hungered for male guidance. Julia could only do so much. Abraham was a good role model for William. If only they could remain with him a bit longer.

Given the opportunity to talk to Jonathan privately, she would ask if they could stay in Yoder. The children were taking to the Amish way of life, and they both liked Abraham. Neither child needed another change in their lives. Julia didn't want to change locations, either. She liked the farm, but she liked Abraham even more. He was a good influence on her children. He was a good influence on her, as well.

Riding to town with Julia at his side and the children in the rear of the buggy made Abraham all the more aware of his feelings for Julia and her family. He glanced at her, seeing her flushed cheeks and warm smile. She took in the surrounding area with the Amish farms and neighbors, some of whom had reached out to Abraham when he first arrived. He had appreciated their welcome and willingness to help if and when he needed extra hands to harvest or bale hay or any of the other jobs a farm demanded. Regrettably, he had remained somewhat aloof and kept to himself far too much.

Julia with her sweet disposition would fit in well with the women in the area. Never once had he heard her complain about the lack of worldly items. She had cooked on the wood-burning stove, made delicious coffee and even baked biscuits that were light and fluffy and so different from the overcooked and flavorless lumps of flour he pulled from the oven.

He glanced over his shoulder at the children who seemed lost in their own thoughts. The breeze blew their hair back from their sweet faces and their contented smiles brought a warmth to Abraham's heart that filled him with joy.

Even Julia seemed more lighthearted today, as if the struggle of the past was over and a new time of peace and happiness appeared on the horizon.

Abraham wanted to fully embrace that new dawn, but he had to be practical. The Philadores were tough adversaries, and until he knew otherwise, Abraham would keep up his guard.

"The grocery downtown has a pay phone," he shared. "We will shop and then call Jonathan."

Julia leaned closer. "But will he know anything about Pablo and his friend?"

"The marshals have informants. We should be able to learn what the Philadores are planning."

"I pray they are planning to stay in Philadelphia and have abandoned any desire to find William."

"You are in danger, too, Julia. You saw the men who broke into your apartment. Plus, you saw Pablo in Kansas City and could incriminate all of them."

"We will trust the gang is concerned about other issues, do you not agree?"

Her smile lit up her face. "I agree. We must trust."

If only Julia could trust him. He had not been able to protect his wife and child. He could not become complacent and make a similar mistake again.

He jiggled the reins to hurry Buttercup along and glanced at the oncoming traffic. Any car passing by could be a threat. He did not want to live his life in fear, but he needed to be cautious and on guard.

"I made a list of some of the things we'll need at the grocery." Julia opened the tote she had placed at her feet in the buggy and pulled out a sheet of paper. "Will the store be different than the groceries I'm used to?"

"More items are sold in bulk. Anything dry, such as flour and corn starch and spices—even powdered laundry detergent—is packaged in plastic bags."

"So I won't find the brands I'm used to?"

"I am sure many of the products you bought in Pennsylvania will be available for purchase. After all, the grocery serves the *Englisch* community in addition to the *Amish*. Although the selection may be more limited."

"What about the meat?"

"The meat market has a butcher. He makes sausage and provides other selections typical to the Amish." He chuckled. "Do you like pig's feet?"

She rolled her eyes. "Tell me it's a Pennsylvania Dutch delicacy."

"Some like it. My mother served it with homemade noodles over mashed potatoes and gravy."

"Noodles and potatoes are eaten together?"

He laughed at the surprised look on her face. "A lot of carbohydrates, but so good. Sarah can teach you to make the noodles."

"She's already done so much. I need an Amish cookbook."

"Perhaps we can find this at the store, as well."

"Is there something I could give Sarah as a thank-you for keeping Kayla?"

"She does not expect a gift for being a good neighbor."

"Still…" Julia thought for a moment. "I want her to know how grateful I am."

"Before you and the children arrived, Sarah had asked me to help her at the upcoming flea market in Yoder. I planned to sell some of my neighbor's furniture for him if he does not return home before then. Sarah will have a table nearby and sell her quilts and other hand-made items."

"We could help her that day."

"First we will see what Jonathan has to say. If the Philadores have eased their search for William, we can attend the flea market. Otherwise, we will stay home and out of sight until all of this is over."

"Will that time ever come, Abraham?"

"I pray it will be over soon."

If the Philadores ended their search for William, the marshals might move the family to a less isolated area and back into the *Englisch* world.

Saying goodbye to the children would be hard. Saying goodbye to Julia would be even more difficult.

Chapter Sixteen

Julia enjoyed visiting the grocery and felt like a child in a toy store at Christmas. As Abraham had mentioned, many of the products she used in Pennsylvania were available for purchase. She placed a number of items in her cart, including canned cherries for the pie she would bake sometime soon.

The dry items, sold in bulk, intrigued her. Powdered chicken stock for soups, flour and sugar, corn starch and a myriad of spices, including pickling spices that she had never used. Just as Abraham had mentioned, they were packaged in clear cellophane bags with a store label.

"I'll need to ask Sarah about canning," she said to Abraham as she browsed the shelves.

"There is time," he assured her. "First we must plant the fields and grow the crops before harvest."

"I have a feeling I'll be busy throughout the summer."

If Jonathan would allow them to stay with Abraham that long. She would talk to him today about her preferences.

The children had noticed the small lunch area at the front of the store when they entered. Kayla kept men-tioning that ice cream was sold by the cone—and candy by the pound.

"We'll shop first," Julia said.

They passed another Amish family and Kayla, always the extrovert, waved at the little girl and smiled at the mother.

"We like this store," Kayla announced to the woman.

"You are new to Yoder?" the Amish shopper asked, eying both of them.

Julia groaned inwardly. She should have instructed Kayla not to initiate conversations, especially with adults. The Amish embraced the adage that children should be seen and not heard.

If only Abraham had been nearby to offer a response, but he and William were in the hardware section, examining nuts and bolts and screws. When had her son started appreciating anything to do with carpentry? Probably since he started hanging around their Amish host.

"We have not lived in Yoder long," Kayla responded while Julia debated whether to nod and hurry on to the next aisle or offer some type of noncommittal reply.

"My daughter never met a stranger," Julia finally said with a stilted laugh. If only the woman would continue shopping without additional comments.

"I have not seen you in town. You are living in the surrounding area?"

"In Mr. Abraham's daddy's house," Kayla explained before Julia could grab her hand and tug her to the far side of the shopping buggy.

"The *dawdy* house," Julia corrected.

"You are his sister?" the woman asked.

Julia shook her head. "Not family. I'm…"

Why was it so hard to provide the story Jonathan had told her to use? "I am the housekeeper. He lives alone and has a large farm. He needed someone to cook and clean."

The woman raised a brow. "You have known him before?"

Kayla opened her mouth as if ready to answer.

"Do you know his sister?" Julia asked the woman.

"She does not live in Yoder so I have not met her. I believe her name is Susan."

Julia smiled. "Susan knew her brother needed domestic help."

The woman nodded, satisfied with an explanation that Julia hadn't actually provided.

"Enjoy your shopping." Julia pushed the buggy and pulled Kayla along behind her. They did not stop until they had rounded the corner and were headed to a far aisle.

"Do you know Mr. Abraham's sister, Mama?"

"I didn't say I did, Kayla."

"The woman thought you knew her."

"We will let that woman think what she would like to think. Next time, I do not want you providing information to strangers. We have talked about this before."

Kayla looked at the floor, her bottom lip coming out in a half pout, half cry that stabbed Julia's heart. She hated that her overly friendly daughter had to be reined in like Abraham's horse.

"In Philadelphia, you told me not to talk to strangers," the child said. "I thought it was okay here, especially if they were Amish."

"Strangers can wear any type of clothing, Kayla. I do not want you to be unduly frightened, but you need to be able to trust someone before you engage in a conversation. Do you understand?"

"Do you trust Mr. Abraham?"

"Why do you ask?"

"Because you started talking to him and let me talk to him right from the first morning we met."

"Mr. Jonathan had told me about Mr. Abraham so I knew he was a good man."

"But did you trust him?"

Did she trust him now?

"I trust him enough to talk openly to him, Kayla, and you can, as well."

"What about Miss Sarah? You must trust her, since you let her take care of me while you and Mr. Abraham were trying to find William."

Circumstances had made it necessary to leave Kayla with a woman Julia had only just met. Did she trust Sarah? The question was difficult.

"Miss Sarah seems very kind. She's Abraham's friend, and he said she is to be trusted. Still, she does not need to know everything about us." Julia stared down at her daughter. "You didn't tell her about witness protection, did you?"

"I did not." Kayla made a cross on her chest. "Cross my heart."

"Do you know who I trust?" Julia asked. She put her arm around Kayla's shoulder. "I trust you. And I love you very much."

"I love you, Mama." Kayla thought for a moment and then added, "I love William, too. And Mr. Abraham."

"Did I hear my name?" Abraham and William turned the corner and stood in front of them.

"We were talking about loving you, Mr. Abraham."

His face brightened. He looked at Julia with expectation. "Such a nice thing to be discussing in the grocery. I am happy to know that I am loved."

"It was Kayla." Julia tried to backtrack. "She said she likes you very much."

"I believe the word she used was love," Abraham teased. He appeared to be enjoying Julia's embarrassed discomfort.

"The word love has a number of meanings," Julia informed him.

"Hmmm?" He tugged on his jaw. "I thought love was love."

"No, it's not. You can love ice cream or you can love a child." She pointed to the ice cream area near the restaurant and then at both the children.

"Or you can love a woman," Abraham added, "because she brings joy to your life and makes you a better man."

Julia's heart thumped. Her cheeks burned. Abraham stared into her eyes and wouldn't avert his glance. Everything around them faded, and all she could focus on was the intriguing half smile that curved his lips, the lips she had wanted to kiss last night.

"Did you say ice cream, Mr. Abraham?" Kayla tugged on his hand.

The spell was broken. He glanced at the child. "What is your favorite flavor?"

"Guess," she said.

"Chocolate."

Kayla giggled. "Mama told you, right?"

"Your mother and I have never discussed ice cream, but I know what little girls like."

"Do you know William's favorite flavor?"

Abraham thought for a moment and then raised a brow. "Mint chocolate chip when available, otherwise strawberry."

Kayla's mouth dropped open. "You know everything, Mr. Abraham."

"I know when it is time to check out so we can get ice cream cones for two very special children."

He turned to Julia. "Have you finished shopping?"

"I still need a cookbook."

"The next aisle over. The children and I will take the shopping cart to the checkout stand and meet you there."

"I'll stay with *Mamm*," William said. Julia had a feeling he thought she needed someone to protect her in case there was a problem.

"We won't be long," she assured Abraham.

They found the book section and she quickly decided on a cookbook.

"*Mamm*." William lowered his voice. "Abraham and I talked about ice cream before we saw you and Kayla. That's how he knew my favorite flavors."

"I thought as much. Kayla will find out soon enough, but right now she is impressed with Abraham's uncanny knowledge. Letting her believe a bit longer isn't a bad thing, William, and knowing Kayla, she will probably come to that conclusion on her own."

"She told me she wants to call him *datt*."

Julia stared at her son, perplexed. "What does she want to call him?"

"*Datt*," William repeated. "The Pennsylvania Dutch word for dad."

"She struggles to remember your father," Julia said. "She was barely five when he left."

"I remember him."

From the look on her son's face, Julia knew the memories weren't good. "Your father loved you, William, even though he did not know how to show that love."

"I would rather he loved me less and showed it more."

"Of course you do. My own father did not show his love so I had to trust my instincts. He was my father, therefore he loved me."

"I can't do that. I know he was my father, but too much happened. I can't trust him and I can't love him."

"I wish my love was enough for you, William."

"Aw, Mom, it is enough. It's just that I would also like to feel loved by my father."

"Maybe someday."

William shook his head. "It's too late." He motioned her to follow him. "Let's go to the cash register. Then maybe we can buy ice cream."

Ice cream might smooth over a little irritation, but not the deep-seated feeling of being abandoned and unloved. Julia had struggled with both throughout her life. She hated that William had the same feelings of unworthiness.

They walked together to the checkout counter. Kayla was helping Abraham take the items from the shopping basket and place them on the conveyer belt. Kayla laughed while Abraham smiled at her with a look that Julia would have loved to have seen on her own father's face. Abraham was providing what both children needed, a strong bond with a good man who seemed to care deeply about their well-being, and for that, Julia was grateful.

"We would like two double-dip ice cream cones," Abraham said to the lady scooping up ice cream. "Chocolate and mint chocolate chip."

He looked at the children. "Waffle or cake cones?"

"Waffle," they both answered in unison.

"What about you, Julia? Surely you would enjoy an ice cream cone."

She laughed. "One scoop of butter pecan, if they have it."

He glanced at the flavors. "They do, but make that a double."

"And you, sir?" the lady asked as she handed the cones to the children.

"Not today." He paid for the cones and then headed everyone outside where they loaded the groceries onto the buggy. "You children stay here and eat your ice cream. Your mother and I need to make a phone call."

"May we sit in the buggy?" William asked.

"Of course. We will be on the phone just inside the grocery if you need anything."

Abraham lifted Kayla into the buggy and placed her on the front seat. William crawled in next to her.

"I'll play like I'm driving," the boy said as he licked his cone.

"Before long you will know how to handle the buggy, William. Plus, Buttercup takes to you. Be patient now and all that you wish will come to be soon enough."

He and Julia walked back inside to place the call.

Jonathan answered on the second ring. "I was just thinking of you, Abraham, my friend."

"I hope good thoughts. We came to town to use a pay phone in case Pablo's brother has given my neighbor's number to the Philadores."

"You no longer need to worry. The gang is focused on other issues. We have had no mention of their search for William in the last twenty-four hours."

"I am not sure that means anything."

"It will when I tell you what we learned from Kansas City."

Abraham pushed the receiver closer to his ear.

"Pablo Davila," Jonathan continued, "and his friend, Mateo Gonzales, were killed in the gunfire that erupted the night you were in the city."

"Both men are dead?"

"That's it exactly. The police haven't confirmed the details, but our sources are reliable. Plus, there's an added bit of information that's come out of the shootout."

"Tell me the Philadores have all been arrested, and I will be very happy."

"If only. That's what I dream about at night."

"I thought you would dream about your pretty wife and the children you will have someday."

Jonathan chuckled. "Actually, Celeste is pregnant."

"Congrats, buddy. You will make a great dad."

"I appreciate the vote of confidence." Jonathan hesitated before adding, "Here's what we've learned about the Kansas City street fight. The word is that a young kid was killed in the shootings. Some sources say the kid is William."

"I am confused."

"And rightfully so. For whatever reason, the word from Kansas City is that Pablo and Mateo were gunned down. A young teen who was with them died, as well. The name I hear is William Bradford."

"William is outside, waiting in the buggy."

"But our informants claim he was killed. The Philadores called off the search for William because they believe he died in the crossfire. I hate that anyone had to die, but having them call off their search plays into our hands perfectly."

"So someone else's loss is good news for us?"

"We're not even sure a teen died, Abraham. Rumors can start that are completely unfounded. We'll learn more as time passes. But you can all breathe a little more easily. Tell Julia."

"She is here with me and wants to talk to you."

"Great. Before you put her on, I just wanted to say thank you, Abraham. You've done an outstanding job keeping the family safe. I told you William would be a problem."

"The issue has turned around," Abraham assured him.

"Only because of your guidance, I have a feeling. I apologize about leaving you high and dry in Kansas City, but we couldn't buck Mother Nature. Who would think we'd have a snowstorm this late in the season or that it would stop everything on the East Coast? Thankfully, you handled it."

"A guy named Grant is a regular at the Fellowship Church shelter we stayed out. He was instrumental in getting us out of a very bad situation and deserves the praise. The manager of the shelter—a woman named Muriel—does, as well, if anything can be done on your end. Either a financial contribution to the shelter or connecting Grant with agencies that can help him as he reaches out to the kids on the street. They both took a liking to William and were instrumental in keeping us safe and ensuring we left the city unharmed during a very dangerous time."

"You've got me thinking, Abraham. Either of your Good Samaritans could have started that rumor about the kid's death so no one would follow you back to Yoder."

And to ensure William remained safe. Abraham nodded, realizing Jonathan might be right.

"I'll contact some folks in Kansas City," the marshal continued, "and put in a good word for both of them. We'll see what can come of it, although your name won't be mentioned."

"I do not want to be connected in any way, Jonathan. Julia and I need to remain completely out of the picture."

"I hear you and agree completely."

Abraham lowered the phone from his ear and motioned Julia closer.

"The kids are sitting in the buggy as if they're an Amish couple leaving the market," she said.

"I will check on them while you talk to Jonathan."

A smidge of ice cream hung on the edge of her upper lip. Abraham used his thumb to lift it off. Touching her sent a jolt though his body. Their eyes connected and more was exchanged in that one glance than they had said last night at the house.

What was wrong with him? He felt like a pool of wet cement when he was around Julia, unable to get back into the form he used to be. Now all he could think about was her, and how much, even in this grocery store, he wanted to wrap her in his arms.

Abraham handed her the phone and then stepped away to keep from reaching out to her and embarrassing both of them. There was something magnetic about Julia, something that made him feel stronger and more protective when he was around her. He had never felt that way before. Perhaps it was because he knew how fleeting love could be and feared it as much as he wanted it in his life.

"Jonathan?" She raised the receiver to her ear. Her

voice sounded strained as if she, too, had felt that pull between them.

Abraham needed fresh air and space away from Julia to think straight again. She and her children were with him for a limited period of time. With the Philadores no longer looking for William, the family would probably leave the Amish area and take up a new residence after William testified at the gang leader's trail. Once they left Yoder, they would never return.

They would live their new lives free of the gangs, and Abraham would be left alone to remember all the special memories and blessings they had brought to his life. He needed to remain strong. Later he would grieve their leaving, which was bound to happen. Without the children and Julia, life would not be the same. Life would never be as good as this again.

Chapter Seventeen

"I'm not ready to leave Yoder," Julia said to Jonathan. She moved the receiver closer to her ear, grateful that Abraham was heading outside so she could have the chance to speak truthfully.

"I don't understand."

"I'm not sure how long you planned to leave us here, but I wanted you to know that the children have bonded with Abraham. He's had a positive influence on them and I hope you'll let us stay in Yoder."

"That's good to know, Julia. I thought Abraham would provide a welcome refuge for you and the children. Hold on a minute." Someone spoke to him before he came back on the line. "Sorry to cut our conversation short, but I need to get to a meeting. Have Abraham tell you what we learned about the Philadores."

Julia hung up and started for the door, but when she stepped outside her heart stopped, seeing the chaos that had had erupted.

Buttercup was running wild, galloping down the middle of the street, eyes wide and ears back, pulling the buggy with Julia's two children in it at breakneck speed. The buggy creaked and shimmied as if ready to snap apart.

Kayla's frantic screams filled the air. William sat in the front, ashen-faced, his hand stretched toward the dropped reins that dragged along the road. Abraham ran alongside, arms flailing to stop the runaway horse.

Julia dropped her half-eaten cone and ran after them. "God," she cried. "Help my children."

A car approached from the opposite direction driving much too fast. Didn't the driver see the buggy?

"No," Julia screamed. The car turned onto a side street and accelerated.

Abraham grabbed Buttercup's mane and leaped onto the horse's back. Grabbing the harness, he pulled back. "Whoa. Whoa, Buttercup. Calm down, girl. Whoa."

The horse fought his control, but slowed and eventually came to a stop.

Julia gasped with relief and ran toward the buggy.

"Mama," Kayla cried, her arms outstretched.

Julia pulled her daughter into her embrace and offered a hand to help William down. His palms were sweaty, his face white. He leaned into her embrace, visibly shaken.

"You're okay," she soothed.

Abraham slipped off Buttercup's back and patted the horse. He reached for the reins that had fallen to the ground and guided the horse and buggy to an asphalt parking lot at the side of a nearby building. He tethered the horse to the hitching rail and continued to speak calmly to the frightened mare.

Julia, still holding Kayla in her arms, approached the buggy. William followed, his head hanging.

"What happened?" Abraham asked.

The boy said nothing.

"How did Buttercup come unhitched, William?"

"I…I was pretending to drive the buggy."

"Which I told you we would work on at a later time. Were you holding the reins and did you encourage Buttercup forward?"

"I held the reins, but I didn't tell her to go. It was the car."

"What car?"

"It came up from behind us and swerved close. Someone threw something from the window at Buttercup. It hit her rump. That's when she spooked and started to run wild."

"You pulled back on the reins?"

"I tried. I had my ice cream and somehow the reins slipped out of my hold."

Kayla wiped her eyes and wiggled to get down. "William's right, Mr. Abraham. We were in the buggy, licking our ice cream cones, and then the car came so fast."

"What color was the car?"

"I think it was red," Kayla said.

William nodded. "It was a red sports car. The driver looked like the guy the sheriff stopped the first time we came to town. There was another man, standing on the sidewalk. I didn't see him until the buggy jerked forward. He had a camera in his hands."

Abraham studied the street. "Wait here. I want to find whatever was thrown."

"You're both all right," Julia told the children. She needed to be strong for them, but her heart was pounding so hard, thinking of what could have happened.

Abraham returned carrying an unopened beer can. "I did not see the man with the camera, but I found this on the side of the road, near where I had left the buggy."

"Who would throw a beer can at the horse?" Julia asked.

"Someone who wanted to make trouble."

Julia groaned, realizing who would have wanted to harm her children. "It was Pablo. He must have checked the bus schedule in Kansas City and realized where William's bus had originated."

Abraham motioned Julia away from the children so they would not hear their conversation. "Jonathan assured me that Pablo and his friend were involved in the gang shooting the night we escaped. It escalated and they were killed."

Julia gasped. "As much as I wanted Pablo stopped, I hate to think of his poor mother. Oh, Abraham, there's been too much bloodshed."

"The Philadores have stopped searching for William."

"But why? Although I'm grateful."

"Jonathan's sources claim a teen was killed in the Kansas City shooting," Abraham said, his voice low. "They got word that it was William. Evidently the Philadores thought Pablo had apprehended the boy and was taking him back to Philly."

"I don't like to hear of any child dying."

"Neither do I, Julia. The report could be bogus. Grant and the two men who helped us could have started the rumor to ensure we eluded the gang members."

"You think Grant would have done that?"

"If he thought William was in danger. No matter how the rumor started, I am relieved that the Philadores are no longer looking for your son."

"I'm relieved, too," Julia said. "But who threw the beer can?"

"The children mentioned a red sports car. It could

have been the guys we saw outside Trotter's Dry Goods. But they are not the only ones who might cause trouble."

He shook his head with frustration. "The Amish are frequently attacked by teens or people who find our way of life strange. They try to cause problems. Amish on bicycles have been run off roads and crashed while drivers of cars laugh at the damage they cause. Some of the so-called pranks can be dangerous, if not deadly. The world does not like people who are different, Julia."

"You can't generalize about the world, Abraham. Some people are intolerant. They don't have a strong moral compass and are inconsiderate of others. Those people have hate in their hearts, but that's not everyone. The world is filled with good people, I have to believe that."

She sighed, feeling sad and unsettled. "Let's go home. We have groceries to unload and dinner to cook. Perhaps on the farm we can forget what happened today. It's time to think good thoughts and to heal from the past."

"The children are upset," Abraham said, glancing at them.

"Fresh air and caring for the animals will help them see another side of life, Abraham. That will be *gut*, very, very *gut*."

He smiled and her heart skittered in her chest.

"Now you are talking like an Amish woman."

She glanced down at her long dress. "If I dress Amish, I must learn to speak Pennsylvania Dutch and embrace your culture. *Gut* is one of the few words I know, along with *danke*. Thank you, Abraham, for providing for us and for keeping us safe. You've gotten us through a hard time, but that's about to change, especially with the news Jonathan provided today. I'm relieved and rejoicing that all of the hardship is behind us." She held out her hand and took his. "Let's think of better things than hateful people, whether they are in Philadelphia or Kansas City or Yoder. Let's focus on all that is good and wholesome."

He nodded. "That sounds *gut* to me, Julia."

"*Yah*," she sighed. "That sounds *gut* to me, as well."

They climbed into the buggy and headed back to the farm. The sun peeked through the clouds and warmed them. Kayla and William were quiet but seemed to have moved past the incident at the grocery. They were ready to embrace their new life, just as Julia was.

Chapter Eighteen

For the next few days, Abraham refused to think about Julia and her family leaving Yoder. The children had eagerly accepted life on the farm. William rose early each day to help Abraham care for the livestock. Kayla gathered eggs and fed the goats and chickens. The children were flourishing. Color filled their cheeks and their eyes twinkled.

Julia's eyes twinkled, too, and each moment that they were together brought Abraham joy. He could not think about what would happen when she and the children were moved to another location. He had not called Jonathan again, although he and William checked for messages at the phone shack when they cared for his neighbor's animals.

Julia rang the bell, calling them to their noonday meal. He and the children finished the chores they were doing and washed their hands at the pump.

"*Mamm* says we can wash up inside," Kayla announced as she lathered soap in her small hands. "But I like using the pump. It reminds me of the olden days."

Abraham had to smile. "By olden days, do you mean a few years ago?"

She giggled. The sound of her laughter filled him with delight.

"No, I mean the really olden days, like the books I read written by Laura Ingalls Wilder. Do you know her, Mr. Abraham?"

"I do not know her, Kayla. I am not *that* old."

She giggled again. "In her stories, the people wash their hands in well water, too."

"Soon we will go to the library and get more books for you to read."

"William wants books on farming. He says he's going to buy land and grow corn and wheat."

The boy nodded. "And raise horses."

"You are good with the animals, William. In fact, you will make a fine farmer or anything else you chose to do with your life."

"I want to be a teacher when I grow up," Kayla announced. "Sarah's daughter said she will teach at the Amish school. Do you think I can go there next year?"

Abraham handed Kayla the towel. "Your mother will decide about next year. Right now you should study hard and learn as much as you can. Teachers must be very smart so they can teach their students. Therefore you must work hard to learn everything you can."

"Farmers have to be smart, too," William added as he reached for the towel. "Plus they get hungry. Let's go eat."

"I'll race you," Kayla said.

She took off running, but William hung back a few seconds. Abraham appreciated the boy's efforts to let his younger sister win.

Arriving at the porch first, Kayla cheered for herself before she opened the door and stepped into the kitchen.

Abraham approached William and patted his shoulder. "You are becoming a man, William. You put your sister before yourself, which is the mark of a considerate person."

The boy beamed with the praise. "*Mamm* said she is proud of me."

"As she should be." Abraham placed his hand on the boy's shoulder. "I am proud of you, too."

William stood a little straighter. He removed his hat before Abraham pushed open the door.

"It smells like your mother has something good prepared for us to eat."

"I feel like I could eat a bear." William laughed.

"Look at you, William." Julia fussed as she glanced at the door. "You are getting so tall. Each day you grow more."

"Abraham said I am growing faster than the calves."

"The baby chicks grow fast, too," Kayla added. She poured milk for herself and William and waited at the table for her brother to pull out the bench for her.

"Kayla, someday you will have to seat yourself again."

"*Mamm* says it is nice to have a man hold her chair."

Abraham glanced at Julia, who quickly turned toward the stove, but not before he saw her blush. "Your *mamm* is right, Kayla. It is nice when a woman is given the attention she deserves. Your mother works very hard for all of us. If we can find little ways to make her life brighter, we should do that."

"You are much too kind, Abraham."

"Just truthful, Julia." He held her chair as she took her seat.

Julia had fixed sloppy joe sandwiches. The meat and tomato mixture filled the kitchen with a spicy aroma that made his mouth water. Chips, pickles and potato salad waited on the table.

"We will give thanks." Abraham bowed his head.

They lowered their heads and prayed silently. Once he glanced up, Kayla caught his eye and then lowered her head again.

"Did you add an extra prayer?" he asked.

"I asked God for us to stay here with you, Mr. Abraham, forever."

He caught himself as he reached for his glass of water. "Forever is a long time."

"*Yah*." The child gave the reply as if she had been raised Amish her whole life.

"Did God answer your prayer?" Julia asked.

"He said He's working on it."

Julia glanced at Abraham, but she was not smiling. He worried she was wondering how much longer she would have to hole up in Yoder. He had been wrong in not calling Jonathan. Another trip to town might be necessary.

"The Yoder flea market is tomorrow," he announced. "The whole town will be there, along with the people who live in the surrounding area."

Julia passed him the potato salad. "You mentioned agreeing to help Sarah before we showed up on your doorstep."

"I had told her I would help." He dropped a heaping spoonful of the potato salad onto his plate. "You wanted to do something nice for her, Julia. We could help transport her items, and I could also take a few of my neighbor's things to sell."

"I've never been to a flea market." Julia took a bite from her sandwich.

"It would be fun to see the other families," Kayla added.

"William and I will ride to Sarah's house to let her know. You will drive the buggy, William."

The boy's eyes widened. He said nothing but his smile was answer enough. "Should we hurry through lunch?"

Abraham held up his hand. "We have plenty of time. Enjoy the food your mother has prepared."

"There will be a lot of people at the market?" Julia asked.

"Many. I will man a booth. All of you can help me. And we will help Sarah."

"What about our chores?" William asked.

"I like the way you are putting the farm first, William."

The boy smiled at the comment.

"We will rise early and get our work done before we leave."

"Kayla and I can make a picnic lunch," Julia suggested.

"That would be nice, but sometimes it is enjoyable not to cook. There will be food to buy, corn dogs and hamburgers, pizza and apple fritters and funnel cakes."

"I like pizza." Kayla's eyes were wide.

"I do, too," Abraham said. "It is agreed. We will eat lunch there."

Everyone was excited, and Julia seemed to be even more excited than the children.

"You have been holed up here on the farm without having an opportunity to talk to other women," he told her. "I should have thought more about your needs."

"You have thought of nothing other than our needs since we have come here, Abraham. Although I must admit a day in town will be fun. The children are looking forward to it, and so am I."

"Before it gets too late, I must have William drive the buggy to Sarah's house as I promised him."

"He will enjoy the opportunity to guide Buttercup, but are you sure he is ready?"

"Most boys around here are driving teams by age seven or eight. The girls learn early, too."

Julia held up her hand. "Let's wait on Kayla."

"As you wish." He reached for his hat on the peg by the door. "We will not be gone long."

"Tell Sarah I am looking forward to seeing her."

"This I will do."

After giving William thorough instructions on how to handle Buttercup and what to be aware of, he climbed into the buggy seat next to the boy and sat back to enjoy the ride. Julia and Kayla stepped onto the porch and waved farewell.

"We will be back soon," Abraham assured them as the buggy headed away from the farm and onto the main road.

Julia hurried Kayla inside after the buggy drove out of sight. Abraham and William were not going far, but after a couple of hours, Julia became concerned. Probably because her son was holding the reins, and she remembered all too well what had happened outside the grocery.

She checked that the doors to the house were locked and then sat with Kayla at the table to do her lessons. As the child read the directions and marked her workbook, Julia kept glancing at the clock on the wall.

The distance to Sarah's house could not be far, yet at the end of the next hour, when she went to the window to watch for the buggy's return, she saw nothing and no one on the road.

Her stomach flip-flopped as troubling thoughts floated through her mind.

"May I color?" Kayla asked.

"First, read aloud to me."

Kayla pulled a favorite book from the box of school supplies, a story in the *Little House on the Prairie* series, and turned to where she had placed her bookmark.

As her daughter read, Julia fidgeted due to the pent-up energy with which she had trouble dealing.

"Would you like a glass of lemonade?" she asked when Kayla came to the end of the chapter.

"Could we make cookies?"

"Why not?" Anything to keep her mind off the time, and her son and Abraham's failure to return.

Julia turned the baking into a teachable moment. Kayla had to measure the ingredients and then they talked about fractions and how the various parts made up the whole.

Kayla grasped the concepts quickly, although her arm tired when she mixed the dough.

"Will you help me, *Mamm*?"

"Of course. You've done such a good job with measuring everything into the bowl."

"The dough is too stiff," Kayla said as she handed the spoon to Julia.

Mixing the cookies helped Julia get out some of her own frustration.

"Pull the cookie sheet from the cabinet, Kayla."

Using spoons, they dropped round balls of dough onto two baking sheets and placed them in the oven.

"Quickly, now, we must clean up our work area."

Julia wanted everything to look nice when Abraham got home, but as twilight began to fall, she was overcome with worry. She stood at the window peering down the lane and forgot about the cookies until a burning smell alerted her to a problem.

Pulling the pans from the oven and seeing the crisp edges on many of the cookies made her spirits sink even lower. She put the cookies on a rack to cool, thankful some of them were salvageable.

"May I eat one now?" Kayla asked.

"Of course. Sit at the table. I'll pour milk."

As Kayla enjoyed her snack, Julia returned to the window and stared at the road, longing for sight of the buggy.

"Mrs. Fielding told me a watched pot never boils." Kayla brought her plate and glass to the sink and put her hand in her mother's. "I had to ask Mrs. Fielding to explain what that meant. Do you know what it means, Mama?"

Julia looked down at Kayla. "You tell me, honey."

"It means you need to stop worrying about William and Mr. Abraham. They will get home soon, but it won't seem like it's soon if you keep staring out the window."

Julia let out a deep sigh. Kayla was right. Staying busy would help to pass the time and calm her frayed nerves. "Let's get dinner ready," she suggested.

But when the table was set and the pork chops were fried and the leftover potato salad from lunch were all on the table, Julia feared even more for her son and Abraham.

Without a phone, she had no way of contacting them.

Even if she used the neighbor's phone, who would she call? Sarah didn't have a phone.

If only she knew how to catch a horse in the pasture and harness it to the other buggy. As much as she enjoyed Amish life, she didn't know the first thing about horses or buggies or how to get herself to Sarah's farm without walking.

She turned to look at Kayla, who was coloring a bright picture of spring flowers. The child could not walk that far, which meant Julia was stuck in the house and would remain here until Abraham and William returned or until someone came to tell her what had happened.

Because she was sure something had happened to them.

Tears burned her eyes. She blinked to keep them back, her heart pounding and her pulse beating much too fast. The top of her head felt like it would explode with the tension that had built up over the last few hours.

Tears wouldn't help, but still they slipped from her eyes. She stepped into the main room so Kayla wouldn't see her. Pulling a tissue from a box, she wiped her eyes and braced her spine, determined to be strong.

But when the door opened and Abraham walked into the kitchen with a smile on his face and a twinkle in his eyes, followed by William who seemed equally jovial, she could no longer hold back her emotions.

"Is everything okay?" she demanded before they had time to hang their hats on the wall pegs.

"*Yah*, why do you ask?"

She pointed to the window. "Because it is almost dark. William was driving the buggy. Anything could have happened."

"William is a *gut* driver. He did a fine job. You would be proud of his ability."

"I am proud of him, but I am not happy about being left in this house and not knowing what was happening."

"Sarah had work that needed to be done," he explained. "She does not have a husband. Some of the neighbors lend a hand, but everyone is busy with their own farms. We loaded the boxes of the items she will sell into her buggy so she will be ready tomorrow. Then she insisted we have a piece of pie."

"Did you not realize I would be worried?"

Abraham stared back at her, clueless. He hadn't realized anything. He probably hadn't thought of her. She was acting like a temperamental child—she knew it—but she couldn't change the way she felt. All the anxiety that had built up, the worry that had turned to fear and eaten at her over the long afternoon came pouring out in a flood of tears.

Confusion covered Abraham's face. William looked worried. Kayla put away her coloring and stood by her mother.

"Mama thought something bad had happened. She has been scared. You should not have been gone so long."

When Abraham failed to say anything, Julia refused to stand in front of him overcome with embarrassment and a mix of frustration and even anger at herself for thinking the worst when they hadn't thought to come home as quickly as possible. She was glad they could help Sarah. She was a beautiful woman, plus she was Amish and she baked delicious pies. Julia couldn't compete—not that they were in competition.

Abraham and Sarah would be good together. Both Amish. Both had lost their spouses. She could see a look of attraction on Abraham's face when he talked about today's visit and that made Julia even more upset with herself and with him.

"Dinner's on the table," she said, rushing past them and hurrying upstairs. She ran to her bedroom and slammed the door behind her. Then she dropped onto her bed and let the tears fall, knowing she was being foolish and childish and irrational, but she couldn't stop the tears and she couldn't stop the concern that something, someday, would happen to one of them. She had lived with fear for so long that she never seemed able to escape its insidious hold.

In the *Englisch* world, medical personnel would claim she needed counseling. In reality, she just needed to feel safe and secure, and not have to look over her shoulder or worry if her son was late coming home.

She thought things had gotten better, but they hadn't changed. She was still fearful. Danger, even if it wasn't gang related, was rampant in the world. It would never end, and she would never feel safe again.

Chapter Nineteen

Abraham had not wanted the pie, but Sarah had cut slices and set them on the table when he and William finished loading her carriage. She had seemed so eager to offer her thanks that Abraham had agreed to eat quickly. He had seen the twilight and even wondered if Julia would be worried. Why had he not said no to Sarah and come home after the work was done?

The children were silent as they ate dinner, both concerned about their mother.

"She is tired today," Abraham offered as an excuse. "And we stayed away too long. This is a good lesson for all of us to be considerate of your *mamm*."

"I told her about pots boiling," Kayla added, looking older than her years. Although Abraham did not understand her comment, he trusted it had something to do with Julia's upset.

"You children should get to bed early this evening. I will do the dishes. Tomorrow we will rise before dawn. Your mother will feel better, and we will have a wonderful day in town."

"I hope I can sleep, Mr. Abraham, because I'm so excited," Kayla admitted.

He hugged her. "Say your prayers and you will soon be asleep. I will see you in the morning."

She wrapped her arms around his neck and hugged him tight. The warmth of her sweet arms and the smell of her brought back memories of Becca, but instead of overwhelming pain and sorrow, he felt the joy of this precious child who was so forthright and giving. Kayla had captured a part of his heart. Not that she had usurped his own daughter's spot, no one could do that, but his heart was big enough to make room for both of them. That was what made love so special. It did not exclude. The space love held in a person's heart only grew larger, which allowed the capacity to love to grow greater.

Once she had hurried upstairs, Abraham turned to William. "You have worked hard today, you must be tired."

"I am ready to sleep. Thank you, Abraham, for letting me drive the buggy. That is something I never would have learned if we had stayed in Philadelphia."

"You have learned much here."

"Because you have taught me. Don't get upset with Mom. She was worried. I could tell from the look on her face. She would look at me like that when we lived in the city, if I was on the street when she wanted me home. It was the fear of losing me. After what happened in Kansas City, I understand that now."

"Your mother was worried about you today. We should not have stayed so long."

"But Miss Sarah needed help."

"I know. Next time we must think of your mother first."

"Mom likes you, Abraham."

"What?"

"I can tell. Maybe you don't see it because you didn't know her before, but you make her smile, and she's happy here. Even though she was upset today, she is usually less worried here than in the city. I even hear her singing sometimes, which she rarely did before."

"Singing is good." Abraham did not know what else to say. He felt like he was conversing with a peer instead of a boy who could see a change in his mother.

Abraham wished what the boy said was true, but he could not fool himself. Julia was concerned about her son's well-being. Abraham was secondary.

"Tomorrow you need to tell her you're sorry," William said, rising from his chair.

The boy was right. Abraham had not apologized. Shame on him.

William held out his hand. Abraham grasped it, then pulled the boy closer and patted his shoulder. "Sleep well. I will see you in the morning."

"We will not mention that we talked about Mom," William added. "It will be our secret."

William was as wise as his sister, even if he was more reticent. Both children, if they continued on the same path, would do well in life—Abraham felt sure. If only Abraham could remain in their lives long enough to see them mature.

With a heavy sigh, he cleared the table and washed the dishes. He pulled a kitchen towel from a drawer, wiped the plates and utensils dry, and returned them to the cupboard.

After folding the towel, he hung it on the rack by the

sink and was ready to leave when he heard footsteps on the stairs.

Julia appeared, her hair loose and flowing around her shoulders. Her face was splotched from her tears and her nose was red, but she looked beautiful.

Drawing in a deep breath, he crossed the kitchen to stand in front of her.

"I am sorry," he said. "I was not thinking of you and only thought of getting the work done. As you mentioned, we were both grateful for Sarah taking Kayla in, and I wanted to help today so she would be ready for her sale tomorrow."

"I'm glad you helped her."

"But I never should have had the pie. That was a mistake and one that took more time and made you even more concerned. I will not make that mistake again if you can forgive me."

"Oh, Abraham, I acted like a foolish teenager. Although, thinking of the fine man William seems to have become, that's probably doing an injustice to teens. I let my fears get the best of me. You must forgive me for that. My head knew you were probably safe, but my heart kept asking—if something happened, how would I endure? I was thinking of myself and not you, so I am the one begging to be forgiven."

He opened his arms and she stepped into his embrace. The world stood still, and all he could see was her beautiful face and her upturned lips. Everything within him wanted to pull her even closer and kiss her—not once, but over and over again. He wanted it more than anything, and as he looked more closely, he realized that was what she wanted, as well, which made his knees weak and his heart pound all the more quickly.

"Julia, would you mind if—"

"Kiss me, Abraham. It's what we've both wanted for too long."

As he lowered his lips to hers, he felt a sense of home-coming, as if everything that had caused him pain in the past was over and only the future, a future of hope and happiness, lay ahead.

"Mama?" came Kayla's voice. "I can't sleep."

Julia pulled back, surprise written on her face.

Abraham's euphoria plummeted as she stepped from his arms. The warmth he had felt dissipated until he was chilled and confused and not sure why he had kissed her.

What was happening to his peaceful life? He had come back to the Amish way to hide out from life, but Julia had opened the door he shut when Marianne and Becca died. Julia had brought light and sunshine and love and laughter back into his broken heart, but he did not deserve any of what she had given him. He had not been able to protect his wife and daughter. He could not be trusted to protect Julia and her children, even if the Philadores had given up their search.

He needed to talk to Jonathan. Perhaps he would call him tomorrow. Julia and her children needed to leave. As soon as possible.

As she hurried to comfort Kayla, Abraham let himself out through the kitchen door into the cool, crisp night. He walked to the lonely house where he would stay for the rest of his years. The only things he would hold onto were the memories of Julia and her children, and the memory of her in his arms tonight.

Julia woke with the feeling of Abraham's kiss still on her lips. Tired though she was, she had slept little and had tossed and turned for most of the night, wondering what she needed to do. As much as she wanted to stay with Abraham, she knew he didn't need to be saddled with a woman and two children, especially a woman who, although she enjoyed the Amish faith, had a long way to go before she could be accepted through baptism. He didn't need to wait for a wife to care for him when Sarah was so close and so interested in Abraham.

Julia dressed quickly and arranged her hair, grateful that pinning the dress and pulling her hair into a bun had become almost second nature in such a short time.

She hurried downstairs, threw a log on the fire in the woodstove and started the coffee.

William raced down the stairs and into the kitchen as if he were late for a job interview. "Is Abraham already in the barn?"

"I don't know. If so, ask him when he wants breakfast."

The boy grabbed his hat from the wall peg and ran outside without shutting the door. She hurried to close it and spied Abraham hauling feed to the barn. His gaze was warm, causing a tingle to scurry down her spine. For all her concern throughout the night, she couldn't help but smile.

"How long before you'll be ready for breakfast?" she called.

"About forty-five minutes, if that gives you enough time."

"It's perfect. I'm looking forward to the day."

The sun peered over the horizon, its rays as bright as Abraham's smile. "It will be good to be together."

She waved and then closed the door. Being with Abraham would be good, she knew that. Another day together, then she could decide whether to call Jonathan or not. Right now, she wanted to enjoy the moment and enjoy Abraham, no matter how long they had. She would savor this day so she could remember it forever.

Kayla hurried downstairs, wearing her Amish dress. "Can you pull my hair into a bun, *Mamm*?"

"After breakfast, honey. Take the basket and collect the eggs, then see if Abraham needs help with any of the other chores."

The child nearly tripped over her feet in her excitement as she left the house and ran toward the chicken coop. Julia smiled, thinking of the fun her children would have in town. All too soon, she heard a wail from outside and opened the door to see William carrying Kayla in his arms.

Julia's heart lurched with concern. She scurried across the porch and down the steps to join them near the water pump. "Did you fall? Are you hurt?"

"My dress." Fat tears streamed down Kayla's cheeks. She pointed to the raw egg whites mixed with thick yellow yolks and broken shells that covered her clothing. William's shirt was equally soiled from carrying his sister.

"Kayla tried to get eggs from a nest on one of the high rafters," he explained. "The ladder she was standing on gave way. She fell and the eggs in her basket broke."

"Did you hurt yourself?" Julia reached for her daughter and drew Kayla into her arms.

"I'm not hurt," the child said between tears. "But I can't go to town with a dirty dress."

"We can wash your dress," Julia soothed.

Kayla sniffed and wiped her eyes. "But not in time for the flea market."

"You can wear one of the outfits you brought from Philadelphia."

"I won't look Amish and people will wonder why an *Englisch* girl is with an Amish family."

Julia glanced at William's shirt that was stained with egg, and her own bodice that was soiled after coming in contact with Kayla's egg-soaked dress. "We'll all change into our Philadelphia clothes."

Abraham stepped from the barn, no doubt hearing the upset. "Is everything okay?"

"Nothing that can't be fixed with a quick change of clothes. We'll be wearing *Englisch* outfits today."

"Is it okay, Mr. Abraham, if I'm not wearing my Amish dress?" Kayla asked with another sniff.

"What you wear is not important, Kayla. Just so we can all be together."

Julia was grateful for Abraham's calm reassurance that eased Kayla's upset. The child changed into a light-blue dress she claimed was the same color as her Amish outfit. Her face was still puffy and splotched from crying, but she smiled eagerly when they all returned to the kitchen. Abraham and William ate a hearty breakfast, but Kayla was so excited she barely touched her food.

Julia spread butter over a biscuit, added a dollop of strawberry preserves and handed it to her daughter. "Eat this or you'll be hungry later."

"I'm too excited."

"You're excited now, but you'll be hungry later. Sarah and Ella will be here soon. You want to be finished eating and have the table clean before they arrive."

The reminder that work needed to be done before they left for town was all Kayla needed. She quickly ate the biscuit along with a few spoonfuls of egg. Then, after asking to be excused, she cleared the dishes off the table and washed the plates and silverware.

"Thanks for your help," Julia said. "Now go see if Abraham needs you while I wash the pots and pans. If we work together, we'll be ready when our neighbors arrive."

Looking up from the kitchen window, Julia saw William driving the wagon across the road to Mr. Raber's barn. He and Abraham would load the furniture for sale into the rear of it. They returned just as Sarah pulled her mare to a stop by the back porch.

Julia opened the door and called a greeting. "I'll be ready in a minute or two."

She hurried to straighten her hair and slipped a lightweight sweater over her shoulders. When she returned outside, Kayla was talking to Sarah's daughter while the girl's mother laughed at something Abraham had said.

The look that passed between them made Julia realize how perfect Sarah would be for Abraham. Yet his kiss was still fresh on Julia's lips. He probably didn't know what he wanted, an Amish wife or an *Englisch* woman who liked everything about the Amish way of life.

Such thoughts needed to be saved for another day. At the moment, they needed to get to town to claim the two tables that would showcase their wares and draw customers.

Julia hugged Sarah and Ella. "William and Kayla, wash your hands and faces, and then we'll be on our way."

They hurried inside and returned so quickly that Julia wondered if they had complied with her instructions. Wisely, she decided not to ask if they had used soap.

Abraham helped her climb onto the front seat of his

wagon and assisted Sarah and Ella into their buggy. Kayla and William sat behind Julia. With a flip of the reins, Abraham steered Buttercup toward town.

Kayla asked William questions about what they might see. As the children talked, Julia leaned closer to Abraham. "I'm sorry about my upset yesterday," she said, keeping her voice low.

"That was my fault totally, and again, I apologize, but today is a new day, *yah*?"

"It is that and a beautiful day for a drive."

"You said yesterday that you have never been to a flea market."

"Is it like a garage sale?" she teased.

He laughed. "This is far larger with many more things for sale. Produce from the gardens, although only spring vegetables are available now. You will find all types of wares both new and used. Farm equipment and hand-made items."

"Like your neighbor's furniture."

"And the many items Sarah has stitched."

"She is an accomplished seamstress."

Abraham's brow furrowed and his lips turned into an impish grin. "Sarah is a neighbor, Julia. Nothing more."

The look he flashed her took Julia's breath. She glanced at the road and scooted over a bit to distance herself from his magnetism. Why was she so taken at times with him? Yet, at other times, like yesterday, he unsettled her peace and calm.

"How long until we get there, Mr. Abraham?" Kayla questioned from the rear.

"It will not be long. Why not sing us a song as we ride?"

Kayla began singing a child's tune about going to

town and buying a toy so she could give it to a girl or boy who didn't have toys. The song's lyrics were simple, but the message was important for children to embrace as their own.

When she stopped singing, she laughed.

"What's so funny?" Julia asked, turning toward her daughter.

"We have everything we wanted, Mama. William is not in a gang, we have space to run and skip and jump, we have a nice house and food to eat, and a pretty dress for me to wear."

Her daughter's gratitude was contagious. "You're so right, Kayla. We have everything we need."

Chapter Twenty

Abraham was glad they had started for town early. By the time they approached the first intersection, the line of traffic was backed up for an entire block. Slowly they moved forward, part of a long trail of wagons and buggies interspersed with a few cars and pickups that waited to turn into the flea market.

A huge steel barn-type structure stretched across the center of the expansive property. To the side, horses were tethered to hitching poles and more horses grazed in a rear pasture.

As soon as they were able to turn in, Sarah pulled her buggy to a stop behind them. They found the man overseeing the flea market who showed them to their assigned tables. Abraham's area opened toward the stables where he had rented a stall for Buttercup.

He and William hauled the larger pieces from the wagon while Julia and Kayla moved Sarah's quilts and other handmade items into her area. After unhitching Buttercup, Abraham and William settled the mare in the barn and then returned to the table to set up the wares. Julia had already arranged the majority of the merchandise.

"It looks so inviting," she told them as she looked over the two tables.

"Only because of your eye for decorating, Julia. I have a suspicion we will sell a lot of Mr. Raber's items."

"Are you a woodworker, Abraham?"

He shrugged, unwilling to delve into his own talents. "I used to do woodworking and thought I might embrace it as a productive hobby, but after my wife and daughter passed, I gave that up."

"You should start again," she encouraged him. "Especially if it was something you enjoyed doing."

He did like working with his hands, but he had given it up more as a personal sacrifice after what had happened. If Marianne and Becca had lost their lives because of him, he no longer deserved to do anything that lifted his spirits or brought joy to his life. It was ironic that Julia had mentioned something that once brought him pleasure.

"How about a cup of coffee?" Abraham asked, needing to turn the conversation away from his past.

"That sounds perfect."

He hurried to the stall across from them and returned with coffee for Julia and Sarah along with a cup for himself. "Children, would you like hot chocolate?"

"*Yah*," the two girls squealed.

William nodded. "Yes, please."

Abraham laughed. "I should have known." Taking the children with him, he purchased a hot drink for each of them and carried Kayla's back to their table to ensure it did not spill. The children sat on folding chairs and enjoyed their hot chocolate as people started to enter the large, open area.

Sarah's quilts were a hit, and she soon had a gathering of women examining her stitches and admiring the patterns. Julia helped her and then returned to aid Abraham when Mr. Raber's furniture attracted customers.

The children stayed close and helped as best they could. Kayla met some other children who were with their parents at nearby booths, and all of them sat in a circle and ate pizza for lunch washed down with lemonade.

"Could we have a funnel cake?" Kayla pleaded with her mother after she had finished her pizza. The sugary sweet smell of funnel cakes filled the arena, and even Abraham's mouth watered.

"You had a very large slice of pizza," Julia reminded the child.

"But the funnel cake is for dessert."

"Perhaps in a bit."

At the next lull in the crowd of buyers, Abraham grabbed Kayla's hand and walked her to the booth at the opposite end of the market.

"Your mother said you could have dessert in a bit. I do believe a bit of time has passed. Would a funnel cake be good?"

"Oh, yes, Mr. Abraham. Funnel cake would be wonderful."

"You will share with William and Ella?"

"I will share with everyone."

Abraham could not refuse the adorable child who had worked her way so quickly into his heart. William had a spot there, as well. The boy was becoming someone Abraham could count on to help him with the farm. For the last three years, Abraham had worked alone. Having

William with him in the barn, mending fences, checking the cattle, made the days pass more quickly and the work more enjoyable.

Soon the fields would need to be plowed. He was eager to teach William how to guide the draft horses to make straight rows for the new crops.

"You should sit and relax for a while," he told Julia. She was pouring her heart and soul into the flea market, and her ability amazed him. She even took orders for his neighbor, convincing customers who were merely looking that a kitchen table or chairs or a cabinet would be perfect for their homes. Sales continued throughout the afternoon, and they made more money than at previous flea markets.

"You are a natural," Abraham told her.

"I just know a good thing when I see it, and your neighbor's furniture is lovely and is being sold at a reasonable price. Anyone would be foolish to let such an opportunity pass by, which is what I tell people who stop by the table."

"Mr. Raber will be pleasantly surprised that so many pieces sold."

"He has good merchandise, Abraham. Next year you need to have your own items for sale."

Sarah went to get a sandwich and left her daughter and Kayla to watch the table. A man approached with a camera around his neck. Abraham recognized him as the guy who had stopped by the phone shack to ask directions.

"How much is this quilt?" the man asked Ella.

"Three hundred dollars."

"That's too expensive. What about this other one?"

The girl checked the price tag affixed to the label.

"That one is for a king-sized bed. It sells for three hundred and fifty dollars."

"Are there any cheap quilts?"

Julia moved closer to help. "You mean smaller quilts that sell for less?" She pointed to a lovely pattern made in blue calico.

"That's what I mean. Listen, I don't want to cause trouble, but I need some photos. You don't mind if I take pictures of the quilts with that young Amish girl who's manning the table?"

Before she could say anything, he lifted the camera from around his neck and started to snap some shots of Sarah's daughter.

Julia took Kayla's hand and backed her away from the table.

Spying Kayla, the guy smiled and raised his camera. "What an adorable little girl."

"No." Abraham placed his hand over the lens, startling the man.

"What are you doing?" The guy squared his shoulders.

"No pictures. Amish do not allow photographs."

The man looked angry initially and then calmed. "I've heard that before, but the little girl's not Amish."

"She is a friend of the Amish and the same rule applies to her." Abraham leaned closer to the man. "If you have heard of our ways, why did you attempt to take pictures?"

The guy stared at Abraham, slack-jawed. "I…I'm not sure."

"You are not sure because your need for photographs is more important than our desire not to have pictures taken?"

"I didn't mean to cause a problem."

"You need to respect our ways just as we respect yours."

"Look, I'm sorry. A guy told me to get lots of pictures."

"Who is that guy?"

The man shrugged. "He's someone staying at the same hotel. He said I could sell the photos online."

"Did you take any knowingly of the Amish?"

"Just the girl with the quilts, but I'll delete those." The guy held up his camera. "You can check my photo file."

Seeing remorse in the man's eyes, Abraham glanced quickly through the more recent photos, deleted a few that included Sarah's daughter and then handed the camera back to the owner.

The man turned to Julia. "In hopes of making amends, I would like to buy one of the smaller quilts. The green one will look nice in my living room."

"You are from around here?" she asked.

"I flew in on business last week and rented a car so I could see some of this area of the country."

"You are the part-time travel writer," Abraham said, knowing the man had failed to make the connection.

The guy smiled. "I knew you looked familiar. Look, I'm sorry about the photographs, but pictures sell. You know what I mean?"

"Where's home?" Julia asked.

"Philadelphia."

The mention of Philadelphia unsettled Abraham. Even if Pablo and Mateo were dead, William could still be in danger. He should have studied the man's digital photo file more closely.

"Have a safe trip home," Julia said, her face pale and her gaze wary.

The man hurried to another stall. Abraham saw him snap a few photographs, but of the entire area instead of singling out specific people.

By late afternoon, the crowds had started to diminish and Julia and Abraham sat behind their table, sipping coffee.

Sarah was talking to ladies she knew and Ella was visiting with girls her own age.

"You should take Kayla for a walk around the area," Abraham suggested. "I will do the same with William after you return. Outside in the rear, they usually have puppies for sale."

"That's not what we need," she laughed. "Especially when we don't know how long we're staying."

Her face grew serious and Abraham turned away, wishing he had not mentioned the pups.

"Perhaps someday, when you are settled," he added, hoping to smooth over the rough edges of her comment.

"You won't mind us leaving you?"

Abraham hesitated, not sure of what she meant.

"Leaving you here at the table with William?" she hastily added.

"Not at all. In fact, he might want to go with you."

But when she asked, the boy opted to remain with Abraham.

Kayla took her mother's hand and the two slowly made their way from booth to booth, examining everything for sale.

"Have you enjoyed the day, William?" Abraham asked.

"Yah, it is different but *gut*. I heard some of the boys

around my age talking about plowing the fields and planting."

"It is almost that time."

"I wondered if you would teach me."

Abraham nodded. "We will do that together if you are still here when it is time to plant."

"I hope we're still here."

Abraham hoped so, too. He watched Julia make her way through the crowd of people. She stood out, but not because of her *Englisch* clothing. Perhaps it was the way she held herself or her laughter or the way she had found a spot in his life. He wanted her to stay in his life, along with her children.

Abraham handed William a few dollars. "The man in the booth across the way has some carrots for sale. Buy half a bushel and then take a couple to Buttercup. I know she would like to see you."

William face lit up. "*Danke*." He hurried over with the money and bought the carrots.

The barn sat adjacent to the market and the crowd was thinning. William grabbed two of the carrots and left the half bushel beside Abraham before walking toward the barn. Abraham nodded approvingly. Buttercup and the boy would enjoy being together.

Abraham needed to keep focused on today and not think about what might happen in the days ahead. Live life in the present, which was what he was trying to do.

Kayla was enamored with the puppies and begged to have one.

"Someday, perhaps, but right now we are still unsettled," Julia tried to explain.

"Look how little they are."

"You can hold them." The Amish lady selling the puppies placed two in Kayla's arms.

She cuddled the puppies and giggled as they squirmed and licked her neck. "They're so cute."

"And not housebroken," Julia pointed out.

"I could ask Abraham. He bought me funnel cake today."

Julia narrowed her gaze. *"Kayla May,* the funnel cake was a treat. A puppy would be with us for a long time. You will not ask Abraham. He has a big heart, but we do not want to infringe on his good nature."

"He likes animals."

"You're right. I'm sure he likes dogs, but these puppies will find a home with someone else."

Reluctantly, her daughter handed them back to the lady and then took Julia's hand.

"There's William." Kayla pointed to the barn as William entered. "He just went inside. He was holding carrots. He probably went to see Buttercup. May we go too, *Mamm*?"

Visiting Buttercup was a good trade-off, especially if it took Kayla's mind off the puppies. Julia had to admit they were sweet, but she had two children to care for. She wasn't ready to take on a pet.

A number of buggies had already left the flea market. Soon Abraham would want to load the wagon and head home. As much as she and the children had enjoyed the day, Julia knew it was time to leave.

"We'll see Buttercup and then return to help Abraham. He will need to pack up soon," she said to prepare Kayla, knowing it would be hard to have today come to a close.

The barn was dark when they stepped inside. Julia heard a shuffle that worried her. "William?"

He didn't answer. She hesitated, trying to adjust to the darkness.

Someone groaned. Her heart raced. "William, where are you?"

Something heavy slammed against one of the stalls. She ran, fearing for her son.

"Kayla," Julia called over her shoulder. "Get Abraham. Hurry."

The child hesitated, her eyes wide.

"Go! Now!"

Julia raced from one stall to another, looking for William.

A back door opened. Light broke through the darkness.

She stopped, unsure of what she saw. Realization hit hard. A man had his hands around her son's neck and was pulling him through the open doorway.

She raced forward and grabbed his arm.

He turned.

Pablo?

"Let go of my son."

He pushed her away.

She lunged and dug her fingernails into his cheeks.

"Agh!" Pablo's hold on William loosened.

Her son collapsed onto the straw-covered floor, coughing.

A car waited outside, the motor running. Mateo peered at them from the driver's seat.

"What are you doing?" she screamed at Pablo. "You've got a mother who loves you. You're breaking her heart."

"I need to prove that I'm a man." He grabbed Julia and started to drag her out of the barn toward the car. She kicked and bit his hand.

Mateo opened the driver's door. "Where's the kid?"

"Run, William!" she screamed. "Get away."

Dazed, the boy regained his footing and staggered toward her. "Mom?"

Pablo tightened his hold on Julia.

Removing a ballpoint pen from her pocket, she shoved it into his neck. He sputtered, released his hold on her and took a step back.

Mateo reached for William. The boy stumbled away from him.

Footsteps sounded, running toward them. Julia looked up to see Abraham.

Chapter Twenty-One

Pablo and Mateo raced to their car. They climbed in, slammed the doors and squealed away from the barn.

Abraham reached for her. "Are you hurt?"

Julia shook her head and tried to catch her breath. "Only frightened. It was Pablo and Mateo. I... I thought both of them were dead."

She dropped to the ground where William had fallen.

"I'm okay," he told them as they helped him up.

"What happened?" Abraham asked.

"I gave Buttercup the carrots and then heard a noise behind me. Before I could see who it was, Pablo jumped me. He said I needed to go back to Philly with him."

Julia looked at Abraham. "Jonathan's information about Pablo and Mateo was wrong."

"Maybe Pablo started the rumor so we would let down our guard."

One of the deputy sheriffs hurried into the barn. "Someone said there had been trouble."

"A guy was throwing his weight around." Abraham put his hand on William's shoulder. "This young man was in the way."

He provided a description of Pablo and Mateo and the car they were driving. "Both guys are members of a Philadelphia street gang. If you see them around town, haul them in for questioning. They need to be in jail and off the streets."

A crowd had started to form in the stable, which was something Abraham did not want. He gave the sheriff his address and then squeezed Julia's hand.

"I will hitch up the wagon," he told her. "We need to go home."

She wrapped her arm around William's shoulders and walked back to the market.

Abraham had not been able to protect them. If Kayla had not run to warn him, William and Julia could have been long gone before Abraham had realized they were missing.

His stomach soured at the thought.

He had to call Jonathan. Julia and her children were no longer safe in Yoder. It was a good thing they had been wearing *Englisch* clothing today, so Pablo and Mateo would not look for them within the Amish community. At least, not tonight. New arrangements needed to be made for their safety—new identities and a new place to live, far from Yoder and far from Abraham. As much as he did not want them to leave, he wanted them to be safe, and they were not safe with him.

Julia felt like an arctic blast of frigid air had frozen her heart. The temperature was dropping, but more than that, she was cold from the near capture of her son. How could she and Abraham have believed the rumors that Jonathan heard in Philadelphia? Rumors were never reliable, yet they had wanted to have all this behind them so they had bought into the lies that were circulated.

The gangs had said a third person died in the street fight, which had been a lie, too. She had been foolish, again. This time it had almost cost William his life.

Abraham stopped to call Jonathan on the way home. The marshals were working on new identities for them. Hopefully they would leave soon. Maybe Abraham could go with them to another Amish community. Hiding within the plain world would have worked, if William had not called David. At least her son had learned a valuable lesson and would never do anything as foolish or dangerous again.

Sarah and her daughter followed behind them in their buggy. Abraham and Julia made sure they were safely at her house, with the few items Sarah had not sold taken inside, before they said goodbye.

Although they tried to make light of everything, Sarah seemed keenly aware that something was afoot. "Whatever happened, Julia, it has been a joy to get to know you and your wonderful children. We will not say goodbye, for we will meet again."

Sarah knew they would be leaving, even without being told. How many other people would soon know if the sheriff started to put it all together?

Abraham's house and the *dawdy* house were dark against the night when they turned into the drive. A sliver of a moon peered through the clouds and cast the houses in long shadows that made the once-welcoming homes appear sinister and foreboding.

Julia clutched her hands to her heart. She didn't need to give fear free rein, not after the turmoil she had been in yesterday. She had learned her lesson and would take each day as it came.

The children were downcast as they climbed from the wagon. William helped Abraham unload the rest of the neighbor's items and unhitch Buttercup, while Kayla and Julia hurried to fix something light to eat before the children went to bed. Abraham stayed outside longer than expected, and when he entered the house, he nodded to her as if to offer assurance that no one had trespassed on his property.

He remained alert during dinner and excused himself a number of times to step onto the porch and stare into the night. The children played with their food, each somber and concerned.

"Are we leaving?" Kayla asked.

"We will know more tomorrow," Julia told her. "You do not need to be concerned or frightened tonight."

"But that man tried to hurt you and William."

Julia pulled Kyla close. "He didn't hurt us. We are here with you, sweet girl. Do not think of what could have been, think only of the moment and that we are all together."

"If we move, maybe we can get a puppy."

"Did you see puppies today?" Abraham asked when he came back inside. He seemed glad for something to distract them from what had happened.

"The lady let me hold two of them." Kayla rubbed her cheek. "They licked me and cuddled close. One was a wiggle worm, but the other stayed in my arms. That's the puppy I wanted."

"Perhaps someday," he said, which was what Julia had told Kayla.

William wasn't interested in talking about the puppies. He looked scared and tired.

"You need to go to bed, children. Everything will be better in the morning."

At least, Julia hoped it would.

When she checked on the children a few minutes later, William was asleep, and Kayla was drifting off. She had found Annie, the doll that she had ignored for the last few days and had her clasped in her arms as if offering security. At least her daughter had something to hold on to. Julia wished she had something, too.

She stepped back into the kitchen. Abraham had washed the dishes and was drying them and putting them away in the cupboard.

"I have a feeling most Amish men don't wash the dishes," she said.

He smiled. She saw the fatigue on his face and her heart went out to him.

"It's been a long day," she offered.

"I am sorry, Julia."

"Sorry because two men want to do us harm? I'm sorry, too, Abraham, but they have nothing to do with you. You've been our guardian through it all. You took me to Kansas City and found William. Somehow, rather ingeniously, you worked with Grant to get us safely out of the shelter and to the rendezvous with Randy. From everything Jonathan had told us, why wouldn't we think that the search for us was over?"

"I need to check Raber's phone. Jonathan said he would call me back."

"About what happened?"

"About what he thinks we need to do next."

Julia liked his mention of *we.* Whatever the future

held, she wanted it to include Abraham. He was thinking the same way she was, which warmed her heart.

"You'll let me know what Jonathan says?"

"Of course, Julia. It should not take long."

She stood at the door as he left, and then stepped onto the porch and watched as he crossed the road.

The farm was quiet and the moon peered ever so slightly through the clouds as Abraham entered the phone shack. As much as she had enjoyed the farm, Julia was resigned to moving on. As long as Abraham was with her, she could manage anything. Without him, she doubted she could take even one step forward.

She went back inside the house and made a fresh pot of coffee. Sarah had given them a pie in thanks for their help today. The children had been too tired for dessert, but she felt sure Abraham would enjoy a slice while they discussed the news Jonathan would share.

She had been foolish to think Abraham should stay with Sarah, especially when Julia needed him and her children did, as well. God had brought him into their lives for a reason. She realized that now.

The rich aroma of the brewed coffee and the cozy glow of the oil lamp brought a comfortable warmth to the kitchen where she felt so at home. If only the sheriff would apprehend Pablo and Mateo. The marshals could deal with the two gang members while Julia and Abraham went on with their lives.

Then she thought of the Philadores and what would happen if they learned Pablo was still alive. Would they search for William again? And, if so, would they find him?

"This is Jay." The message on the answering machine sounded in the small phone shack. "I'd like to buy a kitchen table in maple with six chairs. Call me to confirm the order."

Abraham deleted the coded message from Jonathan. He called the predetermined number and waited for the marshal to answer.

"I had almost given up on hearing from you tonight," Jonathan said in lieu of a greeting. "We've been in contact with the Yoder sheriff. He hasn't apprehended Pablo, which means he and his friend are on the loose. You need to be careful."

"What did you decide about Julia and the children?"

"We're preparing new identities for them. I'll be there in the morning. Tell them to pack and be ready to leave."

Abraham's gut tightened at the thought of having to say goodbye. As much as he did not want them to go, they needed to start a new life for themselves far from Yoder and the Amish community and far from him. He had been a detriment instead of an asset. Jonathan must have realized that or he would have suggested Abraham travel with the family.

"We will be waiting for you, Jonathan."

He hung up, feeling a huge weight settle on his shoulders. Telling Julia would be hard, but he had been in difficult situations before. Seeing Becca's small casket positioned in the church next to his wife's had been the hardest day of his life. He had survived. He would survive this, too.

He hurried across the road and knocked gently on Julia's door. Her face was filled with anticipation when she opened the door and motioned him inside.

"I made a fresh pot of coffee. I'll pour a cup and slice Sarah's pie. Sit at the table, Abraham. I see the fatigue in your eyes. You can eat while you tell me what Jonathan said."

"A cup of coffee sounds good, Julia, but no pie."

She poured two cups and took them to the table. He sat next to her. "Jonathan talked to the sheriff. He and his deputies are still looking for Pablo and Mateo. So far they have come up empty-handed. Perhaps the two gang members have left town and are headed back to Philadelphia."

"If only, although that seems too good to be true."

Abraham agreed, but he said nothing of the sort. Julia had been frightened today and rightfully so. He did not want to scare her even more.

"The marshals are putting together another identity for you. Jonathan will be here tomorrow morning."

"Then we only have one night to be concerned about our safety."

"Pablo did not know where to find you earlier. It is doubtful he has learned your whereabouts since then, especially with law enforcement looking for him and his buddy."

"I'll pack our bags. Did Jonathan give you any idea of the time he would arrive?"

"I am not sure he knew."

"What about closing down your houses? Who will take care of your livestock?"

Abraham raised his brow. "What are you saying, Julia?"

"I'm saying I will help you with whatever needs to be done before you leave with us."

He shook his head. "I am not going with you. My farm is here. I must stay."

"But you said *we* earlier. What *we* would do. You were going to ask Jonathan what *we* would do next."

"If I said that, I meant it in a general way. You and your children will settle in an *Englisch* community. An Amish man would not fit in."

"I thought Jonathan said we would be safer with the Amish?"

"But that has not been the case, now, has it? You have not been safe here."

"We were fine until William ran away and then Pablo came looking for him. You weren't the problem, Abraham. My son was."

Abraham did not know how to respond. Julia was not thinking rationally. She had relied on him to get her to Kansas City, but Abraham had not been able to get them out of danger. If not for Grant and his buddies, there was no telling what would have happened.

Today at the flea market, Abraham had been oblivious to the danger. He used to be a good cop, but his skills were rusty, and he was no longer a protector or guardian. He could work a farm, but little more.

Surely Julia saw him for who he truly was, and if she did not, he would ensure she did not make a mistake by thinking he needed to tag along with her and her children. Much as he wanted to be with them, it was not a wise decision. Julia would come to her senses and be grateful to be free from him and his Amish community as soon as she settled in her new location.

"It is late," he said. "You need to sleep."

He stood and started for the door. She grabbed his arm. He stopped and turned to face her, seeing the upset in her gaze.

"Don't think of me," she said, her voice breaking with

emotion. "But what about William and Kayla? How can you walk away from them?"

"Julia, it is not what I want, but you are no longer safe here. The children will adjust."

"Adjust." She tried to laugh, but it came out like a cry. "William's father abandoned him and never took time to find out what a great kid his son was. As much as I try to tell him that his dad was mixed-up and thinking only of himself, it still hurts. William opened his heart to you. Don't you see that? Kayla did, as well, only she was more vocal about her feelings."

"I did not want them to depend on me, Julia. They are great kids who will grow into wonderful adults. You have been the one guiding them. You will continue to provide the love and support they need."

"They need a man in their lives, a father figure to encourage them and teach them. You did that all so well, and in just a few days they've bonded with you."

"They will bond with someone else, perhaps someone you will love and marry."

"What?" Julia did not seem to accept what he was saying. "I made a terrible mistake falling in love the first time, Abraham. I will not make that mistake again."

Her words made him bristle. For half a heartbeat, he had thought she was interested in him, but she was adamant about never loving again. He needed to accept what she said as truth.

With a heavy sigh, he turned to the door, removed his hat from the peg and left the house. She locked the door behind him. The sound cut him to the quick as if she were locking him out of her life.

How had he gotten her signals so mixed up?

The temperature was dropping and the clouds covered the moon. He stared at the sky and lifted up a weak prayer. *Lord, give me the strength to carry on.*

Before heading home, he circled the barn, the out-buildings and the *dawdy* house to make certain no one was there, hiding in the shadows, waiting to do Julia and her children harm.

Chapter Twenty-Two

Julia couldn't cry. She was too hurt and too angry, and the tears wouldn't come. All this time, she had sensed a connection with Abraham. Hadn't they kissed, and hadn't the feelings between them seemed to heighten as the days passed? But it was all pretending on his part. She felt embarrassed and foolish to have been so wrong about him.

He enjoyed his Amish life and had probably been longing for the day when she and the children would be gone.

She pulled their suitcases from the alcove in the hallway. Tomorrow they would dress again in *Englisch* clothing. She would leave the Amish dresses and William's slacks and shirt behind. If she had time, she would wash them and hang them on the line to dry. Abraham could pass them on to a needy family or give them back to Sarah.

Perhaps Julia's suspicions had been right. Sarah was in love with Abraham. Before long, she would be back in his life. A friend, he had called her, but many romances started in friendship. With time, Abraham would see the fine qualities Sarah possessed. Plus, she was Amish.

Julia had liked everything she had seen about the Amish faith. If only Abraham had asked her if she would consider being baptized, because Julia would have told him yes. The Amish faith would have been good for her children, as well.

What would she tell William and Kayla? The wall of frustration broke apart when she thought of her children being hurt again. Tears filled her eyes and spilled down her cheeks.

Her father had been a rough guy who never showed love or appreciation. Julia had left him to marry Charlie, thinking he would be a caring and supportive partner to walk beside through life. But Charlie had thought more about himself than his children or his wife.

Reflecting on her life, she realized how God had intervened to help her so many times. The Lord had been there all along. She was the one who had closed Him out of her heart.

Forgive me, Lord. She hung her head, overcome by her own self-centeredness.

How had she been so wrong about everything and everyone? All too quickly she had dropped her guard and opened her heart to Abraham. Was she so needy that she fell for any man who crossed her path?

She packed the few things they had into the suitcases, then laid out regular clothing for them to wear the next day. When she looked at their Amish outfits, her heart broke for all they would leave behind, most especially Abraham.

She hauled the suitcases downstairs and heated water for tea. A cup of the soothing herbal mix would calm her frayed spirit so she could sleep, at least for a few hours. Tomorrow would be a difficult day.

Cup in hand, she extinguished the oil lamp and stared through the window. As she watched, the clouds rolled across the sky and the moon peered down, washing the farm in moonlight. Such a beautiful area, with its green fields and tall trees and the small creek that ran along the edge of the farm.

If it hadn't been so late, she would have taken her tea onto the porch, but with Pablo and Mateo on the loose, she needed to be cautious.

Instead, she stood at the kitchen sink and sipped her tea, thinking of everything good that had happened since she and her children had arrived at the farm. The memories brought a smile to her lips, but also a heaviness to her heart, knowing she would have to say goodbye to this idyllic spot tomorrow.

She placed the cup on the counter and was ready to return to her bedroom when a movement caught her eyes. Leaning forward, she narrowed her gaze. What had she seen?

The clouds rolled across the moon, cutting off the shimmering light. Surely her eyes were playing tricks on her.

She was starting to turn away when the clouds moved again. Her gaze zeroed in on the nearby pasture and two figures who stood in the tall grass.

Even from this distance, she recognized Pablo and Mateo.

Abraham stepped onto the porch. He quietly closed the door behind him and stared into the night. His gaze focused on the two young men approaching the house.

Slowly he moved toward the water pump near the *dawdy* house and waited until they'd rounded the barn.

"Get off my property," Abraham said, his voice raised.

Both guys stopped and stared into the darkness.

Abraham stepped from the shadows. "Get off my property now."

"Hey, man. We wanna talk to Will." Pablo shrugged as if they were doing nothing wrong. "Tell him Davey misses him."

"I will tell the sheriff you are both trespassing."

"And how will you contact the sheriff?" Mateo chuckled. "You Amish don't have phones." He pulled his cell from his pocket. "You wanna use mine?"

"I *wanna* see you turn around, Mateo, and head back to your car parked by the road."

"Oh, man, you're scaring me." Mateo jiggled his knees. "You have me quaking in my boots."

"Leave. Now."

The punk shook his head. "Not without the kid."

"You need better intel," Abraham taunted. "The Philadores called off the search."

"Man, we don't care about the Philadores. We wanna work for the Delphis. Bringing the kid back to Philly will make us important to our *new* brothers." Mateo jabbed his thumb against his chest. "We'll have status."

"Using a kid for your own gain?" Abraham turned to Pablo. "Did your mother raise you to hide behind children?"

"Leave my mother outta this."

"What about your dad, Pablo? Is he proud of you?"

"My dad left me. He didn't care about me or my brother. That's why I have to be *the man*."

"Then be *the man*," Abraham said. "Walk away before someone gets hurt."

Mateo glanced at Pablo. "You're crazy *loco* to listen to him, bro. I'll show him who's in charge." He pulled a nine millimeter from his waistband.

Julia stepped onto the porch.

Abraham raised his hand. "Get back, Julia. Go in the house. Lock the door."

She ignored the warning and moved closer. "Mateo is using you, Pablo. He wants William so he can turn him in to Fuentes. Mateo didn't leave the Philadores. He was in my apartment the night they came looking for Will. The police had Mateo in custody. Ask him how he got off."

"Shut up," Mateo growled.

"Fuentes used his money and power to spring him." Julia took another step forward. "It's true, isn't it, Mateo?"

The punk snarled. "If we can't get your kid, we'll take you back, lady."

"No." Pablo held up his hand. "She's not who we want."

"She's who I want, bro. But I want her dead." He raised his weapon.

Abraham pushed Julia behind the pump.

Mateo fired.

Abraham groaned and grabbed his side.

The door to the house opened. "Mom?"

"No, Will!" Julia screamed. "Stay inside."

Mateo raised his revolver.

Pablo grabbed his arm. "Don't hurt the kid. He's a friend of Davey's."

"As if I care, Pablo. You need to know who's boss."

As the thugs argued, Abraham put his arm around

Julia and hurried her to the porch. He grabbed William's hand and urged both of them into the house.

"We're in this together," Pablo insisted.

"No, bro." Mateo laughed. "I'm in this alone. The Philadores don't think the kid's alive, so when I bring him back, I'll be a hero."

He raised his revolver and pulled the trigger.

Pablo took the hit and gasped. He yanked a weapon from his own waistband and fired.

Mateo's eyes bulged. Blood darkened his shirt. He grabbed his gut and fired again.

Pablo groaned with the second hit. His eyes widened, his body twitched and then fell limp onto the ground.

Mateo turned his weapon on Abraham. He squeezed the trigger. The gun jammed. He threw it aside and ran.

Abraham stumbled down from the porch. He kicked the gun away from Pablo and followed Mateo, his gait unsteady.

"Get the guns, Julia," Abraham called over his shoulder. "Ring the dinner bell, Will."

He grasped his side, feeling the warm blood seep into his hand. He had to get Mateo before he escaped again. The Philadelphia gangs knew nothing about Julia and William hiding with the Amish. Abraham had to ensure they never learned of the family's whereabouts. Julia and William would not be safe until Mateo was stopped.

Mateo tripped. He struggled to get his footing.

The clang of the dinner bell echoed in the night.

Abraham's side burned like fire. His legs grew weak, but he continued on, unwilling to give up.

Mateo's car was parked in a stand of trees near the road. He opened the car door and reached for a back-up revolver on the console.

Abraham grabbed the guy's shoulder.

The punk turned, raised the weapon and fired.

The bullet hit Abraham in the gut. He stumbled back, gasping for air.

Mateo climbed into his car and gunned the engine.

Abraham could not stop him. Once again, he had failed.

The last thing he did was call Julia's name.

Julia ran to Abraham and shoved her hand down on his wound, stemming the flow of blood. He wasn't breathing, wasn't moving. William had found Pablo's cell phone and called 911. But would help arrive in time?

The sound of horses' hooves filled the night. She looked up to see buggies blocking the road. Mateo laid on the horn and swerved around the blockade. His car skidded into a giant oak. He was thrown from the car and landed face down on the ground. Two Amish men ran toward him. They turned him over and shook their heads.

His car horn continued to blare in the night. Over that sound came the shrill scream of sirens.

Two ambulances and the sheriff's car appeared in the distance. One ambulance stopped to check on Mateo. The other skirted the buggies and headed toward Julia.

The EMTs jumped from their vehicle and hurried to her aid. "We've got this, ma'am."

She fell back and stared at her hands covered with Abraham's blood.

William was suddenly next to her, burying his face in her shoulder, crying his eyes out.

"Oh, Mom, he's dead. Abraham is dead."

Chapter Twenty-Three

Kayla clutched her doll. She hadn't spoken since Julia
had awakened her and gotten her dressed. William was
ashen. He refused to eat and had only taken a sip of
water, claiming he felt sick. Julia could relate. Her head
pounded and her puffy eyes burned from the tears she
had shed. She had changed out of her blood-soaked clothing and now wore the jeans and sweater she'd had on
the night she arrived at Abraham's house. Everything
seemed so déjà vu, except in reverse.

They had left the *dawdy* house in a van. Jonathan
told her where they were going, but she hadn't listened
and didn't care. Stacy and Karl sat in the rear, whisper-
ing quietly between themselves. Julia couldn't make out
what they said. She turned to glance at them and saw
their hands entwined. On any other night, Julia would
have taken delight in their new relationship. Tonight, she
could think only of Abraham.

He hadn't died, as William had thought, but he was
holding on to life by a thread. Mateo and Pablo had both
succumbed to their wounds, and the Philadores seem
oblivious to what had happened. Still, Jonathan was con-

vinced they couldn't take chances. Not when William's
life was on the line. As much as she hadn't want to leave
Yoder, Jonathan had given her no choice.

The marshals had pieced together enough information to realize that Pablo thought Mateo was interested
in joining the Delphis when Mateo was only thinking
of a way to get noticed by Fuentes.

Pablo and Mateo had met the guy with the camera at
the Yoder hotel and questioned him about the interesting sights in the area. He talked about a teenage boy and
young girl caught on a runaway buggy. Pablo provided
a photo of William taken in Philadelphia. The man recognized the boy and provided directions to the farm.

Julia didn't have the wherewithal to fight anymore,
except she had to take care of her children. Still, her heart
broke, knowing Abraham might not survive.

*Please, Lord, save him. Guide the doctors and nurses
who care for him. Heal his wounds and let him live.*

"We're here."

She glanced at Jonathan. "I thought we were going
to our new location."

"We will be, eventually, but I thought we should make
a stop first. We'll go in through a rear entrance."

Julia should be used to secretiveness, but she wasn't.
She didn't know what to expect and she didn't want any
more surprises, yet she dutifully followed Jonathan and
guided her children through a heavy fire door and down
a long tiled corridor. Stacy and Karl followed them.

Jonathan stopped in front of an elevator. The doors
opened. He pushed the button, and once the two other
marshals entered, standing a bit too close, the elevator
rose a number of floors. When the doors opened, they
stepped into another corridor.

"The children can wait in here," Jonathan said, motioning them into a waiting room. "This officer will escort you."

Julia didn't understand, but she was too tired to argue. The children settled on a couch and closed their eyes. Stacy and Karl sat nearby.

"How long will I be gone?" she asked Jonathan.

"You can come back at any time," he assured her. "You'll just be down the hall."

She followed the police officer, not sure of where they were going or what she needed to see. He stopped at the third door on the right. She glanced back at the room where the three marshals remained with the children.

The officer pushed open the door and motioned her forward. Then he closed the door behind her.

Her heart stopped. The push and pull of machines sounded in the otherwise still hospital room. A curtain was drawn halfway to provide some semblance of privacy for the patient lying on the bed.

Julia moved silently forward and peered around the curtain, unwilling to believe what she saw.

His eyes blinked open.

"Abraham," she gasped, reaching for his hand and pulling it to her heart. "You're alive."

"Jul…ia."

Tears clouded her view. She wiped them away, unwilling to have anything keep her from seeing him for herself.

"The surgery?"

He nodded ever so slightly. "Okay… I will…be… okay."

She laughed through her tears and rubbed her hand over his forehead. "I thought we had lost you."

"I lived…for you."

His words brought joy to her heart. "And I didn't want to live without you. I knew I had to go on because of the children, but there was nothing left."

"I…I need you, Julia."

"Oh, Abraham."

"I want us to be together…you…me…the children."

"That's what I want, too."

"I…" He struggled to make his voice heard. "I love you and want…to be with you…for the rest of my life."

"Oh, Abraham."

"I…will love…you…forever, Julia."

She lowered her lips to his for one sweet kiss that she wanted to last for a lifetime.

When their lips parted, she sighed. "I love you, Abraham. Sleep now, so you can get stronger."

His eyes closed, but Julia remained at his side, holding his hand and giving thanks that the man she loved was alive.

Chapter Twenty-Four

Julia's stomach was a tumble of nerves that had her running to the window every few minutes. She smiled, thinking of Kayla's admonishment back in Yoder that a watched pot never boiled. Today Julia's proverbial pot wasn't even lukewarm, yet she couldn't sit still so she paced back and forth across the kitchen, grateful for this home and the new Amish community that had welcomed her and her children. In the six weeks since they had arrived, the children had made friends and had started to sink roots. The only thing missing was Abraham.

His surgery had been successful, but his recovery had been long and complicated, marred by a secondary infection that had extended his time in rehab.

She looked around the house to ensure everything was tidy and in its place. The schoolbooks for the children were on the shelf, the sewing she had been working on was folded and put in a chest near her treadle machine, and her Bible—the book she so dearly loved to read each morning when she rose and each evening before sleep— sat on the small table near her rocking chair.

Over the last six weeks, she had fully embraced the

Amish faith. The local bishop was pleased with her progress. Julia was, as well.

Her baptism in the not-too-distant future would be another turning point. She had experienced so many over the last two months—the Philadores' break-in, the flight to Kansas, meeting Abraham and having her life change forever. Now, a new identity in a small Amish community in Ohio.

William had testified. Fuentes had been brought to justice and would remain incarcerated for the rest of his life. The gang that had done so much harm was crumbling without his leadership and, hopefully someday, would be only a painful memory of how young men could seek affirmation and a sense of belonging in the wrong way.

Her hand touched the sideboard, the wood smooth under her fingers. She pulled open the drawer. The letter lay there. Charlie had written both children. In his tight script, he had asked their forgiveness for not being a good father and for the mistakes he had made.

Somehow the sealed envelope had ended up in Jonathan's hands. He had brought it to her on his last visit. Not knowing what it might contain, she had been hesitant at first, but with her new ability to trust the ways of the Lord, she had given it to the children. The letter had started the healing process both of them needed.

Charlie had sent a separate note to Julia, taking full responsibility for their failed marriage. "I didn't know what it meant to be a husband or father," he had written. "The prison chaplain said, in truth, we never had a valid marriage because I didn't know how to love." The note brought comfort and removed the last traces of guilt she had carried for so long.

A car sounded in the drive. Her pulse raced. She closed the drawer and pulled in a deep breath. As footsteps sounded on the porch, she threw open the door.

Her heart nearly pounded out of her chest when she beheld the man standing there. "Oh, Abraham."

Without saying a word, he opened his arms. She fell into his embrace, mindful of his still-fragile wounds.

"I have missed you, Julia."

Her heart soared.

He had lost weight in his ordeal, but he was still the strong man who had protected her and her children.

"Come inside." She motioned him forward, then glancing at the car idling in the driveway, she waved to the driver. "The *dawdy* house next door is open. Leave his bags there."

"Thanks so much," Abraham called to the driver after he had delivered the bags.

"You're staying in the house next door," Julia explained. "It's one story, so you don't have to worry about stairs."

"I can climb stairs, Julia."

"No farm work yet, Jonathan told me. William is handling most of the difficult jobs. He could use your guidance."

"And Kayla?" he asked.

"She's eager to see you. The children went to town with a neighbor. I wanted to get the house ready and have you to myself for a few minutes, knowing they wouldn't let you out of their sight once you arrived."

The car pulled out of the drive and Julia closed the door, then took Abraham's hand. "You could have gone home to Yoder, but Jonathan said you chose to come here and recuperate with us."

"I sold the farm, Julia. The youngest of Harvey Raber's three sons bought the place. From what I have learned, the oldest son has been attentive to Sarah. The matchmakers in the area are anticipating a wedding after harvest this fall."

"Sarah deserves a good man."

"You do, too, Julia."

Her heart fluttered. "I have a good man, Abraham, a man who is trustworthy and caring, hardworking and who loves the Lord. Why would I look for another?"

He touched her *kapp* and smiled. "Jonathan said you are meeting with the bishop."

She nodded. "I still struggle with the *heute deutsch* and the Pennsylvania Dutch, but he assures me that will come with time. He has not questioned my desire to be baptized."

"Once you become truly Amish, Julia, all the men in the area will come courting."

She laughed. "Oh, Abraham, if they look into my eyes they will know that I have given my heart to another."

"Should I be jealous?" His mouth curved into a playful smile.

"Maybe a little," she teased.

"I love you, Julia."

He lowered his lips to hers and time stood still as they melded together. Never had she felt such a sense of completion.

He pulled back ever so slightly.

The seriousness of his gaze threw her off balance.

"Is something wrong?" she asked.

"Not wrong, just unfinished."

She raised her brow.

"I want more than the *dawdy* house, Julia. I want to

be with you and the children in our own house. I want to wake each morning knowing you will be there and that together we will face the day and whatever it brings. I want to be your husband and care for you and protect you as best I can, and to love you and cherish you for the rest of my life."

"Oh, Abraham. I want that, as well."

"You will marry me, Julia?" he asked.

"Yes! It's what I've wanted for so long."

"And the children?"

"They already think of you as their father, their *datt*. Kayla gave her doll to a little girl who had recently lost her father. Kayla said she didn't need Annie anymore."

Abraham was visibly touched by the child's thoughtfulness. "I told you about the boy who was kidnapped years ago?"

Julia nodded. "He was the reason you became a police officer."

"Which is what I always thought. But in the hospital, I realized the little boy I wanted to save was really me, although I never knew what I needed to make my life whole. Not until you and the children came into my world."

"Oh, Abraham, I love you."

They kissed and then kissed again and again until a buggy turned into the drive and the sound of children's laughter filled the air. Julia opened the door. Abraham bent down and Kayla ran into his arms.

"Careful, Kayla, of his side," Julia cautioned.

"Mr. Abraham, *Mamm* said you would be here when we came back from town. I did not think the buggy would go fast enough." She wrapped her arms around his neck and kissed his cheek, her face aglow.

"You have gotten so big, Kayla," he said.

"And I help *Mamm*. Now I can bake cookies almost by myself, and I'm studying hard so I can be a teacher."

He kissed her cheek, then stood and looked toward the door where William waited, as if not sure what to say.

"When did you grow up, William?" Abraham asked, the pride evident in his tone.

"I still have a lot to learn."

"*Yah*, and I have a lot to teach you. Come here. Let me wrap my arms around you, son."

The invitation was all William needed. His smile was almost wider than his face as he stepped into Abraham's embrace.

Kayla pushed between them and Julia stepped closer, her heart bursting with joy as she stretched her arms around the family she loved.

Later, when the children were doing their afternoon chores and dinner simmered on the stove, Julia sat with Abraham, their hands entwined.

"Have you talked to Jonathan recently about the Philadores?" she asked.

"Without Fuentes, they seem to have lost their edge."

"Does that mean William is truly safe?"

"For now, especially living here. Are you sure you do not want to go back to your old way of life, Julia?"

She shook her head. "I have found everything I have ever wanted, Abraham, living Amish. There was only one thing I was missing."

He raised a brow.

"You."

She snuggled closer and turned her lips to his. They would face the future together. Abraham would always be her protector, her husband and her friend.

Someday they would have children of their own. Kayla would be big sister. William would help Abraham with the livestock and the farm and learn to take on more responsibilities as he grew.

Jonathan had mentioned helping other families who would need new identities to escape crime. Julia trusted God would reveal who needed their assistance and support in the future. Right now, she was only interested in the present moment with Abraham by her side. What else could she want? She had everything and more, her children, her faith and a wonderful man who filled her heart with love.

* * * * *

MINDING THE AMISH BABY

Carrie Lighte

For everyone who loves and nurtures the children
of others as if they were their own,
and with special thanks to my brother.

If we confess our sins, he is faithful
and just to forgive us our sins,
and to cleanse us from all unrighteousness.
—*1 John* 1:9

Chapter One

"Soup from a can?" Tessa Fisher's mother, Waneta, asked incredulously. "None for me, *denki*. I'll just have bread and cheese."

If her mother turned her nose up at canned soup, Tessa figured she wasn't going to have an appetite for store-bought bread, either. She racked her brain for something else to offer her parents, who had arrived unexpectedly for Sunday dinner.

It was an off Sunday, meaning Amish families held worship services in their homes instead of gathering as a community for church. Tessa should have anticipated guests, since Sunday visiting was a cherished Amish tradition. But the truth was, as a woman living alone, Tessa was more likely to be the one dropping in on others than the one receiving visitors in the little *daadi haus* she rented from Turner King. Still, she hadn't imagined her parents would travel all the way from Shady Valley, which was two towns over, to Willow Creek, Pennsylvania. Since Tessa returned from worshipping at her sister's house only a few minutes before they arrived, she was caught unprepared.

"I'm sorry, *Mamm*," Tessa apologized as she set a bagged loaf on the table. "If I had known you were coming, I would have made something ahead of time, like a dessert."

"From a mix?" her mother half jested, untwisting the tie from the plastic bag.

When Tessa put her mind to it, she could bake and cook as well as any Amish woman, but those weren't her favorite responsibilities and she didn't see much point in laboring over large meals when she had only herself to feed. She'd much rather spend her time socializing or working extra shifts at Schrock's Shop, the store in town where she was employed as a clerk selling Amish-made goods primarily to *Englisch* tourists. Besides, it was the Sabbath. No one prepared a big dinner on the day of rest.

"Probably," Tessa admitted. "It's quicker that way."

"Since when is quicker better?" Waneta frowned. "It sounds as if the *Englisch* customers at Schrock's Shop are influencing our *dochder*, Henry. I think it's time she moved back home."

Tessa's father grunted noncommittally as he served himself several thick slices of bologna. At least the bologna was homemade, although not in Tessa's home; she purchased it the day before at Schlabach's meat market.

Tessa stifled a sigh. A little more than two years ago she and her sister, Katie, who were the youngest children and the only girls in their family, moved from Shady Valley so Katie could serve as a replacement for Willow Creek's schoolteacher, who resigned to start a family. Although Katie was twenty-three at the time, Henry and Waneta were reluctant to allow her to live alone, something Amish women in their area seldom did. So, they sent Tessa, who was nearing twenty-one, to live with her. Early last November, Katie married Mason Yoder, a farmer, and moved into a small house Mason built on the Yoder family's property. Ever since then Tessa's mother had been pressuring Tessa to return home, which Tessa was reluctant to do. Although she loved her parents deeply, Tessa sometimes felt stifled by their overly protective attitude, and she cherished her friends and job in Willow Creek too much to leave. Yet, she also knew the Lord ultimately required her to honor her parents, no matter how old she was or how much she disagreed with their opinion.

"The customers aren't influencing me, *Mamm*," Tessa protested. "Besides, I couldn't leave Joseph Schrock shorthanded at the shop, especially since I didn't have any experience when I first applied for a job there. You remember? He hired me with the agreement that if he took the time and effort to train me, I'd remain a loyal employee for as long as he needed me. I can't walk away now—you and *Daed* always taught us to abide by our commitments."

Tessa knew her mother wouldn't argue with her own instructive advice. As Henry silently chewed his bologna, Waneta slathered a slice of bread with butter and then held it up in front of her.

"The way to a man's heart is through his stomach," she said. "You'll never catch a husband with food like this."

To Tessa, it sounded as if her mother were discussing laying a trap for a wild animal. If she had known serving store-bought bread was going to result in a discussion about her likelihood of matrimony, she gladly would have baked a dozen fresh loaves to avoid the topic. Most of the area's Amish youth were discreet about if and who they were courting, and their parents seldom interfered in their children's romantic pursuits. But, at nearly twenty-three years old, Tessa knew her mother feared she'd never wed, and Waneta's strongly worded hints were gaining in frequency.

"I'm in no hurry to get married," Tessa replied. She'd had her share of suitors over the years, but in the end they didn't seem compatible enough for her to imagine devoting herself as a wife to any of them. Nor could she imagine taking on the duty of raising a family. Not yet, anyway. Not when she'd just begun to experience the rare opportunity of being a single Amish woman living entirely on her own, without the responsibility of cooking, cleaning or taking care of anyone else in her household. She added, "There aren't many eligible bachelors in Willow Creek, anyway."

"Which is exactly why you ought to *kumme* home. I've been talking to Bertha Umble and her *suh* Melvin isn't walking out with anyone."

Melvin Umble? It was hardly a wonder. The last time Tessa saw him when she was visiting home, Melvin seemed far more interested in sprucing up his courting buggy than he was in an actual courtship, and he'd spoken endlessly on the topic. Tessa let her mother's comment hang in the air.

"Would you like a cookie, *Daed*?" she asked. "They're packaged, but they're tasty."

"How can I refuse? Apparently, it's the way to my heart," her father replied with a grin, and Waneta playfully swatted at him with the back of her hand.

"Henry!" she exclaimed. "I'm only trying to help our *dochder*."

Deep down Tessa knew it was true that her mother

was trying to help. But that was just it: Tessa didn't need help because she was perfectly content in her present circumstances. More than content, she was *happy*. As far as she was concerned, she could live as a single woman indefinitely.

"Please think about what I said," Waneta advised later as the three of them bundled into their woolen coats. They planned to spend the rest of the afternoon at Katie and Mason's house. No doubt Tessa's sister would serve a full supper in the evening. Although cooking a large meal wasn't permitted on the Sabbath, Katie's Saturday leftovers were bound to be savory and numerous.

"I *always* think about what you've said, *Mamm*," Tessa replied, hoping to reassure her mother that she needn't worry about her daughter living alone. "Nothing you and *Daed* taught me is ever far from my mind."

"Nor are you ever far from our hearts and prayers," Henry said.

"That's very true, but I still wish she weren't far from our *home*, either." Waneta couldn't seem to resist dropping one more hint as they stepped outside onto the small porch, but Tessa sensed it was far from her final one.

"Hallich Nei Yaahr," Turner King greeted Tessa and her parents as he approached the *daadi haus* on the front corner of his property.

Although January was soon over, because they hadn't seen him since the New Year began they wished him a happy new year, too. He extended a few colorful envelopes to Tessa. Since they technically lived at the same address, they shared a mailbox at the end of the lane. Usually, they gathered their own mail separately, leaving each other's items behind, but these messages appeared to be belated Christmas cards and there was wet weather on the way. Turner didn't want them to get ruined, so he delivered them on his walk back from the mailbox. "These were piling up," he said.

Tessa's mother clucked as her daughter accepted the mail. "She'd forget her own head sometimes," Waneta commented. "What if one of those had been an urgent message from home, Tessa? It's a *gut* thing we have Turner nearby to look after you."

Turner noticed Tessa's olive complexion breaking out in a rosy hue. As she stood next to her father, it was plain to see she'd inherited her prominent cheekbones and long, elegant nose from his side of the family. Turner bristled when his sister-in-law Rhoda once made the superficial remark that she wasn't sure if she thought Tessa was the most striking woman in Willow Creek or just plain homely.

But observing Tessa and her father now, Turner understood what Rhoda meant: one couldn't help but notice their unusual features, which differed drastically from those of most of the Amish *leit* in their district. For his part, Turner found their uniqueness becoming, and it was enhanced when father and daughter stood side by side. For a moment, he was distracted by how winsome she appeared. *I shouldn't be entertaining such a thought— Tessa's closer to my little sister's age than to mine.*

"*Denki* for bringing these to me," Tessa said sheepishly.

"It's not a problem. I forgot to collect my own mail until today, too."

"All the same, you will keep an eye on her, won't you?" Waneta persisted, as if talking about a *kind*. "Especially now that she's living alone, without Katie. We don't want her getting into any kind of trouble."

Tessa's dark, deep-set eyes flashed with apparent anger before she averted her gaze. Clearly, she was as uncomfortable with this conversation as Turner was. One of the reasons he didn't mind having renters was the Fisher girls mostly kept to themselves—at least, they did after he declined several of their invitations to supper when they first moved in. He valued his privacy and didn't relish the idea of increasing his interactions with Tessa beyond the brief greetings they exchanged whenever their paths crossed.

"Tessa knows where to find me if she needs assistance," he responded vaguely. Then he excused himself and hurried along the narrow lane leading up the hill to the larger house where he lived by himself.

As he walked, he marveled over the irony of Tessa's mother asking him to keep an eye out for her daughter. If only Waneta knew Turner hadn't been able to keep his own sister, Jacqueline, away from a world of trouble, she wouldn't entrust Tessa to his watch.

Not that Tessa needed monitoring anyway. During the two years Tessa and Katie lived in his family's *daadi haus*, the sisters always paid their rent on time and they kept the house and yard tidy. Admittedly, they often had visitors, including church members, their parents and female friends for sister days. Turner noticed Mason Yoder used to frequent the *daadi haus*, too, but like any suitor who called on the Fisher girls, he only stayed long enough to pick Katie up and drop her off. Aside from when they hosted a few raucous volleyball games in their yard with other single youth from church, the sisters were courteous, sensible tenants.

Granted, Turner had conversed more often with Katie than with Tessa. The younger sister's effervescent personality frequently made him feel bumbling and dull by contrast. Rather than grow tongue-tied in Tessa's presence, he preferred to interact with Katie regarding any issues that had arisen with the *daadi haus*. Now he wondered if Waneta's comments indicated Tessa was a little too high-spirited for her own good. Maybe there was a reason unbeknownst to him behind the mother's request. He understood how family members sometimes protected each other's reputations; that's exactly what he was doing for Jacqueline.

"It was difficult enough raising my own siblings. I don't need to look after a fully grown tenant," Turner grumbled aloud as he entered his empty house.

He tossed a couple of logs into the wood stove and then washed his hands before preparing a plate of scrambled eggs for supper. He thanked the Lord for his food, adding, *Please keep Jacqueline safe from harm and bring her home soon.*

Before opening his eyes, Turner rubbed his thumb and forefinger back and forth across his brows. It seemed he'd had the same unrelenting tension headache for fourteen years. It started the day his parents were killed by an automobile when he was eighteen and he was left to raise Mark, Patrick and Jacqueline, who was a toddler at the time. If his aunt Louisa, then a young widow, hadn't been living in the *daadi haus* that once belonged to his grandparents, Turner never would have made it through those early years. She helped manage the children, especially Jacqueline, and he supported the family financially by taking over his father's buggy shop. But the year Jacqueline turned ten Louisa married a mason from out of state and moved to Ohio.

With the grace of God, Turner managed to raise his brothers according to their Amish faith and traditions. But bringing up a girl—especially one who was entering her teens—was a challenge exceeding Turner's best efforts. It wasn't that Jacqueline was necessarily unruly; it was more that Turner suddenly was at a loss for how to communicate effectively with her. Having completed her schooling at fourteen, she was no longer considered a child, but neither was she an adult. To Turner it seemed she wanted all the privileges of adulthood without any of the responsibilities, and the brother and sister frequently locked horns. When Jacqueline turned fifteen, she moved to Louisa's house in Ohio. By sixteen, her *rumspringa* began, and she suddenly left Louisa's to live among the *Englisch*. Much to Turner's consternation, it had been nearly eight or nine months since she'd contacted their family.

Raising his head, Turner released a heavy sigh. Try as he did to cast his burdens upon the Lord, lately he felt more overwhelmed than usual. He supposed this was because after his youngest brother, Patrick, married Rhoda and moved out of the house in November, Turner didn't have anyone to distract him from his thoughts on the weekends, when he tended to worry more about Jacqueline's welfare and sometimes took trips to search for her. It was on Saturday and Sunday evenings when he most wished for the loving support and companionship of a wife, but marriage wasn't an option that seemed probable for him.

As a younger man, Turner's time and energy were wholly consumed by raising and providing for his siblings. He'd expected he'd have more flexibility once they entered their teens, but in many ways Jacqueline's disappearance limited him more now than caring for her as a child had done. How could he court anyone when his weekends were spent searching for his sister? Furthermore, he couldn't imagine sharing the secret of Jacqueline's circumstances with anyone outside the family. Although Jacqueline hadn't been baptized yet so she wasn't in the *bann*—or shunned—it was still considered disgraceful for her to have run away to the *Englisch* world.

As for marrying in the future, Turner felt he couldn't risk starting a family of his own, for fear his wife would bear daughters. What if he failed to raise them to stay true to their Amish faith and traditions as miserably as he'd apparently failed to raise his sister? He couldn't bear that kind of heartache again, nor could he allow his wife to suffer through it, either. No, despite his desire to marry, Turner figured the Lord must have willed for him to remain a lifelong bachelor.

Exhaling slowly, he reminded himself the next day was Monday and he'd be back in his shop with his brothers working at his side. Repairing and modifying buggies, crafting wheels and organizing inventory filled Turner with satisfaction. Unlike in the situation with his sister, there was almost no problem he couldn't figure out and fix in his workshop.

He lifted a forkful of eggs to his mouth, but they'd already gone cold. What he wouldn't do for a home-cooked meal—the kind his aunt used to make or his mother before that. He'd received many Sunday supper invitations, but for the past year he'd turned them down, anxious his hosts might question him about his sister. The last anyone in Willow Creek knew, Jacqueline was at Louisa's in Ohio, and he preferred to allow them to think that was still the case. After living among the *Englisch* for over a year, she'd have enough explaining to do and attitudes to overcome when—or *if*—she returned to their community. She didn't need rumors to begin before she'd even arrived.

Unfortunately, his isolation also meant Turner rarely enjoyed a hearty meal, unless one of his sisters-in-law made it for him. They didn't know about Jacqueline's disappearance, either, despite their expressed curiosity about her whereabouts. The three brothers rarely discussed Jacqueline's absence, even with each other, but Turner knew Mark and Patrick felt as concerned about their little sister as he did and they were equally committed to guarding her against gossip, even if their wives' questions—especially Rhoda's—were well intentioned.

As he prepared for bed that night, Turner again reflected on his brief encounter with Tessa's parents. If he'd been as protective as they were, might Jacqueline still be part of their family and community? Or had he been *too* strict? Was that what caused her to leave? There hadn't been any significant conflict between them when she'd gone to live with Louisa. In fact, all three of them had agreed it would be beneficial to have a female influence guiding Jacqueline as she entered womanhood. Turner certainly didn't blame Louisa for his sister's running away, but in retrospect, he regretted allowing Jacqueline to leave Willow Creek in the first place. What if by letting her go he'd given his sister the idea she wasn't dearly wanted, an integral member of their family? Turner shuddered. Once again, he asked the Lord to keep her safe and warm, to guard her against sinful temptation and to bring her home soon.

The pain that had been plaguing Turner all day moved from his forehead down the side of his jaw and into his neck. As his head sunk into the pillow, he decided no amount of distress was worth such physical discomfort. He had to stop worrying, keep praying and start working harder at finding his sister. Meanwhile, he wasn't going to be his tenant's keeper, no matter how insistent her mother was.

When the new day dawned, Tessa practically leaped out of bed. She loved Monday mornings, when she returned to her job at Schrock's. Initially, because her parents sheltered her so closely, she had little experience interacting with the *Englisch*, and she barely spoke a word to the tourists. But after two years as a clerk, she'd grown accustomed to the *Englischers'* ways and she readily struck up conversations as she assisted them with their purchases. Although she missed her close friend, Anna Chupp, who quit clerking when she got married, Tessa enjoyed engaging with the Schrock family and other Amish *leit* who consigned their goods in the shop.

"Guder mariye," she greeted Joseph when she entered through the back door.

"Guder mariye, Tessa," he said, pushing his glasses up the bridge of his nose. "Before you go into the gallery, I'd like to have a word with you."

"Of course. What can I do to help?"

Joseph smiled wanly. "Your willingness to be of assistance makes it very difficult for me to tell you this, Tessa. But you know our holiday sales weren't what I hoped they'd be this year. Now that *Grischtdaag* has passed and *Englisch* schools are back in session, there will be fewer tourists passing through Willow Creek until the weather warms. I'm afraid I temporarily have to reduce your hours."

Tessa's stomach dropped. "By how much?"

"I can only schedule you to clerk on Saturdays," Joseph confessed, shaking his head. "If I had my druthers, I'd keep you on full time and release one of the other employees, but of course I can't do that."

No, because that would mean releasing Melinda Schrock, the clerk who recently wed Joseph's nephew, Jesse. Tessa understood family came first.

"I see," she said plaintively.

"It's only for a season. When spring rolls around, I'll have you back to full time again."

There was only one problem with Joseph's plan: without a steady income, Tessa wouldn't be able to pay her rent. She'd have to move back home before spring ever "rolled around." And once she did that, there'd be no escaping her mother's matchmaking attempts—not unless she got married, anyway.

Some escape that would be, she thought later as she fidgeted in bed long past midnight, mentally calculating her savings and racking her brain for another temporary employment opportunity, some job she could give up at a moment's notice in order to return to the shop. In the end, the only solution she could devise was asking Turner if she could postpone making her rent payments until her work schedule picked up again—something she was hesitant to do. Turner had already been more than generous in allowing her and her sister to live there, renting the *daadi haus* at a fraction of what he could have required. He even reduced Tessa's rent when Katie moved out. Although she'd be asking for only an extension, not a reduction, of her payments, she didn't want to take advantage of his benevolence. Nor did she want him to think she was irresponsible; her mother's recent comments to him on that subject had been humiliating enough.

More than that, Tessa was reluctant to speak with Turner because she harbored a sense of self-consciousness in his presence. When she and Katie moved in, Tessa had developed a full-fledged crush on Turner, who was sinewy and tall and whose tempestuous blue eyes and reticent nature gave him an air of mystery. That he'd been so well respected in the community and so charitable about their rent made her like him all the more. As a result, she tended to become highly animated whenever she spoke to him, sometimes making frivolous remarks because she was nervous in his presence. But he never accepted the sisters' invitations to share Sunday supper with them and their friends at the *daadi haus*, and Tessa suspected he was put off by her obvious interest in him. Eventually, she conceded Turner was too unsociable for her liking anyway and she gave up trying to get to know him better.

Indeed, over time she observed how often he wore a scowl across his face. While Turner wasn't quite ten years older than Tessa, she thought his countenance aged him. It apparently kept people at a distance, too, including his own sister. It was rumored Jacqueline had gone to live with her aunt the year Katie and Tessa moved into the *daadi haus*, and the girl hadn't paid her brother a visit since then. Tessa wasn't altogether surprised. Although Mark and Patrick King were generally congenial, she couldn't recall the last time she'd seen Turner smile. She imagined his somber demeanor would have felt oppressive to his teenage sister, especially since Jacqueline was said to be naturally humorous and outgoing.

In any case, unless the Lord directed her toward another solution, Tessa resigned herself to asking Turner for an extension on her rental payments. Scooting out of bed, she put a prayer *kapp* on over her loosely gathered hair and prayed a simple prayer: *Lord, I don't know what else to do and I really want to stay in Willow Creek. Please reveal Your will for me in this situation. Amen.*

While still on her knees she heard the sound of tires crunching up the snowy lane. Curious, she rose, wrapping a shawl around her shoulders as she made her way toward the kitchen, where she turned on the gas lamp. Meanwhile, a succession of honks came from outside. Tessa couldn't imagine who would be so rude, but when she opened the door, she spotted a car reversing its direction and heading back toward the main road. She figured it must have been desperate *Englischers* who were lost and needed help finding their way. But if that was the case, why had the driver honked as if deliberately trying to wake the household, and then left as soon as Tessa appeared, without waiting to receive directions first?

As she was about to close the door, something at her feet caught her eye. She peered through the near dark. It was a basket of laundry, of all things! Tessa was aware Turner paid an Amish widow, Barbara Verkler, to do his laundry for him, but she was perplexed by the absurd manner and timing of its delivery. She lifted the cumbersome basket, brought it indoors and was about to put out the lamp when something inside the basket moved beneath the light cloth draped across the top. A mouse? She didn't need another one of those getting indoors. Tessa wrinkled her nose and gingerly lifted the fabric.

There, bedded snugly on a pillow of clothing and diapers, was a chubby, pink-cheeked, toothless and smiling
baby that appeared to be about three months old. The
infant kicked her feet and waved her arms, as if to say
"Surprise!" But Tessa was beyond surprised; she was so
stunned she staggered backward. Was this a joke? The
baby flailed her limbs harder now and her smile faded
as she began to fuss. Tessa realized the child wanted to
be held, and as she lifted the baby from the basket, an
envelope slid from the blanket onto the floor.

Sensing it would provide information about whatever
prank someone was playing on her—she didn't think it
was a bit funny—Tessa bounced the baby in one arm and
opened the envelope with her other hand. The note said:

Dear Turner,
I'm sorry to leave Mercy with you in this manner,
but I know I can count on you to take good care of
her for a few weeks until I've had time to decide
what to do next. Please, I'm begging you, don't
tell anyone about this—not even Mark or Patrick,
if you can help it.
Your Lynne

Tessa couldn't believe what she was reading. This
baby was intended for Turner's doorstep, not hers; the
driver must have seen the address on the mailbox and
assumed Turner lived in the *daadi haus*. So, who was
Lynne? Tessa always assumed there was more to her serious, enigmatic landlord than what met the surface, but
she never imagined he was guarding a secret like this.
Before she had an instant to contemplate what to do next,

someone pounded on the door. Had the driver realized his mistake and returned for the child?

"Tessa!" Turner shouted urgently, as concerned for her safety as he was annoyed about the disruption to his sleep. "It's me, Turner. Are you all right?"

When the door opened, Tessa was pressing a finger to her lips. "Shh. You'll upset the *bobbel*," she chastised, gesturing with her chin toward the baby she cradled in her other arm, its face obscured by Tessa's posture.

Taken aback, Turner lowered his voice and uttered, "A *bobbel*? What—"

"*Kumme* inside," Tessa directed. "There's something you need to read."

In the kitchen Turner took the note Tessa thrust at him. He scanned the message and upon noting its signature, a surge of wooziness passed from his chest to his stomach and down to his knees. Lynne—the girlhood nickname he'd given Jacqueline. Feeling as if he was about to pass out, he plunked down in a chair and covered his face with his hands. His first thought was, *I've heard from Jacqueline. Denki, Lord!* But it was immediately followed by a rush of anguish over the circumstances surrounding her communication. His mind was roiling with so many questions, concerns and fears, he felt as if the room was awhirl.

When the dizziness diminished, he opened his eyes. Noticing a torn envelope lay on the table in front of him, he bolted upright again. "Why did you open my note?" he asked.

"If I had known it was meant for you, I wouldn't have!" Tessa huffed, swaying from side to side as she spoke. Turner could now see the baby clearly; her eyelids were drooping and her long, wispy lashes feathered her bulbous cheeks. "But when someone leaves a *bobbel* on my doorstep in the middle of the night, I'll search for any clue I can find."

"Who? Who left the *bobbel* with you?" Turner figured it wasn't Jacqueline—she wouldn't have made the mistake of leaving the baby at the *daadi haus* instead of up the hill.

"I assume by the car the person or persons were *Englisch*, but I didn't see the driver or if there were any passengers," Tessa responded. "Don't you know who Lynne is?"

"Of course I do," he affirmed, without answering what he assumed Tessa really wanted him to tell her: Who *was* Lynne? "I just wasn't sure who dropped the *bobbel* off."

"'Dropped the *bobbel* off' is putting it mildly. This *kind* was *abandoned*," Tessa emphasized. "What kind of person does something like that in the dead of winter? If you want, I can stay here with Mercy while you go to the phone shanty."

"The phone shanty?" Turner repeated numbly. "Why would I go there?"

"I assume you'll want to call someone…like Lynne? Or the *Englisch* authorities?"

"Neh!" Turner responded so forcefully the baby jerked in her state of near sleep. *"Neh,"* he repeated in a whisper.

"Why not?" Tessa pressed.

Turner stalled, studying the baby. Even in the dim light and with her eyes closed, she was clearly his sister's child. With her dark tuft of hair, roly-poly build and snub nose, she looked exactly like Jacqueline did as a baby. "You know we respect the law, but we don't involve the *Englisch* authorities in private matters like these," he said, referring to the general Amish practice of managing their own domestic affairs whenever possible. "Mercy was left in my care because her *mamm* had an emergency. If you hand her to me, I'll take her home now."

Tessa hesitated before placing the baby into Turner's arms. "Okay, but it will be easier for you to carry her in the basket. Let me fix this one so it's more comfortable and secure."

She left the room and when she returned, Tessa emptied the basket before placing a firm cushion on the bottom. Then she showed Turner how to swaddle the baby with a light blanket. She covered the lower half of Mercy's body with a quilt, emphasizing to Turner that it was only for the short walk to his house. "You probably already know this," she said, "but *bobblin* this age mustn't have any loose blankets in their cradles because blankets can cause overheating or even suffocation."

Turner shuddered to realize he *hadn't* known that. What other serious mistakes might he make?

Placing the contents of the basket in a separate bag, Tessa observed, "At least someone took care to pack *windle*, clothes, a bottle and some formula. Look, there are even instructions on how to prepare it and what time she eats."

"*Gut*, then I should be all set," Turner said, trying to project assurance.

Tessa arched an eyebrow at him. "Have you ever cared for a *bobbel* on your own before?"

"*Neh*, but I raised my sister from the time she was a toddler."

"That's not the same as caring for an infant this young."

Turner knew Tessa was right, but what else could he do? He felt duty bound to honor Jacqueline's request not to tell anyone about Mercy, so asking his sisters-in-law for help was out of the question. "That's my private matter to manage and I'd like it to stay that way," he said pointedly, turning toward the door.

"Wait," Tessa said. Surprised by the weight of her hand on his arm and the authority in her voice, Turner pivoted to look at her. The skin above the bridge of her nose was dented with deep lines, and worry narrowed her big brown eyes. "Mercy's sleeping now, but that won't last long. Joseph has temporarily reduced my hours at the shop, so I just work Saturdays now. If you'd like, I'm free to watch the baby during the day while you're at work."

Astonished by Tessa's willingness to help, Turner wondered if the solution could be that simple. From Tessa's brief interaction with Mercy, Turner could see how capable she was, but could he trust her to keep the situation a secret? Then he realized since Tessa already knew about the baby's arrival, he'd have to trust her to be discreet whether or not she cared for Mercy. It would be imprudent to refuse her offer.

"That would be *wunderbaar*," he admitted, "provided you don't tell anyone. I mean it, not a soul. I'll pay you, of course."

Tessa's eyelids suddenly snapped upward like a window shade as she took a step backward. "You needn't *bribe* me to keep this a secret, Turner!"

"*Neh*, I didn't mean I'd pay you for your discretion—I meant I'd pay you for your time."

Tessa softened her stance and reached to fiddle with

Mercy's quilt. "That's not necessary. We're family in Christ, and you've been an excellent landlord to Katie and me. This is the least I can do in return. Besides, I want to help. Really."

Turner's ears warmed at her compliment. "And I very much *want* your help," he said. "But I insist on compensating you for it."

"Perhaps... Perhaps we could work out an arrangement with the rent? Since I won't be earning an income at Schrock's for several weeks—"

"I'll waive the next few months of rent entirely," Turner interrupted. "Now, I'd better get Mercy to the house before she wakes again."

"*Gut nacht*, Turner." Tessa held the door for him, adding, "Don't worry. It's only for a short time. Everything will be all right."

"*Jah*, I'm sure it will," he agreed. But as he trudged up the lane, he didn't feel at all confident about what the next few weeks would bring.

Chapter Two

Tessa lay in bed on her back with her eyes wide open. Who was Lynne? "Your Lynne" the woman had written. Usually that term was used to imply a close connection. Was Lynne a relative? A cousin, maybe? Since the Amish wrote letters in *Englisch* instead of in their spoken *Deitsch* dialect, Tessa couldn't discern from the note whether its author was Amish or not.

She shook her head, trying to stop the ideas that were filling her imagination, but it was no use. She remembered all the times she and Katie noticed Turner leaving on Saturday evenings, either by buggy or in a taxi. She knew it was wrong to speculate about his comings and goings and even worse to jump to unsavory conclusions about his actions and character. *Turner King is nothing if not upright*, she thought, forcing herself to consider the baby instead.

With her pudgy arms and cheeks and her pink skin, Mercy had obviously been well nurtured. At least, she was until her mother abandoned her. Tessa sighed. She supposed she couldn't really say the baby was *abandoned*. After all, it wasn't as if she'd been left with a complete stranger. Turner knew who the mother was, even if he wouldn't say. Tessa could only guess why the mother didn't speak to him directly about caring for the baby instead of just leaving Mercy on the doorstep. Maybe she truly was in a rush, but it seemed if she legitimately had an emergency, she would have called upon other relatives or friends who were better prepared to look after a baby than Turner was. And why did she insist on secrecy, even from Turner's brothers?

The entire situation didn't make any sense, but one thing was clear to Tessa: upon reading the note, Turner's expression changed from one of irritability at being woken late at night to a wide-eyed vulnerability that made him appear almost like a baby himself. Realizing stoic, self-sufficient Turner King was shaken and burdened filled Tessa with a sense of compassion and she was eager to help. Yes, she'd taken offense at his repeated admonishments not to tell anyone about the baby, but his distrust was a small affront compared with waiving her rent for the next few months as payment for caring for Mercy.

Granted, being a nanny wasn't her favorite job, but it was one she had a lot of experience doing. As a teenager the only way she could earn an income had been to mind children. In her community, when an Amish woman had a baby, the family often hired a girl like Tessa to watch the other offspring, so the mother could devote herself to the newborn. While Tessa had doted on the children under her care, she had wished there were other opportunities in Shady Valley for her to earn money. It was expected that most Amish women would marry and give up their jobs when they began families of their own. Even at a young age, Tessa realized she'd probably have her whole lifetime to keep house and care for children, so she'd wanted to experience a different kind of responsibility while she still could. That was why she was so attached to her job at Schrock's.

Yet right before she fell asleep, Tessa realized that although she wouldn't have chosen to be laid off from the shop any more than she'd wish an emergency on Mercy's mother, the timing was mutually beneficial for both her and Turner. It was so uncanny Tessa knew it had to be the Lord's answer to her prayers. He had delivered the alternate solution she'd just requested and she was grateful for it.

When she woke before daybreak, Tessa brewed a pot of coffee and then peeked out the back window of Katie's former bedroom. From this vantage point, she could see a light burning at the house on the hill. Were Turner and the baby awake already? Had they ever gone to sleep the night before? Figuring Turner wouldn't refuse a cup of coffee, she dressed, donned her winter cloak and bonnet, and trudged up the lane carrying the full pot. She heard Mercy's cries before she climbed the porch steps.

"Guder mariye," she said when Turner opened the door. He looked as if he'd spent the night chasing a runaway goat: his posture was crooked, his clothes were rumpled and his eyelids were sagging. "I know it's early but I thought you could use a cup of *kaffi*."

"I'm glad you're here." Motioning toward Mercy, he confessed, "I don't know what's wrong with her. I've fed her, burped her and changed her *windle*, but she keeps screaming."

"She probably misses her *mamm*," Tessa said, setting the coffeepot on the table so she could receive the red-faced baby from Turner's arms. Rather, from his *arm*.

Tessa noticed Mercy was dwarfed by Turner's size; he could have easily balanced her with just one hand. Yet he was every bit as gentle as he was adroit, and as he carefully passed the screeching baby to Tessa, she was aware of the way his arm softly brushed against hers.

While Turner filled two mismatched mugs with coffee, Tessa cooed, "*Guder mariye*, Mercy. What's all this fussing about, hmm? How can we make you more comfortable?"

Mercy's wailing continued as Tessa held the baby close to her chest. She asked Turner to place a quilt on the table and then she set the baby down and took notice of her clothes. Mercy's diaper was lopsided and gaping and her legs were cold and damp. "I think she needs a bath," Tessa suggested. "And I'll show you how to change her *windle* so they're secure."

"I didn't want to hurt her tummy by making it too tight," Turner said, amusing Tessa with his innocent but thoughtful mistake. This was a side of Turner she'd never seen before. "I'll go fill the tub."

"*Neh*, not the tub," she replied, chuckling blithely in spite of Mercy's screams. "She's too small for that. We can bathe her in the sink. You get her ready, please, and I'll make sure the water is the right temperature."

Tessa rolled up her sleeves and set a towel in the bottom of the sink to serve as a cushion. Then she filled the sink part way and tested it with her elbow. She took Mercy from Turner and eased her into the water. Almost immediately Mercy stopped crying. Within seconds, she was smacking the water with her feet and hands, looking momentarily startled each time droplets splashed upward, but then she'd smile and slap the water again.

"She likes it!" Turner exclaimed.

Surprised by the brightness of his grin, Tessa threw back her head and laughed. "Most *bobblin* do, provided the water's not too hot and definitely not too cold," she said instructively.

After she washed, dressed and sufficiently fed Mercy using the supplies Lynne had provided, Tessa rocked the baby up and down in her arms. "She's getting drowsy," she observed. "You look exhausted, too. Why don't you go get a couple hours of sleep before you head to your shop? I'll stay here in the parlor with Mercy, in case she wakes up."

Turner twisted his mouth to the side and shook his head. "*Neh*, that's all right."

Tessa reflexively bristled; why was he so uneasy? It wasn't as if she was going to abscond with the baby to the *Englisch* authorities the first chance she got. "I'll take *gut* care of her and if anyone *kummes* to the house, I'll knock on your bedroom door right away," she assured him. "No one will ever know Mercy and I are here."

Turner rubbed his brow. Was he tired, apprehensive or in pain? It was difficult for Tessa to tell. Finally he said, "*Denki*, I'd appreciate that," and shuffled from the room.

"Now it's time for you to get some sleep, too, little *haws*." Tessa referred to Mercy as a bunny as she lowered the baby into the basket. "When you wake, we'll have a *wunderbaar* day, won't we?"

The comment was more of a wish than a promise. Tessa had spent enough time caring for little ones to know that sometimes it was an enjoyable, fulfilling experience, and sometimes it was tedious, demanding work. Tessa also knew there wouldn't be anyone else around for her to talk to. The very thought made her feel as if the walls were closing in. *It's only a short-term solution to ensure my long-term situation*, she reminded herself. *Besides, it's helpful to Turner and the Lord knows how much he needs that right now.*

Tessa tiptoed toward the kitchen to clean the sink and hang the damp towels, smiling about how loosely Turner had diapered Mercy and how delighted he'd been that she liked her bath. If grumpy Turner King could demonstrate good humor under his present circumstances, she could be cheerful, as well. Yes, she was determined to make today a wonderful day. For herself, for Mercy and for Turner.

Turner clicked the door shut behind him. While he was grateful for Tessa's suggestion to catch a nap before work, he had lingering qualms about her being in the house while he was asleep. Namely, he was nervous someone might stop by—not that that was likely to happen, since it rarely had before—and discover Tessa there, whether with or without the baby. While he knew there was no hint of impropriety in his or Tessa's behavior, he worried her presence there so early in the morning might tarnish their reputations.

But hadn't she promised she'd wake him instead of answering the door if anyone came by? Ultimately, he was too tired to worry an instant longer and he collapsed into bed. He was so exhausted from being up half the night with Mercy it seemed as if his head had just hit the pillow when Tessa rapped on the door. "Turner, it's almost eight o'clock," she called. "Mercy's asleep in the parlor and I'll be in the kitchen."

As he opened the bedroom door a fragrant aroma filled his nostrils and Turner snuck past the dozing baby into the kitchen. "Something smells *appenditlich*," he said.

"I figured you'd need a decent meal to start your day. I made *pannekuche* and *wascht* but since there's no syrup, you'll have to use jam. It wasn't easy preparing something substantial. You must dislike cooking as much as I do—your cupboards are even emptier than mine."

Unlike most of the Amish *leit* in their district, Turner hadn't owned a milk cow, or even chickens, since Jacqueline left home. He relied on the local market for his dairy supply as well as for his other staples, and sometimes he neglected to shop until he was down to the last item in his pantry. He was surprised to hear Tessa's cupboards were often bare, too. Since she said she didn't like to cook, he was touched by her thoughtfulness in preparing their meal.

"Well, *denki* for making this," Turner said, sitting down at the opposite end of the table. It felt strangely intimate to eat breakfast alone with a woman. After saying grace, he told Tessa, "Don't feel as if you need to cook for me in the future."

Tessa's gleaming eyes dimmed. What had he said wrong? He only meant he didn't expect her to do anything other than care for Mercy. If last night was any indication, she'd have her hands full enough as it was.

"Since Mercy was asleep, I didn't have anything else to do and I was getting hungry myself," Tessa replied, helping herself to a sausage.

Turner stacked pancakes on his plate and took a bite. They melted in his mouth. "Do you want to watch Mercy here or at the *daadi haus*?" he asked.

"Here, since I'm far more likely to get unexpected visitors at the *daadi haus* than you are."

Embarrassed Tessa noticed how seldom he received

company, Turner swiped a napkin across his lips. "That probably would be best," he agreed.

Tessa continued, "Monday through Friday I can arrive as early as you like until Mercy's *mamm* returns. For the most part, I can stay as late as you need me to stay, too. But I do have occasional evening commitments I'd prefer not to miss."

Evening commitments. Did that mean she was being courted? It was the customary practice for Amish youth in Willow Creek to court on Saturdays and to attend singings on Sunday evenings, not during the week. But for all Turner knew, it might be different for some couples, depending on how serious they were. He set his napkin beside his plate. "What time do you usually go out?" he asked.

Tessa's cheeks flushed and she swallowed a sip of water before speaking. "I didn't say I was going out."

Now Turner's face burned. He hadn't meant to be presumptuous. "Sorry. I assumed someone like you would be going out."

"Someone *like me*?" Tessa arched an eyebrow. "What am I like?"

Turner sensed he was wading into murky waters. "I only meant that you're young. You're social. You're, you know…carefree."

"Carefree?" Tessa echoed. "I'm not sure that's accurate. But, *jah*, sometimes I like to socialize on Saturday evenings. On Sundays after church, too, although I suppose I could change my plans if necessary."

So then, did that mean she was being courted or not? Turner didn't know why it bothered him that he couldn't be sure. "*Neh*, there's no need for that. I'll watch Mercy on the weekends—my brothers can tend shop on Saturdays, if needed."

Tessa dabbed the corners of her lips. Turner had never noticed how they formed a small bow above her slightly pointed chin. "On Wednesdays, Katie and I usually have supper together at the *daadi haus*. I suppose I could cancel, but I don't know what excuse I'd give her…"

"*Neh*, you shouldn't cancel," Turner insisted. "The last thing I want is for you to be tempted to create a false excuse. I'll be back in plenty of time for you to eat supper with your sister tomorrow evening."

He rose to don his woolen coat for the short stroll to the buggy shop on the western corner of his property. Setting his hat on his head, he hesitated when he heard Mercy stirring in the next room. His brothers were going to wonder what was keeping him and he didn't want them to come to the house, so he reached for the doorknob. Just then, Mercy began wailing in earnest and Tessa moved toward the parlor.

"Don't worry, I'm here," she said as she left the room.

Turner didn't know whether her words were intended for the baby or for him. As grateful as he was for Tessa's help, she also kept Turner on edge. *Is she a little touchy, or am I imagining it?* he wondered, hoping she wasn't temperamental enough to change her mind about protecting his secret or honoring their arrangement. But as he strode across the yard, he again reminded himself he had no choice but to trust her.

By noon, Turner and his brothers finished assembling an order of wheels for the Amish undercarriage assembler who owned a shop several miles away and partnered with the Kings. Although Mark offered to make the delivery, Turner insisted he'd do it himself. His reasons were twofold. First, he'd stop at an *Englisch* supermarket, where no one would look twice if he purchased formula for the baby along with food for himself.

Second, the trip would give him an opportunity to check out the area's minimarkets. According to Louisa, it was rumored among Jacqueline's acquaintances that Jacqueline had recently returned to the Lancaster County area, not far from Turner's home. Although his sister didn't have the required work permit, her peers said she supposedly was working in what the *Englisch* called a "convenience store." The term saddened Turner, especially when he saw what was sold at such shops. But he made a habit of stopping in at the area's stores under the pretext of buying a soda, hoping he'd bump into Jacqueline. He realized this method was about as precise as searching for a needle in a haystack with mittens on and his eyes closed, but it was better than nothing.

As usual, his Tuesday trip yielded no further clues about his sister's whereabouts and by the time he made his delivery, purchased groceries, returned home and stabled his horse, Turner's eyes were bleary with fatigue.

"Look who's here!" Tessa exclaimed when he walked into the parlor, and he grinned in spite of himself. Tessa was holding Mercy against her chest, one hand supporting the baby's legs in a sitting position, the other embracing her across her waist. As if in welcome, Mercy cooed and a long string of drool dangled from her lower lip.

"Let me get that," Turner said. As he gingerly removed the spit cloth from Tessa's shoulder to wipe the baby's mouth, his knuckles skimmed Tessa's cheek. "Sorry," he mumbled, his ears aflame, but she acted as if she hadn't noticed.

After Turner dabbed the baby's mouth dry, Tessa

handed her to him. "I've made a list of items we'll need for the *bobbel*," she said.

A list? "I already bought formula when I was making a delivery."

"*Gut.* Did you pick up extra bottles, too?"

"*Neh*, I didn't think of that."

"It would be helpful to have another spare or two. Also, I'm concerned about Mercy sleeping in the basket. She can't roll over yet, but she's a good little kicker and I wouldn't want her to topple it."

"I might have a cradle stored in the attic. I'll look tonight."

"And then there's the matter of Mercy's *windle*. I'll use your wringer to wash them, but we ought to purchase cloth so I can cut a few more. I could do that in town but it might arouse suspicion."

"You're right," Turner replied, jiggling Mercy. "If you tell me what to get, I can pick the material up in Highland Springs the next time I make a delivery. But I don't have a wringer—I gave mine to Patrick and his wife when they married. Barbara Verkler does my wash for me. She picks it up from my porch on Monday morning and delivers it on Tuesday."

"Uh-oh. I knew about Barbara but I didn't realize that meant you didn't have a washer here at all. I'd better take Mercy's dirty *windle* home with me and wash them there."

"*Denki,*" Turner said, impressed Tessa thought of details about Mercy's care that never would have occurred to him. He followed her to the door and waited while she donned her cloak.

"I'll be glad to see you again tomorrow," she said, tapping the baby's nose.

Turner was surprised but pleased. "You, too," he replied, not realizing until too late that Tessa was speaking to Mercy instead of to him.

As soon as Tessa latched the door behind her the baby let loose a howl Turner couldn't quiet no matter how he tried. Tomorrow might as well have been a month away.

"Supper was scrumptious," Katie raved, cleaning her plate with a heel of bread. "Was the sauce actually homemade?"

"Jah," Tessa confirmed.

On Tuesday, although she'd enjoyed reading Scripture and praying quietly while Mercy slept, Tessa had begun to feel stir-crazy without having any tasks to do or anyone to talk to, so on Wednesday she had toted ingredients with her to Turner's house. Since she had time, she'd decided to forgo the jarred spaghetti sauce she usually bought and use fresh tomatoes and basil to create her own. Tessa had inwardly smirked when Turner gladly accepted the helping of meatballs and pasta she'd set aside, despite what he'd said about it being unnecessary to prepare meals for him.

After spending more time with him in the past few days than during the entirety of the time she'd lived in Willow Creek, Tessa expected to have gained better insight into his personality. Instead, she found him just as difficult to understand. Sometimes his response to her best intentions—such as when she'd prepared breakfast for him—bordered on disapproval. But at other times his appreciation for Tessa was obvious, such as when he'd clumsily indicated he couldn't wait to see her again or when he was retrieving a cradle for Mercy and he'd also brought a rocking chair down from the attic for Tessa to use.

"There's got to be another way you can earn enough money to pay your rent," Katie said, interrupting Tessa's thoughts. She spooned a generous helping of meatballs into a glass container. Both girls appreciated that Mason understood their need to spend time with each other, and they always made enough food for Katie to bring home to him. "I can speak with the *eldre* after school tomorrow. Maybe one of the families needs help around the house, or—"

"*Neh!*" Tessa vehemently objected. "*Denki*, but for now, I can make ends meet."

Katie cocked her head. "Are you certain?"

"*Jah,*" Tessa replied, struggling to come up with an explanation that was both honest and convincing for why she didn't need a temporary job. "I have a little money in savings. Besides, I'm not certain when Joseph might need me back again, so I'd hate to commit to working for someone else and then have to quit as soon as I began."

"I suppose that's true," Katie agreed. "Are you going to tell *Mamm* and *Daed* you're not working at the shop?"

Tessa frowned. "*Neh*, not if I can help it. If *Mamm* finds out Joseph has no pressing need for me—even though it's only temporary—she'll say I'm no longer required to continue working for him and I should return home."

"Don't worry," Katie consoled her. "Unless she questions me directly, I won't say a word about it, but you know she has a knack for figuring these things out on her own."

"*Jah*, and if she does, I might as well pack my bags. There are only two things *Mamm* wants right now—for me to *kumme* home and for me to find a steady suitor and get married. The minute I return to Shady Valley, she's going to arrange for Melvin Umble to call on me. I just know it."

"That's the perfect solution!" Katie exclaimed, clapping. "We need to match you up with a suitor here."

"Oh, you mean so I don't get into an argument with *Mamm* about Melvin once I move back? I'm not sure a long-distance courtship would be enough to deter—"

In her enthusiasm, Katie cut Tessa short. "*Neh*, I'm not suggesting a long-distance courtship in the future. I'm suggesting a local one in the present. Think about it. If *Mamm* caught the slightest hint you already have a suitor here, she'd likely pay the rent for you to stay at the *daadi haus* herself!"

Tessa squinted suspiciously at her sister. Ever since Katie married Mason, she seemed eager to match Tessa up, too. Katie claimed it was because she valued finding a man she loved so much she wanted Tessa to experience something similar, but Tessa suspected Katie may have felt guilty about leaving her behind. There was no need; although initially Tessa was sorry to see her sister go, she quickly adjusted to living completely by herself and now she actually preferred it that way. Especially since Katie and Tessa still visited each other regularly.

"That may be true, but I've already been courted by the only eligible bachelors I can think of in Willow Creek," Tessa complained. *Everyone except Turner, that is*, she mused, recalling how her skin had tingled when his hand accidentally touched her face the previous evening. She immediately banished the peculiar thought.

"In Willow Creek, *jah*," Katie said. "But Mason's sister-in-law Lovina has a brother who just moved nearby to Elmsville from Indiana, and he has expressed interest in remarrying."

"A widower? How old is he? Forty? Forty-five? Sixty?"

"Schnickelfritz!" Katie flicked a dish towel at her sister. "For your information, he's thirty-three."

"Is that how many *kinner* he has, too?"

"Of course not. David only has four *kinner.*"

"Only?"

"Four isn't a lot. I hope to be blessed with at least that many." Katie brought the last of the dishes to the sink. "*Kinner* are a gift from the Lord, Tessa."

"I know that," Tessa replied. "But I can't imagine myself as a *mamm* to one *kind* yet, let alone four at once." As adorable as Mercy was, and as fond as she was becoming of the baby, Tessa had grown antsy after only two days of caring for her. She couldn't wait to get back to the shop where she'd be among people who could talk back to her when she spoke to them. "What do you think I have in common with this David, anyway?"

"I'm not sure," Katie admitted. "But you need a suitor and he wants a wife, so you ought to at least meet him. If you don't strike it off, that's fine, but you need to keep an open mind. You never know who the Lord might provide for you."

"How do you propose I meet him? It's not as if a thirty-three-year-old widower visiting from out of town is going to show up at one of our district's singings."

"That's why you're going to host a potluck supper here the next time he visits Willow Creek. Mason and I will *kumme*, and we'll invite Mason's sister, Faith, and her husband, Hunter. We can also ask Anna and Fletcher Chupp to *kumme*."

Tessa groaned. "But then it will be obvious you're trying to match David and me, which will be uncomfortable, especially if we have nothing in common."

"How about if Anna and Fletcher each invite a single friend, too?"

"I don't know..."

"Have you got any better ideas?"

"Neh."

"Then a Saturday evening potluck it is. I'll find out when David's going to be in town, and then we'll extend the invitations," Katie said, smiling.

Tessa wished she was as optimistic as her sister was, but she felt more dread than hope about meeting David. Still, it gave her the excuse to host a party and she supposed that if there was even the tiniest possibility Katie's plan would help prevent Tessa from returning home, it was worth a try. Somehow, though, when she weighed the option of becoming an instant mother to four children against the option of going home, going home didn't seem so bad after all.

Friday afternoon was especially challenging for Turner. For one thing, the shipment of LED components he'd ordered didn't arrive, which meant Patrick couldn't finish installing the new lighting system for Jacob Stolzfus's buggy. For another, Mark encountered a problem as he was working on the brakes of Jonas Plank's buggy. Unlike most of the buggies in Willow Creek, his used disc instead of drum brakes. Jonas said he kept going through brake pads too quickly, so Mark removed the calipers and when he saw how damaged the pads were, he examined the rotors, which were severely scored. The buggy would need new ones.

Because disc brakes were rarely used among the Amish, Turner had to call several *Englisch* salvage yards to find what he needed. Although it was permissible for the Amish in Willow Creek to use phones for business purposes, Turner didn't have one installed in the buggy shop, so he had to traipse to the phone shanty. It was quicker to walk than to hitch and unhitch his horse, but even so, the trip disrupted his regular work. He finally secured the parts from a place in Highland Springs, but the yard owner was going out of town and told Turner he couldn't pick them up until late the following Thursday afternoon. Jonas Plank pulled a face when Turner explained the situation to him, and it took all of Turner's self-control not to remind him he'd urged the young man to purchase a buggy with drum brakes from the start.

Then on Friday evening, despite Turner's best attempts to pacify her, Mercy cried so long and hard she eventually wore herself out. Between managing the challenges of his shop, taking care of the baby after work and struggling with his concerns about Jacqueline, Turner was bushed. After putting Mercy to bed, he stayed up just long enough to devour a ham sandwich before going to sleep himself.

Not long after, the blaring of a car horn jarred him from slumber. *Jacqueline's back!* he thought and bounded from bed to don his daytime clothes. His heart thumped as he shoved his feet into his boots, flung open the door and bolted outside onto the porch without a coat.

When the horn sounded again, he realized it was coming from the other end of the lane, near the *daadi haus*. A man's voice traveled distinctly across the winter air. "I'm not going to stop honking until you come out, Tessa!"

So it wasn't Jacqueline after all. Turner couldn't quite

catch Tessa's reply to the man's demands, but her tone sounded alarmed so he hurried through the night in the direction of the ruckus. As he neared the *daadi haus*, he could hear Tessa scolding the driver. "I said hush! You're going to wake my landlord, who's a very grouchy person on a *gut* day, so I can't imagine how agitated he'll be if his rest is disturbed at nearly midnight by an *Englischer*. Please leave."

"It's not my fault I'm an *Englischer*," the man argued. "I'll become Amish if it means you'll go out with me. Just once. Please? I'll be a complete gentleman. We'll go out to eat, that's all. If you don't enjoy your time with me, I won't ask for another thing again. I promise."

"*Neh*, Jeremy. You need to leave. Now."

"Not unless you agree to go out with me."

"The only place I'm going is back inside, and I want you to leave."

The moon cast enough light for Turner to watch as Tessa started back up her walkway and onto the porch. Unsure whether he ought to interfere, he hesitated, but when the young man sounded his car horn again, Turner stepped out of the shadows. Suddenly all the frustration he felt about his sister living among the *Englisch* boiled up inside him and he struggled to suppress the urge to direct it toward the driver. The Amish were pacifists and Turner's faith required him to forgive both figurative and literal trespassers.

"Tessa asked you three times to leave. Do I have to ask you a fourth time?" he stated in a deep, gruff voice.

Jeremy's head swiveled in Turner's direction. "Of course not. I'm sorry for causing a commotion. I'll leave right away, sir," he said, his voice suddenly meek.

"Denki," Turner responded. "Please don't return without an invitation from me."

As Jeremy repositioned the car so he could drive forward down the lane, the headlights circled the porch where Tessa stood clutching a shawl around her shoulders. Turner had never seen her dark, glossy hair loosened from its bun and he wasn't surprised Jeremy was smitten with her, considering the emphasis the *Englisch* placed on physical appearances. Still, Turner considered Jeremy's late-night visit an unacceptable intrusion and he wondered if this boisterous *Englischer* was the reason Waneta wanted him to keep an eye out for Tessa. Tessa had been baptized into the Amish church, so she wouldn't dream of becoming involved with an *Englischer* in any romantic capacity—about that, Turner had no doubts. But he worried she may be too guileless to realize her lively personality could be misinterpreted by young *Englisch* men who didn't understand her commitment to the Lord and the Amish way of life.

"I'm very sorry about that, Turner," she said. "Jeremy's parents own the *Englisch* diner on Main Street and he often stops by Schrock's, so I've chatted with him a few times. I'm surprised by his behavior tonight. Usually he's so well-mannered."

"As true as that may be, *Englischers* don't think the same way we do about, er, romantic relationships and courting, so you probably shouldn't give your address to them."

"I didn't give my address to Jeremy!" she protested. "His sister has given me a ride home before so she might have told him where I live, but I certainly didn't invite him here! I'd never do such a thing!"

Her adamant objection made it clear to Turner he was

mistaken to think she would have been so naïve. Wanting her to know he'd stand behind her if Jeremy showed up again, Turner said, "That's *gut*. But he'll have to answer to me if he *kummes* here again without an invitation."

"He won't," Tessa firmly assured him, her chin in the air.

Turner got the sense she was offended, but once again he didn't know why. After saying good-night, he tromped back to the house. To his relief, Mercy was still sleeping soundly, which was exactly what he wanted to do. But when he got into bed, sleep escaped him. All he could think about was whether Jacqueline had been drawn into the *Englisch* world by a boy who promised he wanted only a single date and if she didn't like him, he'd never ask for another thing.

Then Turner questioned if he really came across as disagreeable as Tessa suggested. She had a lot of nerve, didn't she? Perhaps if she bore even a fraction of the kind of concerns and responsibilities he had, she wouldn't be so quick to judge. Or maybe if Turner were a younger man with little to worry about except which Willow Creek *maedel* he should court, he'd walk around wearing a ridiculous grin on his face.

Ah well, there was no sense dwelling on how his life might have turned out if he hadn't had to raise his siblings. He pulled the quilt to his chin and shut his eyes so he wouldn't be "a very grouchy person" come morning.

Chapter Three

Tessa was glad to be working at Schrock's Shop on Saturday instead of caring for Mercy, because she was peeved at Turner for assuming she'd told Jeremy where she lived. As if she would ever—quite literally—flirt with the *Englisch* world! Turner was worse than her parents, to suspect her of such a thing.

How hypocritical could he be, anyway? *He* was the one who'd had a baby delivered to his house by an *Englischer*, yet from the very start, she'd put every presumptuous, judgmental or otherwise nosy speculation out of her mind. She hadn't breathed a single meddlesome word to Turner about Mercy's mother and his relationship with her. But did he extend the same courtesy to her about her "relationship" with Jeremy? No. He'd made a snap judgment based on superficial circumstances.

Yes, it was better she put a little distance between her and Turner, lest she give him a piece of her mind.

Besides, after two additional days of speaking to no one except Mercy, Tessa was relieved to be back in the shop among other adults again. Entering the gallery, she inhaled the scent of homemade candles, soaps and dried-flower wreaths. The large shop also showcased furniture, toys, quilts and other specialty items made by the Amish *leit* in Willow Creek. She relished the experience of helping tourists select their purchases. Although a few customers over the years had been impatient or even rude when speaking with her, the vast majority were respectful. If they asked questions about her Amish lifestyle that she considered too intrusive, she was skilled at refocusing the discussion to the products at hand.

The shop's reputation for delivering high-quality goods attracted local *Englisch* customers as well as tourists, some of whom she knew by sight and vice versa, and they were always pleased to chat with each other. Tessa couldn't imagine ever enjoying a job as much as she enjoyed working in the shop.

Saturday morning was especially busy and she relished being in the midst of the hubbub. During a momentary lull in ringing up sales, Joseph mentioned, "If business keeps up like this, I'll need you back full time sooner than I anticipated."

Tessa smiled at Joseph as she handed him a roll of receipt tape, but her mind was racing. What would she do about her commitment to care for Mercy if business soared and Joseph really did need her back sooner than expected? If he asked her to clerk more hours, she couldn't turn him down, not without offering a good reason. Obviously, she'd never tell Joseph about caring for the baby, but what would Turner do without her help? As galled as she'd been by his comments the previous night, she didn't have any intention of leaving him to manage Mercy on his own—for Mercy's sake, as much as for his. Tessa recognized she was probably being sentimental, but it didn't seem fair to break her budding connection with the baby, especially since Mercy had been left by her own mother once already.

For the rest of the morning she fretted about Joseph's offhand remark becoming a reality. It would be wrong to wish sales wouldn't increase at the shop, but she couldn't think of how else she'd avoid returning to work full time. Finally, after being so distracted she rang up a purchase incorrectly three times, Tessa reminded herself the Lord knew all of their needs—hers, Joseph's, Mercy's and Turner's—and He would provide for those needs according to His sovereign providence and grace. During her lunch break, she retreated to a quiet area in the back room to pray, which alleviated her anxiety.

Her lunch consisted of an apple and a piece of bread thinly smeared with peanut butter, which she swallowed quickly, hoping to use the rest of her break time to purchase groceries at the market a few doors down on Main Street, since she hadn't had an opportunity to shop during the week. But as she headed through the gallery to the main exit, she noted a distraught young *Englisch* woman carrying a crying baby against her shoulder as she perused the merchandise in the soaps-and-salves aisle. Tessa recognized the woman from her previous visits.

"Shh, shh," the woman pleaded as the baby's volume increased. "Mommy only needs a few minutes and then we can go."

"Hi there, Aiden," Tessa addressed the baby, causing the woman to spin to face her. Tessa greeted her. "Hello, Gabby. Is there something I can help you find?"

"Hi, Tessa! I'm looking for goat's milk soap—the scentless kind. My husband has allergies so he can't use anything else, and Schrock's is the only place that carries it."

"It's on the middle shelf. Here," Tessa replied, reaching for a bar of the soap, which was closer to the size of a brick. "Is there anything else you're looking for?"

Gabby shifted the wriggling baby from one arm to the other as his screeching escalated. "I made a list of essential items I couldn't forget. I only have use of the car to get to Willow Creek once a month, but I don't think Aiden's going to let me finish my shopping today."

"Would you like me to hold him while you get what you need? I'm still on my lunch break."

The woman looked a little taken aback and Tessa didn't blame her. It was a forward thing to offer, but she'd grown so accustomed to calming Mercy when the baby was upset that she didn't think twice about volunteering to hold Gabby's baby.

"Or I could take your list and collect your items for you," Tessa suggested.

"Actually, *would* you mind holding him?" Gabby asked imploringly. "I'd be able to think a lot more clearly without him crying in my ear."

"Of course," Tessa agreed. "Take your time and *kumme* find us when you're done. We'll be ambling around in the back."

"I'll just follow the racket," Gabby replied with a weak smile.

As Tessa strolled through the end aisle, she tried to soothe Aiden by rocking him every which way, but he was inconsolable. Mercy usually writhed like that when she had gas and Tessa suspected that was what was bothering Aiden, too. She lifted him to her shoulder and patiently tapped his back until he released a tremendous burp.

"Wow!" Gabby exclaimed as she rounded the corner with a canvas bag full of her purchases. "And I thought his *crying* was loud!"

"He feels better now, don't you, Aiden?" Tessa asked as she turned the infant so they could see his face. He glowered at them as if to ask what they thought was so interesting and then he lowered his eyelids, contented.

"Thank you so much," Gabby raved when Tessa passed the baby to her. "As much as I love him, it's a rare treat to do an errand without toting this fifteen-pound sack of bawling babyhood in my arms."

"You're *wilkom*," Tessa said. She certainly understood why Gabby was so frazzled. Tessa would be, too, if she rarely got out of the house without taking an infant along. Yet at the same time, holding Aiden made her feel a strange loneliness for the heft of pudgy little Mercy in her arms. Regardless of her indignation at Turner's comments the previous evening, Tessa decided after work she'd stop in at his house to see how he and the baby were faring.

Customers lingered in the shop until after closing time and because he needed the business, Joseph didn't hurry them away. By the time the doors were locked, the shelves restocked and the floor swept at Schrock's, the market down Main Street was closed. Tessa's grocery supply at home was limited to a few boxes of pasta, which she supposed she'd have to eat with butter and salt. So, when Melinda Schrock invited Tessa to join her and her husband, Jesse, and several others at the bowling alley, Tessa was tempted.

"Please?" Melinda cajoled. "We only have five people so far, which means we can't pair up for teams."

"I don't know," Tessa stalled. Usually, Tessa would have been the one who suggested the outing, but tonight she felt torn between joining her peers and getting back to see how Mercy was doing.

"It won't be a late night and we'll give you a lift home," Melinda persisted.

Tessa's stomach growled. The bowling alley, a popular location for the Amish in Willow Creek, made fantastic onion rings. Her mouth watering, she agreed, "Okay, if you're sure it's not going to be a late night."

But as it turned out, the only other person to join the trio at the lanes was Aaron Chupp, Anna's husband's cousin, which meant Tessa had to be his bowling partner. She suspected that Melinda, who once was courted by Aaron herself, was playing matchmaker on his behalf. Melinda could have saved herself the trouble. Tessa found Aaron to be unusually self-centered, a perception that was enhanced when he insisted they play several more frames—and then several more after that—when she expressed she wanted to head home.

Finally, they returned their bowling shoes and Melinda yawned exaggeratedly. "I'm so sleepy. Aaron, would you take Tessa home so Jesse and I don't have to go out of our way?"

"I'd be happy to," Aaron agreed, to Tessa's dismay.

All the way home, he spoke about himself and his work as a carpenter, never once asking her a question or pausing to allow her to interject a comment. Tessa found his monologue to be even less engaging than Melvin Umble's discourse about his courting buggy, and she couldn't get inside her house soon enough. It was past twelve thirty, so when she peered through the window in Katie's room she wasn't surprised Turner's house was completely dark. He and Mercy were probably sound asleep, like Tessa should have been by now. As she pulled the shade she grumbled, "Some early night! That's what I get for falling for Melinda's tricks—and the onion rings weren't even that *gut*."

As she was brushing her hair, Tessa decided perhaps she'd drop in on Turner before she left for church the next morning. On Friday he'd indicated he wouldn't be going to worship services himself, but when she asked him how he'd explain his absence, he said that was his problem to address. She hadn't brought up the topic again, but maybe by now he'd changed his plans or his mind. It was possible he needed Tessa's help or input after all. *There's no harm in asking*, she thought as she extinguished her lamp and snuggled into bed.

Turner had been leaning against his porch railing when he heard the buggy coming up the lane some time after midnight. Aware that Tessa and Katie's horse died of old age the previous October, he deduced someone was bringing Tessa home. She'd probably made the most of her Saturday away from him and the baby, staying out as late as she pleased with her friends or possibly with her suitor. He didn't fault her for that. He'd found out early that day just how challenging caring for a baby could be—especially if the baby wouldn't stop whining. It took Turner nearly two hours of trying to pacify Mercy before he realized, upon changing her diaper, that she must have had a tummy ache. No sooner had he given her a bath, dressed her and swaddled her in a blanket than she'd soiled her new diaper, too. Dealing with Mercy's indigestion, the mess and his own frustration with himself at not being better at caring for her, Turner was worn out before the day hardly began.

Yet it wasn't Mercy's intestinal distress that kept him up past midnight; it was his own. His malaise began shortly after lunchtime with what he thought was his usual tension headache. Initially, he dismissed the accompanying upset stomach as a case of nerves because he was so anxious about not being present for the next morning's worship services.

Attendance at the twice-monthly church gatherings was of utmost importance in the Amish community, and he'd never missed a service in his adult life. He agonized over his conflicting commitment to guarding Jacqueline's privacy and to the commandment not to forsake gathering together on the Sabbath. Obviously he couldn't show up at church with Mercy, nor could he leave her alone at home. He considered consulting his brothers, but then he'd not only violate Jacqueline's request, but he might put them in an uncomfortable position, too. Wouldn't they feel torn about keeping the secret from their wives?

The only person he could have brainstormed candidly with was Tessa, but when she broached the subject on Friday morning, he told her he'd work out the details himself. He had to admit the young woman had been extremely respectful about his privacy, never once nudging Turner for more information about the baby's mother or Turner's relationship with her. Over the past week, he'd begun to trust that she wouldn't deliberately betray his confidence. But he still figured the less Tessa knew, the less likely she was to accidentally let something slip. Furthermore, their church family was very close-knit and caring, but some of the *leit*—including his sister-in-law Rhoda—had a habit of asking nosy questions. Turner didn't want Tessa to be tempted to give a deceptive response to their queries.

After growing increasingly nauseated throughout the afternoon, Turner realized he wasn't merely plagued by anxiety: there was a physical cause for his symptoms. After several bouts of retching in the early evening he hoped to experience some relief, but instead his insides cramped tighter, and his torso and head became drenched with sweat. It was all he could do to feed and change Mercy and then put her to bed. He thought the night air might alleviate his nausea, so he wobbled onto the porch where he stayed until Tessa returned. After noticing the lamp go out at the *daadi haus*, he went back inside.

He had almost dropped off to sleep when his insides turned over and he had to bolt to the washroom. This pattern kept up for what felt like an unbearable amount of time. Just as his stomach finally settled down around four o'clock in the morning, Mercy woke up. Turner used his last spurt of energy to change and feed her, but when he returned her to the cradle, she let out an earsplitting objection until he gathered her again. Afraid he'd topple forward, he leaned against the wall, using his arms like a hammock to gently sway her back and forth until her eyes eventually closed. But as soon as he set her down, she kicked and caterwauled.

Turner was too feeble to do anything other than carry her to his bed with him. By the time he'd arranged her safely in his arm, he didn't have enough stamina to turn down the lamp. It didn't matter; he could have fallen asleep with his eyes open.

"Please, *Gott*, heal me soon and keep Mercy from

illness," he mumbled, and the baby winced as his sour breath passed over her face.

This time his sleep was disrupted by a dream of Tessa standing on her porch, her long hair billowing behind her like a curtain in a breeze. "But it's not my fault I'm so grouchy," Turner was saying to her, in much the same way Jeremy had argued it wasn't his fault he was an *Englischer*. "I'll be a happier person if it means you'll let me court you. Just once. Please? After that, I'll never ask you for another favor again, I promise."

Turner woke with a jolt. In his delirium, he couldn't remember whether he'd really asked to court Tessa or if he'd dreamed it. *Either way, she probably said no—I'm not lively enough for her.* He groaned, and sleep overtook him again.

Having forgotten to set her battery-operated alarm clock, Tessa scrambled to get ready for church. Her intention to visit Turner before she left evaporated as she tied her dark winter bonnet over her good church prayer *kapp*. Services were being held at Rachel and Benjamin Coblentz's home, about two miles away. The roads were slick with ice and she'd have to walk quickly to make it in time.

The Coblentzes, like many other Amish families, used their basement for a gathering room, with the men sitting on one side and the women and small children in another area. Tessa was one of the last women to enter the room, sliding into a space on a bench near Melinda.

"Usually *I'm* the last in line," Melinda whispered. "You must have overslept. Does that mean you and Aaron went somewhere else after the bowling alley last night?"

294   Minding the Amish Baby

Staring straight ahead, Tessa shook her head dismissively.

"Ah well, if you're fortunate, pretty soon the two of you will be courting, and you know how quickly courtship leads to marriage. Maybe by next fall you won't have to live all by yourself any longer," Melinda propounded.

Now Tessa was positive Melinda had been playing matchmaker the evening before. Why didn't anyone believe she was genuinely content with her life as it was? Surveying the rows of benches in front of her, she supposed it was probably because most Amish women wouldn't voluntarily choose to live alone. Even the widows remarried quickly or else lived in relatives' homes or in *daadi hauses* on their relatives' properties.

The only other young Willow Creek woman Tessa knew who had ever chosen to live alone was Faith Schwartz, who had lived in an apartment above the bakery she owned. But that was only for a year—at Christmastime, Faith married Hunter, after Katie married Faith's brother, Mason, in early November. Melinda and Jesse were married during last autumn's wedding season, too. Tessa couldn't have been more pleased for her sister and friends, but she had other plans for herself, God willing. Why couldn't people accept that although she lived alone, she wasn't necessarily *lonely*? How could she be, with such a close family and community and relationship with the Lord? She honestly didn't feel like she was missing out on a thing. *Quite the contrary*, she thought for the hundredth time. *I like my life as it is.*

Asking the Lord to quiet her heart, she set aside her ruminations to join in singing the opening hymns and concentrate on the minister's preaching. After the three-hour service, which was conducted in German, Tessa bustled upstairs with the other women to begin preparations for serving dinner. The men flipped and stacked the benches, transforming them into tables where the *leit* could stand as they lunched on cold cuts, cheese, peanut butter sweetened with molasses, bread, pickles, beets and an assortment of light desserts.

Tessa enjoyed chatting with the other women until it was her turn to eat, when she ravenously devoured generous helpings of everything except the beets. Homemade pretzels were also served that afternoon and she ate two of those, as well. Afterward she helped clear the tables and when Faith carried a tray of leftover cream-filled doughnuts into the kitchen, Tessa snatched one from the platter.

"These are so *gut*!" she exclaimed about the delectable treat from Faith's bakery.

"Denki," Faith replied. "I can wrap a few for you to take home if you like."

"That would be *wunderbaar*," Tessa said, munching away. She didn't have any sweets, packaged or otherwise, in her cupboards. Faith wrapped two of the pastries in plastic and then left to help sweep the basement floor after the men loaded the benches into the bench wagon.

Tessa was setting her doughnuts on the side countertop so she wouldn't forget them when Katie emerged from the pantry. "Please don't tell me that's your supper," Katie chided over her sister's shoulder as she gave her a hug. Without pausing to hear Tessa's answer, she continued, "Speaking of supper, how about if we ask Anna and Faith to join us for our Wednesday evening meal? We can discuss our plan for getting together with you-know-who." Clearly, Katie was referencing David.

"You-know-who *who*?" Turner's sister-in-law Rhoda King inquired from where she suddenly appeared in the doorway.

Tessa shot Katie a look before replying evasively, "Oh, no one you know."

"Aha. I get it. It's a secret," Rhoda teased. "You're good at keeping secrets, aren't you, Tessa?"

Tessa's heart thudded. "What are you talking about?"

"A little birdie told us about your late-night surprise visitor last week."

How did Rhoda know about Mercy? Tessa removed a broom from its hook on the wall. She needed to hold something to keep her hands from shaking.

"What late-night guest, Tessa?" Katie asked.

Tessa rolled her eyes and shrugged, as if she had no idea. She wasn't about to lie, but neither was she going to divulge Turner's secret. If everyone at church found out about Mercy, it wouldn't be from her.

"Jeremy Brown showed up at the *daadi haus* in the middle of the night!"

A surge of relief washed over Tessa—*Jeremy* was the late-night visitor Rhoda meant, not Mercy. Tessa bent to sweep crumbs into the dustpan as Katie exclaimed, "*Neh*, he didn't! What did he want?"

"Oh, you know how friendly Jeremy is," Tessa said. Most people in Willow Creek, *Englischers* and Amish both, were familiar with the Browns' diner on Main Street. The family was well liked and hardworking and Tessa frequently told Katie about her chats with Jeremy. "Sometimes he might be a little *too* friendly, perhaps, but he's harmless. On the contrary, he can be very helpful and he's demonstrated *Gott*'s love to his neighbors on Main Street on numerous occa—"

Rhoda interrupted, announcing, "He wanted Tessa to go out with him. Can you imagine? An *Englischer* showing up in the middle of the night to ask to date a baptized Amish woman?"

Katie looked concerned but she defended her sister by saying, "You seem to know a lot about the situation, Rhoda. Were you there, too, or was this information conveyed via the phone shanty?"

Rhoda completely missed Katie's implication her chit-chat wasn't appreciated. "Neither," she answered candidly. "Melinda told me after Donna, Jeremy's sister, told her on Saturday afternoon when Melinda and Jesse ate lunch at the diner. Supposedly, afterward Jeremy was utterly mortified by his lapse in judgment, which might have had something to do with Turner threatening him off the property."

The notion that Turner would *threaten* anyone was absurd. "Turner asked him to leave, that's all," Tessa clarified, emptying the dustpan's contents with a loud tap against the side of the trash barrel.

"Maybe, but you know how menacing Turner looks. One glance at him and Jeremy probably lost sight of the fact the Amish aren't combative like *Englischers* are."

Despite her previous annoyance at Turner and her similar perception of his visage, Tessa reacted defensively to Rhoda's words before she had time to weigh her own. "I don't think Turner is menacing-looking at all. He has thoughtful eyes and a radiant smile!"

"Turner?" Rhoda made a choking noise. "Don't misunderstand. I have deep affection for my brother-in-law, but he's one of the glummest-looking people I've ever seen. Not that I blame him. He had to raise his siblings from a young age, and I suspect he had some trouble with his sister, since she never visits. I've tried to find out more about her, but he's pretty tight-lipped about her circumstances. Patrick is, too."

Remembering what the Bible said about a soft answer turning away wrath, Tessa bit her tongue before quietly suggesting, "Maybe they don't want their sister to be the object of the rumor mill, which can be very hurtful."

Rhoda jabbered on obliviously. "*Jah*, I suppose that could be the reason, but I sense they're hiding something. Of course, I'm only curious because I'd like to help Jacqueline if I could. I don't imagine it was easy growing up without her parents, especially her *mamm*." When her comment was met with silence, she continued, "Anyway, speaking of helping, we noticed Turner isn't in church today. He's never missed a gathering, so he must be awfully ill. We're going to stop at the house to see if there's anything we can do for him. Would you like a ride, Tessa?"

Tessa felt as if her limbs had turned to concrete. Rhoda and Patrick were going directly to Turner's house? She had to get there first. She couldn't let Rhoda discover the baby, not after she'd just released a string of gossip a mile long without so much as taking a breath.

"*Denki*, but I think I'll walk. I feel…lightheaded."

"You do look a little pale," Katie said as she turned from stacking plates in the cupboard. "How about if Mason and I stop by later with some *real* food for you for supper?"

"*Neh!*" Tessa responded. "I mean, the fresh air will do me *gut* and I'll probably take a nap this afternoon." It was no lie; she was suddenly exhausted.

"All right. Well, feel better then," Katie said, touching her sister's arm.

"I will." Tessa forced a smile as she lifted her cloak and bonnet from a peg on the wall. "See you Wednesday evening."

"And Anna and Faith, too, *jah*?"

"Jah," Tessa agreed as she raced out the door in order to reach Turner's house before Rhoda did.

The thin layer of ice on the snow made tromping through the fields and up the hills to Turner's property a treacherous endeavor, but Tessa knew she'd never make it there in time unless she made use of the countryside's off-street shortcuts. She was halfway up the final hill when she lost her footing, landing hard on her knees and hands. Her skin stung where the icy crust tore her stockings and cut into her knees and wrists, but she picked herself up and charged forward. Her breathing was so labored from exerting herself in the cold weather that by the time she pounded on Turner's door, she felt as if her lungs would burst. Then she saw his disheveled, sickly appearance and it nearly took the last puff of her breath away.

Turner was as surprised to see Tessa on his porch as she apparently was by his appearance. Expecting at least one of his brothers and sisters-in-law would come to find out why he wasn't in church, Turner had been bracing himself for their arrival. As valiantly as he'd tried to protect Jacqueline's secret, he'd resigned himself to the fact he couldn't. The inability to honor her request now underscored his sense of having somehow failed her when she was younger. Despite his best efforts, he just couldn't seem to do right by her. The disappointment he felt in himself was even more enfeebling than his illness, and he propped himself against the doorframe for support.

"Turner!" Tessa gasped. "What's wrong with you?"

"The flu" was all he could say. He needed to sit. He wobbled into the parlor and sunk into the sofa.

Following him, Tessa asked, "Where's Mercy?"

From her room, Mercy began to cry, answering for herself. Tessa charged past Turner and up the stairs, returning moments later with the baby, who was dry and clean but restless from being in her cradle for a long stretch. Turner couldn't help it: he'd feared his arms would go limp and he'd drop her if he'd tried to lift her again.

"I expected Mark or Patrick," Turner mumbled as Tessa rocked Mercy, who stopped whining almost instantly. He noticed it wasn't the first time Tessa's actions were having a mesmerizing effect on both the baby and on him.

"They're on their way here any minute. That's why I came—to bring Mercy to my house before they got here."

He appreciated the gesture, but it was too late. "*Denki*, but they're going to ask why I wasn't at church today and I can't lie." His teeth knocked together as a chill rattled his body.

"Oh, look at you. You're shaking!" Tessa leaned over him to feel his forehead with her free hand. Her fingers were as cool and smooth as butter and he wished she'd let them linger there. Covering him with a quilt, she said, "You wouldn't have been able to go to church today whether or not Mercy was here. You're sick. That's the truth and it's all you have to say."

"I suppose you're right," Turner conceded after considering her suggestion. He added wryly, "I guess I should be thankful I'm so sick. Maybe it's a blessing from the Lord?"

But Tessa didn't seem to hear him. She set Mercy on a blanket near the wood stove. Almost as soon as she let go of the baby girl, the child started wailing, but Tessa was undeterred.

"I need to dash if I'm going to make it back to my house without anyone seeing me. I'm going to collect Mercy's things from upstairs and I'll be right back."

She returned with the basket Mercy had been delivered to them in, along with a quilt. She tucked the baby's bottle, formula and diapers into the basket and then tucked Mercy in, too.

Glancing around the room, she announced, "That's everything. As long as your family doesn't go into Mercy's room upstairs, they won't find any sign you've had a *bobbel* in your house."

"Denki," Turner mumbled. Tessa's whirlwind of activity caused him to recognize how devoted she was to keeping his secret. He'd never had that kind of support from a woman before except for Louisa, and if he didn't feel so debilitated, he'd probably be enthralled by her dedication.

"I don't like leaving with the fire dying out and you in such a state," she apologized, "but I know your family will take *gut* care of you. Meanwhile, rest assured I'll take *gut* care of Mercy, too."

Turner wanted to say, "I do know I can count on you, Tessa," but in his weakened condition the words came out as a groan. He'd have to tell her another time how glad he was he'd let her in on his secret and into his life.

Chapter Four

After waking up several times during the night to be sure Mercy couldn't upset the basket she was bedded in, Tessa realized if she was going to get any rest herself, she had to make other sleeping arrangements for the baby. So, on Monday she fashioned a crib by removing a deep drawer from the dresser and setting it atop Katie's old bed. She padded the bottom with a firm cushion.

Confident the sides were high enough that Mercy would be safe as well as cozy, Tessa spent the baby's nap time tending to household chores, including washing diapers. Since they'd be visible to passersby if she dried them on the clothesline with her own laundry, she pinned them to a rope she strung up in the basement. Unfortunately, they didn't dry as quickly there as they would have in the breeze, and Tessa was concerned she'd run out while waiting for them. Turner hadn't yet purchased the bird's-eye cloth Tessa asked him to buy, but she figured once he got better, she'd remind him so she could cut and stitch additional diapers.

Despite her best efforts not to entertain prying thoughts about Mercy's mother, Tessa found herself considering the baby's layette for clues. Although the *Ordnung* in their district didn't prohibit the use of disposable diapers, many Amish women preferred to use cloth. Tessa was aware a minority of *Englisch* women preferred cloth over disposables, too. So, the fact Mercy's mother included cloth diapers in the baby's basket didn't necessarily give Tessa a clue as to whether she was Amish or not. Likewise, Tessa couldn't have guessed whether Mercy's mother was *Englisch* or Amish from the pajamas and outfits she supplied, since the Amish in Willow Creek were given the option of using the same kind of clothing the *Englisch* used for their babies or else dressing them in traditional Amish attire.

"I would love to sew a little dress for you," Tessa told Mercy. The baby was lying on her tummy on a quilt on the floor, where Tessa could supervise her as Mercy used her forearms to raise her head and upper body while paddling the air with her legs like a stranded swimmer. When her strength finally ran out, her head dipped and she rubbed her face into the quilt. Tessa lifted her up and said, "But I don't know if your *mamm* is *Englisch*, and I wouldn't want to offend her by making an Amish outfit."

Mercy smiled and grabbed Tessa's prayer *kapp* strings. Tessa knew she probably held the baby more than some people would say she should, but she didn't care. As long as she gave Mercy plenty of opportunities to develop her muscles and explore her environment on her own, Tessa didn't see any harm in cuddling the child as frequently as time allowed. Mercy's expressions were simultaneously so precious and comical Tessa could have watched her for hours, whether the baby was awake or asleep. It seemed only natural to lavish her with attention and affection.

She was surprised at how quickly time passed and how content she felt staying with Mercy on Monday compared with how antsy she'd been the previous week. *Perhaps it's because I'm in my own home now, where I have plenty of chores and projects to work on when Mercy is asleep*, she mused. She even got an early start on making valentines to send to her friends and family members. Celebrating Valentine's Day by exchanging homemade cards and enjoying a special meal with friends was one of Tessa's favorite traditions, whether she had a suitor or not.

As she cut red and pink paper into the shape of hearts, she decided she ought to host a supper this year and she considered whether she should invite Turner—provided Mercy's mother had returned for her by then. He'd never accepted invitations from Katie and her before, but maybe now that he knew Tessa better he'd want to come? Then she wondered if she should make a valentine for him, too. She dithered about it as she worked, finally deciding it would be appropriate to make a simple but friendly valentine for him. But by then Mercy woke from her nap and clamored for Tessa's attention.

That evening, after she was certain Patrick and Mark had left for the day, Tessa trekked up the hill with Mercy to see how Turner was feeling. When he didn't answer the door, she let herself in.

"Turner?" She inched toward the parlor. When there was no response, she called louder, in the direction of the bedroom, "Turner, are you okay?"

In the moments before Tessa heard him stirring, her knees went rickety and she tightened her embrace around Mercy, imagining what might have befallen Turner. Then Turner shambled into the hall, holding out his hands

palms forward, like an *Englisch* police officer direct-
ing traffic.

"Please, don't *kumme* any closer. I don't want Mercy
or you to catch what I have."

Noting the dark circles beneath his eyes and his pale
skin, Tessa clicked her tongue against her teeth. "You
still look *baremlich*," she said, before she realized it
might be offensive to tell him he looked terrible. "What
can I do to help? Is there anything I can get for you?"

Turner smiled weakly and said, "There's nothing I
need except more rest. I honestly don't feel as bad as
I look."

"It's not that you look bad, exactly," Tessa bumbled,
looking for a way to smooth over her remark. "It's just
that your eyes are kind of faded instead of being their
usual vibrant blue."

Ach! I can't believe I just told him he has vibrant eyes,
Tessa lamented. *That's more forward than telling him
he looks awful!*

Turner apparently took no offense. "How has Mercy
been?"

"She's been a *gut* little *haws*," Tessa gushed, repositioning the baby to face Turner. Mercy lifted her arms
and legs up and brought them down, as if jumping for
joy to see him.

Turner's face brightened a little. "Did she wake up
often last night?"

"*Neh*, she slept like a *bobbel*," Tessa quipped. "Which
is what you ought to do, too. We'll check on you again
tomorrow. I'll pray you'll feel better by then."

She was sorry they had to leave after such a short
visit, but she figured the sooner Turner got to bed, the
sooner he'd get well. And sure enough, when he opened

the door the next evening, it was clear the rest had served him well. Turner's hair was combed, his posture was straight and, while his eyes didn't quite sparkle yet, they weren't as dull as they'd been the previous day.

"I think the worst is past, but I better not hold Mercy yet, just to be on the safe side," he said. "Funny, it's only been two days but I feel like I haven't seen her in a long time."

Moved by his affection for the baby, Tessa balanced Mercy in the crook of her arm so Turner could see her better. Mercy blinked and then tried to cram her entire fist into her mouth.

"I'm hungry, too, Mercy," Turner joked. Reaching to the top shelf of his cupboards, he pulled out two bowls. "Tessa, would you like something to eat? My appetite has returned and I'm heating a pot of the *hinkel-nudel supp* Mark brought me. His wife, Ruby, made it."

"That sounds *appenditlich*. My pantry is so depleted I thought I might have to ask Mercy if I could share her formula," Tessa cracked. Her meals for the past couple of days had consisted of buttered pasta and the leftover doughnuts Faith had given her after church.

"*Ach*, you probably haven't been able to get to the market, have you?" Turner guessed. "You've been too busy taking care of Mercy and me. I'm sorry."

"I'm not," Tessa said, peering at him longer than she meant to before glancing back down at Mercy, who was tugging her *kapp* strings again. "Besides, skipping a few meals is *gut* for my figure. It will help me lose a few pounds."

"I hardly think you need to worry about that," Turner quickly replied and Tessa wondered if he thought she was fishing for a compliment. Why did she make such superficial comments around him? He continued, "You're *wilkom* to anything in my cupboards. I've got plenty of—"

"Neh, neh," Tessa said with a giggle, her embarrassment forgotten. "I appreciate the offer but I'm not going to do my grocery shopping in your pantry! I'm fine. Tomorrow night Katie and a few friends are coming for our Wednesday night supper and it's Katie's turn to bring the meal, so I'll be all set. That is, if you're well enough by then to look after Mercy for a few hours?"

"I'll be well enough. I plan to return to work tomorrow."

"Are you sure you're up to that? You're still on the mend." Even as she asked the question, Tessa realized how much she sounded like her mother. "I'm sorry. I'm clucking like a nervous hen, aren't I?"

Turner chuckled. "No need to apologize. You're much more considerate of my health than I've been about your daily errands. If you'll let me, on Thursday afternoon I'll give you a ride to wherever you need to go."

"What about Mercy?"

Turner lifted his shoulders. "We'll only be gone an hour or so. She'll be fine on her own, won't she?"

Tessa's mouth fell open. Then she saw the glint in his eye: he was teasing. No-nonsense Turner King had actually made a joke. "Oh, you!"

"Mercy will *kumme* with us, of course," he said. "We'll wait for you in the buggy while you make your purchases. I have to pick up a few parts in Highland Springs, but afterward I'll swing back to Willow Creek and take you to the market before it closes."

Usually, Tessa shopped at the market on Main Street, which she could have walked to, but suddenly she didn't want to pass up the chance to spend more time with Turner. Remembering they needed diaper cloth for Mercy, she suggested she and the baby could accompany him to Highland Springs. That way, he could accomplish his business errand and she could go to the *Englisch* fabric store there and shop at the *Englisch* supermarket all in the same trip.

"That's a great idea," Turner agreed. "Now, let's eat."

As Tessa sipped her soup, it occurred to her that although she never especially liked grocery shopping, this time she was looking forward to it every bit as much as gathering with her sister and friends on Wednesday evening.

Because Tessa had taken all of the formula to the *daadi haus* and the baby was getting cranky, she and Mercy left right after Tessa finished eating. Turner piled the bowls in the sink, heated water for tea and ambled over to sit on the sofa, but he was too jittery to stay seated. He wandered onto the porch with his mug and looked up at the stars. Reflecting on the past few days, he realized his illness had been a blessing in disguise in more ways than one. Not only had it given him a legitimate reason for missing church services, but the virus had hit him so hard he hadn't had any ability to worry or wonder about Jacqueline. Nor had he had the wherewithal to pray. But now that he was feeling better, he said, "*Denki*, Lord Jesus, for healing me and for sparing Mercy and Tessa from the flu. *Denki* for using my illness to show me my limitations, even if they're difficult to face. Help me to lean on You for guidance, not on my efforts alone. And if it's Your will, please return Jacqueline to us soon."

As he slowly drank the rest of his tea, he thought about what he could do to show Tessa how much he valued her help, especially while he was sick. He considered paying her a salary in addition to waiving her rent, but he sensed she would be insulted by the gesture. No, he wanted to demonstrate his appreciation in a more personal way, but he didn't know what kind of gift she might like. He didn't even know if a gift would be welcome. Having limited experience in relationships with women, he didn't want to risk making her feel offended or uncomfortable.

Perhaps he could take her to supper after they completed their errands in Highland Springs. Tessa said she disliked cooking, but eating was a necessity, so it wasn't as if he'd be crossing a line by inviting her to have supper with him in a public place. Yes, that's what he'd do. He felt another surge of energy, and he hummed as he went inside and washed the dishes. Then he looked around the parlor and decided it needed tidying, too. By the time he had finished, he felt drained again, but as he lay in bed he realized he'd spent the last hour thinking about something other than his sister's predicament and he didn't even feel guilty. He felt... He felt *hopeful*. With a smile curling his lips, he fell into a sound sleep.

The next day when Turner arrived at the shop, Mark asked how he felt.

"*Gut*. Like a new man."

"Ruby's *supp* has that effect on me, too," Mark said and Turner grinned. It wasn't the soup he was thinking about; it was *sharing* the soup with Tessa.

He smiled again later that afternoon when Tessa and Mercy arrived at his house. He took the basket from

Tessa with one hand and held the door open with the other.

"Look at you!" Tessa exclaimed. "I guess you were ready to go back to work after all—your eyes are absolutely luminous today."

Turner was glad she immediately began unpacking Mercy's things from the large canvas tote bag and didn't notice if his ears were as red as they felt. Was she complimenting his eyes? No woman had commented on his appearance like that before, so he wasn't sure whether to say thank you or not. "What has this *kind* been eating?" he asked, picking up Mercy and weighing her in one hand. "She seems twice as heavy as she was a few days ago."

Mercy cooed at him and he kissed the top of her head, which smelled like lavender; it smelled like Tessa.

"She's been smiling ever since she woke from her nap," Tessa said. "She must be happy she gets to stay at your house with you again."

But Tessa wasn't out the door for more than twenty seconds before Mercy started to snivel. Turner rocked from side to side, trying to pacify her. "It's all right, Mercy. Tessa will be back again soon," he said. Turner's words didn't have any effect on Mercy's whimpering, but they sure made him feel happy.

After Faith, Anna, Katie and Tessa finished eating the yumasetta casserole Katie prepared, along with the marinated carrots and peas Anna brought, they did the dishes and tidied the kitchen together. Then Faith brought out her famous apple fry pies.

"Let's have these in the parlor with tea," Katie suggested.

Wiping her hands on her apron, Tessa replied, "I'm afraid I don't have any tea."

"That's okay. They go just as well with milk."

"I haven't got milk, either."

"No tea and no milk?" Katie shook her head and pulled open the pantry door. "Look, there's nothing in here except a can of soup and half a box of noodles! You call that a pantry? Honestly, Tessa, sometimes I worry about you."

Tessa snorted. "You remind me of *Mamm*. I'm sorry, but I didn't get around to shopping yet this week."

"How could you 'not get around' to shopping for food?" Katie squinted at her. When Tessa didn't respond, she said, "You aren't working at Schrock's, so how have you been spending your days?"

"I'm not sure that's your concern," Tessa replied, "but I've been giving the house a thorough cleaning and catching up on projects I didn't do when I was working."

Apparently, Faith and Anna sensed the hint of tension because they casually moved into the parlor. It was unusual for the Fisher sisters to argue, especially in front of anyone else. Tessa pulled four small dishes from the cupboard, keeping her back to her sister as she placed the fry pies on the plates.

"I'm not as irresponsible as you think I am," she said. *If you only knew how I'd spent my week, you'd understand why I didn't go shopping.*

"I didn't say you're irresponsible," Katie protested. A long silence followed until she said, "Now that I look around, I can see how much work you've been doing. The floors never shone like this when I lived here and they still don't in my new house. I asked how you're spending your days because I worry you're lonely. I understand

you like living alone—but being alone all day? That's
not like you. You've got such a social personality I was
afraid you were… I don't know, depressed or something,
now that you're not working in town. I'm also worried
you might not have enough money for groceries. Mason
and I can help you if—"

"Lappich gans!" Tessa called Katie a silly goose before pulling a tin from the back of the cupboard. She
pried off the top and showed its contents to her sister.
"See? I have plenty of money. But I appreciate your offer
anyway, dear sister."

The pair spontaneously embraced, their rift mended
as quickly as it had begun. "I'm glad you're managing financially," Katie said over Tessa's shoulder. "But
I know you well enough to know you need daily interaction with others. What are you doing for fellowship?
What are you doing for *schpass?*"

Tessa didn't know if caring for Mercy could be considered "fun," and she couldn't have told Katie about
it even if she did, so instead she answered her sister's
question by saying, "For *schpass*, I'm planning a potluck supper with you and Faith and Anna. *Kumme*, let's
eat dessert."

They carried the fry pies to their friends waiting in
the parlor, but Anna declined, saying she felt a bit nauseated. Then she patted her stomach. "Besides, my tummy
is going to be big enough in a few months' time as it is."

Usually the Amish didn't discuss their pregnancies,
sometimes not even publicly acknowledging they were
expecting until the baby was born. But Katie and Tessa
had been tight friends with Anna since they moved to
Willow Creek, and they'd recently gotten to know Faith
better, too, since she was Katie's sister-in-law. Because

neither Anna nor Faith had sisters of their own, the four young women gathered on sister days for quilting, canning, gardening and other projects. Chatting as they worked, they sometimes confided news about their lives they wouldn't necessarily share with others.

"That's *wunderbaar*!" Faith leaned over and squeezed her friend's arm.

"Wunderbaar!" Katie echoed.

"What a blessing!" Tessa exclaimed. "You're going to love cuddling the *bobbel*, feeding her, watching her sleep... Wait until the first time she smiles because she recognizes you've *kumme* into the room. It will melt your heart."

Tessa didn't realize she was crooking her arm the way she did when she held Mercy until Anna replied, "Look at you! You seem as excited about motherhood as I am."

"Neh, not Tessa," Faith objected. "She likes living alone and working at Schrock's too much to ever get married and become a *mamm*. Right, Tessa?"

Unlike the *Englisch*, most Amish women gave up their jobs outside their homes once they got married, and virtually all of them quit working when their babies were born. Some mothers later returned to work in their family businesses, but not until their children were much older, and even then they kept their offspring close by. Faith understood better than anyone the appeal of being a single Amish woman living alone and working outside her home because she'd done it herself for a year before getting married. So Tessa knew her remark wasn't meant as criticism, but she felt prickled all the same. *It's not that I've changed my mind about my plans, but who's to say I won't at some point?* It was a peculiar thought for her to have, considering all she was doing in order to keep her current living situation as it was.

"Well, that might be true right now, but…" she mumbled.

"But first she has to meet a suitor worthy of her devotion," Katie finished for her. "Which is part of the reason we wanted you to join us for supper tonight."

Even in front of her close friends, Tessa was mortified. "I only agreed to host a potluck supper. Don't go planting any celery just yet," she said, referring to the Amish tradition of growing large amounts of the vegetable prior to a wedding. Celery was a main ingredient in many of the wedding dishes, and it was also used to decorate the tables.

As Katie elaborated on their plan to host a potluck and invite David to attend, Tessa could hardly concentrate. She kept watching the clock, hoping there would be time to check in on Mercy before Turner put her down for the night. But her sister and friends were so excited about the prospect of matching Tessa and David on Saturday when he was in town again, they schemed until nine o'clock, and by then, the baby was undoubtedly asleep. After closing the door behind her guests, Tessa headed straight for bed, where she dozed off thinking, *I'm only a night's slumber away from seeing Mercy again. And Turner, too.*

Turner panicked when he heard a knock on the door at seven twenty in the morning. Tessa usually didn't arrive until seven forty-five. Mercy was burbling happily but loudly in the parlor; if Mark or Patrick were on his doorstep, they'd be bound to hear her. He cracked the door partway.

"Guder mariye," Tessa said.

She must smile from the moment she wakes up, he thought and beamed at her in return, opening the door wider to let her in. "I thought you were Patrick or Mark," he explained.

"Neh," she teased. "They're taller and they have beards."

Turner laughed. "What brings you here so early? Is something wrong?" Despite her sunny appearance, he suddenly worried she might have come to tell him she was ill and couldn't take care of Mercy today—or go out shopping tonight.

"Neh, nothing's wrong at all. I came early to ask if perhaps I could watch Mercy at the *daadi haus* instead of up here from now on. That way, while Mercy is sleeping I can keep up with my household projects, as well as wash her *windle*."

Turner hesitated. He understood why Tessa would want to spend the day in her own home instead of his, but he was afraid someone—like a suitor—might visit her unexpectedly.

As if aware of his concerns, Tessa continued, "I'm quite certain no one will stop by. Katie's at school all day, Faith is working in the bakery and Anna's focus isn't on socializing right now. My parents wouldn't come all the way from Shady Valley without telling me in advance. At least, not on a weekday."

"But what if I need to work later than usual, into the evening hours?"

"Katie, Faith and Anna will be preparing their suppers in the evening, so they're even less likely to visit."

Turner realized he was going to have to be more direct with Tessa. "But what if your...your suitor decides to surprise you with a visit some evening?"

"That *would* be a surprise," Tessa said and Turner's mouth drooped, until she continued, "since I don't have a suitor."

"Gut!" he exclaimed and then lowered his voice, stammering, "I—I mean, it's *gut* that no one will be stopping by. *Jah*, it's fine to watch Mercy at your house."

Tessa clapped vivaciously. *"Wunderbaar.* I'll load up the basket with her things and then return for her in a minute."

"Don't be *lecherich*. I'll carry Mercy's basket and walk down with you."

Turner felt so vibrant he could have bounded down the hill in three steps. When Tessa and Mercy were settled into the *daadi haus*, Turner reminded Tessa, "I'll stop in at about three o'clock to take you to Highland Springs."

"We'll be ready and waiting, won't we, Mercy?" Tessa asked and Mercy gave a gleeful squawk.

"I'll take that to mean *jah*," Turner said, tickling the underside of the baby's chin.

He didn't stop whistling all morning, and during their lunch break, Patrick asked, "What's your secret, Turner?"

Turner was devouring his bologna sandwich and nearly choked as he tried to swallow. "What secret?"

"You've been grinning ear to ear all morning, you did more of the wheel assembly than you'd planned and you're wolfing down that lunch like you've never eaten before. Usually when people have been ill, it takes a while for them to get back to their previous state of health and mind. But you seem to have bounced back even better than you were before."

Turner was relieved: Patrick didn't know anything about his secret. He lifted his shoulders and turned his hands palms up. "I suppose I'm blessed," he said before taking another big bite of bread.

"Well, it's *gut* that you're feeling so much better, since you'll be on your own in the shop on Saturday."

Turner had forgotten both of his brothers were traveling to their in-laws' houses for a long weekend, but the reminder filled him with relief. He had planned to see if he and Tessa could somehow take turns caring for Mercy while the other one was at their family's home worship service, since it would be an off Sunday this week. Now he wouldn't have to inconvenience her or ask his family to change their worship time. As for manning the shop on Saturday, that was an impossibility since Tessa would be working and Turner couldn't bring Mercy with him. But keeping it open on a Saturday wasn't an absolute requirement and, as long as all the urgent repairs were completed, his brothers wouldn't be any wiser if the shop stayed closed.

Turner's industriousness didn't wane throughout the afternoon; if anything, he became more enlivened as he worked. By the time he told his brothers he was leaving to pick up the parts for Jonas's buggy in Highland Springs, he had to keep himself from charging out the door. He strode toward his house where he washed his hands and face and put on a clean shirt Barbara Verkler had washed for him, and then he hitched the horse and started down the lane.

Turner's house and the *daadi haus* were separated from the workshop by both distance and a thick stand of trees, but to be safe Turner and Tessa agreed she'd carry the baby outside in the basket, shielding Mercy

from view with a light blanket. Their plan was for Tessa
to sit with Mercy in the back of the buggy, where they
wouldn't be plainly seen if they happened to pass other
buggies.

Concerned Mercy would be bothered by the noise of
the buggy's wheels on the road and the motion of the
carriage as they traveled, Turner paid special attention
to how he handled the horse. As it turned out, the rhythmic motion and sound of the horse's gait put Mercy to
sleep, so Turner and Tessa didn't converse during the
trip to the salvage yard, nor from the salvage yard to
the supermarket.

"I won't be long," Tessa whispered as she stepped
down from the buggy.

"Take your time," Turner insisted.

But she was quick to return with a cart full of food
items for herself and more formula for Mercy. After that,
they stopped at a mini-mall so she could purchase bird's-
eye cotton from the fabric store. Turner's palms went
clammy as she climbed into the carriage the final time.
Traffic was heavy this time of day and it wouldn't be
easy to change direction once they were on their way.
He had to ask her now.

Since Mercy was still asleep, he spoke in a low voice,
woodenly reciting the words he'd rehearsed while she
was in the store. "If you're hungry, I'd like to treat you
to supper so you don't have to wait until we get back
to eat. I've heard the Pasta Palace is a *gut* restaurant."

The parking-lot lights were bright enough that Turner
could see Tessa biting her lip. Was she trying not to laugh
or was she honestly considering his invitation?

"*Denki*, that's very kind of you," she hemmed. "I
just, um…"

Turner could have crawled into a hole. It was clear she was trying to drum up an excuse not to accept his offer. He had been foolish to think she might want to spend time socializing with him. She and her friends were probably going to share a good chuckle over this. "If you'd rather not, that's fine," he said. "I only figured we could avoid the *Englisch* rush-hour traffic if we delayed our return to Willow Creek."

"*Neh*, it's not that I don't want to eat supper with you," she protested. "It's a very thoughtful offer. It's just that I… I've been eating nothing but pasta for the past four days and I'm not sure I could swallow another bite of it."

Turner's morale soared. "Of course you can't," he said. "I should have asked you what kind of meal you'd prefer. Where would you like to go instead?"

They agreed on an American diner, where they both ordered Philly cheesesteak sandwiches and french fries. While they were waiting for their food to arrive, Mercy stirred in Tessa's arms. Squinting one eye open, the baby stretched and yawned and then closed her eye again before struggling to open both eyes. When she did, she blinked as if to ask, "Where am I?" Watching her, Tessa and Turner both chuckled. Within minutes, she was as alert as could be, reaching for the utensils and kicking at the table, gurgling or making an ooh sound. She was clearly enjoying the new environment and being the focus of Tessa's and Turner's undivided attention.

"How old is your baby?" the waitress asked when she brought their order to the table.

Turner's heart skipped a beat as he waited for Tessa's reply, but she nonchalantly answered, "A little over three months," without clarifying that Mercy wasn't her child.

"She takes after her dad—she's got his big blue

eyes. Adorable," the server said, and Turner felt as if he couldn't breathe. If the woman noticed their family resemblance at a glance, Tessa undoubtedly had seen it, too.

"At least she doesn't have my nose," Tessa nonchalantly quipped, but the waitress had already turned away and didn't hear the remark.

After he said grace, Turner hesitated to raise his head and look at Tessa. His cheeks and forehead were burning, as well as his ears. Tessa had never let on if she thought Mercy was his child, but then again she hadn't asked any questions about Mercy's mother, either. Maybe she'd noticed the resemblance and assumed Mercy was his all along. For reasons he couldn't explain, Turner felt compelled to make sure Tessa knew he wasn't Mercy's father. It was embarrassing to even bring up the topic, but he had to set the record straight.

He cleared his throat and said quietly, "Mercy isn't my *dochder*."

Tessa pulled the wrapper off her straw and casually replied, "She isn't mine, either, but we couldn't let the waitress know that, could we?"

Tessa's lighthearted response filled Turner with such warmth he felt like leaping across the table and embracing her and Mercy both. Instead he replied, "*Neh*, we couldn't." He paused to catch her eye before adding, "Although if you were her *mamm*, I think she'd be fortunate to inherit your nose. You have an elegant profile."

"*Denki*," Tessa murmured, dipping her head as she dabbed a french fry into a little pool of ketchup.

Switching the subject, Turner said, "I'm often taken aback by the comments *Englischers* make, but it doesn't seem to bother you."

Tessa shrugged. "I used to be uncomfortable having conversations with them when I first started working at Schrock's. I was always on edge, afraid they'd ask something too intrusive and I wouldn't know how to respond. But then I realized they're just curious about me. Or about the Amish way of life. They intend no harm. And sometimes they even mean to be complimentary, like that waitress."

Turner was skeptical. "Their questions don't nettle you at all?"

"On occasion, *jah*. But when that happens, I switch the topic or respond with a curt but congenial reply. Or else I meet their remark with silence, just like I would when an Amish acquaintance asks a question I consider nosy or inappropriate. Besides, some of the *Englisch* believe in *Gott* and it's interesting to hear them talk about their beliefs, even if they have a different way of living out their Christian faith than we do."

When Tessa put it that way, Turner realized she wasn't being naïve; in fact, she had more wisdom—and charitableness—than he did. He still might not trust most *Englischers*, but his confidence in Tessa was growing by the hour.

Chapter Five

Once again on Saturday there was a long line of customers at Schrock's, some of whom were unusually ill-mannered.

One woman barked at Tessa for giving her the wrong change. When she slapped the money on the counter and demanded Tessa recount it, Tessa obliged, proving she'd given the woman the correct amount due her. The customer then swept the money from the counter, shoved it in her purse and walked away without a word of apology. Another customer toppled a box of candles, and someone else allowed his child to handle one of the wooden tractors while sucking a fat lollipop. When the father was finished browsing, he set the sticky toy back on the shelf, which caused the child to scream and kick until the father promised him a chocolate milkshake at lunch.

"Tessa, you must have nerves of steel not to be fazed by the rush of customers," Joseph commented during a quiet spell. "I appreciate how patient you've been this morning."

"It's my pleasure," Tessa said.

Everything was Tessa's pleasure that day, primarily

because the evening before last Turner had told her she had an elegant profile. Tessa wasn't ordinarily given to thoughts about her appearance, as she knew vanity was a sin, but if there was one physical feature she used to wish she could change, it was her nose.

As a girl, she wasn't even aware she had a prominent nose until a classmate told her it stuck out like a chicken's beak. After that she became self-conscious and frequently stole away to her family's washroom to angle a hand mirror against the mirror above the sink so she could study her nose from the side. Tessa had realized she was being vain, just as she had realized she was growing envious of all the girls at school who had little round noses. But one day when the same boy repeatedly called her "Beaky" under his breath, Tessa asked to be excused. She told the teacher she felt sick, which meant she was lying in addition to being envious and vain. Wracked with guilt, she hid behind a tree in the schoolyard and cried until school let out and Katie walked her home.

"The Lord gave you a nose just like your *daed*'s, and I think it makes him look distinctive," her mother had said when Tessa finally confessed what had happened. "One day someone will think the same way about you. But it's more important to focus on what's in someone's heart than what's on someone's face. Now dry your eyes and help me peel these potatoes for supper."

As Tessa had matured, she was able to brush it off when others commented on the size or shape of her nose until her first suitor asked her, without a hint of derision, how she'd broken it.

"I've never broken my nose!" she'd declared.

The young man had appeared mortified. "I'm sorry. I just assumed…"

Although he hadn't meant to be insulting, Tessa had been offended all the same. So she was delighted when Turner said he liked the very thing about her face other people considered unattractive or peculiar. More than that, she was euphoric Turner was so chivalrous as to treat her to supper, knowing how hungry she'd be if she waited until they returned home to eat.

Far from feeling at a loss for what to discuss during their meal, Tessa had been utterly engaged in conversation with him. Like other young men she knew, Turner talked about buggies, but his emphasis wasn't on the vehicle as a prized possession but on his work at the shop. A spark lit his eyes when he gave examples of the challenges he and his brothers encountered, both with repairs and with their customers. As he spoke, his facial muscles visually relaxed and he leaned back against the booth seat, occasionally using his hands to illustrate an anecdote. It was clear he found his profession fulfilling. Tessa could have listened to his resonant voice all evening, but he was careful not to monopolize the conversation, and asked about her family and clerking at Schrock's. Since Mercy was so content, they took their time eating, lingering over a banana split for dessert, which they shared.

As Tessa reflected on that evening, she couldn't help humming, and the afternoon sailed by even quicker than the morning. When Joseph locked the door behind the final customer, Tessa worked with unusual efficiency to perform the chores that needed to be completed before she left. *The sooner I get home and eat, the sooner I'll be able to visit Mercy and Turner*, she thought.

Tessa was putting a new bag in the trash bin when Joseph invited her to join his family for supper that evening. Usually, she'd jump at the chance to eat one of Amity's delicious meals and spend the evening playing board games with their rambunctious young brood, but tonight Tessa racked her brain for a polite yet truthful way to decline Joseph's offer. Then it hit her like a bolt of lightning: tonight she was hosting the potluck supper. In her giddiness over her evening out with Turner, she'd completely forgotten about the party.

"*Denki*, I would like to but I can't. I'm hosting guests at my house tonight."

"Ah well, perhaps another time," Joseph said. "I'll finish up here since I have to wait for Amity and the *kinner* to pick me up. You can go ahead and go home. Bundle up. It looks like it's snowing again."

Exiting through the back door, Tessa regretted that she hadn't worn her heavier cloak and a scarf when she'd left the house that morning. For a few seconds, she hoped the bad weather might prevent her guests from coming so she could visit Turner and Mercy instead, but she knew that was improbable. The snow was fluffy, not heavy, and even if it kept up, her sister and friends could easily transverse the roads by horse and buggy.

She'd made her way down the back alley and was nearing the parking lot behind the mercantile that was used by cars as well as buggies, when she looked up and noticed a figure waving at her.

"Tessa!" the man called.

As he passed beneath the street lamp, she could see it was Jeremy. Tessa momentarily stopped cold in her tracks before hugging her cloak to her chest and sidestepping him. She didn't have time for his antics. "I'm in a hurry, Jeremy. I need to get home. Excuse me."

"Please wait," Jeremy said, following at her elbow. "I'm not going to make a spectacle of myself again. I want to apologize to you for my behavior last week. I'm very sorry. There's no excuse for my behavior, and it doesn't reflect the respect I have for you and your beliefs. I hope in time you'll forgive me."

Tessa stopped to face him. She was shivering but she wanted to look Jeremy in the eyes. She knew it took humility and courage for him to apologize. "I forgive you, Jeremy."

Jeremy's voice squeaked as he said, "Thank you, Tessa. That means a lot to me."

She nodded. "I really do have to go now—"

"Do you want a ride?" Jeremy offered. "You look cold and you said you're in a hurry. My sister Donna is in the car waiting for me."

Tessa hesitated. The Amish were permitted to accept rides in cars from the *Englisch* and she still had to tidy the house before the guests arrived. She didn't want Jeremy to doubt she was sincere about accepting his apology, and since his sister—who had given Tessa rides in the past—would be traveling with them, she didn't have to worry about the impropriety of riding alone with an *Englisch* man. But Turner had indicated Jeremy wasn't welcome on the property without an invitation from him, and Tessa wanted to respect his wishes.

"That's okay, I'll walk." Her bare fingertips were going numb.

"I can drop you off at the end of your driveway, since I haven't had a chance to apologize to your landlord yet and I know he doesn't want me around."

This time, Tessa didn't refuse. She scurried with him across the parking lot to his car. Since his back seat was stacked with oversize boxes of paper goods for the restaurant, she slid into the front seat next to Donna, who gave her an enthusiastic greeting and scooted closer to her brother. Jeremy had left the car running and the interior was toasty warm. Because she'd accepted a ride, Tessa figured she'd have enough time to prepare lemon squares for the party; they were her specialty, the one dessert she never burned or undercooked. She had forgotten to tell Turner about the potluck, but maybe before everyone arrived she'd run up to his place with a plate of lemon squares for him, too.

Turner stepped down and paced the length of his horse and buggy where he'd parked it in the lot behind the mercantile. Taking several deep breaths, he tried to gather his thoughts. The day had started off so well, with Mercy waking in a pleasant mood, smiling at Turner when he changed her and listening raptly whenever he carried her to the window and pointed out the snowflakes. He knew she probably couldn't understand him, but he was delighted that she seemed enthralled with the sound of his voice.

Still, after spending all day indoors Turner began to feel confined, which made him appreciate Tessa's help all the more. Wanting to be as considerate of her as she'd been to him, he decided to pick her up after work so she wouldn't have to walk home in the cold. He planned to ask if she wanted to share a pizza, which they could pick up on the other side of town and then eat at his house.

Figuring he'd catch Tessa coming down the alley behind Main Street, Turner headed toward the parking lot behind the mercantile to watch for her. Rounding the corner, he spotted her beneath a street lamp. But instead of walking toward home, Tessa was getting into a car. He knew that car; it was Jeremy's. Sure enough, he spotted Jeremy just as he opened the door to get in on the driver's side. Turner pulled into the parking lot entrance as Jeremy's car was driving out the exit at the opposite end.

Now, stomping back and forth next to his buggy, Turner tried to make sense of why he felt so irked. Tessa technically wasn't doing anything wrong; she was probably only getting a lift home. But it seemed inappropriate for her to accept a ride alone with an *Englisch* man. Didn't she know that people might gossip? Turner had come to believe she had more discretion and exercised sounder judgment than that, but apparently he was mistaken. Furthermore, Tessa had heard him tell Jeremy he wasn't welcome on the property without an invitation from Turner. Didn't she have any regard for Turner's wishes?

Suddenly a voice behind him said, "Hello, Turner."

Turner was so lost in thought he hadn't noticed anyone approach the lot. "Hello, Joseph." He fiddled with the horse's reins, as if that were the reason he was idling in the parking lot. "You can't be too careful in this weather."

"*Jah*, that's true," Joseph agreed. "You know, I'm glad our paths crossed. Amity and I were just saying we don't get to see you nearly as often as we'd like to. We hope you'll call on us soon."

"*Denki* for the invitation." Turner kept his response neutral. He felt deceptive enough pretending to adjust a rein that didn't need adjusting; he wasn't going to make false promises to Joseph, too.

Just then Turner heard a faint whining. During the

past week or so his ears had grown finely attuned to the sound: it meant Mercy was waking up. In a matter of two minutes, she might start wailing her lungs out. Turner wanted to skedaddle before Joseph heard her, but it was too late.

"Do you hear a cat?" he asked.

Turner cocked his head as if listening. "*Neh*, I don't hear a cat" was all he could truthfully say. Fortunately, Joseph's wife turned down the alley and the buggy made enough noise to drown out Mercy's mewling.

"I see Amity is here to pick you up," Turner commented. "Better not delay. With the way the *Englisch* drive in snow, it's best to get off the roads as soon as possible."

Joseph chuckled as he headed toward his family's buggy. "We'll see you around soon, I hope."

"*Gut nacht*, Joseph." Turner said loudly, hoping his voice blocked out the sound of Mercy's.

As soon as he climbed into the buggy and spoke sweet nothings to Mercy, she quieted. And when the horse trotted back toward home, she sounded out, "Aah," holding the syllable for a long time before repeating it as if it were a song. Turner, however, was far from singing. Rattled that his secret had nearly been exposed, he kneaded the muscle in his neck, which was tighter than it had been since before he'd gotten ill.

Because his plans for the evening were ruined anyway and Mercy seemed satisfied to be nestled in her basket in the back, Turner decided to stop at the phone shanty. He situated his buggy so it obscured him and Mercy from view, lest any other buggies pass by. It had been weeks since he'd spoken to Louisa and, although it was unlikely, he hoped she might know more about Jacqueline's current situation than he did. He could usually count on a teenager to pick up the phone at this time on a Saturday and today was no exception.

"You must be very quiet," Turner said to Mercy as he waited for the girl who answered the phone in Ohio to fetch Louisa from her house close by. The phone shanty Turner used was enclosed on three sides, more like a booth than a room, and Turner held Mercy in a seated position with her back to his chest, the way he'd seen Tessa do it. Tessa had crocheted a pink cap for the baby, and she was wearing it now. Snuggled in Turner's arms, Mercy was content to watch the snowflakes as he wiggled her up and down.

After exchanging brief pleasantries, Louisa said, "I'm afraid I've heard disturbing news. Remember I told you an acquaintance of Jacqueline's recently said her cousin in Elmsville told her about an Amish *maedel* who ran away with an *Englischer* during her *rumspringa* and now works in a convenience store near Willow Creek?"

"Jah." Of course Turner remembered; that's why he'd been searching the markets in his area. He sensed Louisa was reluctant to report whatever new information she'd heard.

"I'm sorry to tell you this, Turner, but the *maedel* supposedly gave birth to a *bobbel*."

Louisa's news would have shattered him, had Turner not already known about it. Although he felt guilty because Louisa was clearly in anguish over the rumor, Turner didn't confirm what he knew. He couldn't, not when Jacqueline had asked him not to.

It sounded as if Louisa was sniffing. Turner had always known his aunt cared deeply for Jacqueline, but he'd been so absorbed by his own concerns he hadn't fully considered that Louisa felt like a mother to the young girl. She was probably as grieved by this news as he had been. On top of that, her husband was ailing after suffering a series of small strokes, so she was worried about him, too. Turner tried to think of something to say to console her.

"As devastating as it would be if Jacqueline bore a *bobbel*, if the rumor is true at least we'd know she was still alive," he said. Turner had never allowed himself to hint at his deepest fear until now. Soothed by Mercy's presence, he added, "At least we'd still have hope she might one day return to us."

"*Jah*, that is our prayer." Louisa continued slowly, "But supposedly this *maedel* is considering leaving the Amish altogether. The *bobbel*'s *daed* is a *kind* himself and doesn't want anything to do with the *bobbel* or with her. It's said she's thinking of moving out of the region altogether. Maybe even giving up her *bobbel*."

Turner's legs were jelly. Jacqueline wasn't going to return? She was going to leave Mercy behind? The possibility caused his throat to burn and his lungs to constrict. He couldn't fathom how Jacqueline could even contemplate leaving Mercy behind permanently. Just then the baby grunted and kicked her legs to let Turner know he'd stopped bouncing her and she wanted to keep moving. He automatically complied.

"Turner?" Louisa was prompting him from his silence. "You know how rumors start in small communities. This one could be completely false. Or perhaps it's not about Jacqueline at all."

"Perhaps not," Turner managed to say. He pressed Louisa for more details about who Jacqueline's acquaintances heard the rumor from; maybe he could track the person down and ask more questions. But apparently the gossip had been passed along so many times, even those repeating it weren't sure where it originated. Turner finally bade Louisa good-night and then he and Mercy continued on their way. When he pulled up the lane to his house, he didn't notice whether Jeremy's car was at Tessa's. He had far more pressing things on his mind.

Tessa was concerned when she looked out Katie's window and didn't see a lamp on at Turner's house. Was he napping because he felt ill again? Tessa's guests would be there within the hour and her dessert was still baking, but she darted up the hill and rapped on Turner's door. There was no answer so she knocked again, loud enough to wake Mercy from the soundest slumber, but there was still no stirring within the house. She sped to the stable. Pulling the door open, she saw the horse and buggy weren't there. Where could Turner and Mercy have gone?

Making a mental list of Mercy's supplies, Tessa tried to determine if Turner urgently needed to purchase something for the baby. But even if he did, Turner wouldn't have gone into a store alone with Mercy. Tessa wondered if he took the baby for a ride in the buggy to calm her, since it had had a tranquilizing effect on her on Thursday. But it was unlikely he'd have gone out with Mercy on a snowy evening—unless something was wrong with the baby and he needed help. A dozen scenarios flitted through Tessa's mind, each one more disturbing than the first.

As concerned as she was, Tessa realized even if something upsetting had befallen Turner or Mercy, there was nothing she could do about it now except pray. Once she was home, she bowed her head and beseeched the Lord, "Heavenly Father, please keep Turner and Mercy healthy and safe, wherever they are, and bring them home soon."

By the time she'd pulled the lemon squares out of the oven and slid the corn bread muffins onto the rack in their place, her guests had arrived. To Tessa's dismay, in addition to the married couples, there were two single men, but no other single female guests present. Hunter and Faith brought David, the widower, who was short and portly and wore glasses. Anna and Fletcher brought a tall, muscular young man with sandy-blond hair named Jonah, who just moved to Willow Creek from Ohio to work on Fletcher's carpentry crew. After introductions were made and the men stamped off their boots and were settled in the parlor, the women retreated to the kitchen to tend to a few last-minute food preparations.

"I'm sorry, Tessa," Anna whispered. "I invited the daughter of my stepmother's childhood friend who is visiting her from out of state, but the entire household, including their guests, came down with that nasty stomach bug that's been going around."

Recalling how sick Turner had been, Tessa sympathized, "That's too bad she's ill, but I understand. *Kumme*, let's go play a round of charades while the corn bread bakes and Katie's chili simmers."

The group broke into two teams: David, Tessa, Jonah and Faith against the others. Every player jotted the name of a person from the Bible on slips of paper, and then the two teams exchanged the slips. The teams took turns and each person had two minutes to act out the character they'd chosen; if their team guessed it before the timer went off, they scored a point.

When it was Tessa's turn, she chose a slip that

said Queen Esther. As she pretended to don a crown, Jonah and Faith called out the names of every king and ruler they could imagine. King David. Saul. Caesar. Nebuchadnezzar. Each time Tessa vigorously shook her head no, Faith's and Jonah's subsequent answers grew louder and more urgent as they attempted to guess the correct person. Tessa continued to mime Esther praying, fasting and preparing a banquet for the king. By this time, Jonah and Faith were both standing as well as shouting, whereas David was silent and immobile, a blank look on his face.

"It's Cain, preparing stew!" Jonah yelled.

"Cain wasn't a king," Faith said with animated disgust.

Tessa was so exasperated they assumed she was a male that she threw her hands in the air and grimaced exaggeratedly at them to indicate they were on the wrong track.

"You're Moses and you're frustrated with the Israelites' idol worship!" Faith said loudly, interpreting her gesture to be part of the game. The other team realized Tessa hadn't been acting out a role, and they all cracked up at Faith for continuing to guess who Tessa was imitating. Tessa laughed so hard she bent over, clutching her stomach.

As the timer sounded, Jonah hollered triumphantly, "You're King Solomon falling on his sword! Am I right? Did I guess it? I'm right, aren't I?"

Tessa was too breathless to reply and the others howled with amusement. When the rumpus subsided, Tessa good-naturedly groaned. "Neither of you really had any idea who I was?" she asked Faith and Jonah.

"*Neh*, but at least we were guessing," Faith said, zestfully chastising David. "One of our team members didn't say a word."

"I thought perhaps she was being Queen Esther," David replied, eliciting a cheer from Tessa.

"I was! Why didn't you call it out?"

David's shrug caused Tessa to wonder whether he was incredibly self-conscious or just bored with their game. Either way, his reservation didn't bode well for them being a match; humor was important to Tessa. Until she played charades with her friends, she hadn't realized how long it had been since she'd had a good, hard belly laugh herself. She'd missed that.

"Do I smell something burning?" Hunter interrupted her thoughts.

"*Ach*, my corn bread!" Tessa yelped. Acrid smoke filled the air after she darted into the kitchen and removed the charred muffins from the oven. But when everyone gathered around the table, they politely ignored the thin blue haze hanging overhead.

"Sorry about that," Tessa said, utterly chagrined. "My *mamm* says I'd forget my own head sometimes and I'm afraid it's true."

"That's okay," David consoled her. "My Charity frequently does the same thing herself."

"Who's Charity, your wife?" Jonah asked.

"*Neh*, my daughter. She's eleven," David replied.

Tessa cringed to hear her skills being compared to those of a girl eleven years of age, but David continued obliviously. "Most of the time she's done a *wunderbaar* job preparing our meals ever since my wife passed on, although there have been a few mishaps. I'm sure with a little more female guidance Charity will grow to be a fine cook."

Could it be any more obvious he's looking for a wife? Tessa wondered. David might have expressed such a sentiment subtly to Tessa in private if he wanted to court her, in order to gauge her interest in him by how she responded. Making such a bold remark in front of her close friends was downright embarrassing.

Fortunately, Katie quickly changed the subject, asking, "Jonah, how do you like Willow Creek so far?"

"It's all right," he said, reaching for the butter. "But the *Ordnung* is different from my home district's. For instance, it seems there are more restrictions here on buggy modifications."

"Anything you need to know about that, you can ask Turner King, my landlord," Tessa suggested. "He and his brothers run a buggy shop, so obviously he's an expert. He's always been very generous to Katie and me as renters, so if you need modifications to your buggy, I'm sure his prices would be reasonable." As soon as the words were out of her mouth, Tessa realized she'd been praising Turner effusively and she wondered if anyone noticed her breathlessness.

To her relief, Jonah asked a question about the use of leaf springs compared with air suspension on the buggies, and all of the men joined the discussion until Katie gave a tiny cough. Tessa knew her sister was politely signaling Mason that they needed to change the conversation to a subject the women could participate in talking about, too.

After supper was over and the dishes put away, everyone said they were too full to eat dessert yet.

"Are you just saying that because you're afraid I burned the lemon squares, too?" Tessa joked.

"I'm sure dessert will be delectable," David said. His

flattery felt awkward to Tessa in light of the blatant remarks he'd made about his daughter needing a female
influence to help her cook.

"I know!" Faith exclaimed. "Instead of the usual board
games, why don't we go outside and play cut the pie?"

"Isn't it still snowing?" David questioned.

"If it is, we won't melt," Faith ribbed, already lacing
up her boots.

The group tramped to the flat area at the base of the
hill behind the *daadi haus*. The clouds had cleared and
the moon lit their path. As they shuffled through the
snow, etching a big circle crossed with lines forming
eight sections of "pie," Tessa realized it was a good thing
there was a fresh layer of snow atop the scant amount
beneath it; otherwise someone might have noticed her
footprints leading up the hill to Turner's porch. Glancing
toward his house, she saw a lamp on. She'd been having
so much fun she'd momentarily forgotten how worried
she'd been because Turner and Mercy hadn't been home
earlier that evening. *I guess everything must be fine*, she
thought. Denki, *Lord*.

"Not it!" Hunter suddenly shouted and the rest cop-
ied him.

"Looks like you're it, David," Fletcher said when
David was silent.

"*Neh*, I'm going to sit this game out," he said, patting
his stomach. "I'm too full to move."

Tessa thought if Katie held any hope of her sister and
David being a match, she should let it go entirely: Tessa
couldn't see herself with a spoilsport.

"I'll keep him company," Anna offered and her husband gave her a knowing nod.

"I'll be it," Jonah gamely volunteered, moving to the

middle of the circle as the other players scattered along the lines.

Tessa grinned beneath her scarf. Jonah's personality matched hers more closely than David's did. And although he appeared a year or two younger than she was, he was still closer to her age than David was. *Not that that matters*, she thought. *Turner's nine years older than I am and we get along just fine.* But while she intuitively liked Jonah's character and good humor, for whatever reason she couldn't quite picture him as a suitor.

"No fair!" Katie yelled when Jonah jumped a pie "slice" to tag her. "You can't jump from one piece of pie to another. You have to run within the lines."

"That's not how we play in Ohio," Jonah objected.

"You're not in Ohio any longer," Mason jested, molding a snowball and lobbing it in Jonah's direction. But Jonah dodged it and it hit Katie instead, disintegrating into a chalky cloud upon impact with her forehead.

"Hey!" Katie indignantly scolded Mason.

"Sorry, I was defending your honor," Mason laughed, just as Faith pitched a snowball at him from behind.

An all-out snowball fight broke out after that, with everyone taking aim at whomever they could hit. The snow was too powdery for anyone to get hurt and, although David stayed on the sidelines, even Anna joined in. When their shouts and squeals became especially loud, Tessa reflexively warned, "We ought to quiet down. We're going to wake the—" but she stopped short of completing her thought.

"The what?" Katie asked. "The only other person nearby is Turner and his lamp is on, so he's not sleeping."

Tessa was at a loss for what to say, but David took advantage of the pause in the snowball fight to interject,

"Speaking of people being asleep, I'm almost ready to hit the hay. Are we going to have dessert soon?"

Although the others seemed reluctant to go indoors, Tessa was secretly glad David made the suggestion, and she rewarded him with an especially large lemon square. Not only had he rescued her from Katie's question, but he'd moved the party toward its end. Now that Tessa knew Turner and Mercy were home again, she was eager to find out how they were and where they'd been.

Turner stayed in the shadows on his porch long after he'd watched Tessa and her guests return to the *daadi haus*. He had come out there after putting Mercy to bed because his head ached so severely he felt nauseated and he hoped the fresh air would calm his stomach. But upon realizing Tessa was holding a party, his queasiness worsened.

Rationally, Turner knew he shouldn't be disappointed in her for having fun with her friends. Apparently, that's what people her age did. They nonchalantly accepted rides from *Englischers* and played in the snow with their Amish friends as if they were children. For the second time that day, he felt foolish for ever thinking Tessa might have been interested in his company as a man. He was too old and he had too many responsibilities. Why would she want to spend time with him when she could frolic with her friends?

Their voices traveled clearly across the yard and Turner had tried to discern whether Jeremy was among them, but he couldn't. From what he could distinguish from their shouting, there was one man in the group who was either visiting or had moved from Ohio. Turner wouldn't be surprised if Katie was trying to match him with Tessa.

Turner felt like a fool for mistaking Tessa's effervescence at the restaurant for genuine happiness to be with him. She'd told him how much she disliked cooking—her conviviality on Thursday was probably mere relief she didn't have to prepare supper that night. Or else she was glad to be with Mercy; the bond between the pair was undeniable. Perhaps she felt she had to humor Turner's suggestions, since technically he was her employer as well as her landlord. As far as Turner knew, maybe she'd accompanied him only out of a sense of duty.

His disenchantment might not have felt so severe if Louisa hadn't just told him the rumor about Jacqueline possibly leaving Willow Creek. The entire evening's events seemed to emphasize Turner's life and responsibilities were in stark contrast to Tessa's. Once again, he reminded himself of the urgent need to concentrate solely on finding his sister. He never should have been distracted by his passing feelings for Tessa in the first place.

Heading back inside, he checked on Mercy and slumped into a chair at the kitchen table. He hadn't eaten, but he wasn't hungry. He bowed his head and prayed for a long while, asking the Lord to move Jacqueline to come home. He lifted his head and then rose to stoke the fire in the wood stove. Upon hearing a knock at the door, he felt his heart gallop with hope: Was God answering his prayers already? But no. It was Tessa, not Jacqueline, who appeared on his doorstep. She was holding a plate wrapped in tinfoil.

"It's *gut* to see you," she said cheerfully. "You weren't here when I stopped by earlier. I was worried."

Turner wasn't about to humiliate himself by telling

her about how he'd gone to pick her up, and he couldn't tell her about stopping at the phone shanty, either. "Well, I'm here now," he stated. He didn't intend his words to sound so acerbic, but he offered no further explanation.

Tessa took a step backward, cocking her head. "*Jah*, I can see that. How about Mercy? Is she all right?"

"She's asleep, which is a wonder, considering how much racket you and your guests were making outside."

Tessa's eyes widened. "I'm sorry about that. I tried to keep everyone fairly quiet."

"*Jah*, well, judging from the noise, I'd have guessed you invited *kinner* instead of adults."

"Why is that? Because adults shouldn't have *schpass*?"

Tessa tipped her chin up, as if challenging him to argue, but Turner's head was pounding and he was too tired to quarrel.

"Why have you *kumme* here at this late hour?" he asked directly.

"I thought you might like these lemon squares," she said, "but I see your disposition is sour enough already. *Gut nacht*, Turner."

She whirled around and stormed down the hill. When she slammed the door to the *daadi haus*, he winced at the sound as if he'd been clocked upside his head with a wrench.

Chapter Six

$\sim$

Tessa felt completely humiliated and she couldn't get back inside the *daadi haus* quickly enough. She slapped the plate of lemon squares onto the table. Recalling her mother's adage about the way to a man's heart being through his stomach, she ranted to herself, *That assumes the man actually* has *a heart!*

Not that she wanted to get to Turner King's heart—not anymore, anyway. He was acting like a completely different person than he had on Thursday night, simply because her guests had been a little rowdy. It was as if he was enforcing an ordinance against adults having fun! Tessa doubted they'd made enough noise to wake the baby, but even if they had, she'd apologized for it. If Turner held a grudge for such a small offense, she couldn't imagine how unforgiving he'd be for a substantial one.

His attitude is no different than David's, the old stick-in-the-mud, she thought. How could she have ever entertained romantic notions about Turner? She must have gotten swept up in the drama of his secret about the baby. Or maybe it was that she was so enamored of Mercy she imagined she had developed feelings of affection for Turner, too.

She thought she'd come to understand him a little better over the past couple of weeks and she'd hoped he'd come to understand her better, too. But he obviously didn't, otherwise he wouldn't have acted as if she was prying about where he and Mercy had gone. It wasn't necessarily that Tessa thought she had the right to know, but couldn't Turner at least have given her the courtesy of an explanation? He should have understood her well enough by then to recognize she was worried about what may have happened to Mercy, instead of shutting her out as if she were a snooping pest.

In a way, Tessa was glad Turner had reminded her what he was really like and how he apparently viewed her. It underscored just how much she didn't need a suitor because she didn't want to get married, especially not to such a fuddy-duddy. But he was also a fuddy-duddy who was her employer and landlord as well as a member of her church, and as Tessa prepared for bed she knew she'd have to apologize to him for her flippant remark. But first, she needed to confess her resentment to the Lord. She knelt by the bedside and admitted her transgression, ending her prayer by asking, *Please let my words be acceptable to You and loving toward others.*

When Tessa woke on Sunday morning, her bitterness had melted but she was glad she wouldn't have to see Turner that day. Perhaps all the time she'd spent engaged in his predicament had contributed to her false sense of attraction to him. Although she regretted missing even a single day of seeing Mercy, a little break would do Tessa good. Maybe it would give Turner a new appreciation for her, too.

Tessa joined Katie, Mason and the rest of the large extended Yoder family, including Faith and her husband, Hunter, at the Yoder farmhouse for off-Sunday worship. Afterward, Tessa and Katie helped prepare a light lunch.

"Well?" Katie asked when she and Tessa finally had a moment of privacy as they walked back to Katie's place together while Mason pulled his nephews around the Yoder's yard on a sled. "What did you think?"

"About David, you mean? I think you know what I think."

"Okay, I'll admit he didn't seem like a *gut* match for you. But what about Fletcher's crew member, Jonah?"

"He seemed congenial," she said thoughtfully. "I liked how easygoing he was."

Katie rubbed her gloved hands together in delight. "*Jah*, he was definitely more energetic than David. I think it would be worth it for you to get to know each other better, don't you? Your birthday is coming up on the eighteenth. I could host a party for you and invite him so the two of you could spend more time together."

Tessa had been so consumed with caring for Mercy and protecting Turner's secret, she had forgotten her birthday was drawing near, but she didn't want Katie turning the celebration into another matchmaking opportunity.

"*Denki*, but the truth is I really don't want a suitor, especially not a pretend one. It wouldn't be fair to act as if I'm interested in someone just because I'm afraid *Mamm* would tell me to *kumme* home otherwise," she said as she followed her sister into Katie's house.

"I never suggested you should pretend anything— that would be very deceptive," Katie clarified. "But you just said yourself Jonah possesses qualities you like, so why not get to know him better in a casual setting and allow him to get to know you, too? You never know—"

"I said *neh*," Tessa snapped. She'd kept an open mind about meeting David and she'd even entertained the possibility of Turner as a suitor, but look where that had gotten her. This time her position wasn't going to change. "Why can't you understand I really don't want to be courted? Just because you're married doesn't mean I want to be. Not now, anyway."

Katie's eyes welled. "It's not that I want you to get married, Tessa," she said. "At least, not until you want to. It's that I really don't want you to have to leave Willow Creek. I'm trying to think of every possible way to help you stay here."

Tessa felt awful. She hung her cloak on a peg and took her sister by the shoulders. Katie wouldn't look at her as a tear trickled down her cheek. "I'm sorry, Katie. I'm being so defensive and self-centered I didn't even think about how my leaving Willow Creek might affect you. I can't even express how much I'd miss you, too. But I'm sure it's not going to happen. In a few weeks, Joseph will need me back again and *Mamm* will never know there was a break in my employment."

"I hope that's true." Katie pushed a tear off her cheek with her palm. "Because I'm going to need you here now more than ever. It's too early to say for sure, but I'm pretty certain I'm with child."

"Katie! That's *wunderbaar* news!" Tessa's joy was immediate and genuine.

"I'm going to the clinic in Highland Springs after school on Wednesday to find out for certain, so I won't be able to have supper with you. Do you suppose we could meet on Friday instead? Say, around five o'clock?"

"*Jah*, whatever works best for you."

"So, about your birthday… Are you at least *open* to the idea of my giving you a party and inviting Jonah?"

Tessa rolled her eyes, but she conceded, "Maybe. We'll see."

"One last thing," Katie added. "If you happen to write home, please don't mention to *Mamm* I'm expecting. I want to tell her in due time."

"Of course I won't," Tessa promised. She and Katie had always shared their deepest secrets with each other before telling anyone else. "But you know *Mamm*—she probably somehow knew about the *bobbel* before you did!"

The two sisters giggled and gave each other a long embrace. But as happy as Tessa was for her sister, an uncomfortable feeling passed over her. It wasn't sadness, exactly. It was more like…like envy. *That's* lecherich, Tessa scolded herself later as she walked home. *Getting married and starting a family is the last thing I want to do right now.* Yet when she opened the door to her empty *daadi haus*, Tessa experienced a sense of loneliness that was so deep she curled up in a ball on her bed and wept until she eventually fell asleep.

Turner was worried about Mercy. She was unusually temperamental and she didn't seem interested in her bottle. He first noticed her mood shortly after he'd finished reading Scripture and praying that morning. She grew increasingly cranky throughout the afternoon and Turner had such a difficult time getting her down for a nap, he ended up holding her the entire time she slept. At first he thought perhaps she'd just become too accustomed to Tessa cuddling her, but when Mercy kept refusing her formula, he became concerned. He hoped she hadn't caught the stomach flu he'd had.

Now it was evening and as he rocked her in the chair he'd brought down from the attic for Tessa, he studied her face. Even in sleep her bottom lip curled over in a pout and her eyelids were squeezed into two lines curving downward like frowns. Observing her discomfort, Turner felt more anger than forbearance toward his sister for the first time since Jacqueline left Louisa's home. How could she even think about abandoning this vulnerable little child? Having grown up without a mother herself, she ought to have known how important it was for a girl to have a female to nurture and guide her. Some might have argued Jacqueline was only a youngster herself, but Turner figured if she was old enough to give birth to a baby, she was old enough to accept the responsibility for her. After all, he had raised his siblings when he wasn't much older than Jacqueline himself.

But his anger quickly turned back to concern again. What if Jacqueline really did leave town? If Turner hadn't done right in raising her, how would he do right raising her daughter? He couldn't bring Mercy up by himself, nor could he ask Louisa to take the baby, not after all she'd already done and not when her husband was ailing. Turner supposed Rhoda or Ruby would help, but they'd be starting families soon, too. He wasn't confident Mercy would be treated like one of their own children. Turner wanted Mercy to be dearly loved—the way Tessa loved her.

As the thought occurred to him, Turner acknowledged he needed to apologize for the way he'd treated her when she came to visit him. His churlishness had been uncalled for. Yes, Turner's nerves had been frayed because of what Louisa told him, but Tessa had been extraordinarily supportive these past couple of weeks and she deserved better from him.

Deep down, Turner was aware it wasn't merely the news about Jacqueline that had contributed to his boorish behavior toward Tessa. It was also that when he saw her cavorting with her friends in the snow, it shattered his illusion she fancied him the way he was drawn to her. He couldn't blame her for that. He was too burdened with responsibilities, too stodgy and probably too old for someone as vivacious as Tessa. Not that he'd seriously considered the possibility of courtship, exactly, but he had allowed himself to imagine there was a spark of romance between them.

How embarrassing, he thought. *I haven't courted for so long I misinterpreted Tessa's attentiveness as attraction.* While he couldn't tell Tessa where he'd gone on Saturday because it would mean either admitting he'd intended to pick her up from work or confiding he'd contacted Louisa, he at least could apologize for how he'd behaved when she paid him a visit.

His mind made up, he gently lowered Mercy into her cradle. After praying over her, he crept to his room as quietly as he could. Tending to an upset baby had been more grueling than his most difficult day at the shop and he was beat, but he was still too worried about Mercy to fall asleep. So he pulled a pillow and a quilt into her room and arranged them on the floor, where he eventually drifted into slumber.

Turner was awoken hours later by the sound of what he thought was a coyote yipping and he leaped to his feet, confused about where he was. Then he realized it was Mercy who was howling. Stumbling to the crib in the dark, Turner murmured, "I'm here, Mercy. Your *onkel* is here."

He slid his hand beneath her back and drew her to his chest. Her clothes were damp so he turned on the lamp to change her diaper. Although he hurried through the task as quickly as he could, she cried the whole time. When he lifted her again, his cheek brushed her head. It seemed hot. *She has a fever!* Panicking, Turner wasted no time with a coat—he simply bundled Mercy in the quilt from the floor and charged out of the house down the hill to Tessa's. She'd know what to do.

He was startled to find her waiting with the door open and the kitchen lamp on. Her luxurious hair hung loosely past the blue shawl draped around her shoulders.

"What's wrong, my *schnuck* little *haws*, hmm?" she purred to Mercy and extended her arms to take the baby from Turner.

Turner handed Mercy to her, spouting, "I'm afraid it's the stomach flu. She's been fussy all day and she didn't finish any of her feedings. She has a fever—feel her head. She's hot, isn't she?"

Tessa put her lips to the baby's forehead. Mercy was already quieting, as if she knew she was in good hands again. "She seems a little warm, but I don't think she's actually hot. See how she just rubbed her ear? She might have an earache," Tessa said.

"An earache? She'll need to see a doctor for that, won't she?" Turner asked, but he didn't allow Tessa to answer. "Can it wait until the morning, or should we take her to the emergency room? But if we do that, how will we explain whose *bobbel* she is—*neh*, *neh*, I don't even care about that. I'll go hitch the horse—"

"Shush!" Tessa demanded, carrying Mercy toward

the parlor, lightly jiggling her as she walked. "An earache doesn't necessarily mean an ear infection. Some
babies pull at their ears when they're tired. Or she might
be teething."

"How can we tell what's wrong with her?"

Instead of answering, Tessa ran her finger along Mercy's bottom gum. "*Jah*, there it is, right there in front.
It's a little early, but my sister-in-law's son started teething at three months, too. Or it's possible Mercy is older
than I think she is."

"You're sure she doesn't have a fever?" Turner asked.
He hoped his question wouldn't offend Tessa but he'd
never forgive himself if he neglected to help Mercy while
she was under his care.

Tessa pressed her lips to Mercy's forehead a second
time before replying thoughtfully, "As I said, she seems
a little warm, but not really feverish. Sometimes babies
run warm when they're teething. But if it makes you feel
better, we can take her temperature. I don't have a baby
thermometer, do you?"

"*Neh*, but I could go get one. Some of the *Englisch*
convenience stores are open until midnight."

"It's already twelve forty-five," she told him. "But
there's a convenience store on the border of Highland
Springs that's open twenty-four hours a day. Instead of
turning onto the main route, you follow Old County Way
all the way until you come to a fork in the road. Bear left
and the store is on the right."

In all of his searching for Jacqueline, Turner had never
been to the store Tessa described and he wondered how
she knew it was open all night. It hardly mattered. "You
don't mind staying up with Mercy until I return?"

"Of course not. I've missed her," Tessa said. "But first

I'll need you to bring an extra pair of pajamas down from your house. I've got *windle* but I'll need more formula and spare bottles. It probably makes sense for us to keep her supplies at both houses anyway, instead of carting them back and forth."

Shooting out the door and up the hill to his house, Turner gathered the items Tessa required and sprinted back to the *daadi haus*. When he returned, Tessa was swaying in half twists with the baby in her arms. Mercy's cries had stopped completely and she was gripping a lock of Tessa's hair.

"I think you're going to have to untangle me," Tessa told Turner. "She won't let go."

Turner spoke in a soothing voice. "*Neh, neh*, Mercy. Don't pull. We mustn't hurt Tessa."

His hands trembled as he gingerly pried Mercy's fingers, one by one, from Tessa's tresses. He was close enough to smell Tessa's shampoo, and whether it was the fragrance, the nearness to her or his anxiety about the baby, he felt heady with nervousness.

Once he freed Tessa's hair from Mercy's clutches, Turner uttered, "I'll be back soon," in a husky voice and started toward the door.

"Turner, wait," Tessa said, stopping him midstride. "I'm confident Mercy will be fine—she seems more comfortable already. Getting a thermometer is only a precaution for your sake, so there's no need to rush. You must slow down or you'll have an accident. Go put on your coat and hat, and don't forget to take money with you or you'll end up making the trip twice."

As he turned and faced her, Turner ruefully thought she had never appeared as lovely to him as she did in that moment. It wasn't her glossy hair, chocolate-colored eyes or flawless complexion that made her so: it was her gracious care about him, despite his cloddish behavior toward her. He felt like falling to his knees to ask her forgiveness, but there would be time for that later.

"*Denki* for the reminders," he said. "You always seem to think of everything."

Tessa's directions led him straight to the convenience store. It wasn't surprising he'd never visited this particular shop; it wasn't one of the chain stores he usually frequented and from the outside it looked deserted. Inside, he discovered it wasn't as well kept as the other stores and he searched the dusty aisles hoping to spot the kind of baby thermometer Mercy needed.

"You need help finding something?" a young *Englisch* woman asked. She wore heavy eye makeup and ripped jeans, and her left nostril was pierced with three silver hoops.

"I'm looking for a baby thermometer," Turner said.

"Oh, yeah, they should be right over here," the woman replied, leading him to an assortment of gauze, aspirin and antiseptics. She scanned the items hanging from small metal rods, but didn't find what he was looking for. "Zander," she called to a blond guy wearing a sweatshirt monogrammed with the letters of a local college. "Do we have any baby thermometers?"

Please, Gott, *let them be in stock*, Turner prayed.

"Try the next aisle over, the one by the diapers," he shouted from his perch behind the cash register. "Jackie was shelving inventory. She probably messed up again."

"Yep, here it is," the girl said, holding a box up victoriously. "Somebody needs to train that girl better."

Zander snickered. "Not gonna happen. Artie canned

her on Saturday. She barely made it through the trial period."

"Oh, that's too bad," the girl replied, bringing Turner's purchase to the counter for him. "I really liked Jacqueline. She was sweet."

Jacqueline? Turner felt as if his legs were made of rubber. His hand shook as he reached to give Zander a twenty-dollar bill. "Is Jacqueline Amish by any chance?" he asked casually.

Zander's laugh exposed white, perfectly aligned teeth. "She didn't dress like it, but that would explain a lot if she was. Like why she always asked me to ring up the magazines and booze."

Turner steadied himself against the checkout counter. "Do you know where she lives?"

Zander squinted at Turner suspiciously. "Why? Is she your wife? Kind of young for you, but I guess that's the Amish way, huh?"

Turner held his tongue. If he weren't so desperate to find Jacqueline, he would never disclose his personal situation to a stranger, especially not to an *Englischer* with a foul mouth. "I think she might be my sister." He repeated, "Do you know where she lives?"

"Never asked." Zander handed Turner his change, pushed the plastic bag containing the thermometer across the counter and said dismissively, "Have a good night."

But Turner wasn't going to be dissuaded so easily. "Listen, my sister is… She's missing and I think the girl who worked here might be her. Did she have long dark hair and blue eyes?"

"Nope, this Jacqueline is a blonde," Zander said. "With green eyes. There's no way she's your sister."

The young woman tipped her head. "Why are you telling him she—"

Zander cut her off. "You'd better go reshelve Jackie's mistakes, Chloe. Artie won't be pleased if he finds out you've been standing around yapping instead of working."

Chloe opened her mouth but then closed it again and disappeared into the back room. Turner got the sense she was about to tell him something about the girl who worked there, but he couldn't very well follow her. Besides, he needed to get back to Mercy. Deciding he'd return the next day to talk to the staff again, he exited the store.

He wasn't halfway across the parking lot when a female called to him.

"Hey, mister!" Chloe was carrying a big plastic bag of garbage. "Listen, I've got to be quick or Zander will come looking for me. That girl, Jackie. She does too have dark hair and blue eyes."

Turner knew it! *Denki, Lord,* he immediately prayed, his hopes burgeoning. But why did Zander lie about what Jacqueline looked like?

Chloe continued speaking as they walked toward the dumpster. "I don't know where she lives, but our manager, Artie, might. He usually shows up between five thirty and six each night. But the thing is, well, he's paying some of us under the table, 'cause we're minors. Not everyone has a valid work permit, if you know what I mean."

Turner understood. "So he might not be willing to tell me anything about her?"

"Right." Chloe hurled the bag over the side of the dumpster and wiped her hands on her jeans. "I know

Amish people don't usually do this kind of thing, but you could mention the licensing authorities. I mean, please don't really report him—if he gets into trouble I could lose my job and I really need the money. But you know, you could drop some hints."

He smiled widely. This young girl with thick makeup and tattered clothing was going out of her way, even risking her job, to help him. Would he have done the same for her or for any other young *Englischer*? His attitude had to change.

"Denki," he said and added the blessing, *"Gott segen eich,* Chloe."

"Your sister's a good kid. I hope you find her." She scrambled back to the store.

I do, too, Turner thought. *I do, too.*

After easing Mercy's pain by placing a cold cloth on her gums, Tessa was able to prompt her to take a bottle. After she burped a couple of times, the baby seemed content to cuddle, taking in Tessa's face with her big, innocent eyes.

"You feel better now, don't you, Mercy?" Tessa murmured. "I feel better, too, now that you're in my arms again. Two days away from you is two days too many."

"Ah-ah-ah." The baby seemed to agree.

"But I'm not so sure our friend, Turner, feels better. And he probably won't until he takes your temperature and is assured you don't have a fever, but that's just because he cares about you so much."

Tessa continued talking to Mercy until the baby's eyelids closed. Sitting on the sofa in the dim light, she listened to Mercy's rhythmic breathing and thought about Turner. She had never seen him so alarmed. Rather, she hadn't seen him so alarmed since the night Mercy arrived on the doorstep. He'd worn the same aghast, defenseless expression tonight as he'd worn then. Once again, her gall over his curt behavior was superseded by deep sympathy for his situation.

She couldn't help but wonder if Lynne knew what a burden she'd placed on Turner by leaving the baby in his care. Yes, Tessa was there to help, but Lynne wouldn't have known that. On the contrary, by requesting Turner not tell anyone about Mercy, Lynne essentially ensured the burden would fall entirely on him. Lynne undoubtedly knew he'd accept the responsibility with unflinching commitment, but Tessa could see it was taking a toll on him. Whoever Lynne was, Turner must have cared about her deeply to make such a sacrifice. And it was clear he cared about Mercy every bit as much. *Despite his sullenness, his devotion is admirable*, Tessa mused.

Then she admitted to herself it wasn't merely admirable—it was attractive. Turner's commitment to those he loved was more appealing to Tessa than a sense of levity in someone like Jonah could ever be. Which wasn't to say she didn't appreciate a sense of fun in a man, but that she was surprised by how drawn she was to Turner, in spite of his serious nature.

It hardly matters, she thought. *He's obviously preoccupied with bigger concerns. And even if he was interested in courting someone, he's made it clear he thinks I'm too... What was it he called me? Young and carefree.* What would it take for him to see that, while she might be cheery and social, she was also thoughtful and responsible?

Tessa was so deep in thought she didn't hear Turner's quiet arrival some time later. His pallor was no longer as white as milk and he projected renewed energy when he presented Tessa with the sterile thermometer.

Taking it from him, she said, "While I'm doing this, why don't you fix us a cup of tea? I think we could both use a little refreshment."

Turner followed her suggestion and when he returned with the cups several minutes later, Tessa grinned. "99.2," she announced. "That's completely normal for a baby her age."

"*Denki*, Lord!" Turner yawped, nearly spilling their hot beverages. "And *denki*, Tessa. What would I have done without you? I don't know how I'll ever repay you."

"As I told you from the start, I *want* to help," Tessa emphasized, hoping Turner would hear the sincerity in her tone and understand she was speaking as a friend, not merely as a hired nanny. "You're not indebted. You don't owe me a thing."

"Actually, I do. I owe you an apology." Turner sat on a chair across from Tessa, took a sip of tea and then set his cup aside and cleared his throat. His eyes were the color of thunderclouds. "I'm sorry about how I treated you last night. You must have been appalled by my rudeness—I know I am."

Hearing Turner openly admit his shortcoming filled Tessa with warmth. She met his gaze and said, "I forgive you. And I'm sorry I made an insulting comment about your disposition. I was hurt by your attitude, but my remark was very immature."

"It was also accurate. I can be a real killjoy sometimes," Turner confessed. He picked up his teacup and stared into it. "You and your guests weren't making too much noise at all. I think maybe I was envious."

"Envious? But why?"

"Because you all were having *schpass* and I was… Well, I wasn't."

"That's understandable. You've had a lot on your mind lately."

Turner shook his head. "You have no idea."

Tessa realized he might think she was being nosy, but she had to ask, "Do you want to tell me about it?"

Tessa's voice was so sympathetic and her presence so reassuring Turner took a deep breath. He knew his sister wouldn't want him to tell Tessa that Jacqueline was Mercy's mother, but this was no longer about what Jacqueline wanted. It was about what Turner *needed*. And what he needed was encouragement and support from someone he trusted. From Tessa. He sighed and then his words rushed forth like the creek's current in springtime. He confided everything, beginning with his parents' death to the time Jacqueline moved to Louisa's home in Ohio and straight through to his conversation with Chloe at the convenience store. Twice in the telling he had to stop and blink back tears, but Tessa's mild expression never changed. Her eyes reflected kindness and sensitivity. She softly patted Mercy on the back, but other than that, she didn't move an inch. When Turner finally finished sharing his burden, he simultaneously felt fifty pounds lighter yet completely wrung out.

To his grateful relief, Tessa didn't speak a word of criticism against Jacqueline, she didn't give him unsolicited advice and she didn't ask him any questions, save one: "What can I do to help you find your sister?"

"You're already doing it," Turner said. He paused before adding, "If possible, I'd like to talk to Artie right when he gets to the store in the afternoon. Chloe said he usually arrives between five thirty and six. I'm not sure when I'll be back. I suppose it depends on if I find out where Jacqueline is living and whether she's home when I get there. Do you think you could—"

"I'll watch Mercy for as long as you need me to," Tessa offered. "So please take your time. And as for the rest of tonight, I think Mercy should stay here since I know how to treat her gums."

"She's not going to let you get any sleep."

"We'll be fine. I'm more concerned about *you* getting sleep. You should go home and get to bed. You need to rest so you can think clearly."

"All right," Turner agreed reluctantly.

"I'll be praying for you about your conversation with Artie," Tessa said as she walked him to the door where they both paused at the same time. They were standing so close he could hear Mercy breathing.

"*Denki*, I appreciate that. And I'm so grateful you knew how to ease Mercy's discomfort." Turner put his hand on the doorknob. Before twisting it, he asked, "By the way, how is it you were still awake when we showed up?" he asked.

"Sunday is visiting day, so the last of my unruly guests had just left and I was cleaning up after them," Tessa said with a wink.

A grin curled Turner's mouth for the first time all night.

Then Tessa said in a more serious tone, "To be honest, I wasn't actually awake until I heard Mercy crying."

Turner was incredulous. "You heard her from all the way up at my house?"

Tessa shrugged. "Either that, or I heard her as you were running down the hill. All I remember is I was startled awake and I knew right away Mercy needed my help."

"Really?" He was impressed. "I guess that's what they call maternal instinct," he said.

"Maternal instinct?" Tessa repeated, wrinkling her forehead. Then a smile sparkled across her face. "*Jah*, I suppose that's exactly what it was."

Turner wasn't sure what he'd said to make her appear so pleased, but whatever it was, he hoped he'd say something like it again very soon.

Chapter Seven

Tessa returned to the parlor and ruminated over Turner's disclosure. Suddenly, everything made sense: his guarded exterior, the trips Katie and Tessa saw him making, Mercy's resemblance to him. What was especially clear was why he seemed so intolerant of *Englischers*. Tessa regretted making unfavorable assumptions about his character, but at least those thoughts had been fleeting—she felt worse for holding a longstanding opinion he was fundamentally sullen. It was no wonder he was slow to smile; his burdens were greater than any she had ever carried.

As troubled as she was about Turner's heartaches, Tessa simultaneously felt honored he'd confided in her about them. He didn't have a choice when it came to telling her about Mercy, since she knew about the baby even before he did. But telling her about Jacqueline was of his own accord. Surely this meant he trusted her deeply? Now more than ever Tessa intended to show him how worthy she was of his confidence.

Sighing, Mercy scrunched her face in her sleep. Over the course of a short time Mercy had grown noticeably, becoming even chubbier if that was possible. Tessa's muscles ached from holding her, but she was reluctant to put the baby down. It occurred to her if Turner was able to locate Jacqueline and convince her to come home with him, Tessa no longer would be taking care of Mercy. She hadn't realized how attached she'd grown to her until she had to face the imminence of letting her go. Tears streamed from her eyes and she tried to wipe them away with the corner of her apron, but they came too fast. She cried noiselessly so as not to wake Mercy.

I must be overly tired, she told herself. But she knew that wasn't what was wrong, not entirely. The fact was she'd come to treasure her relationship with Turner as much as she cherished her bond with Mercy. They'd become a family of sorts and she didn't want their time together to end, just as she previously hadn't wanted her days living alone to end. *How did that happen?* she lamented. *How did I change from wishing I could stay single indefinitely to yearning for a husband and* bobbel? She knew the answer to her own question: Turner and Mercy were what happened. As a tear rolled from her cheek and dribbled onto Mercy's forehead, Tessa realized if she didn't go to bed now, her sobs would get the best of her and she'd wind up waking the baby.

Since she was too tired to take out the big drawer she used as a crib for Mercy, Tessa arranged a place on her own bed where she could safely lay the baby for the night. Before she settled next to her, Tessa pulled her prayer *kapp* from the bedpost and knelt beside the bed. She thanked God for easing Mercy's discomfort and asked Him to help Turner find Jacqueline and to know what to say when he did. She ended by saying, *Lord, I understand it's best for* mamm *and* bobbel *to be reunited, but it hurts to let go of Mercy, so please give me Your peace.*

In the morning Tessa woke to Mercy making gurgling sounds next to her. She reached over and placed her hand on the baby's belly. "I'm glad to hear your teeth aren't bothering you this morning," she said. "Is there any chance you'd let me sleep a few more minutes?"

Every time Tessa closed her eyes and fell silent, Mercy animatedly waved her arms and made lip-smacking noises Tessa recognized meant she was hungry, so Tessa picked her up and ambled into the kitchen. As coffee percolated on the stove top, she cracked two eggs into a pan and then prepared Mercy's formula so they could leisurely eat their breakfast together.

"Look, Mercy," Tessa said later that morning as she pulled construction paper from a drawer. "I've been making Valentine's Day cards. Maybe when you take a nap this afternoon, I'll make more. I might even make one for your *onkel*."

But just after Tessa put Mercy down for her late afternoon nap, Turner arrived. "I didn't stop by this morning because I thought you girls might need your sleep," he said. "I wanted to see how Mercy is and ask if there's anything you need before I head to Highland Springs."

"She's sleeping soundly after a very active day. You'd never know she was in pain from teething, although it's bound to come and go."

"It was probably just a ploy to visit you last night," Turner joked.

"She doesn't need a ploy—she's *wilkom* any time."

"Does that go for me, too?" Turner asked.

Tessa couldn't tell if he was earnestly uncertain or if

he was being flirtatious. Erring on the side of caution, she said, "Of course that goes for you, too."

"In that case, I'll stay for a visit after I return from Highland Springs." There was a hint of apprehension in Turner's voice. Tessa understood: she was probably as nervous about what he might discover as he was. She didn't know if he could bear the dejection if he learned Jacqueline had already left the area.

"I'll be waiting," she said. "I'll even make supper."

"I might not be back until late."

"That's okay, it will keep," Tessa said. Then, to encourage him, she added, "I'll make plenty, in case your sister is hungry, too."

This time Turner's voice sounded optimistic when he replied, "*Denki*. We'll look forward to that."

Turner had possessed an abundant amount of nervous energy all day. With his brothers away, he had hoped to use the quietude to concentrate on reconciling the bookkeeping, a project he kept procrastinating, but he was too wound up. Since there were no repairs scheduled he had poured himself into filling their next wheel order. But now, as he headed toward the convenience store, he suddenly felt depleted, as if he could hardly lift his horse's reins.

To distract himself from the whorls of dread twisting in his stomach, he reflected on Tessa's hopefulness he'd find his sister. *This must be how Patrick and Mark feel to have the faithful reassurance of their wives. Whoever Tessa chooses to marry will be a very blessed man.*

Even as the idea crossed his mind, Turner felt a stab of sorrow, knowing *he* could never be that man. Yes, Tessa knew his deepest secret yet seemingly held no judgment against Jacqueline or him. But knowing what happened in someone else's family and having it happen in one's own family were two different matters. Even if his far-fetched dream came true and Tessa was willing to accept him as her suitor, Turner could never marry her, so courting her was futile.

Considering what happened as a result of him raising his sister, Turner was absolutely panicked at the possibility he might have to raise his niece. He'd do it, if it came to that, because he loved her and because he had no other choice, just as he'd had no other choice but to raise Jacqueline. But he could choose whether or not to raise a daughter, because he could choose not to marry and thus spare a potential wife from the kind of affliction he was experiencing now.

Turner shook his head and reminded himself he had to stay focused on the task at hand. He thought about what he was going to say to Jacqueline when he found her. He'd tell her he loved her, of course, and that she always had a home—she and Mercy both—as well as a family who wanted to help her. He'd urge her to return, letting her know that although she might wish she hadn't made certain choices in her life so far, she could make better decisions now. He'd say he thought she'd regret leaving the Amish, but she'd never regret anything as much as she'd regret leaving Mercy. And he would remind her that although she might turn her back on the Lord, God would pursue her with His unfailing love.

Although he arrived at his destination later than he intended, Turner took the time to pause before entering the convenience store, asking the Lord to help him demonstrate grace and patience to the *Englisch*.

"Artie?" Turner questioned when he approached an

overweight, middle-aged man with a moustache and thick-rimmed glasses standing behind the checkout counter.

"Who's asking?" The man was obviously surveying Turner's clothes and hat.

Turner swallowed, knowing if he wanted information from the man, he'd have to be forthcoming. "My name is Turner King. I believe you know my sister, Jacqueline."

Artie stopped counting the bills he was holding long enough to cock his head and say, "Jacqueline? Can't say I've met anyone by that name."

"You might know her as Jackie. Or Lynne," Turner said, realizing Zander probably warned Artie about their early morning conversation, and the manager might feel threatened by Turner's presence. "I'd just like to speak with my sister."

"Sorry. Wish I could help." Artie wrapped an elastic band around the wad of bills before pocketing them.

Turner felt desperate. *Lord, please guide me.* "I think you can," he persisted. "If you tell me where she lives, I'd appreciate it."

Artie squared his shoulders. "She didn't mention where she lives."

Turner pointed out Artie's slip of the tongue. "Then you admit she *did* work here! She must have given you her address when she filled out an application."

"My filing system is a mess," Artie claimed.

Suddenly, it dawned on Turner that anyone who paid his employees under the table wouldn't have made them fill out legitimate applications. "Someone here must have seen her arriving at or leaving work. Was she within walking distance, or did she get a ride in a car?"

Artie lumbered out from behind the counter. He was even taller than Turner and twice his width. He pointed to a No Loitering sign hanging on the wall. "I've told you I don't know anything about the girl, so unless you're going to buy something, it's time for you to leave."

Averse as he was to contacting the *Englisch* authorities, Turner recalled Chloe's advice and said, "She's a minor and she's missing, so if I can't find her myself, I'll have to visit the police. Perhaps by then you'll have found her address, and you can tell them when they question you and your staff about her employment here."

"Ha," Artie scoffed, but he dropped his shoulders. "The Amish don't get involved with the police."

"Not as a rule, no," Turner said, heading for the door. "But we do when conscience dictates or we have no other recourse."

"Hold on." Artie's tone was urgent. "Payday starts tomorrow night at six and it ends the second I walk out that door at seven fifteen. The kids know there are no substitutions, no excuses, no exceptions. I pay in cash so they need to come in and pick it up in person. If your sister was working here—and I'm not admitting she was—that's her one chance to collect her wages. And if she doesn't, you might try asking Skylar when he comes in for his pay. Muscular guy, curly hair like a lion's. You'll recognize him because he wears cargo shorts, even in winter. But I'm warning you—no drama in front of my employees or customers."

"You have my word I won't cause any trouble," Turner said emphatically, extending his hand to shake Artie's the way the *Englisch* did. "*Denki*, sir. You've been very helpful."

* * *

It was only a little after six o'clock when Tessa heard a knock. Surprised Turner was back already, she wiped her hands on her apron. She alternately had been fearing and looking forward to this moment. If Turner hadn't found Jacqueline, he'd likely be overcome with sorrow. If he had found her and convinced her to come back with him, he'd be elated. That was exactly what Tessa wanted, but it would also mean her responsibility to care for Mercy had come to an end. She smoothed her hair and tried to relax her posture before tugging the door open.

"Hello, Tessa." It was Melinda Schrock. "I hope I didn't catch you in the middle of eating supper?"

Because Mercy was wide awake and gumming a cold cloth in the parlor, Tessa stepped outside onto the porch, pulling the doorknob close to her back. "Actually, I am in the middle of making it," she said honestly, hoping Melinda would take the hint and keep their conversation short. "What can I do for you, Melinda?"

"It's more like what I can do for you," Melinda boasted. "I'm here to offer you my shift tomorrow at Schrock's."

"What? Why?" Tessa stalled, trying to come up with a truthful reason she couldn't work the following day.

"I have the opportunity to visit Jesse's relatives in your hometown, Shady Valley, tonight and tomorrow," she said. "His brother was in town for business today and he invited us to a party for his wife. Sort of short notice, but Joseph said he didn't mind, as long as you fill in for me."

Tessa hugged her torso to keep warm. Without knowing whether Turner had located Jacqueline, she couldn't risk not being available to watch Mercy. "I'm sorry, but I can't."

"Why not?" Melinda asked. "I thought you'd jump at the chance to earn a full day's pay."

"Ordinarily, I would. *Denki* for thinking of me," Tessa said in a sweet tone so Melinda wouldn't be too angry. "But not this time."

"Why not?" Melinda demanded.

Tessa knew from experience Melinda didn't take the word *no* easily. "I have a…family matter to take care of this week," she said. Perhaps it wasn't *her* family matter, but it was the closest reason to the truth she could offer.

"What kind of family matter?"

Tessa worried she was running out of time before Mercy began crying. "It's private, so I'd rather not discuss it. I'm sorry you'll miss your trip. At least it wasn't something you were anticipating for a long time, so I hope you'll get over your disappointment quickly."

Melinda's eyes widened. It was clear she was curious but since Tessa had put her foot down firmly and Melinda probably understood she couldn't get more information out of her, she resorted to cajoling. "Joseph's the one who will be disappointed. He always talks about how willing you are to help. Wait until he finds out you turned down the chance to work for an entire day without even really giving a reason. He's going to feel slighted."

Tessa recognized Melinda was only trying to manipulate her, but her comments hit a nerve anyway. What if Joseph really was offended Tessa didn't fill in for her? And what if he decided he didn't want Tessa to come back to her job when business increased? The efforts she'd made to stay in Willow Creek would be for nothing—she'd end up back in Shady Valley after all. *But*

Joseph would never fire me over something like that.
Would he? she wondered. Right then she resolved to pray
that wouldn't happen but to accept it if it did. It would
break her heart, but she'd rather lose her job and have
to return home than to let Turner down when he was
this close to finding Jacqueline. Tessa's commitment to
him—and to Mercy—was more important than her own
plans and desires.

"That's not my intention at all and I'd feel terrible
if he was offended," Tessa finally replied. "But Joseph
understands about family commitments, so I think it's
unlikely he'll feel put out. If anything, I'd think he'd feel
slighted by you, since he gave you the privilege of working full time instead of me, and now you'd rather go to
a party than honor your work commitment."

Melinda looked dumbfounded and Tessa took advantage of her silence to say, "As I mentioned, I'm cooking
supper, so I need to say *gut nacht* now, Melinda."

She could hear Melinda stomping down the stairs
like a child throwing a tantrum, so when heavy footfalls
sounded on the porch a few minutes later, she assumed
her coworker had returned to badger her again.

"I'm sorry, but the answer is still *neh*," she said as she
swung the door open.

"What was the question?" Turner asked. He was
standing alone but he was grinning—a good sign.

"*Ach!* Turner, *kumme* in," she prattled. "You look
pleased. Did you find Jacqueline?"

"Not yet, but I'm getting closer," he announced, wiping his feet.

"That's *wunderbaar* news!" Without thinking,
she reached out and squeezed his arm for emphasis.

In response, he placed his hand over hers and gently squeezed back.

"*Jah*, it is," he agreed exuberantly.

Sensing everything was about to change, Tessa memorized the way she felt with Turner's large calloused hand enveloping hers while the baby cooed happily in the next room. When she could preserve the moment no longer she pulled away, saying, "How about if you go get Mercy while I put supper on the table? Then you can tell me all about your trip."

Whether it was from what he'd just discovered concerning Jacqueline or from the silkiness of Tessa's fingers beneath his, Turner felt lighter than he had in years. It was as if all the tension he ever carried in his head, jaw and neck had metamorphosed into a fluttering hopefulness, and he was bursting at the seams to share his exciting news with Tessa.

She insisted on holding Mercy so he could eat, and he dug into his plate of shepherd's pie with gusto. In between bites, he recounted his interaction with Artie, ending by telling Tessa how confident he was he'd see Jacqueline the next day.

"I'm sure she's in need of money, so she'll be there," he said, helping himself to a second serving of pie.

Tessa placed her prayer *kapp* strings over her shoulder so Mercy couldn't yank them as she fed the baby her bottle. "Your *mamm* is going to be surprised at how pudgy you are now, little *haws*," she said to the baby.

"That's provided I can persuade her to *kumme* home," Turner said. When Tessa squinted, biting her lip, he asked, "What's wrong? You look doubtful."

"I have no doubt you'll find Jacqueline. But is talking to her the most effective way to persuade her to return?"

Turner was baffled. "What do you suggest? I can't *insist* she return and I'm not going to call the authorities."

"Of course not. But have you considered bringing Mercy with you?" Tessa asked. "My intuition tells me it was excruciating for her to leave this little *bobbel* the first time, and as soon as she sees her *dochder* she'll never want to part with her again."

"Aha. And since Jacqueline doesn't have a job to support a baby, much less to support herself, she'll be more than willing to return home." Turner marveled at the wisdom of Tessa's suggestion. "That's a terrific idea."

Tessa moved the baby to her knee and tapped her back until Mercy released a most unladylike belch. Turner and Tessa both chuckled.

"There is a favor I'd like to ask," Turner said. "Would you be willing to *kumme* with us?"

Tessa didn't hesitate. "Sure. I'd be happy to keep Mercy calm during the trip."

"It's not just Mercy you keep calm—I feel more tranquil in your presence, too."

A smile dawned across Tessa's features. Turner was pleased she seemed to accept his compliment. "Please pass the salt," she said as she scooped shepherd's pie onto her plate.

"Salt?" he taunted, holding the shaker just beyond her reach. "This meal is perfectly seasoned. Why do you need salt?"

"Perfectly seasoned? You should tell my *mamm* that," Tessa replied, tugging the salt shaker from his fingers. "She doesn't exactly consider me to be a very *gut* cook."

"Really? I knew you didn't *like* to cook, but there's

no question in my mind you *can* cook. Your meals prove otherwise."

"*Denki*, but only a bachelor could say that about my meals," Tessa teased. "According to my *mamm*, the reason I'm not being courted and haven't gotten married yet is because of my culinary skills. 'The way to a man's heart is through his stomach,' she always says."

"I hardly think your cooking is the reason you aren't married yet," Turner said.

"*Neh?*" Tessa asked coyly. She paused to lick gravy from her fork. "So what you're saying is there are far more obvious reasons a man wouldn't want to court or marry me?"

"*Neh, neh,* I didn't mean it that way!" Turner protested. "I only meant the meal is very *gut.*"

Tessa's eyes met his. "I'm glad you like it."

"I like you very much." Chagrined, Turner immediately corrected himself. "It. I like *it* very much."

To distract Tessa from his blunder, he quickly changed the subject. "So, are you going to tell me what you meant by what you said when you answered the door tonight?"

When Tessa was done explaining about how Melinda asked her to cover her shift at the shop, Turner said, "*Ach!* As much as I appreciate you turning down a shift to watch Mercy, in the future please do what's best for you. If you wanted to work tomorrow, I would have found a way to watch Mercy. That's one of the advantages of being a business owner—especially a business owner whose brothers recently took time off from work. They owe me extra hours at the shop."

"But what excuse would you have given them?" Tessa asked.

"It would have taken a little creativity, but I would have worked it out."

"Speaking of working it out," Tessa began, "Katie can't meet me for supper on Wednesday evening, so she wants to meet me on Friday night instead. I already told her *jah*, but now that we're so close to finding—"

"Don't be *lecherich*. There's no need to cancel on Katie. Who knows? By Friday evening, we both might be eating supper with our sisters!"

"*Gott* willing," Tessa said.

But the following evening, after arriving early, parking at a gravelly rest area across the street from the convenience store and waiting for what felt like days, they still hadn't spotted Jacqueline. Instead, they witnessed a handful of adults who appeared to be customers going into and out of the store, as well as several youth, including Chloe, who entered and exited a couple of minutes later with their hands shoved into their pockets or clutching their purses. Meanwhile, Mercy's fussing erupted into a full-scale lamentation. It seemed the more her volume increased, the more Turner's hopes decreased.

"I need to stretch," he said and leaped down from the buggy. Treading back and forth along the shoulder of the road, he trained his eye on the door to the convenience store. Turner didn't wear a watch, but he figured it was at least seven, maybe later. Hadn't Artie said the employees needed to collect their pay by seven fifteen, no exceptions?

Right when he was about to rejoin Tessa in the buggy, Turner noticed a silver car pulling into the lot. It parked halfway between the buggy and the mini-mart and it was angled in such a way it partially obscured Turner's view of the store's entrance. Since the driver got out on the other side of the car to enter the shop, Turner couldn't get a good look except to notice it was a male. *Why hasn't Jacqueline* kumme *yet?* he wondered, shaking his head.

A moment later, a large man exited. Turner would have recognized Artie's shape anywhere. The manager plodded to a sports car, squeezed into the front seat and drove away. Recalling Artie's rule that payday was over once he left the premises, Turner's hopes were completely dashed.

"Turner!" Katie stepped down from the buggy, clutching Mercy. "Look! Isn't that the kind of car the person who dropped off Mercy was driving? I'm almost sure—"

Turner didn't wait for her to finish. He raced across the lot and reached the vehicle at the same time a curly-haired young man wearing shorts came out of the store.

"Skylar!" Turner shouted, stepping in between the man and his car. "I need to talk to you about my sister, Jacqueline."

"Sure, no problem," the man replied, but they were interrupted by the sound of the baby's diminished cries and Tessa's approaching footsteps. "Is that Mercy I hear?"

So Tessa was right: Skylar *was* there the night Mercy was dropped off. Or at least his car had been. Turner nearly committed the sin of physically harming another person when he gripped the young man by his shoulders, spinning him so they were eye to eye. "What do you know about my sister's baby?"

"Turner," Tessa cut in. A car had driven up and its high beams illuminated the two men.

Turner released his hold on Skylar. "Why don't we walk over to my buggy to talk?"

"That's a good idea. Let me ask my wife to join us," Skylar said. Until that moment, Turner hadn't realized a woman was sitting in the passenger's seat. Opening the door, Skylar bent down and said, "Charlotte, these folks want to talk to us about Jackie and Mercy."

The woman emerged from the car and she and Skylar glanced over their shoulders at the convenience store before accompanying Turner and Tessa to the buggy, where Charlotte and Tessa facilitated an awkward round of introductions.

"What do you know about my sister's baby?" Turner repeated impatiently. "Did you leave Mercy on my doorstep or do you know who did?"

"I understand the situation is upsetting, but if you give me a moment, I'll tell you everything I know," Skylar promised. He explained how he and Charlotte led a kind of underground ministry for runaway teenagers. Skylar worked at Artie's because he believed the best way to help kids in trouble was to build relationships with them. Since Artie mostly employed minors who didn't have work permits, the store was an ideal place to reach youth who needed help, although Skylar had to be careful Artie didn't find out about their ministry.

Turner was skeptical. "You have a ministry for Amish runaways?"

"For *any* underage runaways," Charlotte answered. "We primarily help *Englisch* kids, but you'd be surprised how many Amish teens we come into contact with, too."

Turner *was* surprised to hear that, but his urgent concern was finding out more about Jacqueline, not about their ministry. He pushed them to answer his questions.

"We don't know where she lives—she was extremely guarded about it," Skylar told him. "Charlotte and I left Mercy with you at Jackie's request. She was conflicted about whether she was going to return home or try to start over in Philadelphia."

Turner's blood was boiling. "You said you *help* runaways. How is separating a *mamm* from her *bobbel* and her family helpful? What gives you the right to—"

Tessa cleared her throat, which Turner recognized as a reminder to keep his temper in check. He let his sentence drop.

"You've misunderstood, Turner," Charlotte said softly. "We weren't trying to *separate* Jackie and Mercy. We were trying to keep them together. Jackie was... She was in a bad way. Whether it was reasonable or not, her biggest fear was social services might take the baby from her. We asked if anyone in her family could care for Mercy until she was thinking straight again. Meanwhile, she had to get a job to support herself."

"Our hope for her was that she'd reunite with her family and her Amish community," Skylar asserted. "Unlike some of the kids we meet who suffer abuse at home or who are struggling with addiction—and worse—we knew Jackie comes from a stable, loving family. It seemed the only thing keeping her from returning home was her sense of shame."

"We spoke with her about the forgiveness we have in Christ," Charlotte said. "And she told us she'd repented and asked for God's forgiveness, but she was having a difficult time forgiving herself."

Skylar concluded, "She seemed to miss her family and community a lot. So when Artie fired her, we thought for sure she'd finally return home."

"She didn't," Turner stated flatly, his voice hoarse. He was so deflated he feared he might cry in front of everyone.

"It's possible she'll show up for one of our Sunday night dinners again. If not, we'll continue to keep our eyes peeled for her," Charlotte offered. "We have contacts throughout the state, so if we find out she's left the area, we can enlist their help, too."

"Yeah, we'll definitely do that, but my guess is without her final pay she probably can't afford a bus ticket," Skylar reasoned. "So she won't go far. Not unless she borrows money from someone."

Turner was willing to clutch at any straw of hope. "That might be true…"

"On the off chance she does borrow cash or had any savings, you might want to stake out the bus depot," Skylar suggested, pulling out a cell phone. He tapped the keyboard before lifting the phone to his ear. "What time does the bus run to Philadelphia from Highland Springs?" he asked. "Monday, Wednesday and Friday nights at seven thirty-eight? Okay, thanks."

Turner blew air through his lips. Zander said she was fired on Saturday, so the first bus she could have caught left on Monday evening. They might have missed her by a day.

Tessa immediately offered consolation. "I think Skylar's right—she probably doesn't have the means to leave. But just in case, there's another bus running tomorrow night. We can watch for her on that one."

Turner massaged his neck. It seemed he was no closer to finding Jacqueline now than he'd been when she first left Louisa's, and he was exhausted.

"Why don't we head back to Willow Creek, Turner? We can check the phone shanty for messages on the way," Tessa coaxed.

"All right," he agreed. Then he clapped Skylar's

shoulder, shook Charlotte's hand and said, "*Denki* for all you've done. I'm sorry for taking such a hostile tone."

"I understand," Skylar replied, handing him a small card. "It's my phone number and address. Keep in touch so we can update you on what we find out."

Charlotte produced a pen and slip of paper so Turner could jot down his address for them, too, but Turner hoped there would be no need to contact each other. He prayed that, when he returned home, he'd discover Jacqueline had used the spare key they'd always kept hidden by the birdfeeder and she was waiting in the parlor for Mercy and him. Barring that, he hoped he'd at least have a message from her at the phone shanty.

But there was no hint at either place to indicate his sister was still in town. And since Tessa insisted on keeping the baby with her another night, Turner's house, like his heart, felt particularly empty and stark, so he dragged himself upstairs and collapsed into bed.

Chapter Eight

❧

For all the emotional toil Turner was suffering, Tessa was glad Mercy was none the wiser. The baby could almost manage to roll over from her back to her tummy—no small feat, considering her plumpness. She drew her knees to her belly and then kicked her legs straight, using the momentum to twist her lower body to the side, but her head and shoulders didn't follow, so eventually she'd fall to her starting position again. Tessa giggled as she watched her try repeatedly until Mercy finally became so frustrated she let out a holler, as if to accuse Tessa of not helping her.

"It's just as well you don't roll over for the first time yet," Tessa said, scooping her up. "Your *mamm* will want to be around to witness it when you do."

Mercy was drooling and pulling her ear again, sure signs her gums were bothering her. Since Tessa was accompanying Turner to the bus depot that evening, perhaps on the way they could stop to purchase a teething ring. "Meanwhile, I'll do my best to make you comfortable," she cooed to the baby.

Figuring her time caring for the baby was nearly over,

Tessa wanted to make the most of every moment, and she nuzzled her cheek against Mercy's soft hair. Even after Mercy fell asleep, Tessa held her, memorizing the strawberry pucker of her mouth and the fleshy roundness of her cheeks, until her arms were nearly numb and she had to lay the baby in her makeshift crib.

It's not as if I'll never see her again. Tessa tried to assuage her loneliness so she wouldn't start weeping again. *If Jacqueline is as overwhelmed as Skylar and Charlotte indicated, she'll probably be glad to have me care for Mercy from time to time.*

She padded into the kitchen where she opened the icebox and considered preparing stew for supper. She and Turner could bring it with them in thermal mugs and eat it while they waited at the bus station. Or was that a bad idea? Did it seem like she was making a picnic of an occasion that felt more like...well, not like a funeral exactly, but like a hospital visit? Given Turner's state of mind the previous night, Tessa wondered if he'd even be able to eat. His disappointment had been almost tangible as they'd traveled from Highland Springs to Willow Creek. She'd taken no offense when he'd hardly spoken, because she could barely form a sentence, either.

Like Turner, she'd been positive they'd catch Jacqueline at the convenience store. If Tessa felt so woefully letdown when they didn't, how must Turner have felt? No wonder he seemed pessimistic about going to the bus depot tonight—after so many stymied attempts to locate his sister, he probably had to keep his expectations in check. Admittedly, it seemed unlikely to Tessa they'd see Jacqueline there, either, but she wanted to be encouraging so she urged Turner to give it a try.

Deciding against making stew after all, Tessa peeked

in on Mercy and then donned her cloak to dart down the lane to the mailbox. Valentine's Day was the following Monday and she had several cards ready to mail to her cousins in Indiana. She chortled when she removed the pile of mail that had accumulated in the box; it was a good thing her mother couldn't see how negligent she'd been in collecting it. After depositing her cards and raising the red metal flag on the side of the box, she strolled toward the house, flipping through the letters to separate hers from Turner's, since he apparently had forgotten about the mail for several days, too. Not surprisingly, most of them were hers, including one from her mother postmarked the day before.

Once inside the *daadi haus*, she put a kettle on for tea and then sat down in a square of sunlight to read her mother's letter, hoping the envelope didn't contain its usual number of recipes for her to try.

Dear Tessa,

My hand is shaking as I write this letter. This morning I crossed paths with Melinda Schrock in the mercantile.

Tessa's own hand began to tremble; she had a feeling about what was coming next.

You can imagine my shock when she expressed concern about our "family matter" that kept you from covering a shift at the shop!

While I'm sure you'll come up with an excuse for not telling your father and me you were temporarily relieved from your duties at Schrock's, I can think of no justifiable reason why you'd lie to Melinda in order to avoid returning to work when the opportunity presented itself.

Not only is deception harmful to your relationship with God, but it undermines other people's trust in you, as well. You've long insisted you're mature enough to live on your own, but your recent behavior indicates otherwise. Your father and I have discussed the matter and we believe you'll behave more responsibly if you live with us, where we and our community can support you by holding you more accountable for your words and actions.

As a courtesy to Joseph, you may work for the next two Saturdays. By then he should be able to find someone else to fill your part-time role. We will pick you up after your shift ends on Saturday, February 19, but of course we hope for an apology before then.

Your loving (but disappointed) Mother

Tessa wanted to scream, but instead she ripped her mother's letter in half and then ripped it in half again and again and again. *How's that for immature behavior?* she railed to herself. She rose to her feet and turned the gas burner off; she was too upset to drink tea. She was too upset to do anything, except pace from the kitchen to the parlor and back again, stewing.

She should have known this was coming; after all, she had taken her chances when she turned down Melinda's shift. At the time, losing her job was a sacrifice she'd been willing to endure for Turner and Mercy. But deep down she'd doubted Joseph would feel so ruffled Tessa turned down a shift that he'd fire her. In the event she miscalculated and he did let her go, Tessa had counted on her ability to finagle another arrangement that would convince her parents she still needed to stay in Willow Creek—even if that meant being courted by Jonah. Or David. She'd never imagined the scenario she was facing now. Knowing things would turn out this way, Tessa still would have made the same decision again if it meant helping Turner find Jacqueline, but she was stunned by the reality of what the decision had cost her.

It suddenly occurred to her Melinda had gone to Highland Springs on Monday even though Tessa had refused to take her shift, which meant Joseph had been left shorthanded at the shop. Tessa had automatically assumed Melinda would have forgone her trip rather than to put her employer—and her relative—in that position. Then another thought struck Tessa: What if Melinda had never actually told Joseph that Tessa had turned down the opportunity to work? What if she'd simply allowed him to think Tessa would be there? If so, when Tessa failed to show up at the shop it would have looked like Tessa was the one who didn't honor her commitment. Under those circumstances, Tessa wouldn't have been surprised if Joseph fired her before she had the opportunity to tell him she was moving back to Shady Valley.

Sitting back down at the table, she buried her head in her arms. *What does it matter if I leave Willow Creek? There's nothing for me here anyway*, she lamented. Not only was she going to lose her job, but she was about to lose Mercy, too. As for Turner, well, she never had him to lose in the first place.

I might as well resign myself to becoming Tessa Umble and making pot roasts for Melvin while he tin-

kers away on his buggy, she thought. But then she decided if returning to Shady Valley was the price she had to pay for helping Turner find his sister, she was going to make their efforts worth her while. She blotted her eyes with her apron, stood up and resolved to do whatever it took to reunite Mercy with her mother. And if Tessa had anything to say about it, she was also going to enjoy Turner's company while she still could.

"How was your visit with Rhoda's family?" Mark asked Patrick during their dinner break on Wednesday.

"It was enjoyable, but my stomach aches."

"You think you caught the bug?" Mark questioned.

"*Neh*, my stomach aches because every time I turned around, Rhoda's *mamm* was sliding another plate of food under my nose. I ate so much I'm surprised I could finish my sandwich just now."

Mark chuckled. "I face the same problem—Ruby's *mamm* always tempts me with food, too, which wouldn't be so bad, but Ruby is just like her. If this keeps up, I'll gain another ten pounds before summer." Mark patted his bloated stomach for emphasis.

"Some problem," Turner muttered. His brothers didn't know how blessed they were.

"What was that?" asked Mark.

"I don't think being well fed is something to complain about," Turner retorted. "You're fortunate your wives and their *mamms* are so attentive. Not everyone has someone in their lives to help provide for their physical needs as well as to encourage them emotionally and spiritually."

"I wasn't really complaining," Patrick protested. "I meant it more as a joke."

"*Jah*, well, it wasn't funny. *Kumme* on. Let's get back to work."

Turner noticed his brothers exchanging baffled looks before he walked away. He knew he was being irascible, as well as unfair. Mark and Patrick would have willingly shared the burden of Jacqueline's situation with him if Turner had told them about it. And he was just as blessed as they were—he had Tessa's help and support. But try as he did, he could neither release his anger about his circumstances nor summon any enthusiasm about going to the bus depot that evening. So, his own willpower failing him, he prayed, *Lord, please help me change my attitude. And please give me hope to keep searching for Jacqueline, just as You keep pursuing us when we turn astray. Lead her home, Lord.*

God must have answered his prayer tenfold, because by the time he arrived on Tessa's doorstep, he was humming with eagerness for their trip to the bus depot to begin.

"Hello, Turner. I didn't expect you quite this early. If you'll take Mercy to the buggy, I'll get my cloak and we can be on our way." Tessa's eyelids were puffy and her nose was pink, but she smiled at him before turning away.

When the trio was snugly situated in the buggy, Turner angled toward Tessa. If she felt ill or was upset, he wanted to give her the option of staying behind. "Are you okay?"

"*Jah*," she said. "Why do you ask?"

"You seem a little tired," he replied. "Or as if you've been crying."

Tessa shook her head, not looking at him. "It's nothing. I'm fine."

"You're fine now, but you were upset earlier today, weren't you?" Turner asked. In the near dark he could see Tessa's profile but he couldn't read her expression. "Don't you want to tell me what was troubling you?"

"*Jah*, but not now. It's a long story."

"Please?" Turner countered.

Tessa covered her face with her hands and cried. "I'm sorry. I told myself I'd keep my composure."

Knowing there was plenty of time to get to the bus depot before boarding began, Turner set the reins on his lap. Then he did something that surprised himself: he pulled Tessa's hands away from her eyes and gently turned her head so she was facing him. "No matter what it is, you can trust me," he whispered, "the way I've trusted you."

Tessa tucked her chin toward her chest and shook her head, sobbing harder. "Not yet," she uttered. "We have to find your sister."

No. For once Turner was determined to put Tessa's needs above his own need to find his sister. "Then you'd better tell me soon, because we're not leaving until you do," he said tenderly.

In tearful snippets, Tessa described her interaction with Melinda and the letter she'd received from her mother that afternoon demanding Tessa return to Shady Valley the following Saturday. When she was finished, she sat straight up again and sniffed, saying, "I'm sorry. You really didn't need to hear my problems when you've got enough burdens of your own."

"My burdens have *caused* your problems," Turner replied remorsefully, stroking his jaw. "If you weren't helping me, you wouldn't be in this predicament."

"That's not true!" Tessa declared. "If it weren't for

you and Mercy, I would have had to leave Willow Creek weeks ago, because I wouldn't have been able to make my rent payment *and* buy groceries. A person can only survive for so long on pasta, you know."

Turner chuckled in spite of how guilty he felt. He'd seen enough evidence of Tessa's determination to know she would have found another way to meet her financial responsibilities if she'd had to. He was far more indebted to her than she was to him, and he was determined to help her stay in Willow Creek. Not just because he felt he owed her that much, nor because he might still need her to care for Mercy, but because he couldn't bear the thought of her leaving. "There's got to be a way we can convince your *eldre* to change their minds."

"I'm sure I'll think of something," Tessa said, although her voice lacked conviction. "For now we'd better get on the road if we want to get to the depot on time."

"All right." Turner wished there was something else he could say to buoy Tessa's mood the way she always encouraged him. But words failed him so instead he passed his handkerchief to her, picked up the reins and signaled his horse to walk on.

Inwardly, Tessa doubted there was anything she could do to stay in Willow Creek now that her *mamm*'s mind was made up. To be fair, Tessa acknowledged she hadn't been forthcoming about her situation to her parents, even if she'd withheld information for good reason. But right now she couldn't dwell on her own situation, lest she start blubbering again. As commiserating as Turner was, she didn't want to break down in front of him twice in one night. She was determined to be a help, not a hindrance, especially since she feared their trip to the depot wouldn't result in a reunion with Jacqueline, and Turner would need as much succor as she could offer.

"Ah-ah-ah," Mercy sang from her basket, snapping Tessa out of her thoughts.

"Someone's happy to be traveling," Tessa said. "Mercy loves being on the move. Have you noticed she's almost able to roll over now?"

"*Neh*, I haven't seen her try that yet. But I have noticed she's almost too big for some of her clothes."

"You're right," Tessa agreed. "*Ach!* I forgot—I meant to ask if we could stop on the way to the depot to get her a teething ring. I think her gums may be a little worse."

"Maybe on the way back," Turner suggested. "I don't think we'll have enough time now."

It felt so natural talking about mundane errands with Turner that Tessa quickly forgot her embarrassment about crying in front of him. The closer they got to the bus depot, however, the quieter Turner became. The depot was nothing more than a square building containing a ticket booth, two bathrooms and a row of plastic seats bolted to the floor on the periphery of the room. Passengers could enter and exit the depot from a door on one end and make their way to and from the buses through the door on the other end.

"Why don't you and Mercy wait in here where it's warm and I'll go talk to the bus driver," Turner said. "I should be right back, but *kumme* find me if you spot any young women with long, dark hair. It might be *gut* to stay off to the side. I'm afraid if Jacqueline catches a glimpse of the baby, she'll know I'm here and she'll turn around and leave before I have a chance to speak to her."

Tessa nodded, even though she suspected that with her Amish attire and Mercy's babbling, which sounded especially loud in the high-ceilinged room, they were too conspicuous to be overlooked. She chose a seat affording a view out the glass door so she could watch Turner speaking to the bus driver beneath a bright overhead light. Even from a distance she could tell how tense he was by the way he massaged the back of his neck.

A few minutes later he reported the bus had just arrived from Peaksville and it was being cleaned before continuing on to Philly. No one was allowed to board until seven twenty. He said passengers could reach the bus by coming through the depot or by walking right up to it from outside. He decided to stand outdoors while Tessa and Mercy waited inside to be sure they wouldn't miss Jacqueline at either location.

Tessa watched as passengers trickled through the door. Some bought tickets at the booth; others took seats or milled about the room. She saw a businessman, an older couple and a family of five, as well as three women who appeared to be college age. When a dark-haired woman who appeared to be in her fifties and was wearing a prayer *kapp* entered the building, Tessa's heart skipped a beat. She and Turner had been so focused on finding Jacqueline, they hadn't considered what they'd say or do if they bumped into someone else from their district. Fortunately, Tessa didn't recognize the Amish passenger as being from Willow Creek. From then on, she kept her head lowered and her gaze focused on Mercy, except to furtively scan the area whenever the door opened and another person entered.

As small as the depot was, the attendant made his announcements over a loudspeaker. "Now boarding, Highland Springs to Philadelphia," he said and then repeated himself.

Tessa's heart raced. *Please, Lord, let Jacqueline show up. Please, please, please*, she pleaded silently as she wiped the drool from Mercy's chin. Tessa had put a cloth in her tote for soothing the baby's gums, but she didn't want to go wet it with cold water for fear Jacqueline would arrive while they were in the restroom.

"Now boarding, Highland Springs to Philadelphia," the attendant announced again, even though everyone except Tessa and Mercy had already filed outside. The loudspeaker crackled with static and Mercy began to whimper.

Please, Lord, I don't think Turner can take the despondency of being disappointed again, Tessa prayed. Then she got up to pace, gently joggling the baby as she circled the room. She avoided looking through the glass door—if Turner was in view, she didn't want to see the expression on his face.

"Final call for all passengers traveling from Highland Springs to Philadelphia," the man in the booth said twice and Tessa winced at the words.

A few minutes later she felt the rumble of the bus pulling away from its bay, and shortly after that a burst of cold air swept through the room when Turner opened the door. His hat was angled so Tessa couldn't see his face, but she didn't have to see it in order to know how he felt.

"Let's go," he said, his voice so low at first she wasn't sure he'd said anything at all.

Tessa stayed planted where she was. "Are you sure? Maybe she's running late. Maybe she'll show up in a minute, hoping she didn't miss the bus."

"*Neh*, she won't." Turner picked up the tote and walked to the door, holding it open for Tessa to pass through.

"I'm sorry, Turner," she said once they were on the main thoroughfare.

"Me, too."

There was nothing more either of them could say, but Mercy cried for the next ten minutes, as if to speak for them both.

"Why are we stopping here?" Tessa asked when they pulled up in front of an *Englisch* store that sold groceries, home goods and clothing.

"For the teething ring, remember? I'll calm Mercy if you'll go in. And if you see pajamas in the next size, please get a couple of pairs of those, too. There's no sense postponing it. She's growing fast." Turner handed Tessa a couple of bills.

Tessa heard the forced nonchalance in his tone, but she understood his need to focus on practical matters and deny his despair because she had tried to do the same thing that morning after reading her mother's letter. His pain would come out sooner or later and Tessa hoped she'd be there to listen to him express it, just as he'd been there to listen to her.

"I'll be right back," she said as she disembarked the buggy.

She'd hardly taken four steps through the automatic doors when she heard someone from behind calling, "Tessa! Wait up!" It was Rhoda, Patrick's wife.

"Hello, Rhoda. How are you? Chilly evening, isn't it?" Tessa spoke rapidly, hoping to distract Rhoda from asking any questions in return.

"It's not so bad because we turned the heater on," Rhoda replied. "That's one of the really *gut* things about being married to someone who knows everything there is to know about buggies. Patrick modifies ours for as much comfort as the *Ordnung* allows. Does Turner have a heater in his buggy, too?"

"Turner?" Tessa played dumb.

"*Jah*, didn't I see you getting out of his buggy just now? Patrick will want to say hello to him before we leave."

"*Neh!*" Tessa responded sharply. "That's not a *gut* idea right now. He's…he's…" She was at a complete loss for an explanation.

"Sorry for the wait," Patrick said to Rhoda as he breezed through the doors. "Oh, hello, Tessa."

"Hello, Patrick," Tessa replied. "Don't let me keep the two of you. I think the store closes at nine."

If Tessa waited until the couple walked farther into the store, she could run back to the buggy to warn Turner. That way they could leave before Patrick and Rhoda came out to talk to him. They'd find out about Mercy soon enough, but tonight of all nights, Turner was in no shape to tell them about the baby and Tessa was going to do her best to help protect his secret for as long as she could.

"*Neh*, doesn't close until ten," Rhoda corrected Tessa. To Patrick she said, "Tessa and I are having a little chat, so you go ahead in and look for those work gloves you need. I'll meet you near the checkout counter."

Tessa sensed Rhoda wasn't going to let her question about Turner go ignored, so she confessed, "You're right, that was Turner's buggy you saw me get out of. He was so kind as to transport me here, since there's something I urgently need to buy and this is the only store that carries it."

Rhoda raised her eyebrows, leaned forward and

touched Tessa's arm. "It's okay, Tessa, I won't tell any-one, not even Patrick. Your secret is safe with me."

"Tell them what?" Tessa asked, doubting there was much of anything Rhoda wouldn't tell.

"You know." Rhoda winked. "I won't tell them Turner is courting you."

"Pah!" Tessa sputtered, the air knocked out of her.

"Don't look so nervous," Rhoda giggled. "I mean it when I say I won't tell. After the last time you and I spoke at church, I had a very unpleasant experience be-cause someone implied something about me that wasn't true. I believe the Lord used the situation to show me how harmful my own nattering could be. I'm sorry for anything I've ever repeated that I shouldn't have, and I'm committed to not sharing other people's information in the future. Even if it's something *wunderbaar*, like the news you and Turner are walking out. Trust me, you'll see. With *Gott*'s help, I'm keeping my lips sealed."

Tessa uttered the only words she could manage, "*Denki*, Rhoda," before hightailing it away from her.

Even though he had directed the horse to the farthest corner of the parking lot, Turner sat in the back of the buggy where he could cradle Mercy without being seen by any passersby. He was glad to have a few minutes to gather his wits; he'd been close to either punching some-thing or crying back at the depot. The act of pacifying Mercy was calming to him, too.

"I know you're upset," he sympathized with the baby in a low voice. "We both are."

Upset didn't begin to cover the range of emotions he felt right then. He was also angry, grieved and down-cast because they hadn't found Jacqueline—doubly so because of Tessa's news. He didn't know what else he could do to search for his sister and he hadn't any clue about how to help Tessa stay in Willow Creek, either. He felt so powerless he couldn't even muster the will to pray.

"Giddyap," he said to Mercy, bouncing her on his knee. "This is how you ride a horse, Mercy, up and down, just like this. Giddyap."

By the time Tessa returned, the baby was squealing with delight. Turner felt a small measure of satisfaction knowing he could at least make his niece happy, even if he couldn't solve the other problems he faced.

"Quick," Tessa urged, taking Mercy from him. "We have to leave right away, before Patrick *kummes* out of the store."

Turner scrambled to take his seat again. In his haste, he momentarily forgot about his disappointment; he just wanted to flee before his brother finished shopping. When they'd put a good distance between themselves and the store, Turner eased up on his horse.

"That was close," Tessa said. "Here's your change. And an oversize heart-shaped cookie cutter."

"An oversize heart-shaped cookie cutter? Why would you buy me such a thing?"

In his peripheral vision, Turner saw Tessa dabbing drool from Mercy's chin with a cloth. "I crossed paths with Rhoda. She saw me getting out of your buggy, so I told her you brought me here to help me find a special item. Which you did, right?"

"Technically, I suppose I did. But what has that got to do with the cookie cutter?"

"I couldn't very well purchase a teething ring and baby pajamas with Rhoda and Patrick in the store because they might have seen me. But they also might have seen me leave without buying a specialty item. So, I purchased the first thing I saw that I knew the mercantile doesn't carry. I'll pay for it and keep it myself if you don't want it."

"Don't be *silly*," Turner chuckled. "Of course I want it. What man doesn't want a heart-shaped cookie cutter?"

Tessa laughed, too. "Mind you, it's not just *any* heart-shaped cookie cutter—it's an *oversize* heart-shaped cookie cutter!"

"I'm sure this will *kumme* in very handy when I host my annual Valentine's Day party," Turner joked.

"Your annual Valentine's Day party? Why haven't I ever been invited to that?" Tessa crossed her arms as if she was pretending to feel slighted.

"Because this is the first year I'm having it," Turner replied without missing a beat. Then it was as if all of the tension he'd held pent up inside him came rushing out in the form of laughter. He cracked up so long and hard he thought he might need to bring the horse to a halt.

"Don't tell me—Mercy and I will be your only guests," Tessa jibed.

"*Neh*, just you. Unless Mercy's tooth cuts through by Monday, she won't be able to eat the oversize heart-shaped cookies I plan to bake."

Tessa giggled and wiped the corner of her eye with her free hand. "There's something else I have to confess about my discussion with Rhoda. I hope it doesn't offend you."

Turner was curious. "What's that?"

"First off, let me assure you she absolutely promised not to tell anyone and I think she'll honor her word."

Now Turner was worried. "She couldn't have found out about Jac—"

"*Neh, neh*, she doesn't know anything about Jacqueline," Tessa said. "But because I told her you'd given me a ride to the store, she made the assumption you were courting me."

"That's all?" Turner asked. "Why would that offend me?"

"Because I didn't deny it. I allowed her to think you wanted to keep our courtship a secret, otherwise she would have brought Patrick over to the buggy to greet you."

"While I'm sorry my circumstances put you in that position, I understand. But as long as you're not upset about Rhoda making that assumption, then neither am I."

"I'm not upset," Tessa confirmed, repositioning Mercy on her lap.

Why? Because it isn't true so it doesn't matter what Rhoda thinks, or because you'd accept me as a suitor? Turner wondered. Merely discussing a courtship between them caused warmth to course through every fiber of his body. Turner was too flustered to say anything else until they'd almost arrived home.

"In spite of not finding my sister tonight, it felt so *gut* to laugh. *Denki*, Tessa, for helping me through such a difficult time." Turner wanted to say more, so much more, but what words could express the depth of his feelings?

"I'm not gone yet and we haven't found Jacqueline yet, so I'm not done helping you," she reminded him. "I intend to accompany you to the depot Friday evening, too."

"I'm glad," he said, but the knot in his throat at the mention of her leaving Willow Creek was so large his sentiment was barely audible.

As he brought the buggy to a stop in front of Tessa's place, she offered to keep Mercy overnight again. But

Turner knew what a blow it had been for Tessa to receive her mother's letter that morning and he figured
she needed a good night's rest. When he said as much,
she didn't argue. So the baby wouldn't get too cold, he
dropped Mercy and Tessa off at the *daadi haus* while
he stabled the horse.

When he walked into the parlor, Tessa had just finished changing Mercy's diaper. He looked down at the
baby, who was batting her arms and kicking her legs as
if trying to get their attention.

"You're a happy *maedel*, aren't you? Is that because
your *mamm* is coming home soon?" Tessa asked and
Turner was heartened by her positivity. Tessa grinned a
wide grin at Mercy and ran her fingers up her tummy,
repeating, "*Jah*, you're a happy *maedel*, aren't you?"

Just then Mercy made a giggling noise. Turner and
Tessa both looked at each other, raising their eyebrows.
"Did she just laugh?" he asked.

Right on cue, Mercy undeniably gave them the sweetest laugh he'd ever heard.

"She did! She laughed!" Tessa said and she and Turner
spontaneously threw their arms around each other.

Turner wished the moment—and the embrace—would
never end. Right then he wanted to kiss her more than
he ever wanted anything—even more than he wanted
to find Jacqueline. Yet the very thought of his sister reminded him why he couldn't entertain any more notions
of romance, so he dropped his arms and in a single motion lifted Mercy from where she lay.

"Say bye-bye to Tessa," he instructed Mercy, but he
felt as if he could have been speaking to himself.

Chapter Nine

Tessa squirmed beneath her quilt, trying to find a position that would facilitate sleep. So much had happened that day she didn't know how to make sense of it all.

Instead of focusing on the upsetting events she couldn't control and problems she couldn't solve, she tried to reflect only on the good parts of the day. Such as the moment when Mercy laughed, and especially the moment after that, when she and Turner embraced. As if those two occurrences weren't splendid enough, there was a third happening in the sequence—the moment when Turner's face was so close to hers, and his eyes were filled with such yearning, Tessa had been certain he was about to kiss her. The mere thought of his lips on hers made her catch her breath; if he had actually kissed her, she probably would have fainted from bliss.

Of course, he hadn't actually kissed her. They hadn't actually found Jacqueline. And she was nowhere near coming up with a reason strong enough to convince her parents she ought to stay in Willow Creek.

As her thoughts looped back to the dilemmas she and Turner were facing, Tessa allowed herself to consider the possibility it might be a long time before he found his sister; worse, he might never locate her. Either way, Turner eventually would have to tell his family and the community about the baby. Rhoda or Ruby might care for Mercy on occasion, but who was better suited to be her full-time nanny than Tessa? She didn't have to divide her attentions between other familial responsibilities like they did. Surely her parents would allow her to remain in Willow Creek to care for a baby who was essentially orphaned, wouldn't they? Just as she drifted into sleep, Tessa envisioned another possibility: Turner would ask to marry her and the two of them would raise Mercy together as their own...

But in the bright sunlight of a new day, Tessa realized how preposterous her wish was. When Turner knocked on her door, his forehead was ridged with worry lines and Tessa suspected romance was the last thing on his mind, much less marriage.

"Is it okay if I'm a little late collecting Mercy tonight?" he asked.

"Absolutely. I'd also be happy to keep her overnight again if that would be more helpful."

"*Denki*, but that's not necessary. I only need you to watch her so I can stop by the convenience store. I want to give Artie a note for Jacqueline in case she shows up there for some reason."

While Tessa was glad Turner was demonstrating renewed determination to find his sister, she was dubious about his plan. Since Charlotte and Skylar indicated Jacqueline was wrestling with other types of shame, Tessa imagined the girl would also be too embarrassed to return to the store after being fired. Besides, Artie said payday was one day and one day only. So what reason would Jacqueline have to go back there? But Tessa supposed anything was possible; besides, Turner needed as much encouragement as he could get, so she held her tongue.

Turner seemed to know what she was thinking. "Don't worry about me getting my hopes up," he said. "I don't believe she's going to visit the store, either, but I'll feel better if I do something instead of just waiting until it's time to go to the bus depot again."

"Why would you assume I'm worried? I'm *glad* you're keeping your hopes up!" Tessa protested.

This time it was a smile that caused Turner's forehead to wrinkle. "You didn't say you were worried, but you were thinking it," he bantered. "I'm getting better at reading your expressions, Tessa."

With Turner gazing at her like that with his big, soulful eyes, Tessa completely lost her train of thought and she couldn't come up with a witty response.

Fortunately, Mercy butted in. "Ah-ah-ah-ah."

"*Jah*, we see you. We know you like to be the center of conversation," Tessa said with a laugh and Mercy squawked in response. Glancing back up at Turner, Tessa asked, "Would you like to eat supper here tonight? I have all the makings for stew. I can let it simmer, so it won't matter what time you arrive."

Turner accepted her invitation, and then cupped Mercy's fat cheeks in one hand and kissed the top of her head good-bye. After he left, Tessa carried the baby into the parlor, where she pointed out the window at the tree branches swaying in the wind and the sun dappling the frozen ground with shadows. Tessa neglected her housework to hold, play with and sing to Mercy for the rest of the morning.

"There will always be floors to sweep and windows to wash," she told the baby, "but you and I won't always be togeth—" She couldn't bring herself to finish the sentence aloud. If Turner could keep his hopes up about his situation, she could keep her hopes up about hers.

Later, when she'd put Mercy down for her afternoon nap, Tessa chopped vegetables and cut the meat for the stew. She was cleaning up when she suddenly remembered Katie was supposed to visit her the following night for supper and it was Tessa's turn to cook. *But I told Turner I'd go with him to the bus depot*, she fretted. She'd have to go tell Katie tonight she needed to cancel. Since it probably would be late when Turner returned, perhaps he'd offer to give her a ride to Katie's house after supper. Tessa smiled at the thought; traveling side-by-side with Turner beneath the moonlight was so romantic, no matter their destination. But what excuse would she give her sister for canceling? Then she remembered Katie had an appointment with the doctor on Wednesday afternoon; surely she was eager to talk to her sister privately about the outcome. Tessa didn't want to hurt Katie's feelings, nor did she want to let Turner down. What was she going to do?

After brooding about it through the rest of her household chores, Tessa realized she'd have to tell Turner about the predicament. Meanwhile, there was nothing she could do now except to pray, and once she did, she felt so reinvigorated she decided to bake a pan of lemon squares. This might be one of his last opportunities to taste them. Maybe he'd be so pleased she took the time to make her specialty dessert for him, he wouldn't be able to resist kissing her.

"Ach!" she said aloud. "I'm becoming more like my *mamm* every day!"

"Rhoda called on us early this morning to say Patrick has the stomach bug and he won't be here today," Mark said after removing his hat and hanging up his coat. "I guess it wasn't his mother-in-law's cooking making his belly ache yesterday after all."

"Jah. He was well enough to be out and about last night, so that means the worst of it probably hit him during the early morning hours," Turner said, distracted by the paperwork mounting on the desk in the corner of the shop.

"What were you two doing out and about last night?" Mark asked.

Turner jerked his head up. What did Mark mean, "you two?" Had he seen Tessa and Turner on the road? Aloud he asked, "What?"

"You just said Patrick was out and about last night. Where did the two of you go?"

Turner exhaled. "Nowhere. Not together, anyway. I crossed paths with him at the *Englisch* store in Highland Springs."

Dodging questions, hiding Mercy and trying to outpace Jacqueline's movements was wearing Turner out. He wondered if it was time to tell his brothers about the situation. Not only for his sake, but because they probably didn't know what to make of his ups and downs and he owed them an explanation for his recent moodiness. But, illogical as it was, he felt if he didn't tell them, it would mean he hadn't given up hope—hope that Jacqueline would return and hope that Tessa would be able to stay in Willow Creek. For a fleeting moment he again allowed himself to think of courting her...

"Did you hear me?" Patrick questioned loudly.

"Sorry. What did you say?"

"I asked if you want me to make the wheel delivery tomorrow morning."

"*Neh*, I'll do it," Turner replied. "And unless any new repairs *kumme* in this afternoon, let's get this order finished and then you can call it a day. I'll stay here and catch up on the accounting."

"Really?"

"Don't look so surprised," Turner chuckled. "I haven't been that demanding lately, have I? *Neh*, don't answer that. Just leave early and take your wife out to supper. You deserve a break and Ruby does, too."

Mark left at three thirty and Turner took advantage of the hushed environment to tackle the paperwork he'd put off. His progress was slow, however, and he barely made a dent in it before it was time to head to the convenience store. Tearing a piece of paper from a pad, he wrote:

Dear Jacqueline,

If you are planning to leave the area, I'd urge you to reconsider. You didn't have a choice about losing your parents, but you do have a choice about your daughter losing her mother. Mercy needs you. God forgives you. And Patrick, Mark and I love you. We'll work things out together.

Please come back to us.

Your brother,
Turner

He folded the sheet thrice and slid it into an envelope, which he sealed. Then he hitched the horse to the buggy and journeyed to Highland Springs, arriving in the lot at the same time Artie was parking his car.

The stocky man held his hands up. "She didn't come in for her pay, so I haven't seen her," he stated gruffly before Turner had a chance to greet him.

"I know. I'm here to ask if you'll give her this if she does stop by." Turner extended the envelope.

Artie shook his head but accepted the letter. "You're not going to give up, are you?" he asked.

"*Neh*. Not yet," Turner answered. *Although sometimes I sure feel like it.*

Artie galumphed into the store and Turner returned to his buggy. Although he hadn't performed much physical labor in the shop that day, Turner was tuckered out. At least he had Tessa's and Mercy's smiles to anticipate seeing at the end of his trip. But when he sat down to share Tessa's savory stew with her, her eyes appeared lusterless and she was quieter than usual.

"Patrick was out sick today," Turner said conversationally toward the end of their meal. "He came down with the stomach flu. I'm relieved you and Mercy haven't caught it."

"I guess that's one *gut* thing about being so isolated—we're not exposed to as many germs," Tessa replied as she rose to take their plates to the sink.

So, was that what was wrong? Was she tiring of being alone in the house with the baby all day?

"Is something on your mind?" he finally asked, holding Mercy while Tessa brought dessert to the table. She paused in the middle of pulling back the tinfoil covering the pan.

"*Jah*, I'm afraid there is." She reminded him that earlier in the week she'd agreed to meet with Katie for supper on Friday. "She's going to arrive at five and she usually only stays for an hour or an hour and a half at most. But if she doesn't leave until six thirty, that will be cutting it pretty close for us to get to the depot in time. I think I should cancel our supper altogether, but I don't know what excuse to give her."

Thinking it would be unfair for Tessa to change the plans she'd made with her sister so he could keep plans he'd made concerning *his* sister, Turner said, "*Neh*, don't cancel your supper. As long as Katie leaves by quarter of seven, we'll have time to spare. In fact, even if we encounter a brief delay on the road after that, we'll be fine. But if your sister stays longer than expected and you can't *kumme*, Mercy and I will make the trip by ourselves."

"I don't know." Tessa was biting her lower lip. "Are you sure about this?"

"It's all settled." Turner wiped Mercy's nose with a napkin. "So stop looking so concerned. For a minute I thought you were going to tell me something awful had happened. Like that you'd burned dessert."

Tessa's countenance lifted noticeably and a mischievous twinkle lit her eyes. "*Neh*, lemon bars are the one thing I rarely burn," she said as she cut a large piece for him. "But I'm warning you—they're extra lemony, so they'll make your lips pucker."

She blushed as soon as she said the words, as if she'd just had the same thought he did—the thought that had nothing to do with lemons, but everything to do with lips.

As Mercy slept on Friday afternoon, Tessa surveyed the food in her cupboards and icebox. She wanted to make beef stroganoff, but she discovered she didn't have any noodles in the pantry—that was a switch! She figured she could serve the stroganoff over mashed potatoes instead, until she found she didn't have any potatoes, either. She realized she had little choice but to make a haystack supper, which essentially consisted of seasoning whatever meat and veggies she had on hand and serving them over a layer of crushed crackers. Then she'd top the "haystack" with salsa and cheese. Not the fanciest meal she'd ever prepared, but Katie wouldn't mind.

When she finished chopping onions, she melted a thick pat of butter in a pan and added the onions to it. As she worked, she considered whether or not she should tell Katie about the letter from their mother. On the one hand, she thought it was only fair to prepare her sister for the probability Tessa had to return home. On the other hand, if Katie confided the doctor confirmed she was with child, Tessa didn't want to dampen her sister's joyful news. Besides, there was still time to think of some way to convince her parents she needed to stay in Willow Creek, wasn't there?

Tessa sighed heavily. She wouldn't tell her sister tonight, but she knew she ought to give Joseph the courtesy of telling him tomorrow—if he didn't fire her first. For the fourth time that day, tears rolled down Tessa's cheeks. She reflexively lifted her hand to brush them away and the onion juice on her fingers stung her eyes, causing her to weep harder. She was in the bathroom washing her face when Mercy began crying in the bedroom. The baby had soaked right through her clothes and the bedding was wet, too. Tessa knew she wouldn't have time to bathe her before Turner arrived to pick her up, so she used warm water and a cloth to clean her as well as she could. Mercy was not pleased.

"Uh-oh, Mercy," she said in a singsong voice, trying to mollify her. "It looks like we're out of clean *windle*. I need to dash to the basement and get a fresh one, okay? I'll be right back, little *haws*."

But Mercy was screaming so loudly Tessa didn't want to put her down. Because the diapers were hung so high she had to stand on her tiptoes to reach them, Tessa knew she wouldn't be able to unclasp them from the rope while holding Mercy. Instead, she one-handedly fished through the tote bag she used to carry Mercy's belongings.

"Sh-sh-sh," she said, bouncing Mercy, but the baby's cries escalated. Exasperated, Tessa dumped the tote over so she could see at a glance whether it contained any diapers. Fortunately, there was one left. As Tessa finished changing Mercy, she smelled something burning and she tore into the kitchen. Nothing was aflame but the onions were blackened and smoking in the pan. Careful to angle Mercy away from the burner, Tessa turned off the gas. At that very moment, Turner knocked.

"*Kumme* in," she shouted louder than she intended as she rinsed the pan under the tap. A cloud of steam rose around her, causing her eyes to water even more.

"Here, let me help you," Turner said when he entered, lifting Mercy from her arms.

"*Denki.*" Tessa excused herself to go into the washroom, where she washed her face a second time. *I'm a wreck*, she thought as the mirror reflected her pink nostrils, blotchy cheeks and mussed hair. At that moment, she wished Katie wasn't coming over and Mercy and Turner would just leave already. She would have preferred to spend the evening taking a hot bath, eating a store-bought pizza she heated in the oven and working on her final Valentine's Day cards.

Instead, she dried her eyes and took a deep breath. When Tessa returned to the kitchen, she found Mercy cooing to Turner. *That little scamp!* she thought wryly.

"Sorry about that," she said. "One minute I was chopping onions and the next minute…" She spread her arms to indicate the chaos.

"You must be tired," Turner replied. "Even if Katie leaves in time, are you sure you want to *kumme* with me tonight? I could go alone. It might be better if you stayed here with Mercy anyway. I can see her tooth is almost breaking through. It might make her cross."

"Neh!" Tessa answered sharply. She felt guilty for thinking it, but at that moment she decided if she couldn't stay home alone, she didn't want to stay home at all: she needed to get out of the house. "We made our plans and we should stick to them. I'll meet you at your house by six forty-five at the latest—if I don't, it means Katie is still here and you and Mercy should leave without me."

Turner seemed to be scrutinizing her and he scratched the back of his head, but he didn't argue. As soon as he and Mercy left, Tessa regretted the tone she'd taken. Then she walked into the parlor and saw the contents of the tote strewn across the floor and she became irritable all over again. First because she'd made a mess and second because Turner had neglected to ask for the tote, which contained items he'd probably need for Mercy during the next couple of hours. "Do I always have to be the one to remember everything?" Tessa grumbled.

She returned Mercy's belongings to the bag and then scoured the kitchen, washroom and parlor twice to be absolutely sure her sister wouldn't find any trace of Mercy.

Then she crammed the bag under Katie's bed since Katie would never have reason to look under there. As long as she was on her knees, Tessa figured she'd better pray; otherwise, she was likely to snap at Katie just as she'd snapped at Turner.

When she was done asking the Lord for grace, as well as for Jacqueline to arrive at the bus depot that night, Tessa stood up. But Katie's bed looked so inviting she thought she'd steal a fifteen-minute catnap before starting supper—rather, before starting it a second time. *A little sleep and I'll be as fresh as a daisy*, she thought as her head sunk into the pillow.

The next thing she knew, someone was pounding on the door. She sat up, dazed. Her sister usually tapped the door twice and then walked right in. Had Turner come back for the tote bag? Tessa hoped not: she could only imagine how disheveled she appeared. Trying to pin her prayer *kapp* into place, she swung her legs over the bed and scurried toward the door. The pounding continued and then she heard footsteps scurrying from the porch; Turner probably was afraid of being caught at her house by Katie, so he didn't want to wait any longer.

"Don't go. I'm here," she announced, swinging the door open. But he'd already left. She took a step out onto the porch. "Turner!" she called, just as she glimpsed movement from the corner of her eye.

"Surprise!" a chorus of voices shouted. Suddenly several people were singing "Happy Birthday" to her.

Tessa stayed frozen where she was, one foot inside the house, one foot outside. *I must be dreaming*, she thought. *This can't really be happening.*

But sure enough, when they'd finished singing, Katie, Mason, Faith, Hunter, Anna, Fletcher and, last but not least, Jonah gathered around her, laughing at what Tessa knew was the stunned expression on her face. She managed to squeak out the words, "*Denki*, everyone, but my birthday isn't until next Friday."

"We wanted to surprise you by celebrating early. And it looks like we did!" Katie was practically warbling with delight.

"Are you going to invite us in or are you just going to stand there gawking?" Mason ribbed and Tessa moved to the side to let them pass.

Once indoors, Katie directed the men into the parlor and then she, Anna and Faith bustled around the kitchen, uncovering the dishes they'd prepared and pulling plates from the cupboards. Tessa absentmindedly washed the burned onions from the pan, trying to surmise a reason they had to leave by six forty-five. She couldn't. It would be too insulting, too ungrateful. Turner was going to have to go to the depot without her, and he was going to have to bring Mercy with him. *But her gums are sore. She needs me to comfort her and Turner does, too*, Tessa thought, and a tear trickled down her cheek. She felt as if she'd abandoned them both.

"The birthday *maedel* needs to freshen up," she said. Katie followed her as she darted to her room.

While Tessa let her hair down to brush it, Katie confessed. "I...I got a letter from *Mamm* and I know you did, too."

Tessa nodded, not trusting herself to speak.

"That's why I wanted to have a party now, instead of next week. It's kind of a last-ditch attempt to help you get to know Jonah."

Tessa shook her head. "It's too late for that," she said

as she gathered her hair into a bun. "I think it's time to give up."

"*Neh*, not yet. I'm going to tell *Mamm* she has to let you stay here because next fall Willow Creek will be short a teacher again. If you have a suitor *and* a job, she's sure to change her mind."

Tessa clapped her hand over her open mouth. Willow Creek would need a new teacher? That could mean only one thing: Katie would be resigning because she was with child. Tessa had been so shocked by the surprise party she completely forgot to ask about Katie's doctor appointment.

"Katie! What a blessing!" she exclaimed and encircled her sister with her arms. Tessa doubted their mother would change her mind, even if Tessa did wish to become the new teacher and Jonah wanted to walk out with her. But for Katie's sake she said, "*Denki* for the party. And, who knows, maybe your plan will work."

Katie beamed. "Great. But if you're going to capture Jonah's attention, you might want to put on another dress first. Otherwise he'll be focused on that blotch on your shoulder instead of your winning smile."

Tessa peered sideways at her shoulder, which was damp with Mercy's drool. Her arms suddenly ached with loneliness. She could have started weeping again but her eyes were already puffy enough, so instead she changed her dress and then joined the others in celebration.

Turner was getting nervous. It was six thirty. He couldn't wait any longer to hitch his horse to the buggy; maybe by the time he was finished, Tessa would be walking up the lane. He bundled Mercy and carried her to the stable in the basket, which he secured in the back of the buggy and then hitched the horse. Still no Tessa. He waited a few more minutes, figuring he could guide the horse into a swift trot if necessary. He had really hoped Tessa would be able to accompany him, but when he feared he could wait no longer, he started down the lane.

As he approached the *daadi haus*, Turner noticed lamps shining from several windows. Then he spotted Katie and Mason's buggy secured to the hitching post he and his brothers built primarily for Katie and Tessa's use back when they still had a horse. *I wonder why Katie hasn't left*, Turner mused. *Of all evenings, it had to be tonight that she chose to stay late.*

He sighed as Mercy fussed behind him. He assumed she was irritable because her gums hurt, but without Tessa's input, he couldn't be certain. He hoped once they were on the main road, the motion of the buggy would calm her. He was nearing the end of the lane when he spied a buggy hitched to the fence straight ahead, blocking his way. He brought his horse to an abrupt stop. Who would have been so rude as to block the lane and so reckless as to tie a horse to a flimsy fence railing instead of to the hitching post?

Then it dawned on him: whoever was in his way was a guest at Tessa's house. It was probably one of the Fishers' relatives or their friends from out of state joining them for supper, because anyone local would have known the lane was shared by both Turner and Tessa; it wasn't meant for Tessa's use alone. Now what was he going to do? Time was of the essence. He couldn't leave Mercy alone in the dark buggy at the end of the lane, nor could he risk Tessa's guests seeing her. Since fencing lined both sides of the narrow lane, there wasn't enough room at this particular juncture to turn the buggy around. So he directed his horse to walk backward toward the *daadi haus*.

It was a slow process, but when he arrived at a spot close enough for him to keep an eye on the buggy, he jumped out of the carriage and bound up the porch steps. He repeatedly rapped the door. A moment later, Tessa appeared.

"Turner, you're still here! What's wrong?" she asked in a surprised voice. "Is Mercy—"

"Hush!" He put his fingers to his lips. What was she thinking? Her guests could have heard her.

"Who is it, Tessa?" Katie asked over Tessa's shoulder. "Oh, *gut*, it's Turner. I haven't seen you for a long time. Please, *kumme* join our party. We were just about to serve cake. Faith Schwartz baked it, so you know it will be *appenditlich*."

"*Neh*, I can't," he gruffly declined. "There's somewhere I need to be and one of your guests is blocking the lane."

"*Ach*, that must be Jonah's buggy. I'll get him."

When Katie left the room, Tessa hurriedly whispered, "I'm so sorry I can't go with you. You see, my sis—"

Turner cut her off. "No need to explain, but tell *Jonah*—" Turner practically spat out Jonah's name "—to hurry it up. I'll be waiting outside." Over his shoulder he added, "And in the future, I don't ever want to find a horse hitched to the fence again."

Turner wasn't angry simply because the buggy was blocking his way; he was also miffed because the fence wasn't at the correct height to tether a horse. The animal could become agitated and try to rear, snapping the wooden rail and injuring itself.

Furthermore, he was piqued Tessa was hosting a party

when she'd promised to accompany him to the depot. He knew she wouldn't have deliberately misled him about her plans, so he suspected she'd made the party arrangements long ago and had since forgotten about them. Even so, she knew how important it was for him to get to the depot in time. She should have made doubly sure there were no obstacles to slow him down. Better yet, she shouldn't have invited a guest who was so irresponsible and inconsiderate he'd tie his horse to a fence railing unsuited for hitching purposes.

A very tall young man jounced past his buggy. Jonah, no doubt. Turner couldn't help but speculate about whether he was also at Tessa's the night the group played Cut The Pie. It seemed to take him forever to reposition his horse and buggy, but once the lane was finally clear, Turner wasted no time hurrying past him and onto the main road.

Turner's horse accelerated into a swift gallop and within minutes, Mercy's whining subsided. He knew without looking at her she'd fallen asleep. Turner's jaw ached but he pleaded aloud with the Lord to deliver him to the depot on time or else to delay the bus's departure.

When they arrived, he rapidly but securely hitched his horse and lifted Mercy from her basket. She stirred but didn't wake. He clutched her to his chest with both arms to shield her from the cold and sprinted to the bus depot.

Panting, he asked the ticket booth attendant, "Has the seven-thirty-eight bus to Philadelphia left yet?"

"Yes, sir. It departed right on time. You missed it by two minutes."

Groaning, Turner shut his eyes and pinched the bridge of his nose. He felt as if the room was tilting. He couldn't fall over, not with Mercy in his arms. Steadying himself against the ledge of the ticket counter, he asked, "Did you notice if a teenage girl boarded it? She would have had long dark hair and she was probably traveling alone. She's slim and about this tall." Turner indicated the height of his shoulder.

"I see so many passengers after a while they start to look alike," the attendant said. "But, yes, there might have been someone matching that description who boarded the bus. I only remember her because she counted out her change down to her last dime in order to purchase the ticket. She must have been awfully desperate to get away from here."

Turner staggered backward as if he'd been shoved. His voice reverberated in the empty room as he repeatedly moaned, *"Neh, neh, neh!"*

Jolted awake, Mercy raised her voice, too, so Turner returned with her to the buggy, where he tucked her into the basket as she continued to holler. He wanted to holler, too. His disappointment this time was threefold: he was disappointed in his sister, disappointed in Tessa and, dare he think it, disappointed in God. It was time to give up searching and praying he'd find Jacqueline, and it was definitely time to stop depending on Tessa or imagining any kind of romantic future with her. *I'm all done*, he thought and headed for home.

Chapter Ten

Tessa waved to her guests from the porch, calling "*Denki* for the *wunderbaar* party!" Her cheerfulness belied how bad she felt about Jonah blocking Turner's path.

But how could he have known she shared a lane with Turner? The two times Jonah visited the property it had been too dark for him to see that the lane continued past the *daadi haus* and up the hill. According to her sister, Jonah had traveled alone, and she and Mason transported Anna, Fletcher, Faith and Hunter to the party. Katie had instructed Jonah not to bring his buggy to the hitching post at the *daadi haus* until after they sang, because if Tessa spotted it their surprise would be ruined. Jonah had intended to tie his horse to the fence for only a minute, but in all of the excitement, he'd forgotten to return to it and move his buggy.

It was a perfectly understandable mistake, but Tessa didn't blame Turner for being brusque. He was probably already on tenterhooks when Tessa hadn't shown up in time to accompany him to Highland Springs. But recalling that Turner said he'd have plenty of time even if he encountered a delay, she assumed he'd reached the depot before the bus departed. The question now was whether he'd seen Jacqueline or not. Was his sister up the hill right now, visiting with him? If she was, Tessa didn't want to interrupt them, but if Turner hadn't found her, Tessa wanted to offer consolation.

I know—I'll bring Mercy's tote bag up to the house. Tessa figured if Jacqueline was there, she'd give Turner the bag and leave them to their privacy. Otherwise, she'd stay to explain about the party and the fiasco with Jonah's buggy, and help Turner devise a new course of action. She pulled the tote from beneath Katie's bed, put on her cloak and hurried up the hill.

Before she had a chance to knock on the door, she heard Turner's voice from the other end of the porch. "Don't knock. You'll wake Mercy."

"You startled me," she said, making her way to him in the dark as a cloud passed across the moon. "Is… Is Jacqueline home?"

"Neh," he replied tersely.

"Ach, I'm sorry to hear that, Turner. And I'm sorry I couldn't accompany you. I was—"

"You were having a *wunderbaar* party, I know. I heard." In the moonlight, Turner's profile looked as if it was chiseled from stone; his jaw was hardened in an uncompromising line.

Despite Turner's accusatory tone, Tessa responded softly, *"Jah,* my sister and friends threw a surprise birthday party for me. I felt terrible I couldn't accompany you, but asking them to leave early would have been rude."

"Not half as rude as it was for them to block my way."

Tessa's eyes smarted but she understood how shattered he must have felt because Jacqueline wasn't at the depot a second time. She hesitantly explained, "Jonah didn't know we share the same lane. He moved the buggy as quickly as he could."

"It wasn't quick enough." Turner's voice was flinty with resentment when he said, "The bus departed two minutes before I arrived. Two minutes, Tessa. And according to the station attendant, Jacqueline was on it."

"Oh, *neh. Neh!*" A spasm gripped Tessa's stomach and she felt woozy. If she was this devastated, she could only imagine how Turner felt. She took a deep breath and said, "That's *baremlich*, but at least we know she went to Philadelphia. Skylar and Charlotte said they had contacts throughout—"

"Enough!" Turner yelled, facing her. "Enough is enough. I'm done looking for her, but even if I weren't, I don't want Skylar and Charlotte's help."

"Okay. We don't have to involve them. We'll find her ourselves. I still have a week here to keep helping you." Tessa touched Turner's shoulder but he jerked his arm away.

"*Helping* me?" he ridiculed. "If it weren't for *your* party, *your* guests and *your* insatiable need to have *schpass*, Jacqueline would be here right now! What kind of help is that?"

Now it was Tessa's turn to flinch. "What are you saying? You can't possibly be blaming me for *your* late arrival at the depot! You said you'd allow yourself plenty of time to get there, even if there was some kind of delay. Besides, I had no idea about the party and no idea about the buggy."

"Maybe not, but that doesn't make you any less responsible. A person is known by the company she keeps, and it's not the first time you've associated with someone who behaves in a harebrained, juvenile or otherwise feckless manner!" Turner pivoted to walk away, adding, "It's no surprise your *eldre* want you to *kumme* home where they can monitor your behavior."

Tessa darted ahead of him and planted herself in front of the door, glaring. Her words were like knives on her tongue when she snarled, "Do you want to know what's no surprise, Turner? What's no surprise is that your sister ran away and won't *kumme* home. Who would ever want to live with such a judgmental, unappreciative, boring old man?"

Then she pushed past him and stormed down the hill, slamming the door so hard the windows rattled. She marched straight to her bedroom, picked up her pillow, pushed her face against it and screamed until the back of her throat burned. She had dedicated the last three weeks to protecting Turner's secret and caring for Mercy, day or night, whenever he needed. She had risked her job so Turner could look for Jacqueline. And she had lost the privilege of living alone as a result of putting Turner's and Mercy's needs ahead of her own. How could Turner have the nerve to imply she'd rather have fun than help him find Jacqueline? How could he imply she was immature or undependable? Tessa covered her face with the pillow and screamed again.

Then she pulled her suitcase from the closet and flung her dresses, capes and aprons atop the bed. She yanked her good church prayer *kapp* from the peg on the wall and emptied her drawers of their stockings and hair pins. She wished she didn't have to wait until next Saturday to leave. She had half a mind to call her parents from the shanty and ask them to pick her up on Monday.

Turner won't last three days without me to help him care for Mercy, she gloated. But at the thought of leaving Mercy abruptly, just as Jacqueline had done, Tessa's emotions turned from outrage to anguish. She sat on the edge of the bed and a torrent of tears washed down her cheeks. She sobbed so hard she could barely breathe and she knew she'd make herself sick if she didn't stop.

By the time she washed her face and donned her night-clothes, Tessa was too drained to hang up the clothes and put away the items she'd flung on her bed, so she shuffled into Katie's old room. As she lay her head down, she felt a soft lump beneath her neck. She was about to turn on the lamp to see what it was when she realized she was holding the cloth Amish puzzle ball she'd made for Mercy. "My little *haws*, what are you going to do without me?" she murmured. "And what am I going to do without you?" Then she cried herself to sleep.

Turner checked on Mercy and then reclined on his bed with an extra pillow folded beneath his neck to ease the pain. It wasn't helping much but he wouldn't have been able to sleep anyway. After missing the bus's departure by two minutes, Turner didn't think he could possibly experience any more dejection that evening, but Tessa's words had wounded the rawest, most vulnerable part of him. They wouldn't have hurt so much if they hadn't been true: he'd always known if only he had been a better father figure or a stronger role model of their Amish lifestyle and Christian faith, Jacqueline would have made different choices.

As insufferable as that reality was, Turner had to face the fact he couldn't do anything about the past. But he could try his best to make sure he didn't fail Mercy the way he'd failed Jacqueline, and he resolved to tell his brothers and their wives about the baby. Since Patrick was still recovering and business was slow, Turner had told Mark not to come to the shop on Saturday, which meant Turner would have to wait to talk to his brothers until he could pay them a visit after church on Sunday. Together as a family, with counsel from the deacons, they'd decide what was best for Mercy. Although Turner still felt conflicted about betraying Jacqueline's confidence, in a way it would be a relief he didn't have to hide Mercy from his brothers or the community any longer. Now maybe he'd have someone other than Tessa to count on for help.

The next afternoon while Mercy napped, Turner opened the ledger he'd brought home on Friday so he could continue trying to reconcile their accounts at home. When he finished, he took a brief snooze until Mercy's jubilant babbling woke him. To Turner's surprise, when he entered her room, she was lying on her stomach. *Wait until I tell Tessa Mercy rolled over.* The thought instantly flitted through his mind before he remembered what happened the night before.

When he picked Mercy up, he noticed her clothes were damp. "Let's change your *windle* and then you can show me your new trick," he said as he searched her dresser for a clean diaper. When he couldn't find one, he brought the baby downstairs to check the tote Tessa left on his porch the previous evening, but he didn't find one there, either.

Turner glanced at the clock: it was a little past four. Tessa wouldn't be home from Schrock's until after five and Mercy's clothes were soaked through. Even if he could wait until Tessa returned, he didn't want to speak to her if he could avoid it. He wrapped the baby snugly and lifted the spare key to the *daadi haus* from the hook near the door. Ordinarily, he wouldn't think of enter-

ing the house without Tessa's permission, but he figured under the circumstances it was permissible. Tessa
wouldn't even have to know he'd been there.

Tessa trudged home from Schrock's, completely
spent. On the way to work that morning she'd planned
what she'd say to Joseph if he was upset about being
short staffed the previous Tuesday, as well as how she
was going to tell him she was resigning, in the event he
didn't fire her first. But when she arrived at the shop it
was Amity, not her husband, who greeted Tessa in the
back room. She said Joseph and the children had come
down with the stomach bug, as had Melinda and Jesse,
and she asked if Tessa could possibly manage the store
on her own.

"The shop only needs to stay open until the three-
o'clock-tour-bus customers leave. You know how important their sales are to our success," Amity had explained.

"Of course," Tessa had agreed. She owed Joseph that
much. Besides, waiting on customers would keep her
mind off her own queasy stomach, a nausea that wasn't
caused by the flu.

"*Denki.* Joseph said he knew he could count on you."
Amity had confided, "He wasn't pleased when Melinda
asked you to take her shift on such short notice, and he
was even less pleased when she went to Shady Valley
even though you couldn't cover for her."

While Tessa was relieved to discover Joseph knew it
wasn't her fault he was left on his own in the shop on
Tuesday, she'd been abashed at Amity's praise. Joseph's
gratitude was going to make it that much harder for her to
tell him she was leaving Willow Creek. She'd agonized

over it most of the day, and by the time the final customers left she had a headache as well as a stomachache.

She was slogging up the lane to the *daadi haus* when a female voice called, "Excuse me, please."

Standing beneath the big willow tree near the porch was an *Englischer*.

"Jah?" Tessa replied warily. The last thing she needed was for Turner to see another *Englischer* on his property. Who knew what conclusions he might jump to about "the company she kept."

"I'm looking for Turner King. I checked at the house but he's not there. Do you know if he's in town?" As the girl approached, Tessa caught sight of her eyes. She knew those eyes: they were Turner's eyes. Mercy's eyes. Tessa felt her heart fluttering within her ribs.

"He was here as of last night. He's probably running an errand," she replied, although she couldn't imagine him going out with Mercy. "Why don't you *kumme* inside with me to get warm while you wait for him."

Jacqueline nodded and followed Tessa indoors. Tessa offered the girl a chair by the wood stove in the parlor and then she put on a kettle for tea. As she waited for it to boil, she prayed that God would guide her conversation with Turner's sister. Tessa didn't know whether she should reveal that she knew who Jacqueline was or not. As angry as she was at Turner, Tessa had given him her word she wouldn't tell anyone she knew about Mercy, and Tessa figured that meant not telling Jacqueline, either.

"Sorry, the cookies aren't from scratch," Tessa said nervously a few minutes later as she carried the tray into the room. The men had gobbled up all of the homemade goodies the night before, so there weren't any leftovers.

"*Denki*. I like this kind," Jacqueline replied. Her hand trembled so much her teacup rattled in its saucer. Tessa was quiet, allowing her to lead the conversation. "How long have you lived here?"

"About two years. My sister lived here with me until she got married last November."

Jacqueline set her cup on the end table. "Then I believe you must know about my *dochder*, Mercy?"

Tessa's cheeks burned as she nodded.

"It's okay. From what my friends told me, I realize they'd taken Mercy to the wrong house. I don't care about any of that. I just want to know if she's all right."

Tessa nodded again before finding her voice. "She's thriving."

"Are you sure? You've seen her again since that night?"

"I… I've been helping care for her. Your *dochder* is just the sweetest baby. She laughed at us the other day for the first time. She can almost roll over and she's cutting a tooth. I'm Tessa Fisher, by the way," Tessa jabbered.

"I'm Jacqueline," the girl said, even though Tessa already knew her name. "*Denki* for looking after my Mercy while I was…while I was away. I'm glad Turner had your help."

"It was my pleasure. And rest assured no one else knows about you or the baby."

Jacqueline hung her head. "Turner must be so ashamed—I certainly am. I wouldn't blame him if he's really angry to see me traipsing back here again after leaving Mercy with him all that time."

"Angry to see you? Are you kidding me? Turner can't wait to see you!" Tessa knew she was raising her voice but she couldn't help herself. She had to impress upon

Jacqueline how keenly Turner wanted to welcome her home. "I don't think you have any idea how deeply he's grieved your absence and worried about your well-being! I don't think you understand how steadfastly he's searched for you!"

Jacqueline's eyes were tearful and her chin quivered, so Tessa rose, crossed the room and leaned down, placing her hands on the girl's shoulders. "Turner didn't tell anyone about the baby because of *your* request. He was also trying to shield you from gossip. Believe me, there were plenty of times when it would have been easier for everyone if he had disclosed your secret. But he didn't because he's so loyal and protective and loving. Angry? *Neh.* He's going to be *thrilled* to see you. There's nothing he's wanted more than to *wilkom* you home."

Jacqueline wiped her cheeks with the back of her hand. "I'm glad, because I've *kumme* back for *gut*."

"You have? That's *wunderbaar*!" Tessa spontaneously embraced the girl as if Jacqueline was her own sister and Jacqueline hugged her back. After they let go, Tessa started to say, "Why don't we—" but she was interrupted by a faint noise coming from the basement.

She jerked the door open to discover Turner standing at the bottom of the staircase with Mercy in his arms.

Shocked, Tessa yelped, "What in the world?"

"Ah-ah-ah," the baby chanted.

From the parlor, Jacqueline squealed, "Is that Mercy? My Mercy?"

Turner rushed up the stairs and squeezed past Tessa to get to his sister, who sobbed upon seeing her child.

"Mercy, my *bobbel*," she kept repeating, taking the

baby from Turner and kissing her all over her cheeks and head. "Look how you've grown!"

Meanwhile, Turner cried, "Oh, Jacqueline, how I've prayed for your return." He embraced both mother and child, closing his eyes as he hugged them. Tessa noticed a tear dribble down his face and she glanced away, feeling as if she was intruding on their reunion.

When he finally let go of Jacqueline and Mercy, Turner said, "Mercy needed clean *windle*, so I let myself in. Then I heard voices coming from upstairs and I didn't know who it was. Since I didn't want anyone to find out about Mercy, I just stayed where I was, hoping they'd leave. I didn't mean to startle anyone."

His tone was more informational than apologetic and Turner neither looked at Tessa nor addressed her by name, so she responded by simply murmuring, "Hmm," without looking at him, either.

He quickly said, "*Kumme*, Jacqueline, let's go to the house."

"Okay," she agreed. Her face was tear streaked. "Tessa probably doesn't want us blubbering in her parlor all evening. I'll change Mercy's clothes and *windle* at your house."

Turner glanced around the room. "Do you have a suitcase?"

"*Jah*, I left it on your porch."

At the door Jacqueline swiveled to face Tessa. "I can't express my gratitude enough, Tessa. Mercy is going to miss you. But you can *kumme* up the hill to visit us every day, can't she, Turner?"

"*Neh*, she can't," he said sharply. Opening the door, he explained, "She's moving next week."

But Tessa knew the real reason he didn't want her to visit. He shouldn't have worried; she had no intention of darkening his doorstep again until she returned the key to the *daadi haus*.

Bit by bit over the next several hours, Jacqueline told Turner about the *Englisch* boy she'd met during *rumspringa*. Once they learned she was with child, the boy dumped her. Jacqueline was so humiliated and ashamed she left Louisa's and secured a job as a live-in nanny for an *Englisch* Christian family in Ohio, who knew of her plight and provided her with medical care as well as room and board and nominal wages. Although they encouraged her to return home, Jacqueline was convinced once the baby was born, the boy would want to marry her. Instead, he denied knowing her and his parents threatened to call the police if she continued "stalking" him.

Disgraced and deserted, Jacqueline boarded a bus to Willow Creek, but on the way she lost her nerve and made it only as far as Highland Springs. She spent most of her savings to sublet a dingy room in a rundown house. After the landlady somehow found out Jacqueline was from an Amish family, she took to disparaging her faith.

Around that time—because she needed to save every cent she could for formula—Jacqueline began attending the free suppers Skylar and Charlotte hosted at their home. They encouraged her to stay in the area and think things over, even if she wasn't ready to return to her family. That's when she left the baby with Turner—or rather, Skylar and Charlotte did. Meanwhile, Jacqueline took a job at the store where Skylar worked. By then she was so ashamed and downtrodden, she figured Mercy would be better off without her, and she decided she'd board a bus and move to Philadelphia on her own. Right around the time she made up her mind to leave, she got fired.

"I'm so glad you didn't have enough money to pay for a ticket," Turner said, sighing heavily.

"Oh, I had enough money—*just* enough. And I mean down to the penny," Jacqueline replied. "In fact, I even bought the ticket. I was going to leave on the seven-thirty-eight bus last night."

Turner suppressed a gasp. "Then what stopped you?"

"I love Mercy too much," she said, gazing at the baby as she rocked her. "I'm so sorry for what I did. I know it was wrong. But that doesn't mean I regret giving birth to Mercy. It doesn't mean I don't love her with my whole heart."

"I know."

"Turner, I am so sorry for what I put you through, too. Will you forgive me?"

"*Jah*, I forgive you. Will you forgive me for…for failing you?"

Jacqueline's eyes flashed as if he'd said something insulting. "Failing me? How have you ever failed me?"

"I—I didn't know how to raise, how to guide you once you became a teenager. I probably made a lot of mistakes when you were younger, too. I'm to blame for—"

"For *nothing*!" Jacqueline stopped rocking the chair and leaned forward. "Turner, my running away had absolutely nothing to do with you. It had nothing to do with Ant Louisa. I was being headstrong. I was following my own will instead of *Gott*'s will for me!"

Turner was surprised by Jacqueline's perspective; she

demonstrated so much more accountability than he'd expected.

"Why do you think I left Mercy with you?" Without waiting for an answer, Jacqueline spouted, "Because I knew you'd be as *gut* of a parent to her as you have been to me."

Overwhelmed, Turner's eyes filled. After all this time of blaming himself for somehow failing Jacqueline, and after all this time of thinking he never ought to marry, he could hardly believe his ears when Jacqueline called him a good parent.

She continued, "And because of my upbringing, I realize it's time for me to grow up and admit my wrongdoings. So I've confessed them to the Lord and I'm prepared to speak to the deacons. I want to be baptized into the church, Turner. I want to raise Mercy the way you and Louisa raised me."

Denki, Lord, Turner prayed, wiping his sleeve across his eyes.

Jacqueline fawned over Mercy, "I can't get over how much you've grown. And look at that smile! Your *onkel* took *gut* care of you, didn't he?"

"I couldn't have done it without Tessa's help," he replied. Despite their argument the previous night, Turner had to give credit where credit was due.

"Hey, I know! Monday is Valentine's Day. Let's invite Tessa over for a special supper. We'll ask Skylar and Charlotte to *kumme*, too."

Turner hedged. "Uh, I don't know if that's a *gut* idea…"

"Why not? I'll take care of all the arrangements, I promise. Besides, don't you think we should do something nice for them, as a way of expressing our gratitude?"

Put like that, Turner couldn't say no, but he cautioned, "I don't know if Tessa will *kumme*. She probably has packing to do."

"She'll *kumme*. She's crazy about Mercy, and from the way she talks about you I would have thought you were courting her."

Turner coughed. "What? Why do you say that?"

"Well, for one thing, when I was nervous about how you'd feel about seeing me again, Tessa reminded me of how loving, protective and loyal you are. But it wasn't just what she said. It was also the way her face looked when she said it. You could tell she really meant it."

As Turner recalled their argument on Friday night, a searing pang of compunction rendered him speechless. At the same moment, the baby curled her fingers around Jacqueline's hair, which hung loose in an *Englisch* style.

"You'd better get used to that," Turner said. "She was always pulling Tessa's *kapp* strings and she's bound to pull yours, too."

"I don't mind at all. But I do mind that *schtinke*—I'd better change her *windle*. After I put her down, I think I'll turn in for the night."

Turner retired to his room, too, where he sat on his bed and mulled over his sister's remarks. Did Tessa really mean it when she'd said he was loving, loyal and protective? That wasn't how he had acted toward her on Friday night. That wasn't how she'd described him on Friday night, either. *Of course, she may have been speaking in anger, reacting to the vicious, unfounded comments I'd made about her*, Turner reluctantly admitted to himself.

It's time for me to grow up and admit my wrong-

doings, Jacqueline had said. How was it possible his seventeen-year-old sister was behaving more responsibly than he was? Turner dropped to his knees and spent the better part of the next hour confessing his transgressions and thanking God for bringing Jacqueline safely home. Before climbing into bed, Turner asked the Lord to ease the hurt he'd caused Tessa to suffer and to soften her heart toward him so they could be reconciled.

The next morning he traveled alone since his sister and the baby wouldn't be attending church until Jacqueline spoke to the deacon and bishop. He was glad to see Patrick sitting a few benches in front of him; Turner assumed he was no longer contagious, which meant he could carry out the plan to visit his brothers later that afternoon. After eating dinner and helping the other men stack and carry the benches to the bench wagon, Turner tried to track down Tessa, but by then she must have either left with Katie and Mason or walked home through the fields. He'd have to wait until evening to speak with her.

Turner stopped at his house only long enough for Jacqueline to climb into the buggy with Mercy. As they rolled down the lane toward the road, he sighted Tessa walking in their direction.

"Stop," Jacqueline demanded. "I want to tell Tessa about the party."

So Turner brought the buggy to a halt and held the baby while Jacqueline hopped down to speak with Tessa. He could hear their conversation clearly.

"*Guder nammidaag*, Tessa," his sister chirped. "I'm so glad I caught you, because I want to invite you to our Valentine's Day party tomorrow night at six o'clock."

Turner saw the look of utter disbelief on Tessa's face.

He wondered if he should step down and say something to encourage her to attend. But what would he say?

Jacqueline must have noticed her expression, too, because she pleaded, "Please *kumme*. After all you've done for me, the least I can do is have you as my special guest for supper."

"*Denki*, that's very kind, but I have chores to take care of before I leave."

Jacqueline wasn't giving up. "But Mercy has been asking where you are. She really wants to see you."

Turner chuckled: his sister was hitting Tessa's soft spot.

At that, Tessa conceded, "All right, but I won't be able to stay long."

"See?" Jacqueline said when she was seated beside Turner again. "I told you she'd *kumme*."

When they arrived at Mark's house, he and Patrick were astounded to see Jacqueline and they couldn't stop hugging her. Amazingly, neither Ruby nor Rhoda asked any questions—they were too busy oohing and aahing over Mercy. Before their visit was over, Jacqueline had invited all of them to the Valentine's Day party, too.

By the time they returned home, it was nearly nine o'clock and there were no lamps shining at the *daadi haus*. Disappointed, Turner slipped out onto the porch after Jacqueline and Mercy went to bed. He rubbed his jaw—why was it hurting so badly? He shouldn't be tense; he should be overjoyed. Jacqueline was home, safe and sound, which was the only thing he wanted. Or was it? Peering down at the darkened *daadi haus*, he had to acknowledge there was something else he desired: he desired to walk out with Tessa. But how could he? He didn't even know if she'd forgive him, much less accept him as a suitor. Not to mention, she was leaving Willow Creek in less than seven days.

Suddenly, Turner recalled Artie asking, *You're not going to give up, are you?* And he was emboldened by the memory of his own response, *Neh. Not yet.* Right then and there he decided he wasn't going to give up on his dream of courting Tessa. *Not yet*, he thought. *Not ever.*

But the next evening, as he waited for Tessa to arrive at the party, he felt his resolve giving way to nervousness. He didn't suppose he'd get a chance to talk to her in private until after the party, but he intended to try to put her at ease in his presence until then.

His brothers and their wives showed up first, followed by Skylar and Charlotte.

"I'm so glad you're here!" Jacqueline squealed when she saw them.

"*We're* so glad *you're* here," Charlotte answered.

Jacqueline ushered them into the parlor to meet the rest of the family, while Turner lingered in the kitchen until Tessa knocked on the door.

He grinned and said, "Happy Valentine's Day, Tessa."

"Hello, Turner," she replied, neither warmly nor coolly. "There's a car parked in the lane, but it's got nothing to do with me."

Remembering how harshly he'd spoken to her about Jonah, Turner felt his ears burning. "*Jah*, in daylight you'd recognize it belongs to Charlotte and Skylar. They're in the parlor."

"You've invited *Englischers* into your home?"

"Why not? As a very wise young woman once told me, they just have a different way of living out their faith than we do." Turner's remark elicited a quick smile from Tessa and his confidence surged.

During supper everyone complimented Jacqueline on the meat loaf, brown-butter mashed potatoes and broccoli bake she'd prepared, but by that time Turner had grown nervous again and he could hardly taste the food. For dessert the group devoured yellow cupcakes with red-and-pink buttercream frosting Rhoda purchased from Faith Schwartz's bakery, as well as strawberries dipped in chocolate Ruby brought. Afterward, the women shooed the men into the parlor. Turner tried to focus on their conversation to no avail, so he was glad when he realized the stove would need more wood soon and he went outside to fetch it.

By the time he'd returned, the women were sitting in the parlor, too, and Jacqueline was handing out slips of paper for a game of charades. Hoping he could be on Tessa's team, Turner set the wood in the bin. "Where's Tessa?" he asked, looking around.

"She just left. She said she had to call it an early night."

Turner didn't bother to excuse himself. He bolted out of the house, hurtled down the porch stairs and zoomed down the hill, reaching Tessa just as she was shutting the door behind her.

Breathless, he choked out the words, "Tessa, please wait. I need to talk to you."

She gave him a curious look but opened the door for him to pass through. They went into the parlor and she took a seat on the sofa. He knelt in front of her but she looked down at her hands instead of into his eyes. This time he hadn't rehearsed what he was going to say; he wanted it to come straight from his heart.

"Tessa, I am so sorry for the *baremlich* things I said Friday night. I didn't mean a word of them. I was so disappointed because I thought I'd missed Jacqueline and I needed to blame someone. So I blamed the Lord and I blamed you—the very ones who faithfully helped me all along. But the truth was, *I* was the one to blame. I didn't leave enough time to get to the depot because I kept hoping if I waited long enough, you'd be able to accompany me."

Tessa bit her lip and nodded. The delicate tip of her nose was turning pink and it seemed she might begin to weep, but instead she said haltingly, "I understand. And I...I forgive you, Turner." When she finally lifted her head, her expression was fraught with candor. "I'm sorry I called you judgmental, unappreciative and boring. You're not any of those things. I never once heard you condemn your sister the way most people in your situation would. You've always expressed your appreciation of me, in both word and deed. And I've never had such interesting conversations with a man as I've had with you."

A smile crept across Turner's face, but he still had more to say. "You've helped me so much these past few weeks, Tessa. Now it's my turn to help you. If you'll allow me, I'd like to speak to your parents."

"And say what?"

"Say what I should have said as soon as I found out about the letter you received from your *mamm*. I'll tell them about Jacqueline and Mercy. I'll say you're the most thoughtful, capable, mature woman I've ever met. Not only that, but your sense of *schpass* has lifted my mood when I've needed it most. I'll remind them they asked me to keep an eye out for you, but instead you kept an eye out for me." Turner paused to catch his breath. "I'll tell them how much I want you to stay here."

Tessa's eyes glistened. It felt like months had passed since the last time Turner beheld her face. "But why?" she asked. "Jacqueline is home now. You don't need my help anymore."

He swallowed, gathering courage. "I want you to stay because I want to court you, Tessa."

She blinked. She blinked again. A smile flickered across her lips, slowly at first, but then spread like wildfire from her mouth to her cheeks to her eyes, until all of her features were illuminated by its brilliance. "I want to be courted by you, Turner."

He kissed her then. And then again. When he pulled away he gently traced her exquisite nose with his fingertip.

"Do you know something?" he asked. "Your *mamm* is wrong."

Tessa knitted her eyebrows. "Wrong about what?"

"The way to a man's heart isn't through his stomach. At least, that's not the way to my heart."

Tessa giggled. "*Neh?* Then what is the way to your heart?"

"The way to my heart—" he murmured, pausing to kiss her a third time "—is through *your* heart."

This time, Tessa kissed *him*. "Happy Valentine's Day, Turner," she said.

Epilogue

"These cookies are enormous!" Jacqueline exclaimed to Tessa. "Where did you get such a big cookie cutter?"

"It was Turner's, if you can believe it," Tessa answered, winking at her husband before she bit into a heart-shaped confection.

"It's a *gut* thing Mercy's asleep, or she'd be asking for a bite," Jacqueline said, looking at Mercy, who had fallen asleep on her lap. She finished the last of her cookie and then slowly stood up, careful not to rouse her daughter. "*Denki* for supper, Tessa. It was yum-yum, as Mercy would say. I'd better head down the hill now."

"I'll walk with you back to the *daadi haus*," Turner offered.

Last year, after he and Tessa explained the situation with Mercy and Jacqueline to Tessa's parents, and in light of the fact Joseph restored Tessa's full-time schedule as well as gave her a promotion, Waneta and Henry agreed to allow their daughter to continue living in the *daadi haus*. When Turner and Tessa married in the fall, Jacqueline moved into the *daadi haus* and Tessa moved up the hill.

"Could you please retrieve the mail, too?" Tessa requested. She hadn't forgotten to collect it; she'd deliberately left it in the box for Turner to find.

She was rinsing the last pot when he passed through the kitchen with a stack of wood in his arms. A few minutes later he returned from the parlor, rested his chin on her shoulder and hugged her around the waist from behind.

"I love you," he whispered into her ear.

Tessa wiped her hands on her apron and turned to face him. Wrapping her arms around his neck, she said, "I love you, too." Eager to have him read the card from her, she barely paused before asking, "Did we get any mail?"

"One for you, one for me. I must be becoming more social—this is the first time I've ever received as much mail as you," Turner joked, holding a pink envelope above Tessa's head. "A kiss for the mail carrier first."

"Silly," she said, standing on her tiptoes to kiss him and grab the letter at the same time. "This one looks like it's from my *mamm*. Please let me read it before you open yours."

They moved to the parlor where Tessa sat beneath a lamp and Turner wiggled close to her on the sofa. The card had a picture of a cupcake on the outside. Printed inside was the message Hope Your Valentine's Day Is Extra Sweet. Tessa smiled at the irony: the card was store-bought instead of handmade.

On the back Tessa's mother had written a note, which Tessa silently read to herself:

Dear Tessa,

I trust this letter finds you and Turner well. Please give him warm regards from your father and me.

As you know, Katie, Mason and little Michael are here for a visit. Your brothers' children enjoy entertaining their newest cousin with silly faces and chasing him as he crawls around the house. It reminds me of how your brothers and sister used to dote on you when you were a baby.

To a mother, her children will always be her babies in some way, no matter how old they are. (You'll understand when you have one of your own.) We all wish you and Turner were here with us. We look forward to visiting you next.

Your loving Mother

PS The enclosed recipe for boneless pork roast with vegetables is from Bertha Umble. I think ten cloves of garlic is too much, so I only use half that many and it turns out fine.

Tessa dabbed her cheek; she was touched by her mother's sentiments. Even the recipe card made her lonely.

"Are you okay?" Turner gave her a squeeze.

"*Jah*, just a little homesick. Can you imagine—I'm homesick for Shady Valley?"

"We can go there whenever you want."

"*Jah*, it would be fun to surprise my *mamm* and *daed*," Tessa said. "Now it's your turn. Open your card."

Turner let go of her so he could open his mail and Tessa watched his expression as he pulled the card from its envelope. On the front, she'd used red and white construction paper to form two interlocking hearts. On the inside were three of the same type of hearts. Beneath them she'd written a rhyme:

Husbands are sweet.
Babies are, too.
I'll soon be blessed
And so will you!

Turner's mouth fell open as the meaning of the verse sunk in. "R-really?" he asked.

"Really," she confirmed.

"Oh, Tessa, my Tessa!" he shouted.

He hugged her so tight she giggled and said, "I can't breathe."

Turner immediately loosened his grip. He slid one hand behind her head and tenderly caressed her cheek with his thumb as he looked into her eyes.

"I wonder whether *Gott* will bless us with a girl or a boy. Either way, I'll be happy. But I do hope our *kin* inherits your profile," he said. Then he added, "Your *mamm* and Katie will be thrilled. So will Jacqueline. But poor Joseph—wait till he finds he's going to lose his assistant manager!"

Tessa giggled. "Well, we don't want to tell anyone about the *bobbel* just yet. Let's wait a while, okay?"

"Of course," Turner said. He rubbed his nose against hers and then gave her a kiss. "It will be our little secret."

* * * * *

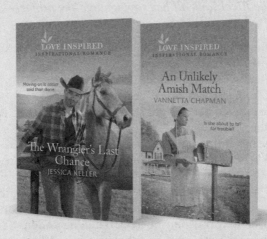

*Intent on reopening a local bed-and-breakfast,
Addie Ricci sank all her savings into the project—and
now the single mother's in over her head. But her high
school sweetheart's back in town and happy to lend a
hand. Will Addie's long-kept secret stand in the way of
their second chance?*

*Read on for a sneak preview of
Her Hidden Hope by Jill Lynn,
part of her Colorado Grooms miniseries.*

Addie kept monopolizing Evan's time. First at the B and B—though
she could hardly blame herself for that. He was the one who'd insisted
on helping her out. And now again at church. Surely he had better
places to be than with her.

"Do you need to go?" she asked Evan. "Sorry I kept you so long."

"I'm not in a rush. I might pop out to Wilder Ranch for lunch with
Jace and Mackenzie. After that I have to…" Evan groaned.

"Run into a burning building? Perform brain surgery? Teach a
sewing class?"

Humor momentarily flashed across his features. "Go to a meeting for
Old Westbend Weekend."

What? So much for some Evan-free time to pull herself back
together. "I'm going to that, but I didn't realize you were. The B and B is
one of the sponsors for the weekend." Addie had used her entire limited
advertising budget for the three-day event.

"I thought my brother might block for me today. Instead he totally
kicked me under the bus as it roared by. He caught Bill's attention and
volunteered me for the hero thing." The pure torment on Evan's face was
almost comical. "I want to back out of it, but Bill played the 'it's for the
kids' card, and now I think I'm trapped."

"Look, Mommy!" Sawyer ran over to them. A grubby, slimy—and very dead—worm rested in the palm of his hand.

"Ew."

At her disgust, Sawyer showed the prize to Evan. "Good find. He looks like he's dead, though, so you'd better give him a proper burial."

"Yeah!" Sawyer hurried over to the patch of dirt. He plopped the worm onto the sidewalk and told it to "stay" just like he would Belay. That made both of them laugh. Then he used one of the sticks as a shovel and began digging a hole.

"He's like a cat, always bringing me dead animals as gifts. I'm surprised he doesn't leave them for me on the doorstep."

Evan chuckled while waving toward the parking lot. She turned to see his brother and Mackenzie walking to their vehicle.

"Do you guys want to come out to Wilder Ranch for lunch? I'm sure they wouldn't mind two more. It's a happy sort of chaos there with all of the kids."

Addie's heart constricted at the offer. No doubt Sawyer would love it. She wanted exactly what Evan was offering, but all of that was off-limits for her. She couldn't allow herself any more access into Evan's world or vice versa.

"We can't, but thanks. I've got to get Sawyer down for a nap." Addie wasn't about to attempt attending a meeting with a tired Sawyer, and she didn't have anywhere else in town for him to go.

Evan's face morphed from relaxed to taut, but he didn't press further. "Right. Okay. I guess I'll see you later then." After saying goodbye to Sawyer, he caught up with Jace and Mackenzie in the parking lot.

A momentary flash of loss ached in Addie's chest. A few days in Evan's presence and he was already showing her how different things could have been. It was like there was a life out there that she'd missed by taking the wrong path. It was shiny and warm and so, so out of reach.

And the worst of it was, until Evan, she hadn't realized just how much she was missing.

Don't miss
Her Hidden Hope *by Jill Lynn,*
available May 2020 wherever
Love Inspired books and ebooks are sold.

LoveInspired.com

LIEXP0420

IF YOU ENJOYED THIS BOOK
WE THINK YOU WILL ALSO LOVE

LOVE INSPIRED
INSPIRATIONAL ROMANCE

Uplifting stories of faith, forgiveness and hope.

Fall in love with stories where faith helps
guide you through life's challenges, and discover
the promise of a new beginning.

6 NEW BOOKS AVAILABLE EVERY MONTH!

SPECIAL EXCERPT FROM

LOVE INSPIRED SUSPENSE
INSPIRATIONAL ROMANCE

Someone is trying to force her off her land, and her only hope lies in the secret father of her child, who has come back home to sell his property.

Read on for a sneak preview of
Dangerous Amish Inheritance *by Debby Giusti, available April 2020 from Love Inspired Suspense.*

Ruthie Eicher awoke with a start. She blinked in the darkness and touched the opposite side of the double bed, where her husband had slept. Two months since the tragic accident and she was not yet used to his absence.

Finding the far side of the bed empty and the sheets cold, she dropped her feet to the floor and hurried into the children's room. Even without lighting the oil lamp, she knew from the steady draw of their breaths that nine-year-old Simon and six-year-old Andrew were sound asleep.

Movement near the outbuildings caught her eye. She held her breath and stared for a long moment.

Narrowing her gaze, she leaned forward, and her heart raced as a flame licked the air.

She shook Simon. "The woodpile. On fire. I need help."

He rubbed his eyes.

"Hurry, Simon."

Leaving him to crawl from bed, she raced downstairs, almost tripping, her heart pounding as she knew all too well how quickly the fire could spread. She ran through the kitchen, grabbed the back doorknob and groaned as her fingers struggled with the lock.

"No!" she moaned, and coaxed her fumbling hands to work. The lock disengaged. She threw open the door and ran across the porch and down the steps.

A noise sounded behind her. She glanced over her shoulder, expecting Simon. Instead she saw a large, darkly dressed figure. Something struck the side of her head. She gasped with pain, dropped the bucket and stumbled toward the house.

He grabbed her shoulder and threw her to the ground. She cried out, struggled to her knees and started to crawl away. He kicked her side. She groaned and tried to stand. He tangled his fingers through her hair and pulled her to her feet.

The man's lips touched her ear. "Didn't you read my notes? You don't belong here." His rancid breath soured the air. "Leave before something happens to you and your children."

Don't miss
Dangerous Amish Inheritance *by Debby Giusti,*
available April 2020 wherever
Love Inspired Suspense books and ebooks are sold.

LoveInspired.com

HARLEQUIN

*Heartfelt or suspenseful,
inspiring or passionate, Harlequin
has your happily-ever-after.*

With new books published
every month, you are sure to find the
satisfying escape you know you deserve.

HNEWS2020